# Last of the Famous International Playboys

It must be confessed at the outset that my impressions of *Last of the Famous International Playboys* (an unfortunate title) will, no doubt, be biased (though in which direction I prefer not to disclose) due to the protagonist's frequent habitation in a certain neighbor woman's modest next-door dwelling during lengthy portions of his formative years; and, while I found the boy to be limited intellectually, I read with great interest the advance copy provided to me by the publisher. Having completed my task, this commentator would simply stress once again that "offensive" is frequently nothing more than a synonym for "authentic" and that any great work of art will always have an ethical impact on any serious reader.

— John Ray, Jr., Ph.D., author of Do the Senses Make Sense? and winner of the Poling Prize

It makes you laugh; it makes you cry. It's all that shit.

— J. D. Salinger, author of The Catcher in the Rye

It's a love letter from the 80s.

— John Hughes, screenwriter of The Breakfast Club

*Last of the Famous International Playboys* is a dizzying pastiche of cultural and literary references all shot out of a cannon. The whole thing moves at breakneck speed, and it doesn't stop until it hits the target. Thoroughly entertaining!

— F. Scott Fitzgerald, author of The Great Gatsby

I was wholly absorbed by *Last of the Famous International Playboys* and its delicate portrait of the human experience. It did me an enormous amount of good in giving me back a little energy, or rather the desire to climb back up again from the dejected state I'm in, except the ending. The ending was very sudden.

— Vincent van Gogh, artist

It's a Rorschach test. Which one is the hero?

> — Norman Mailer, author of *Tough Guys*
> *Don't Dance*

It's like if a Morrissey song was a novel.

> — random Smiths fan

Unsurprising. I think colorblind is fine... as long as you don't want to see anything.

> — el-Hajj Malik el-Shabazz, Minister

*Last of the Famous International Playboys* has the courage to be simply what it is—a genuine snapshot of a specific grotesque delivered in a circular form that takes all the liberties it wants with grammar and punctuation. Now will the cowards who would interpret it as something else or the charlatans who would deconstruct it into dust have the courage to leave it alone?

> — Susan Sontag, author of *Against Interpretation*

The process of art is painstaking. Something like *Last of the Famous International Playboys* doesn't happen overnight... unless you work on it all night.

> — Len Tukwilla, driftwood sculptor

Can I borrow your towel for a sec? My car just hit a water buffalo.

> — John Cocktostin (aka Irwin M. Fletcher),
> *Los Angeles Times*

# Last of the Famous International Playboys

Adam Lenain

CHRISTMAS LAKE PRESS

This is a work of fiction. Names, characters, places, and incidents are products of the author's imagination or are used fictitiously and are not intended to be construed as real. Any resemblance to actual events, locales, organizations, or persons, living or dead, is entirely coincidental.

Published by Christmas Lake Press 2023

www.christmaslakecreative.com



ISBN 978-1-960865-12-0



Interior layout by Daiana Marchesi
Cover art: Vincent van Gogh
Cover design: Nskvsky
Title page photo: Thomas G. Fiffer

For Jill, Buggy, and T. T.

*Every thing that you love you will eventually lose, but in the end, love will return in a different way.*

— Franz Kafka

# Last of the Famous International Playboys

# Chapter 1

The dream starts peacefully enough. It's stupid though. I still don't understand it.

I'm in the first row of the grandstand at Yale Field... right behind the on-deck circle on the third base side. I'm wearing home whites. My feet are up on the railing, and you can see the blue of my stirrups, but I don't have any cleats on. I'm just sitting there, you know, just watching the game in white sanitary socks. Then Eddie Canelli pokes his head out from under the dugout overhang and when he sees me, he just looks at me for a second like I'm an idiot, and then he says in his whiny fly voice, "What are you doing? You need to hit."

The grandstand is packed. All these people are waiting, and it's like the only thing they want to see now is me, so I stick a hand in my duffle bag to grab my cleats, but they're not in it. I don't even want to hit, but I have to now, so I get up and look under the seat, only there's nothing there besides some ketchupy hot dog wrappers. I look under the seats behind me. I look in the aisle. I look on the other side of the railing. I look everywhere, but I can't find my shoes, and I can't stop looking for them either. That's pretty much the whole dream.

The thing is I'd already had it at least a dozen times. It was boring a hole in my head, and right then, when nothing made any sense, it was all I could think about. I barely remember the drive. I was probably going eighty miles an hour with the headliner of my dad's piece of shit Buick sagging in my face, but the only thing I could really see out the windshield was me frantically hunting for shoes. I usually wake up right about then—all sweaty and hyperventilating—but this time I just zoned out. What was it all about, you know? Why wasn't I in the dugout? Why wasn't I wearing cleats? Why did I keep looking even after no one was paying attention? I mean, the game finally just goes on without me.

It all seemed so important, like the reasons for everything were buried in that dream somewhere, but I couldn't figure it out, and by the time I took the exit to my grandmother's assisted living facility, I was miserable again—worried about where I was going, worried about what to say when I got there. I'd fucked up everything imaginable, and my grandmother was the only one left who could help me, but I didn't know what to say to her. I didn't know how to tell her what I'd done.

# Chapter 2

*Fall 1988*

It was something about a student loan. It was right there in the letter. I couldn't go to class until my tuition was paid, so I had to wait in a line that stretched out the front door of this old colonial building all the way to the street before I could see the bursar. Red brick stuck in the middle of all that gray Gothic architecture. The building didn't belong there any more than I did. It's embarrassing to think how nothing it is to wait in a line, how easy it is for a normal person to just stand there.

My dad used to say I was fidgety when I was little. And I was. I bit my fingernails constantly. I was forever scratching a hole in my chest. I used to turn the light switch in the downstairs bedroom on and off a couple hundred times a day because I was afraid of what might happen if I didn't. I had this one tic where I'd drop to a knee every few steps. I don't even know why. I was a nervous, weird little kid. But all the weirdness seemed to calm me down, so I lunged around the house. I lunged from classroom to cafeteria. I even lunged down concrete sidewalks until finally my knees were so bruised and sore I couldn't walk anymore. I've always been this way. There isn't a time I can remember when I wasn't anxious about something. You'd never know it to look at me now. I'm six foot two. I weigh a hundred and ninety-five pounds. My grandmother's friend, Helen, used to tell me I looked like Rudolph Valentino. She even showed me a picture once. I don't know shit about Rudolph Valentino, but I'm pretty sure he never stood at the end of some innocuous line suffering like a pussy.

The thing is, you grow out of the tics. You can't keep doing weird shit forever, only when you stop, it's like you're on your own to figure out how to manage what's in your head—the low grade, everyday bullshit that makes you inept around other people, the dread of an uncertain future. It doesn't matter. Either way, the thoughts keep coming. It's like they're not even yours after a while—worried thoughts, anxious thoughts, irrational thoughts—until finally there's no room left for anything else.

The skinny girl in front of me in line smiled. She looked friendly, and she was wearing pink flip-flops all covered in white plastic daisies. They looked like something a little girl might have on her feet. I wanted to be friendly too. I still knew no one there, and no one seemed interested in knowing me. I thought maybe she was from India. I wanted to ask, but it sounded lame in my head, so then I wanted to say something about her flip-flops, but I couldn't think of anything funny, so I just stared at her feet for a while trying to come up with something good. When I looked back at her, she didn't seem so friendly anymore, and the window to say something was gone. That's when I realized more friendly people had piled up behind us. I was trapped between strangers in a line that wasn't moving. Do you see what I'm saying? Do you see how ridiculous this is? I did my best to appear normal, and I'm pretty good at it, but it's exhausting—pretending unwanted thoughts aren't racing through my head at a hundred miles an hour—and I wasn't sure I could do it anymore. I mean, I was pretty convinced all these people were about to find out something was seriously wrong with me.

I started to mumble. It's something I do when I'm lost in my own head. I mumbled about how out of there I was, about how I didn't want to be there anymore. Then the guy behind me tapped me on the shoulder.

"You dropped this," he said.

He was about my height, but he had blond hair and blue eyes and looked a little like the drummer for The Police. He was wearing khakis and a blue button-down oxford like most of the other prep schoolers I'd met there, only for some reason he actually seemed concerned about me. When I showed my freshman roommate, Derek, the letter I got from the bursar, all he said was "Sucks to be you" before he pushed past me out the door.

"I'm Jonathon," he said, handing me my letter.

Jonathon Vandershar III's grandfather (the first Jonathon in the series) invented something to do with vulcanized rubber, so there will never be enough Vandershars to ever spend all their money. A few years ago *Town & Country* dubbed them American Royalty, but as far as I could tell, the Vandershars were all just completely unreliable. Jonathon was actually in line to square away his own tuition bill—which no one had bothered to pay.

I was still wobbly. Jonathon steadied me with a firm grip on the shoulder until he was sure I was okay. Then he turned his attention to the strangers. For the most part, they were all staring now—at least the ones close enough to have heard me talking to myself. He focused on the Flip-Flop Girl first.

"I like those daisies," he said. "Where you from?"

She still seemed wary, oddly self-conscious about what was on her feet, so when she didn't answer, he looked around again.

"I think we're all gonna be here for a while," he said. Then he shrugged. "We might as well get to know everybody."

I'd never met anyone like Jonathon Vandershar. He was this polished heir to an endless fortune who somehow still made you feel comfortable in your own skin by not taking himself too seriously. They were all facing him now. He was like gravity. No one could turn away. They all seemed to forget they were in a line that wasn't moving. Jonathon drilled them with question after question, somehow managing to have a conversation with one of them and all of them at the same time. I learned their names and where they were from (the Flip-Flop Girl turned out to be Puerto Rican—more evidence that I don't know shit about anything) and where they went to high school, all their common friends, all their shared interests. By the time we reached the front door of the bursar's building, my heart was no longer racing and Vandershar had talked me into hanging with him in the City.

I met him a couple hours later in front of the post office. He popped open the rear door of a black Lincoln Town Car and invited me inside, only instead of heading south on I-95, his driver took us across the Quinnipiac Bridge toward East Haven where a helicopter waited at Tweed Airport. I'd never even been on a plane. Now I was strapped into the black leather seat of a luxury chopper lifting off for New York City. It was incredibly loud, and I had to sit facing backwards, so I pretty much just concentrated on not barfing the whole time. Jonathon pointed down at the sprawling Vandershar estate as we passed over the Connecticut shoreline, just this thick, massive house even from ten thousand feet, and then he picked out the tennis courts and the pool and the dock where the property met the water. We landed on top of some skyscraper in midtown before we jumped in a cab that took us to a building on the Upper East Side.

There were like five doormen, and they all seemed to love Jonathon, so there was a lot of Jets and Giants banter as we headed into the elevator. His parents owned an apartment on the twelfth floor. It was just a one-bedroom, but the living room was huge and filled with an enormous brown L-shaped leather couch and a baby grand piano that sat on an oriental rug-covered hardwood floor. It wasn't dark yet either, so with the blinds open, I could see Central Park through the windows that went all the way from the floor to the ceiling, and on the wall above the couch, blown up so big it had to be five feet tall, was a framed photograph of a rail-thin, wrinkled butcher with a little nub of cigarette dangling at the edge of his mouth as he cut the head off a chicken.

"I shot that in Jakarta," said Jonathon as he sat down on the piano bench.

He referred to it like it was a work of art, but all I saw was a skinny old man about to cut the head off a chicken.

"What do you like?" he asked.

"What do I like about what?"

"What kind of music do you like?"

He started to play, but it looked so effortless he almost seemed bored.

"I don't know," I said, since I don't know shit about classical music.

"You don't know?" He stopped playing. "What kind of an answer is that?"

I didn't say anything else. I was still trying to understand what that enormous photograph was doing there. I could see Jonathon out of the corner of my eye, but I was still sort of facing the butcher.

"Where are you from anyway?" he said.

He'd spared me in front of all the strangers in line to see the bursar. He didn't ask me a single question. It was like he shielded me from any more attention, but now that we were alone, he was asking, and it was a question I never knew how to answer.

"Outside the City," I said.

"What does that mean?"

"We have a house on Lake Anna though."

I'm not sure why I said this. It sounded better than New Jersey, I guess. It was no estate in Greenwich, but it was something. It's true that my dad's parents lived there, and it was better than New Jersey. The house had seven bedrooms and a wraparound porch, but I was definitely not from Lake Anna. That house was a place where I was the butt of jokes and cousins made fun of my tics while aunts and uncles and grandparents did nothing to stop them.

"Where the fuck is Lake Anna?" he said.

"Virginia."

"That's pretty far outside the City, don't you think?"

"My dad lives in Newark."

"Bullshit. No way you grew up in Newark. You're from a McNeighborhood of brown stucco somewhere."

"I grew up in New Brunswick."

"Now was that so hard? What's your dad do?"

"He coaches high school football."

"You play football?"

"I play baseball."

"Siblings?"

"I have two brothers."

"Older or younger?"

"Older."

"They play football?"

"They used to hunt me with pellet guns."

He smiled when I said that like I'd passed a test of some kind.

"I have a sister," he said as he went back to the piano. "She's younger though. Also a pain in the ass."

"My little brother died from meningitis," I said.

He stopped with the piano again.

"Jesus. How old were you?"

"Ten."

"You can die from meningitis?"

I finally turned away from the wrinkled butcher to face him.

"What's *your* dad do?" I said.

"He fucks the housekeepers at our estate in Greenwich."

"Does your mom know?"

"Why do you think she spends all her time in places where no one knows her?"

We hopped in a cab downtown after that. Vandershar leaned forward and gave the driver the name of a club I no longer remember. Then he flopped back into the back seat and rolled his window down.

"You're gonna like this place," he said. "Very talented."

I wasn't sure what he meant. Then I watched him fumble for something in the front pocket of his khakis. He finally had to contort himself sideways to free a tiny vial of cocaine, which he showed me hopefully, holding it between his right index finger and thumb.

"You want some?"

"I'm good," I said.

"Maybe next time."

Then he spooned a little up his nose.

Jonathon had a habit of quoting movies, and he'd just busted out some *Fletch*, so with the garbagey stink of midtown wafting its way into our cab, I said, "You never do get used to the smell, do you?"

He was impressed I'd picked up the reference.

"Manure spreader jackknifed on the Santa Ana," he said in a funny voice as he returned the vial to his pocket.

Then he stuck his head out the window like a happy golden retriever.

The drive got increasingly dangerous after that. We passed a slew of burned-out buildings and any number of hookers and street thugs and flaming trash cans as we wound our way through the desolation of the Lower East Side. We stopped suddenly in front of an unremarkable gray facade with a line that stretched out the door—a line we didn't wait in. Vandershar knew somebody, so we just walked right into another universe—this cavernous, tired ballroom, half-empty even though there were at least a thousand people in it, a loud driving music I'd never heard, a photo of some Italian fountain projected twenty feet tall onto the far wall, dilapidated chandeliers and balconies and stairs leading to other strange rooms with faded gold paint peeling off the walls like an abandoned palace that had been taken over by these night creatures—bankers, street urchins, socialites, celebrities, drag queens, college kids, white, black, brown, whatever—all bound together by an unmistakable desire to be something other than what they were.

I looked like a mark in my Levi's and faded green Bobo's Billiards T-shirt. Vandershar handed me a vodka tonic and a shot of tequila. The vodka smelled like lighter fluid, and the tequila was worse. I wasn't much of a drinker before that. The first time I got drunk I had a run-in with a newspaper dispenser that didn't turn out so well. I'd pretty much steered clear after that, but I couldn't turn down both the coke and the booze, so I did the shot with him. Vandershar wouldn't stop talking about a band he'd just seen there, some new sound that blew his mind, but he was talking a hundred miles an hour, and it was kind of hard to hear him, so I just stood there with my back to the bar, sipping vodka drinks as his voice receded into ambient noise and a strange calm came to me. It reminded me of the moment school let out every summer when there was no more bullshit to worry about and I would be at my grandparents' soon. I drank another and then another (first with tonic, then with cranberry, then with grapefruit, then back to cranberry again—anything to mask the lighter fluid), and the whole time, I watched a pink-haired girl pole dance topless against a backdrop of empty picture frames and disinterested bystanders that I'm pretty sure included Judd Nelson and a transvestite who had to be seven feet tall.

We chased Eastern European models in and out of the nooks and crannies of that decrepit building most of the night. Hardly any of them spoke English. Vandershar didn't care. It was like watching a hyena snap at a herd of racing gazelles. He finally found a couple who spoke French—a language he claimed to speak too—and then I watched him happily stumble through a conversation that was nothing but misunderstanding and confusion. He kept introducing me as his *bel ami*, like he was inviting me into the conversation. "*C'est mon bel ami!*" he'd say with an arm around my shoulder, and then he'd laugh like a fool while they waited for me to say something. I just stood there with an idiotic smile on my face. Jonathon kept at it though—working it, pressing on when it seemed hopeless, and right when it appeared he was about to make some progress, right at the moment when he seemed to be moving in for a kill, a Go-Go Boy, wearing nothing but tighty-whities and tan hiking boots, appeared behind him and lifted a galvanized steel bucket into the air before he dumped about five gallons of water over Jonathon's head.

I thought the Not Welcome Police had finally caught up to us, but a crowd gathered almost instantaneously around Jonathon. He calmly righted himself, all dignified, before he turned, soaking wet and smiling, to face the Go-Go Boy. Then—just like that—he ripped his own shirt off. Brooks Brothers buttons went flying in every direction as he showed off a washboard stomach to the approval of an adoring crowd. Before I even knew what was happening, we were at the center of it—because Jonathon was always at the center of it.

The music seemed louder now, penetrating my core, chasing the Dread—or whatever you want to call the shitshow that lives inside of me—into the shadows, and as the vodka took root, I melted comfortably into the crowd, content to watch Jonathon's show, happy for the first time since I'd arrived at Yale. He was posing. He would face one direction, strike a pose and hold it. Then he would shift mechanically to face a different direction and take on a different pose, and with his shirt off like that and his blond hair wet and flopping all around, he looked almost statuesque, less Stewart Copeland and more like the Greek God of Who Gives a Fuck.

I was the happiest bystander of all. Then, out of nowhere, the Go-Go Boy's wingman snuck up behind me and dumped a bucket of freezing water over my head too. It knocked the breath out of me. I pushed the wet hair away from my face, and when I did, all I could see was Jonathon looking right at me the same way he had when he offered me the cocaine. I looked around. They were all staring now, waiting for me to do something, all these strange faces—bankers, and street urchins, and socialites, and celebrities, and drag queens, and college kids, white, black, brown—all of them just staring. But suddenly I didn't care. It was like I wasn't even me anymore, like I could be someone else too, so I lifted that soaking wet Bobo's Billiards T-shirt over my head and flexed for every last one of them like I was some muscle-bound freak on display at a carnival sideshow. Vandershar loved it. The crowd went berserk, so I kept at it, feeding on the energy with that music blaring and all these strangers screaming, and only when I noticed what had to be two people fucking in the balcony above me did the Go-Go Boy lean in to tell me I'd just won a contest that required I remain shirtless for the rest of the night.

I was absolutely hammered by the time we ran into these art history majors from Barnard. They were twins from Wisconsin named Leslie and Lisa, but I could never tell them apart. It was hard to understand what they were even doing there. They seemed so serious, not to mention skeptical of every word out of Vandershar's mouth. They didn't want anything to do with either of us at first, but Vandershar wouldn't give up. He kept probing and prodding the edges until finally he found a tiny crease, and then he charmed his way in with a mini-dissertation on Vincent van Gogh and some museum in Amsterdam, about how if you stood right in front of a van Gogh it looked like one thing, but if you walked away from it, if you got far enough away, it looked like something else, and this got them to talking, and then it got them to laughing, and then they were serious again, only this time fascinated by everything Vandershar had to say. He explained the genius of van Gogh's vision, his ability to hide God's truth in plain sight, the inescapable preeminence of perspective in great art (even though the two of them looked exactly the same from any distance), and what it all meant in the grand scheme of things. It was a masterpiece of bullshit is what it was. It was like there was nothing he didn't know. All I did was stand there the whole time with my shirt off. I'm not even sure which one I ended up with.

# Chapter 3

I barely made it to baseball practice the next day. I woke up around noon in the pullout section of that milk chocolate living room couch with a throbbing headache. Vandershar was gone and so were the twins from Barnard. It was just me, the old wrinkled butcher, and that chicken. I had to take the train back to New Haven.

You need to know I hit a couple home runs off some poor fuck about to pass out from the heat during a summer league game, and afterward an assistant coach from Yale pulled me aside to ask what I got on the SAT. That's how they recruit you in the Ivy League. You hit a couple home runs off the guy they're actually looking at and then they ask you what you got on the SAT.

You also need to know that when I was eleven, I stopped talking. The Dread had convinced me that if I opened my mouth, I would make everything worse, so I kept it shut—for days. My dad didn't know what to do with me anymore, so he sent me home with my grandparents. Not the Lake Anna grandparents, but my mom's parents. They lived in a rickety, faded-white, two-story house in Widworth, Massachusetts—a quiet New England town, generally unremarkable except for my grandmother's neighbor, who had achieved a small amount of fame by writing two books about white male confessional literature before living out his last days in obscurity.

This grandmother looked a little like Betty White, except she had broad shoulders, big, strong hands and the calves of a woman who walked twenty miles a week because she never learned to drive. My grandfather was quiet and bald as a Ping-Pong ball. He'd spent his entire adult life in the same job running a radio station, and when he retired, all he did was fish, watch baseball, and tend to his yard. He was easily the happiest man I've ever met. I was only supposed to stay with them a few days—just long enough to get my head on straight—but after the few days, I didn't want to leave. I didn't know them very well yet, but I felt comfortable there—no annoying people asking me stupid questions about things I didn't want to talk about, no one making me speak, no one laughing at my tics or whispering about my strangeness. They just seemed to meet me where I was, probably because that's where they were too, and that made me feel better for some reason, so the few days turned into the entire summer and then every summer after that. Every chance I've ever had I owe to those summers in Widworth. My grandparents basically raised me, and Gram didn't want me missing out on summer league games just because I wasn't with my dad in July and August.

She found a league for me to play in and a team close by, and as I got older, she found me a better team, and then a better team after that. They were always there too, in lawn chairs right behind the screen, so when somebody in the stands said something about a scout from Yale, Gram marched over to a guy who looked like

Ichabod Crane in a Yale hoodie and asked him what he was doing there. He said he was there to see the other team's pitcher. She told him he was watching the wrong kid, and after I bombed two home runs off the guy, Ichabod Crane wouldn't leave until he had all my information. That's when he asked what I got on the SAT. I told him I hadn't taken it. Gram looked horrified and did all the talking after that. She assured him I was a whiz at math and that a test like that wouldn't be a problem. She figured out where I could take it that summer. I ended up with a 740 on the math and a 520 on the verbal, which makes me about the dumbest fuck ever to get into that place.

Yale Field is one of those old-fashioned ballparks. The outfield fence is lined with an evergreen hedge that's split in dead center by a twenty-foot, green sheet metal, hand-operated scoreboard. The infield is orange clay. Then there's this ivy-covered grandstand that wraps around the infield from first to third, and in the stands rows and rows of weathered, wooden seats with olive drab paint cracked and faded by God knows how many years of baseball. Everybody loves the place. I spent some of the most miserable days of my life there fouling off fastballs through the sleet.

Baseball is actually a spring sport, so fall practice amounted to nothing more than a two-month tryout to see if any of the freshmen would make varsity, but the seniors on that team—and there were twelve of them—wanted nothing to do with any of us. We were more like intruders—a distraction on their way to the Eastern Intercollegiate Baseball League title (the Ivy League, plus Army and Navy) and a trip to the Northeast Regional of the College World Series. They didn't need us, so mostly they ignored us, and if anyone ever did bother to say something to a freshman, it was usually to get some help moving something heavy.

Our practices ran like clockwork. We were divided into eight groups. Each group rotated from one station to the next for a total of one hour and forty-five minutes. Each station was thirteen minutes. You did whatever you were supposed to do for thirteen minutes, and then you had sixty seconds to haul ass to the next station. It didn't matter if you were making any progress either. Progress always seemed sort of beside the point. It was really the appearance of progress that mattered, so you kept moving like you knew what you were doing no matter what. It was all modeled after the program at the University of New Haven, a school not five miles away that went to the Division II College World Series just about every year.

So with my head still pounding from a night in New York, my group was supposed to hit from 3:43 to 3:56, and I was expected to take ten swings in the hundred and eighty seconds of those thirteen minutes that had been allocated to me, only I was still trying to reconstruct the prior night as I waited for my turn. It seemed finite somehow, like I would never see Vandershar again, and this made me wonder if his world was even real.

The other groups were scattered all over the field—pitchers in the bullpen, another group running from foul pole to foul pole, another at the soft toss station up the first baseline, another group on the tees in front of the third base dugout, a group taking ground balls at second base, a group taking ground balls at third base, another lazily shagging fly balls in the outfield. But there were also two strays—two groupless freshmen. One of them was standing next to a five-gallon white plastic bucket up the first baseline, catching baseballs back from the third basemen as they took infield. He was semi-out of shape, all soft edges with a roll around his waist and a little nub of a chin. His name was Norman Forsh, and he was a pitcher from Chicago. The other groupless freshman was just up the third baseline, standing next to a similar white bucket, catching baseballs back from the second basemen. His name was Larry Zayger. Larry was constructed from blocks and squares and rectangles, and he had a giant head. The seniors called him "Head" because he had the biggest head in the history of Yale baseball. He wore a size eight hat.

They had nicknames for all of us. They called Norman "Ass" because he was always right behind Larry, and they called me "Spazio" since I couldn't remember the bunt defenses. (We had a defensive playbook an inch thick. You had to be a mechanical engineer to read it.) Larry hated the nicknames. It wasn't so much the nicknames to be honest. It was the total lack of interest in our real names that bothered him. He tried to rally us in revolt, but it was all too new and no one wanted to make waves, so Larry (with only Norman behind him) confronted our team captain—this senior pitcher who had a scar that cut diagonally through both lips like he'd tried to lick a weed whacker—but the Weed Whacker Scar told him to fuck off, so after that, Larry (with Norman right behind him) went straight to our head coach, Eddie Canelli, with a list of atrocities and an equally lengthy list of demands, but Canelli blew him off too, and the net result of all this complaining was a job standing next to a white plastic bucket.

I had to keep my head absolutely still to avoid what now felt like rolling on the deck of an overmatched dinghy. My hangovers are debilitating. A lot of them are two-dayers, and this one was no different. The vodka was still in me. On the train back from New York, I spent a fair amount of time on my knees heaving into the public toilet of a railway car, but the door of my chosen bathroom didn't lock, so when the train gained (or lost) momentum the door would fly open (or shut), and there, opposite me on the other side of the car, I would see (or not see) a pony-tailed girl of no more than eight in a bright flowered sundress, Band-Aid on her shin, looking right at me, and I wondered the whole time if I was somehow scarring her childhood. What I really needed was a quiet place to close my eyes, but it was my turn to hit.

When I finally stepped into the cage, it was a relief to see Canelli with his back turned in the bullpen. He was checking out one of our left-handed relief pitchers, but of course when he realized I was up, the evaluation ended, and he turned to watch me.

Canelli's gut was all round and stiff like a bug abdomen. He had spindly legs and scrawny arms, and he wore these oversized bifocal glasses that looked just like the eyes of a giant fly. The first time I met him was on my recruiting trip. His redheaded secretary led me back to a cramped office in Ray Tompkins House. I hardly said a word. It didn't matter. He just went on and on in his high-pitched fly voice about how great Yale was and how all his players graduated and went off to Wall Street to make their millions. He told me about Ron Darling, and how he taught Ron Darling to throw a slider, and how he made Ron Darling a major leaguer, and how he could make me a major leaguer too if that's what I wanted. He told me he thought I was a legitimate fifth-round draft pick, and then he said he liked my name: Spencer Mazio. He said he liked hard-nosed pricks whose last names ended in vowels. He said he could win with guys like me. He'd never even seen me play.

The Weed Whacker Scar was on the mound throwing live batting practice, so I dug in and got as ready as I could, but my hangover had robbed me of certain basic motor skills and there didn't appear to be any end in sight. My eyeballs were marinating in vodka fourteen hours after I'd stopped drinking it, and I could smell cranberry with just a hint of grapefruit. I was in no condition to hit. I took a feeble hack at his first pitch and was a mile behind it. Our hitting coach, Danny Puzzo, looked like he'd just whiffed a pile of dog shit.

Puzzo always stood right behind the cage during BP. He was a stocky little man with a helmet of sandy blond hair who played

Double-A ball somewhere in the middle of nowhere for about half an inning. He made me queasy even when I didn't need my stomach pumped. His job was to make it clear that I didn't know shit about anything, least of all hitting. He also seemed to yell "Be tough out there, kid!" about three hundred times a game. Dicky Janice, the Ichabod Crane-looking coach who'd recruited me, wasn't far away either, just up the third baseline next to Larry, hitting fungoes to the second basemen from in front of the third base dugout. His job was to hit wicked in-between hops at infielders and bark "Battle him now!" every time Puzzo yelled "Be tough out there, kid!"

I swung and missed at the next pitch too. That's when the batting cage started to spin around me. I would have cut my own head off to be rid of the sickness. I was sweating vodka, so I stepped out of the box to keep from barfing, and for some reason, I looked at Larry again. He appeared so oddly determined. He just refused anyone the satisfaction of his humiliation, so he caught each ball back from the second basemen with an air of dignity before he dropped it into his bucket. His sense of purpose was unsettling, and it rattled me when he finally looked over, but he just seemed to be urging me on, encouraging me to do something, you know. That's when the big dumb asshole behind the plate made somebody get him an egg crate to sit on just so he wouldn't waste his knees on such a useless douche.

I swung and missed at the next pitch too.

"What *are* you good at, Spazio?" said the Big Dumb Asshole from his egg crate.

Larry caught another baseball and dropped it into his bucket. Janice hit an in-between hop and asked for another ball. Catchers' mitts popped in the bullpen while Canelli watched, arms folded. Pitchers jogged from foul pole to foul pole. Norman caught a baseball and dropped it into his bucket. Bats pinged at the soft toss station up the first baseline as the seconds of my turn in the cage wound down. It was all like clockwork—inevitable, indifferent, never-ending. We were cogs in a meaningless machine, at once useful and expendable. How many days had it been like this? How many more would there be? I wanted to hit the next pitch so far over the left field fence that nothing would ever be the same, but I had to stop moving or I'd puke for sure, so I took the next fastball instead.

"Good," said Puzzo. "Be patient. Wait for yours."

"He's not gonna walk you," said the Big Dumb Asshole.

"I guess that wasn't my pitch," I said.

Then I threw up a little in my mouth.

I could see this other freshman, Billy Clark, standing next to Puzzo now. He was waiting for his turn to hit, only he seemed to be sizing me up. The seniors called him "Nut." Billy played right field, and if you stood next to him long enough he would tell you that he was the MVP of the American Legion team that won the American Legion World Series when he was fifteen and that his lifetime batting average in high school was .436. He was from a coal mining town in Western Pennsylvania, and he always had a couple of days of growth on his face and a load of Skoal in his mouth, and when he was nine years old he lost his left testicle in an accident that involved a garden hoe and a jackrabbit.

I was running out of time. There weren't more than twenty-seven seconds left in my turn. I would see only one more pitch, so I closed my eyes to visualize bombing it all the way to the batting cages beyond the left field fence, but the nerves got to me first. I didn't want to swing and miss again. I didn't want to fail. The Dread is a shape-shifty thing made of shadow, so I never know what form it will take or what it might do to me. This time it smoldered up into my hangover and somehow made it worse. My throat thickened. My airway narrowed. There was a blackness coming, and with my eyes shut, I receded further and further into the yawning dark space where my little brother haunts me.

I could see him now, scrambling to pick up the fish food flakes, the excitement in his face as the garage door rattled open and our mom pulled in with the balloons and cake. Nathan was sick all the time and allergic to just about everything, but meningitis isn't what killed him. That's a lie I've told so many times it's somehow blotted out the truth.

My little brother died in the downstairs bedroom on his seventh birthday. We were feeding the fish, but he got so excited when he heard the garage door open that he dropped the fish food. It was everywhere, so we scrambled to shove all the flakes back into the little yellow plastic container before anyone saw the mess, only they were sticking to everything, so it was sort of impossible, and by the time I looked up our older brothers, Troy and Anthony, were in the room with us. I had no idea what would happen next. Troy and Anthony were unpredictable, a tornado that could demolish anything, so it was weird when all Anthony did was tell Nathan a present waited for him high on one of the bookshelves behind the desk. Troy looked right at me, and I could feel my heart in my mouth, but he just smiled. It was barely a smile at all really, and it was the strangest thing. I got real calm all of a sudden, like for the first time I was a part of something.

I guess it was supposed to be funny—Nathan holding our dad's .38 caliber revolver right as our mom walked in—and I was in on it now, so I stood there and watched Nathan climb onto that chair, and then I watched him reach up over his head to grab the first thing he could touch, and then I watched him drag it over the edge where his thumb caught the trigger and it went off in his face. The bullet entered his head just above the left eyebrow and made a perfect round hole before it ripped through his brain, tore open the back of his head, and left a chunk of skull just sort of dangling there. He was dead before he hit the ground.

When I opened my eyes the Weed Whacker Scar was already into his windup, but I couldn't move. I stood frozen, and from inside that drunken, wistful delirium I failed to realize that the Weed Whacker Scar had aimed his next pitch right at my head. I could hear the seams whizzing toward me, and I could see the baseball, but I couldn't move, or at least I don't remember moving. Somehow it missed me and I ended up in a heap on top of home plate.

"How was that one?" said the Big Dumb Asshole. "Was that your pitch?"

He was standing over me now since he had to get up from his egg crate to catch a baseball that was intended for my earhole. I used to run from my older brothers. I'd never even been in a fight, but I felt something different now—something volcanic, something I didn't even know existed before I took my shirt off in front of a thousand strangers—so when the Big Dumb Asshole went to toss the baseball back to the Weed Whacker Scar, I grabbed his front leg mid-stride and yanked him off balance. He hit the ground twisted and sort of helpless, so I jumped him and ripped his mask off. I just remember how shocked he looked right before I hit him in the face, like it was unthinkable, like it couldn't possibly be happening to him, but that first punch didn't hurt nearly as much as I thought it would, so I hit him again as he tried to wriggle away, only that's when I heard all the *fuck yous* behind me.

I stopped and turned to see a mob swarming the infield, Larry hacking his way through the middle of it to get at the Weed Whacker Scar, and when he finally reached him, he threw a wild haymaker before he disappeared into a sea of blue jerseys. Unfortunately, the distraction was enough for the Big Dumb

Asshole to get ahold of his catcher's mask. He hit me in the face with it. It knocked me senseless and opened a huge gash inside my mouth. He cocked to take another swing, but before he could finish me off, Billy Clark leveled him with a cross-body block that knocked him into the batting cage netting.

You could hear Eddie Canelli at this point, his high-pitched squeal cutting through the *fuck yous* as he raced in from the bullpen, but it was like trying to put an end to a prison riot. I was bleeding all over home plate now. The Big Dumb Asshole had managed to drive my lower lip through my lower teeth with his catcher's mask, and I was feeling woozy again, but the Ass was standing over me now, wielding a thirty-four-inch Black Magic like a broadsword to keep the mob away, Larry still somewhere in the middle of it, the *fuck yous* still flying, Billy and the Big Dumb Asshole tangled up together in the batting cage net as Canelli pleaded for it stop. But I didn't want it to stop. We were in it together now, and I didn't want anything to put an end to that.

# Chapter 4

The gash in my mouth needed twelve stitches to close, and the doctor insisted I stay the night in the infirmary in case I was concussed. The Yale infirmary was in the Department of University Health on Hillhouse Avenue. It had eight beds and smelled like bad things covered up with bleach. It was a pretty familiar smell actually. My little brother spent hours on end hooked up to machines, having blood drawn as they frantically tried to figure out what was wrong with his immune system. There were long conversations with doctors behind closed doors, me by myself out in some waiting room full of sick people. My lower lip was now about double its normal size and crusted over with dried blood and spit. I just wanted to sleep, but I couldn't stop running my tongue in there, tweaking the stitches and making it worse.

There were just two of us in beds—me and the kid next to me who I recognized from Durfee Hall. He was connected to an IV, and his dark hair was all matted to the back of his head like he'd been in there forever. He was holding a worn paperback copy of *The Violent Bear It Away* that had a yellow "USED" sticker on the spine.

"I'm John Henry," he said as he put the book down.

John Henry was the name of a giant, bald Black man who raced a steam engine through a mountain with a sledgehammer in a book my mom used to read Nathan when we were kids. The John Henry in the bed next to me was five foot eight, scrawny and white. The idea of him holding a sledgehammer, let alone racing a steam engine through a mountain with it, made me smile, which pulled the stitches and hurt like a motherfucker.

"What happened?" he said.

He seemed curious about everything, like he was always right at the edge of asking a question.

"I got hit," I said.

"With what?"

"It's hard to talk."

He nodded, so I know he heard me, but he didn't seem to care. He kept right on talking anyway like he'd known me his whole life—a torrent of random thoughts, a stream of consciousness that busted over the top of a barrier in his head that could no longer hold it back and before long he and the Vicodin had me happily talking right over the top of my fat lip.

"You ever read this?" he said, picking the book back up and waving it at me.

"No."

"I can't get into it."

"Then why are you reading it?"

"I followed a girl into this class." He was staring at the cover now. "It was right at the end of shopping period. She had nice calves. Now I have to read this."

"I once ran over a Jack Russell terrier checking out a girl's ass," I said. "It was chasing a pigeon."

"You kill it?"

"No, it came out the other side. It turned out to be her dog."

He seemed to consider that for a second.

"I think you learn more about a girl from her calves. Anyway... we were just supposed to talk about Flannery O'Connor."

"Who's that?"

"She wrote this," he said, waving the book at me again. "You've never heard of Flannery O'Connor?" He waited a beat for an answer, but then he kept going. "It doesn't matter. We didn't really talk about Flannery O'Connor. That's the problem. Then I got this shit."

"What do you have?"

"Staph. Actually, that's a lie. We did talk about Flannery O'Connor. We were on her bed. She lives in Welch. There were spiral ring notebooks everywhere and paper... just paper all over the bed. This girl takes more notes than anyone I've ever seen, and she had these glasses on that she only wears for reading, but they're like... they were killing me. So she was explaining the meaning of the title... and I kissed her."

"She didn't want you to?"

"No. She did."

"Then what's the problem?"

"I think it ruined it."

"Ruined what?"

"I don't know. She kind of avoided me in Commons the next day, and she hasn't come to see me here once."

"Does she know you're in here?"

"I don't know. Maybe not. But she could find out. I was being not boring."

"Not boring?"

"We wrecked all her notes rolling around."

"How is that not boring?"

"It wasn't the only thing we did."

"How long have you been in here?"

"Five days," he said. "I think boring is the long-term play. Slow and steady wins the race, you know? You need to play the long game. That's the lesson. If you want it to last, be boring. Just not too boring."

"Five days hooked up to that?" I said, nodding at the IV.

"Does anyone know *you're* in here?"

"I doubt it."

"They're not gonna tell anybody. You better make some phone calls. In about five days, you're gonna look like this."

He waved at all his scrawny paleness and bedhead, but I had no one to call besides Gram, and I wasn't about to worry her that I was in the infirmary. I did want to tell her about the Big Dumb Asshole though. He kind of reminded me of the kid who lived across the street from her. That kid was big and stupid too. The day after I got there, he stole my bike right out of Gram's driveway. He painted it blue with a can of cheap spray paint, but it was obviously mine. It had the same frame. The same forks. The same handlebars.

Gram just paid attention, you know? I mean, how hard is that? To pay attention to someone? To make sure they're okay? She pried the truth out of me even though all I could give her was a series of nods and some tears. Then she headed for the garage before I watched her march across the street with a handful of sandpaper and a crescent wrench. She told the boy's mother she'd find red beneath all that blue paint. I think she might have said some other things too, but the part about the paint was the only thing she repeated. She sanded down a stretch of frame, and when she hit red, she hoisted my bike onto one of those broad shoulders and marched it right back to me.

"That boy's no good," she said. The door from the garage into the kitchen swung shut behind her. "You stay away from him."

"I'm sorry," I said, wiping away tears.

She paused for a second since these were the first words out of my mouth in a week.

"It's nice to hear your voice," she said. "But I won't do that again."

Then she went back to mixing a can of tuna fish with a glob of mayonnaise.

I wanted to let her know I'd pummeled that Big Dumb Asshole, but the number of her assisted-living facility was written on a piece of paper now squirreled away somewhere in my dorm room, so I put the thought out of my mind.

John Henry tossed *The Violent Bear It Away* onto the night table.

"I still don't know what the title means," he said. "You ever have a girlfriend?"

"Not really. One... maybe... I guess."

"One maybe you guess? What does that even mean?"

"We never really talked about it. I was in tenth grade. She was a senior."

"So what makes you think she was your girlfriend?"

"I don't know. She used to blow me in the girls' bathroom after fourth period."

"That's definitely some evidence she was your girlfriend. What makes you think maybe she wasn't?"

"I don't know," I said, but I did know.

She used to slip notes through the vents in the front of my locker—sometimes a funny little doodle, other times a joke only I would understand, or gossip about some girl she didn't like, and sometimes all the note would say was *I want to suck your dick*. But they never really went beyond that, and we never really talked much outside school. So one day I wrote her a note, and I slipped it through the vent of her locker. It was about Nathan and how he really died and how she was the only thing that had made me happy since, but she never said a word about it. She never said a fucking thing. I know she got it because she told all her friends what was in it, but she never said one word about that note to me, and I never said one word about it to her either.

"I went out with the same girl for six months last year," said John Henry. "She thought I was boring. She told me I was gonna be a truancy officer, and then she dumped me."

"Mine ended up giving me the Clap."

"Jesus," he said. "Did you tell her?"

"Yeah."

"What'd she say?"

"She told everyone I gave it to her."

"What'd you do about it?"

"I slashed her tires."

"Not her," he said. "The Clap."

"They just give you some tetracycline."

"Your parents say anything?"

"No."

"No advice on how not to get the Clap?"

"You think maybe that's how you got the Staph?"

"How?"

"From the girl."

"The Staph is in my knee," he said.

"So."

"So you can't get a Staph infection in your knee from a hand job."

"You can if it's vigorous," said Larry, crashing into the room with that huge head and all the sharp angles and blocks of his body.

Norman and his little nub of a chin were right behind him.

The matronly, plain-clothes nurse who showed up every now and again to make sure we weren't in need of another pineapple fruit cup intercepted them as they started to make themselves comfortable.

"We can't have visitors after eight," she said.

"Did he even tell you what happened today?" said Larry to the nurse as he pulled a chair over.

"You have one minute," she said.

"Was it random bad luck or intentional act of violence?" said Larry with this goofy look on his face.

Larry and Norman loved to tell stories. It was like telling the story was better than doing the thing itself, but the nurse wasn't interested. She rolled her eyes and went back to her paperwork.

"So what happened to him?" said John Henry.

"Who's this?" said Larry.

"This is John Henry," I said. "He's got Staph."

"It's in my knee," he said.

"He didn't get it from a hand job."

"Can we stay focused?" said Larry. "It started out as just another day of disappointment at Yale Field. You have to understand. We have twelve seniors on our team, and every one of them is a complete asshole."

"What do you play?" said John Henry.

"Baseball," said Larry. "I won't bore you with the list of atrocities, but it's lengthy and littered with disrespect, hard labor, and hazing. It's been going on since the day we got here, and our head coach doesn't seem to give a shit."

"So today," said Norman, "Spencer put an end to it."

"How'd he do that?" said John Henry.

"He got into it with the biggest, dumbest one of all," said Larry.

"What did he even say to you?" said Norman.

I didn't answer because I couldn't stop thinking about how easy it had been, like there was some unfamiliar freedom to be had punching someone in the face.

"It actually looked like you were talking to yourself," said Larry. "Your eyes were shut, and it was like you were psyching yourself up or something."

"You were definitely not in a hurry to hit," said Norman.

"Spencer's pace during batting practice seemed to piss off the big, dumb fuck behind the plate, so he had the asshole on the mound throw a pitch right at Spencer's head."

"You got beaned?" said John Henry.

"No," said Larry. "He ducked it and ended up sprawled on top of home plate, but when the big dumb one went to throw the ball back to the asshole on the mound—"

"Spencer's on the ground," said Norman, "and he reaches back with one hand and grabs the guy like he's a rag doll. This guy weighs two hundred pounds easy, and Spencer just tosses him like it's nothing."

"It was superhuman," said Larry.

"And before that big, dumb fuck even knew what had happened, Spencer's on top of him and dots him right in the nose."

"I see this," said Larry, "and I'm like, *Yes. Fuck... Yes.* This is how the revolution begins. So I went after the motherfucker on the mound."

"You charged the mound?" said John Henry.

"Oh, I charged the mound. I wasn't wasting that opportunity."

"You ended up in a headlock with your face scraping the infield dirt," said Norman.

"So what happened to Spencer?" said John Henry.

"He got a couple good shots in," said Norman, "but then he stopped pounding the guy so he could watch Larry take on the varsity infield, and when he wasn't paying attention, the big, dumb one grabbed his catcher's mask and clocked Spencer in the mouth with it."

"Okay, you two," said the nurse. "Time to go."

"We just got here," said Larry.

"Out."

"If you'd like, we can lock up," said Norman.

"There's nothing to lock. Visitor hours are over."

"Well, that's where you have us mistaken," said Larry. "This is official business."

"Do I need to call security?"

"No. No, in fact you've passed our test. We were sent here to make sure you would see to it that the unfortunate souls here in the infirmary are kept isolated and as lonely as possible during their stay. So, well done. This is really good work. We'll report back. Spencer, we'll see you tomorrow. John Henry with Staph, very nice to meet you."

They made me leave the next morning since I wasn't concussed. I looked around that bleach-smelling room with its now seven empty beds, and it occurred to me that I really didn't want to go. The Dread had been gone since I dotted the Big Dumb Asshole, but it slithered back into my head the moment I thought about returning to my freshman dorm and Derek, my dick roommate. I asked the nurse on my way out how much longer John Henry would be in there. She said at least two more days, so I went back to my room—Durfee Hall, entryway B, fourth floor (where Derek was mercifully not home)—took a shower, changed, then headed up to Park Street to grab a couple Philly cheesesteaks to smuggle back into the infirmary about two hours later.

John Henry perked up when he saw me, like I was unexpected, but then he went right back to his questions like he'd been waiting for me the whole time. I think that's when I really knew we'd be friends. He asked all about the baseball team. He wanted to know what position I played. He was curious how we managed school and class while we were on the road. (I had no clue since I'd never done it.) He asked how long it took to get out to the Field House on the bus and how much time I spent at practice, but mostly he wanted to know about Larry and Norman and why Eddie Canelli did nothing about twelve assholes who terrorized us in broad daylight day after day. Then, he grilled me about the classes I was taking and why I wanted to major in math. After that, he asked about my family. He never said a word about himself, never complained one bit about his circumstances or all that time alone spent hooked up to an IV. He just seemed genuinely interested in me, so I kept answering—like for the first time it was okay to be honest—until we got to Nathan. I didn't have many friends growing up, mostly because we moved all the time, but also because there was a loaded gun in our house that occasionally went off, so I told him the lie instead... and instantly regretted it.

# Chapter 5

*Summer 1992*

I sat outside my grandmother's assisted-living facility for a long time after I got there, tapping away at the steering wheel of my dad's piece of shit Buick. I didn't want to disappoint her, but I eventually got out of the car.

The place was divided into wings, two identical brick buildings connected by a white-pillared portico. The parking lot was huge too. It was basically two football fields of empty parking spaces. It made no sense. No one ever visited the Widworth Community Health Center. They didn't need all that parking, but I guess the place had been a real hospital at some point. The white-pillared portico was a reception area. I was still shaking by the time I got in there, but no one was at the front desk to help me. I couldn't remember where Gram's room was. I'd only been there the one time—when I moved her in—so I staggered down a sterile hallway until a pretty young nurse with a short blond ponytail led me around a couple corners to an open door. I think she was

Scottish—at least she sounded Scottish. Maybe Irish. What do I know?

My grandmother looked older when she appeared in the doorway. She was smaller somehow—like a diminished version of the woman who raised me—and she was wearing a frumpy flannel nightgown. I wasn't ready. I didn't know what to say, so I just stood there. I'd been coming up with reasons not to call her for nearly four years, excuses not to make the trip, and now that she was standing right there in front of me, I felt even worse for having left her alone so long.

"Who the hell is this?" she said.

"It's your grandson," said the Scottish Nurse. "He's come to see you."

"My grandson is a criminal."

The Scottish Nurse looked at me, but not like I was a criminal, more like she just felt sorry for me.

I got arrested for pissing on that newspaper dispenser in front of a Friendly's in Widworth the first time I got drunk. I was fifteen. Gram left me in jail for thirty-six hours and told me if I wanted to be an idiot for the rest of my life, I should keep running around with idiots. This is what I got for not calling, and for some reason it made me feel a little better.

"She's not serious," I said. "My brother's the criminal."

The Scottish Nurse turned back to my grandmother hopefully.

"Your other grandson," she said.

"Oh?" But now Gram appeared confused, and she was looking at the Scottish Nurse instead of me. "The one who fought in the war?"

"What is she talking about?" I said.

"She doesn't remember things very well."

"I used to live with her. She knows who I am. Gram... it's me. It's Spencer."

"Oh?"

"I don't think you understand."

"What is there to understand? I'm her grandson. She knows who the fuck I am."

But she didn't.

She had no idea who I was. I'd fucked up so much in the last twenty-four hours I didn't even know where to begin, but it never occurred to me that my grandmother wouldn't be there to unfuck any of it.

"She knows who I am," I said, only this time I sort of mumbled it to no one in particular and stared at the floor.

"I'm so sorry," said the Scottish Nurse. My grandmother disappeared back into her bedroom. "She's been this way for a long time."

There was an unbearable buzzing in my head. I broke out in hives—hives all over my body. The Scottish Nurse could see them forming on my neck and arms, and I think it freaked her out. She just looked so sorry for me. I couldn't even ask her what to do, so I bolted down the hall, but just as I was about to crash through the door of that white-pillared portico to a night spent sleeping in the Buick, I noticed the Admitting Nurse, who was now teetering on a stool as she struggled to stick a file back on a long gray shelf. The Admitting Nurse was actually a little hard to look at. She had a weak chin, and her teeth were hidden behind all this complicated orthodontia. She could have been twenty-five. She could have been fifty. I had no idea.

"Can I help you?" she said, stepping off the stool to face me.

"I need to talk to a doctor."

The Admitting Nurse looked irritated, but she slapped a clipboard down in front of me. She didn't even notice the hives.

"Fill this out," she said.

"It's not for me."

"Doesn't matter."

"These are admission forms," I said.

"You need to fill them out to talk to a doctor."

"Can I stay here?"

"It's not a hotel."

"Yeah, but if I fill these out?"

"Fill them out and you can talk to a doctor."

In my state of mind, I thought any connection to my grandmother would somehow disqualify me from residency, so I strung together a series of lies that in retrospect made my admission less, and not more, likely. I told them my name was Spencer Chase. (Chase is the name of the bank on my credit card.) I gave them the address of the loft in SoHo (a place I never lived), and then I checked the depressed and suicidal boxes. I also said I was on meds. I wrote *the little green ones* in the margin since I still don't know what that shit is called. The Admitting Nurse bitched at me for not having an ID or proof of insurance, so I told her I was the heir to the vulcanized rubber fortune. (In fact, all I got when my dad died was the Buick and a $25,000 federal tax lien.) She was still unimpressed, but she finally went and got a doctor anyway—this Asian intern who reminded me of Kyong the Korean grad student who taught me calculus freshman year. I couldn't understand a word that guy said either. I'm not sure the broken English mattered. They were both so much smarter than me I wouldn't have understood much of what they said anyway. This Kyong smiled a lot, asked me a million questions in enthusiastic but unintelligible English, appeared concerned about my hives, not to mention the depressed and suicidal boxes, then prescribed me twenty milligrams a day of the little green ones before he swatted me on the back and welcomed me to Widworth. The Admitting Nurse looked horrified.

# Chapter 6

*Spring 1989*

I took the Weed Whacker Scar deep over the green wall in center field toward the end of fall practice and that's when all that choreographed clockwork finally came to a grinding halt. It felt like nothing when it left my bat, just a solid ping before it towered into the outfield, but they all stopped to watch it—every single one of those Assholes—and it was dead silence when it finally cleared the wall. Canelli put an arm around me when my turn in the cage was over, and he led me back to the dugout where he said something about Lou Gehrig before he told me he thought I could be All-League at third base. It turned out I was the only freshman to make the varsity, which meant instead of spring break in Cancún with the guys, I got to go to Deland, Florida, with twelve Assholes who talked about nothing but investment banking twenty-four hours a day.

They were all interviewing for jobs on Wall Street, so they couldn't shut up about places like Lehman Brothers and Bear

Stearns, JP Morgan and Goldman Sachs—about how Goldman paid a hundred and sixty grand a year with salary and bonus and how some baseball alum named Fitz worked at Lehman for only five years before he invented a foreign currency trading algorithm and retired at thirty-one with fifty million dollars in the bank and a house in the Hamptons.

My jobs growing up were all drudgery: I bagged groceries. I rode a paper route. I mopped the floors of a pool hall in Newark called Bobo's while the bookie who worked the pay phone in the bathroom flicked cigarette butts at my head. I could barely navigate Yale. The idea that I might have to do something after I graduated I didn't even want to consider, and the thought of Wall Street almost seemed ridiculous. I didn't even like New York. It was filled with ten million strangers, and besides taking my shirt off in front of a thousand of them, the only other memory I had of the place really wasn't that fond.

We had gone to Mount Sinai to see some famous immunologist when Nathan got really sick, and even though we were only supposed to be there overnight, my mom brought enough stuff to stay a week. Besides all our crap, Nathan's hospital room was filled with plastic machines and tubes and flashing lights all over the place. There were also a couple heavy-duty chairs you could sleep in and a TV attached to the ceiling over by the door. They whisked Nathan off the moment we got there to take blood and perform tests no five-year-old should even know exist. Troy and Anthony bolted to roam the hospital, but I was still lunging around, so I couldn't keep up. I stayed put and had a front row seat as the Mazios started rolling in.

First, it was my grandparents. My father's father is tall—six foot three at least—with a full head of white hair, a combination that fuels a douchey confidence that never seems to burn out. He was wearing a charcoal gray suit with a bright red and blue striped tie which seemed unnecessary on a Saturday for a guy who was retired. His last name wasn't really Mazio either. It was Maziotis. He was Greek, not Italian, but there weren't enough Greeks in Trenton in 1947 to make selling life insurance worthwhile, so he married an Italian girl with an enormous family, dropped the "tis" and became the life insurance king of Central New Jersey. He always creeped my mom out. I never knew what he did to her, but it went all the way back to the days before my parents were married, when they were first dating at Hofstra—my mom the basketball star, my dad the backup quarterback. Whatever he'd done, she never liked to be anywhere near him.

My grandmother (the bona fide Italian) was with him and, like most of the women in her family, she was short and squat with monster double Ds. She took an hour to emerge from a fur coat that went all the way to the floor. It was a performance taking that thing off, but so much of what they did felt that way. My grandfather once took me down to the banks of Lake Anna and stuck a fishing pole in my hands so he could take pictures of me holding it. We didn't fish. He just wanted the photo to hang on a wall in the house as if he'd made a memory that would last a lifetime. It never occurred to him that he'd actually succeeded, and even though they wanted you to know they had money (he sold his insurance business and retired to Lake Anna), my grandmother was cheap as fuck. She would fill my bathtub at night with about an inch of lukewarm water and then sit there to make sure I didn't use any more while she asked me shitty questions like: Who do you like better—your mother or your father? Or, why don't you ever spend any time with your other grandparents? But she existed in a bizarro dreamworld where she did no wrong and the truth was nothing more than your opinion because she'd deny ever asking me those questions or that she skimped on the bath water. She even promised to pay for college until I actually got into one.

"Why did you tell them when we would be here?" said my mom the moment they left the room to get coffee.

"How could I not?" said my dad.

He already looked beaten. My dad was tall, but not tall enough. Good looking, but not good looking enough. He was destined to be the backup quarterback, but it wasn't like he wanted to be the starter. It was more like he wanted to disappear altogether. You could tell he didn't want to be there, like he was trapped inside a life he never wanted. He didn't say anything else. He just ducked out to go smoke one of the sixty thousand cigarettes he lit that weekend.

My mom was nearly as tall as my dad, five foot eleven in sneakers, and she had jet black hair that was always pulled away from her face in a tight ponytail, but she was showing the strain of Nathan's never-ending illness. She still had sharp features, but you could see the lines on her forehead now and a few stray, frizzled gray hairs, and the more she poured herself into Nathan's mystery, the more out of control Troy and Anthony got.

Then my Aunt Barbara showed up with her second husband and kids—all three of them: an older blond girl of unknown origin from a man no one ever met, and the two rotten ones. My Aunt Barb had been married once before, but it only lasted six months, and she was pregnant when he left her, so nobody really believed he was the dad. When I was a little older, I learned she'd had an affair with her married boss and that he'd sent her packing with a settlement that included an agreement never to have anything to do with the kid. The two rotten girls were just a little older than me. Their names sounded like "Garbage" and "Wretched" if you said them fast enough, and they both had these upturned little pig noses. They lunged through the hospital hallways making fun of me the whole day—back and forth between Nathan's room and the vending machine where they shoveled down Snickers bars and Ho Hos. I tried to hide from their giggling. I pretended not to hear them. I disappeared into my own head, repeating the words "Garbage and Wretched" over and over to drown them out. Their dad was a total wallflower, a supposed musician, content to sponge off the Mazio money. He was balding and soft—just generally unimpressive. I'm not sure he worked a day in his life. Aunt Barb didn't have a job either. That first kid ended her desire to work as completely as it did her first marriage, and it was like she'd lived every day since waiting for her parents to die so she could inherit their small fortune.

It was getting late that first night. My dad was already gone. Troy and Anthony got in trouble for unplugging medical devices in the rooms of elderly patients, so he had to get them out of there. I just remember the World Series on the TV above me as I dozed in one of those sleeper chairs. Nathan was finally asleep after a grueling, inconclusive day with doctors and nurses coming and going with all the tests and scans. I worried every time they took him away that they would come back with horrible news, but Nathan stayed totally calm the whole time. He was just curious about everything—what was happening to him, what they could do about it—until I finally felt ashamed that I was the one who was afraid, and I wondered what was inside my little brother that wasn't inside me.

"I'm surprised your parents aren't here too, Erin," said Aunt Barb as she pulled the covers over Nathan while my mom put the room back together. "Are you still not speaking to your mother?"

"There's no need for anyone to be here," said my mom as she put the top back on a Tupperware bowl that had been holding potato salad about an hour before.

"My father likes to make sure he's getting what he paid for."

"I already thanked him. Isn't that what he paid for?"

Aunt Barb stood up from the bed.

"I'm worried about my brother," she said.

"Are you?"

"You're not?"

"I think we're all exhausted."

"He seems unhappy… more than usual."

"His son is sick, and we don't know what's wrong."

"Is that really all you think it is?"

My mom stood up straight. She towered over Aunt Barb. She was at least eight inches taller.

"You really don't have to stay," she said. "I have it from here."

"Do you, though?"

"Why don't you just say what you came here to say?"

Aunt Barb paused for a second, but not so much because she was carefully considering her words, more just to savor the moment.

"It's no wonder this kid is sick all the time," she said. "Look at the environment he's in. Your husband is not well. Troy and Anthony are frothing at the mouth, and that one…"

She nodded in my direction like she was embarrassed to be related to me.

"And that one what?" said my mom.

"Let's just say Einstein didn't need to turn a light switch on and off a hundred million times to know what it did."

"Edison."

"What?"

"I think you mean Edison."

"Can't you see there's something wrong in your house?"

I've never really been sure if you're allowed to hate someone in your own family. I mean, do you really have to take this kind of shit just because you're related? I kept waiting for my mom to let her have it. She could've hit Aunt Barb double-barreled. Garbage was a bed wetter and Wretched ate her scabs. We all knew this, but my mom wouldn't say it. She wouldn't say anything. I wanted to stand up and let Aunt Barb know we all knew her kids were as weird as I was, but I was afraid of what either of them might do to me, so I didn't.

"I think I'd like you to leave now."

Aunt Barb looked up at the TV and then down at her watch.

"I hate baseball anyway."

My mom waited for every last one of them to leave before she began to cry. I could still hear the baseball game over my head. The Yankees were ahead 4–2. My mom sat in her chair for a minute staring up at the TV, but then she came over and sat at the edge of my chair, still thinking I was asleep, and she gently pushed the hair up out of my face.

"All I ever wanted was for you boys to be happy," she said. "Happy and healthy. Why does nothing ever turn out the way I want it to?"

She wiped the tears from her eyes and picked up the phone. The call was short and muffled, so I didn't really hear what was said. I just know Gram and Papa showed up the next day. They came with no angles, no axes to grind, and nothing to hide, so you never had to worry if one of them was coming up behind you. The whole place felt different the moment they got there. Papa turned on the World Series again, but the Yankees were getting their asses kicked, so he mumbled some shit about how he hated the Dodgers and sat down in the chair next to the bed. He'd brought with him something in a crumpled brown paper bag, and with the game out of reach for the Yankees, he pulled a framed photo out of the sack. This is when I learned my grandfather was from the Bronx, transplanted to Massachusetts to run a radio station. The man hardly ever spoke—unless you wanted to talk baseball.

"Now this was my favorite team," he said. It was an autographed photo of the 1961 Yankees, and he held it so Nathan could see it. "And you know which of these fellas was the best?"

He pointed to Bobby Richardson. "Not big. Not fast. Hardly ever hit any home runs. Still the MVP of the 1960 World Series. Don't listen when they tell you you can't do it."

Nathan smiled ear to ear.

"Do you have them in sports yet?" said Gram.

"No. Mom. We don't—"

"I'm just asking. As much as you don't want to admit it, basketball was very good to you. It got you into a good school." She looked at me then. "It wasn't as easy for a girl to get into college back then."

"Do you really want to talk about basketball right now?"

Papa gave that framed photograph to Nathan, and I thought to myself: *What do the 1961 Yankees have to do with anything?* But Nathan took that picture and looked at it like he knew exactly what it meant, like he knew it somehow connected him to something, something that made him happy, and within minutes that famous immunologist appeared in the room with good news. Two days later Reggie Jackson would hit three home runs in a single game while Nathan watched in awe, and he would forever after be a Yankee fan. He hung that photograph of the 1961 Yankees on the wall above his bed back home in New Brunswick. It was his good luck charm, and now that good luck charm had led me all the way to Deland, Florida, and twelve Assholes who talked about nothing but investment banking twenty-four hours a day.

I sat quietly toward the front of the bus with no one in the seat next to me as we headed back to our Deland motel. It was dusk as I stared out the window, once again wondering what I was doing there. It made me queasy to think about things that hadn't happened yet. It's like the future just lurks out there somewhere in the darkness waiting to beat the shit out of you, so I hid from it the best I could, but as I reclined in my seat and rested my head against the window, thoughts of a guy named Fitz and his fifty million dollars danced in my head. That future seemed solid. It felt secure—something that would chase the Dread away forever.

I got my first shot at a job on Wall Street later that season. It was a Saturday, and we were all in the locker room getting dressed. Every once in a while the jayvee would have a Saturday game against somebody shitty like Bridgeport University or Housatonic Community College while we played a weekend doubleheader. Our locker room was always cool and musty when you first got there, but you could tell the place would really stink if you gave it a chance—like after practice, when we were all sweaty and the showers were going, and the place smelled like hot feet. There were rows and rows of blue chicken wire lockers, simple, crude, blue wooden benches, and a red rubbery floor. It was pretty unimpressive really. I don't think anything had been done to the Yale Field House since about 1950. I sometimes got the feeling nothing had been done to anything at Yale since about 1950. The whole place felt tired and run down. They're supposedly raising billions of dollars to renovate everything—all the colleges, administrative buildings, classrooms, libraries, everything. I'm sure I'll be getting hit up for money soon to fix the place even though it was a total dump the whole time I was there.

The varsity uniforms were brand new button-downs—home whites and road grays—with "Yale" written in blue, sewn-on block letters right across the chest of both jerseys. Joe the Equipment Guy told me Eddie Canelli used his own money to buy them since Yale wouldn't spring for the upgrades. The jayvee uniforms were from about 1978—these miserably tight-fitting pinstripe pants that went with blue polyester pullover jerseys with white, iron-on script that was all cracked and faded and peeling off. Every day Joe gave you a wad of gray T-shirts, socks, a jock strap, gray shorts and a practice jersey, all held together by an oversized safety pin with your number scratched on it, and on game days you got another pin with your uniform.

I was putting on my home whites as we listened to Larry complain about his summer job.

"I'm not complaining," he said.

"It sounds a little like you're complaining," said Norman.

"Why would you stay here and take Italian all summer?" said Billy, struggling with a pair of scissors to free his combination lock from a glob of Vaseline-slathered athletic tape.

"So he doesn't have to work," said Norman.

Billy had an entire drug store in his locker: deodorant, a toothbrush, toothpaste, shaving cream, razors, aftershave, Band-Aids, Q-tips, hand lotion, soap, shampoo, conditioner, contact lens solution, and about six tins of chewing tobacco. He said that's how they did it in The Show, and he was oddly confident that The Show was where he was headed. He also had four thirty-three-inch Easton aluminum bats with the green lettering (he used those during games), five thirty-three-inch wood Louisville Sluggers (he used those during batting practice, so he'd be ready for The Show), two oversized outfielder's gloves, an infielder's glove, five pairs of batting gloves, sliding pants, and more wrist bands than any one human could possibly hope to use in a lifetime. It was no wonder the seniors hated him the most. One of them had actually encased his combination lock in a knot of athletic tape and Vaseline.

"I want to be able to read Italian," said Larry.

"Who did that anyway?" said Norman, nodding at the tape glob.

"Who do you think?" said Billy.

"I don't know. You've narrowed it down to all of them."

"I think it was the Big Dumb one."

"You saw him?" said Larry.

"I didn't see him do it, but he was in here."

"He does look like the kind of guy who might spend some time wrapping your combination lock in athletic tape and Vaseline," said Norman.

"You tell him to go fuck himself?" said Larry.

"No," said Billy.

"Why not?"

"He told me to go fuck myself first."

"And you didn't do anything?"

"What are you gonna read in Italian?" said Billy.

"Dante," said Larry.

"Dante?" said Billy. "Why don't you just suck a dick and get it over with?"

"Spencer takes Italian," said Larry. "Are you saying Spencer sucks dicks?"

"I'm saying Spencer doesn't read Dante."

"What's your dad do anyway?" I said.

"He works at Morgan Stanley," said Larry.

"Is he a banker?"

"He's a prick."

"But it's in the City."

"Is what in the City?"

"The job."

"Where else would it be?"

"You don't want it?"

"Larry wants to read Dante this summer," said Norman as he stood off the bench.

"You know you have your mother's thighs," said Larry.

"It's the pinstripes," said Norman.

"If you don't want the job, I'll take it," I said.

"I'll talk to my dad, which is a favor in and of itself since it's such a pain in the ass, but I can't promise you anything."

# Chapter 7

*Summer 1992*

The Widworth library was a smallish room off the main hallway on the West Wing second floor. It had a single window at the far end, a table with two wooden chairs on each side, and two walls filled with books that were probably donated by rich people cleaning out their attics. There was a paperback set called the Signet Classics. I think it had all the books I was supposed to read in high school but didn't. I don't know when I stopped liking books—maybe when they started to make me explain what was in them. Mrs. Ewing would write red felt-tip notes in the margins of my sixth grade book reports: *Plot summary! What do you think about this? What are the themes? What are the deeper meanings?*

I started in on the Signet Classics not long after I checked in to Widworth. I kept to the short ones at first. *Of Mice and Men. The Sun Also Rises.* A depressing little book of short stories, one of which was about a dude who wakes up one morning to find himself transformed into a giant cockroach—and that was the best thing that happened to him. There was also a book about Freud that I took a look at to see if I could figure out what the fuck was wrong with me. Then I picked up *The Crying of Lot 49*—mostly because a blurb from *The New York Times Book Review* printed on the back cover said: *"The comedy crackles, the puns pop, the satire explodes…"*

That book is 152 pages long, and there is nothing funny in it until page 151. They're right about to auction off the stamp collection. Some lawyer named Genghis Cohen (hilarious) is explaining to Ms. Oedipa Maas that the auctioneer is referred to as a "cryer." The auctioneer "cries" the sale, he says, to which Oedipa responds: "Your fly is open." So I laughed and that drew the attention of my roommate, Leonard, who was trolling the hallway.

Leonard looked like a greyhound from a dog track, and his hair was sticking out all over the place like he'd just pulled himself out of bed. He was holding a plastic container full of applesauce in one hand and a plastic spoon in the other, and he sat down at the table right across from me.

One of the best things about the Widworth library was a little *Webster's Pocket Dictionary*. I kept it with me all the time so I could figure out what I was reading. "Moron" is defined as a person who has a potential mental age between eight and twelve years. An "imbecile" is someone with a potential mental age between three and seven years. And an "idiot" is feebleminded— potential mental age not exceeding three years. Leonard was an imbecile.

Widworth wasn't so bad really, even with all the mental patients running around. I did have to turn in my shoes, and they gave me the standard-issue navy blue half-scrubs/half-pajamas to wear, and of course they put me in isolation for the first seventy-two hours with a psych tech checking in on me every twenty minutes since I'd ticked the suicidal box, but it really wasn't that bad. It also didn't hurt that the twenty milligrams a day of that little green shit went right to work.

The brochure in the reception area said Widworth was built in the "Old Georgian" style—two-story brick buildings, majestic white pillars, white trim here and there, a rolling lawn at the back of the property that seemed to stretch on forever—state of the art in 1971: "Offering a human approach to the treatment of mental disease. Assisted living since 1985." A nurse with absurdly long fingernails gave me my little green pills every morning in a tiny paper cup. It was free, courtesy of the taxpayers of the Commonwealth of Massachusetts, and once I persuaded them I was no longer a danger to myself, they let me come and go as I pleased, which meant I could stay in the West Wing of Widworth and still check in on Gram, who lived in the East Wing, whenever I wanted. The only drag was they kept making me do all the group therapy and random arts and crafts bullshit that was actually for the real wing nuts.

My psych tech (the guy who took my vital signs every six hours and made sure I didn't hang myself with shoelaces) was a great big fat person named Timothy Duddle. Duddle was a tool who wanted to go to nursing school, so he took it personally when I wouldn't do the finger paints, and he'd make me sit in the Widworth library like it was some kind of solitary confinement. The thing about the West Wing of Widworth was there weren't any doors anywhere. It was just open doorways, so it was sort of impossible to confine anyone to anywhere. Duddle had to stand guard outside the library just to keep me from leaving.

"What are you doing?" said Leonard when he finally had the foil lid off the applesauce.

"What does it look like I'm doing?"

"Reading a book."

"Shut up in there," said Duddle.

All this caught the attention of my other roommate, Alan, who then slid past Duddle's considerable flab and thrust himself into the conversation.

Alan looked more like a cross between Charles Manson and Jesus Christ, and he was wearing a pair of latex gloves. I'd been avoiding him since the day I got there, but that only made it worse.

"Pynchon," he said.

"What's with the gloves?" said Duddle.

"*Gravity's Rainbow* is more substantial."

"Alan," said Duddle.

"This place is filthy, and it's nobody's business what I touch."

Alan peeled the gloves off and dropped them at Duddle's feet before he strolled over to one of the bookcases.

Twenty milligrams a day of the little green pills had helped at first. It ground down the spikes, slowed my thoughts, but there's uncertainty around every corner, and the Dread has its ways. It always manages to slither around whatever barricade I erect in front of it. It permeated even the pharmaceutical barrier Kyong had provided. Twenty milligrams a day pretty much stopped doing jack shit about three weeks into my stay. I was uncomfortable sitting there.

"You know I've read almost every book in here," said Alan. "Some of them twice. We have a version of *Crime and Punishment* in the original Russian. Do you speak any foreign languages?"

"No," I said.

"I thought you went to Yale?"

I didn't want to encourage him, so I didn't answer. The only thing they actually make you do at Yale is take a foreign language. I took Italian. I thought it would be the easiest since

I'm a quarter Italian, but when someone says something to me in another language, it's like drinking from a fire hose. Italian made me feel stupid five days a week. And nothing was as demoralizing as the Yale language lab on test day. I would strain to understand the high-pressured torrent of questions, then flounder through four- or five-word answers only to hear through the dampening of my headphones a symphony of voices all around me, stringing together sentence after cogent Italian sentence long after I'd exhausted my own puerile *vocabolario*.

"Memory and facility for foreign language are the best barometers of intelligence," said Alan. "I speak English, French, and Russian."

"If you're such a genius, what are you doing here?"

"You don't know?"

"How would I know what you're doing here?"

"I shot my editor," he said.

"The editor of what?"

"My novel."

"Alan makes up people," said Leonard.

"Why would you shoot the editor of your novel?" I said.

"Because she deserved it. She was ruining my book."

"You people need to shut up," said Duddle.

"She was changing it," he said. "She told me it was offensive and that my protagonist was unsympathetic."

"So you shot her?"

"She was turning it into a lie."

"You shot your editor for editing your book?"

"I didn't kill her," he said indignantly. "The bullet passed clean through her abdomen. She's fine. So is my book by the way. Nobody ever wants to talk about that."

"He's supposed to be in there by himself," said Duddle. "Are you gonna shut up or not?"

Leonard started to scrape the inside of the applesauce container with the plastic spoon, which is about the most annoying sound imaginable.

"What's *your* story?" said Alan.

"I don't have a story," I said.

"Just on vacation at the mental hospital?"

Then Leonard noticed the shiny foil lid sitting on the table top with that one last glob of applesauce stuck to the back of it, and he smiled like the imbecile that he was before he leaned over and licked that glob right off the back of the lid without bothering to pick it up.

"Take your time," said Alan. "I'm not going anywhere."

"Yeah, you are," said Duddle. "I'm gonna call in a takedown if you don't get the fuck out of here."

A "takedown" is what happened when you lost your shit in that place. They'd call in about four other psych techs to drag you to the ground like an animal before they hauled you off to wherever it was they took you when you lost your shit in that place. Duddle seemed to administer about one takedown a week—usually at Leonard's expense—but now I was the one losing my shit. The Dread was creeping, slowly expanding, working its tentacles into every inch of me.

"Do you really need all that help?" said Alan. "You weigh four hundred pounds."

"It's protocol," said Duddle.

"You should have a little more faith in yourself."

"Get out."

"Fine," said Alan. "I'll go. You don't have to get all huffy." But then he looked back at me. "I'll figure you out," he said. "Don't say another word. The story you tell is gonna be full of shit anyway."

# Chapter 8

*Summer 1989*

Larry told his dad he wouldn't graduate in four years if he didn't take Italian over the summer, and since Yale cost twenty thousand dollars a year, I got Larry's summer job. Larry said his dad would've taken Italian himself to save twenty grand. Vandershar hooked me up with an apartment broker in the City and a couple nights at the Yale Club. I was all set to go when Canelli pulled me aside one day after practice. He told me he got me a job through the athletic department and had arranged for me to stay in Morse College all summer with a roster spot on a team in the Ansonia Summer League. He told me I'd had the best freshman season of anyone who'd ever played for him, but Eddie Canelli was like one of those B-movie directors who could step away from a complete piece of shit and declare it a masterpiece, so I didn't think much of it. I told him I'd think about it, but it made me uncomfortable to think about it. There was no way I was giving up a job on Wall Street to watch sprinklers turn on and off at the Yale Bowl for eight bucks an hour just so I could play in the Ansonia Summer League. I left for New York without ever saying another word to him about it.

I waited in the Morgan Stanley lobby for about half an hour my first day. I was so nervous I think I told the receptionist my name was Spazio. I didn't own a suit, so I wore a pair of unpressed khaki pants and a crappy blue blazer that I always threw on whenever I needed a jacket. I also borrowed a pair of scuffed brown loafers from Larry. The Morgan Stanley lobby looked about like I thought it would—enormous, all marble and dark wood with a huge conference room on the other side of a floor-to-ceiling window, and beyond that the endlessness of the City. I sat in a leather chair and picked up a *Fortune* magazine, flipping the pages without reading a thing until Larry's dad finally showed up in the lobby. He lit up like I was the Chief Executive Officer of Citibank. He didn't seem like a dick at all.

"It's nice to meet you, Mr. Zayger," I said as I shook his hand.

His head was as big as Larry's, only it was round. Everything about Larry's dad was round, like a cherub, and his hair was all wild and curly and salt and pepper.

"I really appreciate this," I said.

"It's quite alright," he said. "My son is allergic to work. I'm glad to know that at least his friends are not. Let's take you down. I'll introduce you to Ross."

We headed back out to the elevators where he pressed the down button. We stood there awkwardly for a minute. He smiled. I didn't have anything else to say, so my mind returned to its usual state of blankness as the butterflies roamed free in my stomach. He tried to make small talk related to a story he said was on that day's front page of *The New York Times*, but I had no idea what he was talking about.

"Have you found a place to live yet?"

"Yeah," I said, staring at the numbers above the elevator. "Excellent."

It really wasn't that excellent. I'm pretty sure the apartment broker Vandershar hooked me up with was Chinese Mafia. I met him in the Meatpacking District. He wore a shiny silver suit and immediately asked me for a thousand dollars. When I wouldn't hand it over, he said something that sounded like *fucky bullshee*. But all I had was a thousand dollars. It was supposed to cover a security deposit, my first month's rent, and anything else I needed before I got a paycheck. I told him I had to take a leak. Then I ducked into a restaurant and bolted through the kitchen.

When I got back to the Yale Club after that wasted day, I was pretty rattled, so I stopped at the bar off the Main Lounge, which smelled vaguely of bog water scotch, only to find myself surrounded by a small army of alcoholic oldsters all giving me some side-eye since I was in violation of the dress code. I wasn't about to risk my fake ID there, so I went to bed and got up early the next morning to get back at it. I started with a place uptown between First and Second, advertised as a "huge prewar walk-up with high ceilings and thick walls." It turned out to be four hundred and sixty square feet of roach-infested mold with a view of the fire escape next door. It got worse from there. I ended up in a two hundred and eighty-square-foot studio located uptown in a building owned by Columbia. I think the two hundred and eighty square feet included the bathroom. No matter how I arranged the futon, I couldn't seem to get my head more than five feet away from the toilet. It cost five hundred dollars a month. I didn't even care. By the time I signed the lease, I felt like Kirk Gibson right after he hit that home run off Dennis Eckersley in game one of the World Series.

The elevator doors opened.

"You might have to get a suit," said Mr. Zayger.

He pressed the button to take us to the eleventh floor.

"I need a paycheck first."

"Perfectly understandable," he said, smiling.

"Where we going?"

"To eleven."

"What's on eleven?"

"Ross."

"Who's Ross?"

"So you're quite the ballplayer," he said.

"I don't know."

"My son says you're the best player on the team."

"We have a lot of good players."

"He says you're quite the slugger."

Fortunately, it only took about three seconds to get from the eightieth floor to the eleventh. I think we might have been weightless for a second. We got off at eleven and entered another lobby.

"Lawrence Zayger for Ross Carp," said Larry's dad to the receptionist.

The words "Empire Life & Annuity Company" shimmered behind her in gaudy gold letters.

The job—Larry's job—was not with his dad. And it wasn't at Morgan Stanley either. It was with Larry's dad's life insurance broker at a shithole called Empire Life & Annuity Company. I started to feel hot, and I was suddenly very aware of the collar of my shirt. The receptionist called Ross and exchanged a few words, then set the phone back down and said she'd take me back in a minute. I was struggling to breathe since my shirt was trying to strangle me.

"If you need anything," said Larry's dad, "you can call me."

I never heard from him again.

The lobby at Empire Life & Annuity looked nothing like the lobby at Morgan Stanley. There was no marble. No wood panels. There weren't even any windows. It was dark and lit with neon bulbs hidden behind yellowish, translucent panes in the ceiling. The carpet was beige and dirty, and there was an enormous coffee stain near the door. I sat down in an orange chair, and suddenly I could feel a pressure on the back of my neck like the weight of the entire building was pressing down on my shoulders.

After a couple minutes, the receptionist led me back through a maze of temporary walls and cubicles to a cramped windowless conference room. Three of us started that day: me, this kid Dennis, and this Black kid named Marvcus. Dennis had spiny hair that stood straight up off his head, and Marvcus looked like he was twelve. We sat there waiting for Ross Carp, just the three of us—me now holding back the Dread while Marvcus and Dennis flicked a small triangle of folded paper between goal posts they were making with their thumbs and index fingers.

"Either of you know what we're supposed to do here?" I said.

"I think we're just supposed to wait," said Dennis.

"I mean the job," I said.

"Oh," said Dennis. "I don't know."

"How'd you get it then?" I said.

"How did I get what?" said Dennis.

"This job."

"The ad on the message board."

"An ad on a message board?" I said. "You found this job from an ad on a message board?"

"Uh-huh."

"Where?"

"School."

"What school?"

"Brooklyn College," said Dennis.

"What about you?" I said to Marvcus.

"Same," he said. "We took all the ads and threw 'em in the trash. How'd you find out about it?"

The conference room door blew open, and a guy who looked like Buddy Holly exploded into the room. He wore a pale blue button-down shirt, striped tie, and dark, thick-rimmed Buddy Holly glasses. There were also huge pits of sweat under both of his arms. This was Ross Carp—Larry's dad's life insurance broker.

"Welcome," said Ross. "Welcome to Empire Life & Annuity Company."

He said it like Empire Life & Annuity Company was a destination resort.

"Okay good," he said. "This is good. It's good to start small. You three'll actually have an advantage over the other interns. Feel free to ask questions. That's what I'm here for. Interrupt me if I say anything you don't understand." He smiled. "Great. This is great. This is a great opportunity for you. You'll learn the industry. You'll make some money... and we all like money, right? Right? You're gonna like it here. This is great. This is great."

We remained motionless.

"Okay, good," he said, sitting down sidesaddle on the table. "Why don't we start by getting to know each other? My name is Ross Carp. I'm a lead broker here at Empire Life. I started the same way you will. I summer interned three years in a row. Now I make six figures. I own my own house. I drive a Mercedes. Nice... right?" He looked at each of us with another broad, friendly smile. "Why don't we start with you," he said, nodding at Marvcus, so Marvcus introduced himself. Then Ross looked at Dennis and smiled, so Dennis introduced himself. Then Ross looked at me.

"I'm Spencer Mazio," I said.

"And what brought you to Empire Life, Spencer Mazio?"

"Mr. Zayger," I said. "Upstairs. From Morgan Stanley."

"Ah. Right. Great. It's great to have you. It's great to have all three of you," he said as he stood. "Okay, I don't have all day, so let's do this. Empire Life is a diversified insurance provider. We provide a variety of financial services here, all for high-net-worth individuals." He paced in the narrow strip of dirty carpet between the chairs and wall on the other side of the table. "One of the financial products we sell is life insurance. Any of you have experience with life insurance?"

I was the grandson of the Life Insurance King of Central New Jersey, and I didn't know shit about life insurance. You can bet Marvcus and Dennis didn't either.

"Then today you'll learn about life insurance." He paused, like he expected a question, but we had no questions. We didn't have a thought among us. "There are two basic types of life insurance," he said. "Term life insurance and cash value, or whole, life insurance. The companies we broker life insurance for offer both, but we do not sell term life insurance policies. This is very important. We do *not* sell term life. We sell *whole* life. Term life is probably what you think of when you think of life insurance. With a term life policy, you pay premiums so your beneficiaries receive a certain amount of money when you die, but if you stop paying the premiums, your wife and kids get nothing. We do *not* offer this sort of life insurance. We offer *whole* life insurance. Whole life is an investment. It's an investment in your family's future. Think of it as a combination investment account and life insurance policy. A part of the premiums you pay each month go into a brokerage account and get invested, so they build equity, and a portion goes into a regular savings account and earns interest. But here's the difference. Unlike term life, the premiums on a whole life policy don't go on forever. This is very important. Eventually, a whole life policy becomes fully funded. Do you understand? This is the key. It means no more premiums, but you still have the life insurance." He smiled again. "This is very important. It's life insurance, but after a while you don't have to pay for it. When you die, your family gets the life insurance proceeds, the brokerage account and the savings, and they don't pay a dime in taxes. Any questions?"

I didn't know what he was talking about, and I was the one who went to Yale.

"How do we sell it?" said Marvcus.

"It sells itself," said Ross.

"How's it do that?"

"They need it. That's the beauty of life insurance."

"Yeah, but how do you sell something to a guy when he's never gonna get it himself? He's dead."

"It's for his family," said Ross. "How can you possibly say no to something that's for your kids?"

"That's pretty good, I guess."

"Marcus gets it," said Ross.

"*Marv*cus," said Marvcus.

"Isn't that what I said?"

"No. You said Marcus. It's Marvcus. With a 'v.' Right in the middle."

"Marv-cus?"

"Yeah, Marvcus."

"Well, Marv-cus, my assistant, Beverly, will give you a list every morning of men between the ages of forty and fifty-five who make more than two hundred grand a year. These guys have term life or nothing. You call these guys and give them the pitch."

"You want us to make cold calls," said Marvcus.

"No," said Ross, emphasizing the point with his index finger. "I do not want you to make cold calls. You're not selling Glengarry Highlands for fuck's sake. This isn't pink sheet penny stock bullshit. You're selling something necessary... whole life... to someone who needs it... married, kids, smoker. You're doing some poor fuck a favor. He could be dead next week. He doesn't know. He doesn't know he's throwing money away on a term policy. And if he doesn't have life insurance, well that's just plain irresponsible, isn't it? You're making the call for him. He should be the one calling you. So all you have to do is explain to him what he needs... and you will sell. Okay? You will sell. And there is nothing you will ever fuck, drink, or feast on that will feel better than your first sale. Got it?"

"How do we get paid?" asked Marvcus.

"You make seven-fifty an hour, but you also make a bonus for every policy you sell. You make a call. If you have someone interested, you tell them to hold, and you find me. I'll get on the phone and close the sale. If you can't find me, have me paged, keep them on the phone as long as you can, and if I still can't be found, tell them someone from the office will be getting back to them shortly with more details."

"How big is the bonus?" said Marvcus.

"You ask a lot of questions," said Ross.

"I thought you said you were here to answer questions?"

"Is that another question?"

"Well... yeah, I guess."

"I sold fifteen policies a week," said Ross. "I didn't have a clue what the bonus was until I got my first paycheck. I was just happy to have a fuckin' job."

"So how much is it then?" said Marvcus.

"Twenty-five dollars a policy. My fifteen policies a week added about twelve hundred bucks a month to my pay. Happy now?"

We each got our own cubicle with a telephone, a few random office supplies, and a booklet with a scripted pitch we were supposed to memorize. Life insurance is arguably a worthwhile thing, and this was a list of men I didn't even know. Men I would never meet. People I would never talk to again, and I was fully aware of all this when I picked up the phone the first time. In fact, I was thinking these very things as I dialed, but I still couldn't keep my mind from flushing the words I'd memorized into the darkness where the Dread lurked. I forgot the whole thing and read from the script like a robot.

"Hello. This is Spencer Mazio from the Empire Life & Annuity Company. I'd like to talk to you about life insurance."

Click.

"Hello. This is Spencer Mazio from the Empire Life & Annuity Company. I'd like to talk to you about life insurance."

Click.

"Hello. This is Spencer Mazio from the Empire Life & Annuity Company. I'd like to talk to you about life insurance."

Click.

Every one of those clicks was another gut punch because it meant I had to dial another number. What was I even afraid of? Failing? Sounding stupid? Who cared? But it got worse. I finally committed the script to memory so I wouldn't sound like an idiot, but once I was capable of negotiating the first few beats of the conversation, I always seemed to end up knee-deep in confrontation, facing down some fifty-something-year-old man who inevitably tired of my sales pitch and just wanted to get off the phone. Most of them hung up, but just enough stuck around to tell me to go fuck myself that it made the job feel like charging up a hill every morning with a nest of *fuck yous* waiting at the top.

The Dread fed on those *fuck yous*, and as the summer dragged on, it grew more powerful. I barely left my apartment, and I can't imagine hating something more than I hated that job. Embarrassed every morning getting in the elevator with all that banker larvae—most of them only a couple years older than me—talking like I wasn't even there, spilling the details of the deals they were on and all the models they were banging. Then I'd get off at the eleventh floor like a douche while they rode it all the way up to infinity, and by ten thirty, at least a dozen perfectly decent fifty-year-old fathers would have told me to go fuck myself. Touching the phone made me physically ill. I sold one policy all summer and that was to some guy's wife. The woman had been harassing her husband for weeks to get life insurance. She probably murdered him the next day.

I felt nothing when the sale was complete. No rush. No sense of accomplishment. No appreciation for the extra twenty-five dollars I'd just earned—just Dread—knowing I had to pick the phone up again. It was definitely not better than any of the fucks, drinks, or feasts I'd experienced to that point. I lost weight. My skin broke out. I was a mess, so to protect myself, the time between calls became more and more protracted until finally I couldn't bring myself to make them at all. I just stopped. I gave up and daydreamed of Fitz and his foreign currency trading algorithm as I slumped in my cubicle, pretending to be on the phone in case Beverly was watching, and when I knew she wasn't, I'd dial the people I actually knew.

Billy was mercurial. I never really knew when I might catch him. He wasn't working—at least not in the traditional sense. He was playing right field in a Pennsylvania summer league that had him driving two and three hours to games. Larry was usually pretty reachable around eleven. Italian was five days a week in the summer, but it met from nine to ten forty-five, so he was usually back in his room by eleven. He was mortified (but not surprised) to learn that my job was not at Morgan Stanley. He also confessed he regretted his decision to take Italian. Norman I could usually catch before Larry. He started in on the law firm drudgery around eight Central every morning, Bates stamping in solitude, so he looked forward to our calls as much as I did. We basically traded stories of boredom. Then every day at noon (nine Pacific), I'd call John Henry, who by then would be settled into his seat in the shack next to the driving range at his dad's country club.

"You don't even play golf," I said to him one afternoon.

It was a scorcher toward the end of July, so I had no interest in leaving the air-conditioning of the Empire Life & Annuity Company. I just sat there hunched low in my cubicle instead of heading out to lunch.

"That doesn't mean I can't run a driving range."

"You have no street cred."

"It's a country club."

"So."

"I learned to drive a tractor."

"What's the weather there?"

"Seventy-five... maybe. Sunny. Slight breeze off the ocean."

"It's nine thousand degrees here today."

"You know what you should do."

"No. What should I do?"

"You should quit and fly out here so you can do the drive back with me."

"I still don't understand why your mom is making you drive back to school."

"I told you. She has a fear of aviation."

"I know, but doesn't driving actually increase the odds of your death?"

"Possibly, but I generally like to take the path of least resistance when it comes to my mother."

"Even when it's hazardous to your health?"

"I'm serious. Do it."

"My lease isn't up until the end of August."

"I bet my dad would pay your August rent... and buy you a ticket out here. He wants no part of driving cross-country."

"And you can't do it alone?"

"That would not be the path of least resistance."

"I can't quit," I said.

"Then how bad can it really be?"

"I have a jar of peanut butter and a loaf of Wonder Bread in my desk."

"That doesn't sound that bad."

"You run a driving range," I said. "I sleep with a freezable thing under my pillow."

"Yeah, but you're on your own. You're independent. In the City. Spreading your wings."

Beverly got back from lunch, so I had to slump even lower.

"If you could see me right now, you would not be impressed."

"Where's Vandershar anyway?"

"Europe."

"Europe? Did he even tell you he was going?"

"No."

"That's reliable."

"So there's no one there?"

"Not really."

"You should quit."

"I need the cash."

"Then go talk to your boss."

"And say what?"

"I don't know. Tell him you want to invent an algorithm that sells life insurance."

"That's not a bad idea."

"Just talk to him. Jesus. What's he going to do? Fire you?"

So that's what I did. I went to talk to Ross Carp. His office was an odd rhomboid shape that looked like leftover space between the copy room and the bathroom. There was an institutional gray metal desk jammed up underneath the one window with barely room for anything else besides Ross, his chair, a green metal filing cabinet and a rickety bookshelf full of binders and bucket files, and a tattered paperback called *How to Get Along with People You Really Can't Stand*.

"What do you want?" he said.

"I was kind of hoping to talk to you," I said nervously.

"Kind of?" he said as he spun around in his chair and grabbed a pack of cigarettes off his desk. "What are you *kind of* hoping to talk to me about?"

"I don't think I'm very good at this."

"Not good at what?"

"The calls."

"The calls," he said.

"Yeah."

"What *are* you good at?" he said, lighting a cigarette.

He took a drag, then set the cigarette on the edge of an ashtray littered with the remnants of the other dozen or so cigarettes he'd sucked down that day.

"I don't know," I said.

"You don't know?" He leaned back in his chair and clasped his hands behind his head so I could see that his pits were soaked to the middle of his rib cage. "You're pretty good at fucking off. That's something."

"I was thinking maybe there was something else I could do."

"Like what? I could replace you with a button that does nothing when I push it." He reached for his cigarette. "Do you have any idea how I get paid?"

"Not really."

"I get paid when I sell. I get a commission when I sell. Every minute I don't sell... not getting paid. Sitting here, right now, talking to your sorry ass... not getting paid. Now you on the other hand, standing there in my doorway like a fuckwad. You're making seven-fifty an hour. Do you see the problem? That kid Dennis is nearly retarded and he sells." He smashed the cigarette in the ashtray, then looked at me. "You must be the dumbest fuck at Yale." He spun back around to return to his work. "Do what you want. But you can tell Lawrence Zayger I'm not paying him shit for you."

"Paying him? Paying him for what?"

"You don't even know that much, do you?" he said, looking back over his shoulder. "I told him I'd give him a rebate on a policy if he got his kid from Yale to make cold calls for me all summer, and he brings me your sorry ass. Fuck that. I'm not giving him shit for you. You don't want to make the phone calls, fine, but get the fuck out. There's nothing else for you to do here."

# Chapter 9

Vandershar surfaced about a week later. I didn't have the balls to quit, so I was still slinking into the office, but I was late that morning because the subway schedule was all fucked up. When I finally arrived, there was a message in Beverly's handwriting waiting for me:

*Meet at 645 Fifth Avenue. 11:00 a.m.*
*JVIII*

It turned out to be the Armani store. Jonathon wasn't there at 11:00 a.m. because Jonathon's never been on time for anything in his life, so I milled around a bit, gingerly turning over price tags the way I used to flip the pages of *Hustler* magazine in the back of the 7-Eleven when I was thirteen.

"Life insurance?" he said, reaching past me to knock the $175 plain white T-shirt out of my hand. "What the fuck is wrong with you?"

He was wearing long white linen shorts and an untucked blue oxford, and it struck me how long this made him seem. We were the same height, but he had a much longer wingspan than me, like some monstrous bird of prey.

I followed him up the stairs where a couple model/actresses helped me in and out of tuxedos for about an hour. I ended up with a $1,500 tux and a $300 pair of patent leather shoes. Vandershar stuck it all on a credit card. I have no idea who actually paid for it.

We went to some black-tie thing that night in a ballroom at the Waldorf Astoria. There were massive crystal chandeliers and about two hundred tables, white linen, complicated white flower arrangements, and lots of glasses and forks. I don't know how much money they raised, but if it was half as much as they spent decorating the place, it was a lot. Vandershar introduced me to an endless stream of half-smiling rich people before we sat at a table up near the front as guests of an investment banker named Jerry Sandoval.

Jerry Sandoval looked a little like Richard Gere, except his hair was completely white. His date looked like she belonged in a J. Crew catalogue with all this blond straw hair pulled back away from her face and hardly any makeup on. Her name was Lauren, and she turned out to be the heiress to some dog food fortune. I sat next to her at dinner. She was nice, and she would lean over every once in a while to fill me in on the other people sitting with us. Jerry ran all of fixed-income at Goldman Sachs. The rest of our table were from rich families who stockpiled bonds: Jonathon, on behalf of the Vandershars (his dad couldn't be bothered to attend an event for the benefit of children with cerebral palsy), and two other couples: the Fords and the Garricks.

The Fords were ancient. Mrs. Ford looked skeletal with a surgically tight face and all these greenish-blue veins running through her temples. Carbon dating would've been necessary to determine her actual age. She spent a lot of time trying to keep Mr. Ford from embarrassing her, but the Dog Food Heiress told me that Mrs. Ford had been a famous ballerina and that Mr. Ford had inherited a fortune before stealing Mrs. Ford away from her first husband, who was too busy conducting the New York Philharmonic to pay any attention to his wife.

It just didn't seem possible, not because the Fords were now so old and decrepit, but because it just didn't seem possible for anyone to actually do any of those things. I remember an exchange student at Yale named Guillermo. He was a roly-poly kid with funny hair and bad skin who John Henry and I sat next to one day at lunch in Commons. He and John Henry got to talking and pretty soon John Henry was telling Guillermo how he wanted to be a writer, and Guillermo was telling John Henry how he wanted to go home to become the president of Guatemala. I got all cold and embarrassed for both of them. No one does that shit. No one becomes those things, so I shoved away from the table to go get a bowl of green Jell-O.

The other couple, the Garricks, bickered all through dinner. They were much younger, and they seemed to be arguing about an incident that had happened at brunch. It was hard to understand Marcellite Garrick. She was from someplace in South America, and she spoke about a hundred miles an hour, but Mr. Garrick would talk right over her with a voice that could overpower a pneumatic power sander. He was short with fat hands, a thick neck, and a tremendous barrel chest that made his tux fit funny. According to the Dog Food Heiress, Marcellite Garrick was a stripper from Buenos Aires on her third American husband, and Lionel Garrick made cheap clothes he sold by the truckload at J.C. Penney. He also ate a mountain of food. He ate his salad, and then he ate her salad. He ate his rib eye steak, and then he ate her rib eye steak. He ate his asparagus, and then he ate her asparagus, and while he was shoveling all this down, he was telling us how he was going to win the trip to Bermuda when it came up for auction. He must have said it fifty times. Mrs. Garrick finally told him to shut up, then she called him "a stupid" before muttering something about the smoked salmon from brunch.

I sat there not saying anything for a long time, just taking it all in. Of course, nobody said a word to me, except for the occasional whisper of the Dog Food Heiress, but when the mousse came, there was a lull in the battle of the Garricks, and suddenly Jerry turned his attention to me and asked what I'd been doing with my summer.

"I have an internship at Empire Life & Annuity," I said.

"Life insurance," he said, hopefully. "Give me your pitch."

"My pitch?"

"Yeah. Sell me some life insurance."

He licked a glob of mousse off the bottom of his spoon.

"It's whole life insurance," I said, struggling to remember the script.

"Not buying it," he said. "You'll have to do better than that."

He smiled at Marcellite Garrick.

"You need life insurance," I said. Then I looked at the Dog Food Heiress who gave me an encouraging smile. "It's kind of irresponsible not to have it."

"Now we're getting somewhere. Of course I'll never have a wife or kids, but let's assume... just for the sake of argument."

"With a whole policy," I said as the Dog Food Heiress wilted next to him, "the premiums are deposited into a savings account so after a while you don't have to pay them anymore."

"Is that right?" he said. "And how does that work?"

"Eventually it's fully funded, so you don't have to make any more deposits. There's no more premiums after that."

"Bullshit," he said.

Then he ate more mousse.

"I'm sorry?"

"What you just said. It's bullshit. You're better off with a term policy and a 401(k). Whole life is a rip off. The premiums are ten times what they are on a term policy for the same insurance." He looked at Mrs. Garrick again. "Brokers love whole life because their commissions are based on the first month's premium. The bigger the premium, the bigger the commission. You ever have one of these guys call you? They'll say anything. 'Whole life is an investment.' 'The policies are fully funded.' 'The premiums go away.' They're relentless, and it's total bullshit. The premiums never go away. They get paid from the savings account. Some savings account. They use it to pay themselves. They penalize you if you withdraw from it. They charge you interest if you borrow it. It's more like throwing money away than saving it. Insurance companies want as much of your money as fast as they can get it. About the only good thing you can say about a life insurance company is they don't want you to die."

Mr. Garrick exploded into pneumatic power sander laughter, just this hacking pneumatic power sander laugh that made me feel stupid, and then I thought of the Life Insurance King of Central New Jersey ripping off his friends and family for years with the same bullshit Ross was now peddling. The laughter got so loud the people at the tables around us started to turn to see who was making all the noise, and with about half the room now staring, Lionel Garrick began to paw at the table cloth. His expression changed too as all that barrel-chested pneumatic power sander confidence drained from his face until there was nothing left in his eyes but panic. He was trying to hold himself upright, but his fat little fingers couldn't get a grip on anything. He lurched forward onto the table, and with one last gasp, he keeled over right there in front of us. We all stood as he went to the ground, and I could see him again, face down and lifeless, on the floor at Marcellite Garrick's feet. Luckily for Mr. Garrick there were about a hundred and fifty-seven doctors in the room and a defibrillator in the kitchen, so amidst the resulting chaos and 911 calls, a team of tuxedoed men rolled Mr. Garrick onto his back before a very determined young cardiologist from Sloan Kettering saved his life by electrocuting him. He did not win the trip to Bermuda.

Jerry Sandoval handed Jonathon the key to his suite as they loaded Mr. Garrick onto a gurney.

"Take it," he said. "Maybe you can make some use of it."

I didn't say anything in the elevator. Mr. Garrick still looked half dead when they wheeled him away. Nobody else seemed to give a shit. They were all congratulating the guy who saved him, but I'm not sure it would have been any different if Lionel Garrick had stopped breathing forever—maybe a few slaps on the back for the young cardiologist as if he'd done all there was to do, and that would have been it. You die, and they auction off the trip to Bermuda anyway.

The suite took up half the floor and reminded me of the lobby at Morgan Stanley, except it was freezing from an arctic blast of air-conditioning. I couldn't understand why anyone would ever need a hotel room that big. Vandershar didn't even notice. It was like every hotel room on Earth was the size of the Morgan Stanley lobby.

I plopped down on one of the couches while Vandershar went behind the bar.

"You see his wife?" he said, popping the cork on a bottle of champagne.

"I don't think she wanted him to make it."

"You can bet *she's* got some life insurance."

He handed me a glass and set the bottle on the coffee table before he cranked a window wide open to let the summer heat in, but then he stood there contemplating something as he stared out at the City until slowly, very deliberately, he pushed the screen out of sight.

"Your job nearly killed Lionel Garrick," he said as he headed back to the bar.

"Better that fuck than me."

I don't know why I said this. I didn't even know Lionel Garrick, but then I don't really know why I said a lot of the things I said around Vandershar. The word "fuck" in particular always became a prominent feature of my vocabulary, and it was like a performance every time—me saying things I thought he'd want to hear and doing things I thought he'd want me to do. All that time with American Royalty, and all it did was cause me to slump toward my least common denominators.

The champagne tasted like mildew. Vandershar always said it was an acquired taste, but I don't see how anyone could ever acquire a taste for mildew.

"Why the fuck are you working at that shithole anyway?" he said, now messing around with the stereo.

"I thought the job was at Morgan Stanley."

"How does that happen?"

"Larry's dad is a dick."

"Morgan Stanley doesn't hire freshmen."

"How would I know that?"

"You could've asked."

"You weren't around."

"Why are you even thinking about work? You should be chasing ass, not working."

"You ever hear of a guy named Fitz?" I said.

"No. Who the fuck is Fitz?"

"He graduated a few years ago. I guess he worked at Lehman. Then he invented some foreign currency trading algorithm and made like fifty million dollars."

He stopped what he was doing and looked at me like I was an idiot.

"You have your whole life to punch a clock."

"I'm just saying... "

"Saying what? You want to work on Wall Street? Done. Now stop worrying about it."

"You're gonna hook me up with a job on Wall Street."

"Jerry runs the high-yield desk at Goldman."

"That guy's never gonna hire me."

"Why not?"

"He thinks I'm an idiot."

"You think you're an idiot. That's the problem. You're not an idiot. You just don't know anything. There's a difference. Jerry won't even remember you tomorrow, and he's one of like fifty guys my dad knows there anyway."

"You're serious? You can get me a job there?"

"You need to relax. You're gonna end up like Lionel Garrick."

"Is there something else back there? I can't drink this shit."

Vandershar finally found the music he wanted. Then he twisted open a bottle of Bud Light and handed it to me before he flopped down on the other couch and flicked the bottle cap out the screenless open window by snapping his fingers.

"You want me to let you in on a little secret?" he said, leaning forward to fill his glass with champagne. "Nobody gives a shit." Then he sat back and kicked his feet up on the coffee table. "A guy like Jerry Sandoval... he talks to hear his own voice. He's not paying attention to you. No one is. Nobody cares. Nobody's watching. You might as well do whatever the fuck you want."

He studied his glass—a long-stemmed piece of expensive-looking something.

"We should get an apartment in New Haven," he said.

"I'm living in Berkeley with John Henry."

"I can't live on campus."

"Why not?"

"Come on," he said like I should know.

"I'm serious."

"The rooms are too small."

But it was obvious that wasn't the real reason.

"The rooms are too small?"

"I could fuck a girl's head out the bedroom window of my suite in Welch. It's like living in a shoebox."

"You won't live on campus because the rooms are too small."

He looked at me like he wasn't sure he should say anything else.

"Yale's not exactly what it's supposed to be, is it?"

"I don't know. What's it supposed to be?"

He kept looking at me like he couldn't believe I didn't know the answers to my own questions, like I didn't understand a concept so fundamental it was a waste of his time explaining it.

"Your ticket," he said, only I still didn't get it. "It used to be all you had to do was show up at a place like Yale and the world spread its legs for you. Now... you get to work at Empire Life & Annuity. What the fuck good is that?"

"It's still Yale," I said.

"Then what are you worried about?"

"I'm not worried about anything," I said, still fending off the Dread.

"Really?" He downed some champagne, then set the glass on the table. "My grandfather still waves a white handkerchief around for bullshit that doesn't even exist anymore. He has no idea the place has been hijacked by people who don't even want him around."

"What's wrong with your grandfather?"

"You're not listening. No one gets this. It's not my grandfather. Actually, it is my grandfather, but it's also you."

"What the fuck did I do?"

Now he just looked exasperated.

"No. The idea of you. The idea of me. This," he said as he motioned at the scene—two tuxedoed young men sipping champagne with their feet kicked up on the coffee table in the penthouse suite of the Waldorf Astoria—but I couldn't comprehend a universe in which Vandershar and I were anywhere near the same, so I still didn't understand what he was talking about.

"You think we're different?" he said. "Think again. We're the same to these people, and they want rid of us, so eventually they will come for us... until whatever they think we are, we will be... because what the fuck is the difference?"

"Is this why you're never around?"

"You think I enjoy being force-fed Derrida and Malcolm X?" He paused like he was waiting for me to answer, but I didn't know what to say since I'd never heard of Derrida or Malcolm X. "Fucking Jacobins. I'm not playing by their rules." He took a sip of champagne. "These people aren't clever. They're humorless. How is that even possible? You just go through life and find nothing funny? Everything is offensive? What the fuck is the point of that? If you want to talk shit, talk shit. If it's funny, it's funny. No one should get to hide."

"Easy for you to say."

"What the fuck does that mean?"

"I don't know. I'm just fucking with you."

"I'm serious. This shit makes you soft. They're all fucking soft."

"John Henry wants me to drive back to New Haven with him."

"I thought he was from California."

"His mom doesn't want him flying."

"It's one Halcyon and a nap."

"I guess she has some fucked-up phobia."

"Isn't driving more dangerous than flying?" He downed what was left in that long-stemmed expensive-looking piece of something and tossed it out the window. "Fuck it," he said. "Get him to come with us. I'll pay half the rent."

I went to the window, curious where the glass may have landed, only to find it shattered semi-safely on a stretch of rooftop below.

"You need to open your eyes," he said. "Get the fuck out of there before it infects you."

I leaned over the windowsill and took in a deep breath of the warm summer air, and I couldn't help but notice how different the City looked from up there. It wasn't the City I trudged to work through every morning—the humid, stinking City of concrete and asphalt, dirty subways and scaffolding, horizonless and hopeless and unfriendly. It was the breathtaking City of skyscrapers and glass, the City that stretched on forever, electrifying and limitless where anything seemed possible.

"You ever been to France?" he said.

"About what?" I said.

"Ever heard of Juan-les-Pins?"

"No. What is it?"

"It's a little town on the Côte d'Azur."

"The what?"

"The South of France."

"What's so great about it?"

"There's an all-girls school there." He grabbed the bottle of champagne off the coffee table and took a swig. "Girls from all over Europe go there for summer school. About noon every day they start showing up on the beach. Pretty soon they're everywhere—just girls taking off their clothes for as far as you can see."

"Sounds good."

"I met this one named Imke," he said wistfully, staring at the bottle.

"Eem-kuh?"

"It's Dutch."

"It's kind of hard to say, isn't it. Eem-kuh?"

"She looked like Françoise Hardy circa 1962. The bangs and everything. Fucking stunning, but she wouldn't talk to me."

"Why not?"

"She didn't like Americans."

"So how'd you meet her?"

"I impressed her with my determination. And maybe some very bad French."

"So what happened?"

"We got drunk."

"And then what?"

"She called my bullshit... with impeccable English I might add. We were at an outdoor café right on the water. I will say the more I drank, the better my French got, but she knew a thing or two about the military-industrial complex... a fuck ton more than I do, that's for sure, so for an instant, you know, just for like a heartbeat, she could see me. Has that ever happened to you?"

"What?"

"Someone beating you to your own thoughts?"

I shrugged as he slugged more champagne. Then he took another look at the label on the bottle.

"So that's it?" I said.

"What's it?"

"That's your story about the South of France?"

"No," he said as he took another swig. "I had a three-way in Antibes with some sluts from Texas."

"But you thought I'd want to hear about the Dutch girl who had a problem with the military-industrial complex."

"The other two were boring," he said. "Imke's the one who left a mark."

"So did you see her again?"

"Oh, I saw her again." He stood off the couch. "The next day on some guy's yacht." Then he looked right at me with a wry smile. "Maybe life is more interesting when you don't get the girl." He fired the champagne bottle right past me out the window like it was a German hand grenade. "How can there be any art if no one is miserable?"

I watched the champagne bottle explode a couple floors below, and it was like I could finally hear him. I finally understood what he'd been trying to tell me all along, so I let the half-empty bottle of Bud Light slip from my hand and watched it fall until it smashed next to the remnants of the champagne bottle. It didn't matter. No one was watching. No one cared. So I picked a crystal decanter up off the silver tray that sat next to the open window and tossed it German hand grenade-style into the night too, and when I did, I could feel the Dread leave my body with it—like I was suddenly free.

Vandershar ripped a framed painting off the wall. Then he smiled and shoved it out the window. I grabbed the entire tray of crystal decanters and let them slide one by one into the darkness. We took turns throwing glasses from behind the bar after that. Some made it out the window. Some didn't as a pile of shattered shards rose against the base of the wall, and when we were out of glasses, we moved on to the bottles, and when there were no bottles left, we moved on to whatever fit through the window—lamps, books, pillows, a side table, magazines, a telephone—and when it was over, my stomach hurt from all the laughing.

"You know what you should do," he said, nearly out of breath as he fell back into one of the couches. "You should take John Henry up on his offer and meet me in Dallas on the way back."

"I can't quit my job," I said, a bottle of Jack Daniels now in my hand.

"Why do you have to be such a pussy?"

There was an edge to the way he said it that knocked me back and caused the Dread to bubble up into my gut again.

"What's in Dallas?"

"What do you mean what's in Dallas? The sluts from Antibes are in Dallas."

"How'd you even work that?"

"Work what?"

"A three-way."

"Why? You think you've got a shot? You barely open your mouth when there's one involved. What are you gonna do with two?" Then he tried to walk it back a little. "Don't get me wrong. You're the perfect wingman, but admit it—you have no game. If it wasn't for me, you'd get no ass at all."

"How would you know? You're hardly ever around."

"That girl from Toad's? What was her name? Paisley? I sealed that deal for you. The whores from Barnard. And the only reason you got with that girl in Naples is I already fucked her. You're a fluorescent bug zapper. You just stand there and hope they fly into the light."

We'd just dismantled a $2,500 a night suite—together. We'd been the same only minutes before, and just like that, he had me back in my place, but for some reason, instead of resenting him for it, I felt like I'd somehow come up short.

"I don't just stand there," I said.

"You want to bet on it?"

"Bet on what?"

"I'll make sure the Texas sluts are both in Dallas, but I bet you can't pull that shit off by yourself."

"What do I get if I do?"

"You mean besides the three-way?"

"Besides the three-way."

"Alright." He stood from the couch to make his way to the open window. "You make it happen," he said as he bent down to pick up the broken glass so he could dump it out the window bit by bit, "without the need for my intervention... and I'll pay the rent... we move off campus... you pay nothing... but if you fail... not only do you have to live in Berkeley College with John Henry... but you're gonna run naked from the corner of Elm and Broadway all the way to Naples... and when you get there, you're going to walk inside and order me a slice." When he finally had all the glass safely deposited on the stretch of rooftop below, he turned the crank at the base of the window and spun to face me when it was shut tight. "Now let's get the fuck out of here. It's still early."

# Chapter 10

*Summer 1992*

Philip Nafziger had white hair, huge bulbous eyes, and a set of horse teeth. I thought he was a mental patient the first time I saw him. He turned out to be the medical director at Widworth. All the shrinks I ever met were useless. Total neurotics. The woman from school who came to see us after Nathan died was so nervous she could barely talk, and the loser they made my idiot brother, Troy, see after he stole the next-door neighbor's jewelry left his wife and kids right in the middle of it and moved to Maryland with his secretary.

Nafziger stood in the doorway to the library holding a magazine open to a page that had nothing but oversized capital As, Cs, Gs, and Ts all over it, but I had no interest in talking to him.

"Good afternoon, Spencer."

How he knew my name I have no idea.

"*Saccharomyces cerevisiae,*" he said, shaking the magazine, and then sat down across from me.

I could feel him staring.

"*Saccharomyces cerevisiae*," he said again, only this time he said it like he couldn't believe it.

"I don't know what that means," I said, finally looking up.

He was smiling with those horse teeth.

"It's Latin," he said.

"I don't speak Latin."

"No one speaks Latin."

"Then why are you using it?"

"It's the scientific term for yeast."

"Yeast?"

"Baker's yeast."

"What about it?"

"They will have mapped, sequenced, and catalogued the entire *Saccharomyces cerevisiae* genome within the next two years. For the first time in history, we'll have a complete genetic map of a living thing."

"So?" I said as I closed my book.

"Just think of the implications. You know I once had a conversation with Linus Pauling at a dinner party in San Francisco many years ago. He told me the building blocks of life would be found in a triple helix-shaped molecule located inside the nucleus of each of our cells. Of course it turned out to be a double helix, but that's not the point. The point is I had the audacity to tell him he was wasting his time."

"Yeast," I said.

"Yeast," he said, cheerfully.

"Who gives a shit?"

"Well, imagine how medicine will change when we can treat the root cause of a disease rather than its symptoms."

I cracked the book open again, hoping he might leave.

"You went to Yale, did you not?"

"Yeah… so?"

"Surely you took biology."

"They don't make you take biology."

"Chemistry?"

"They don't make you take that either. I took astronomy."

"Astronomy?" he said. Then he set the magazine on the table and leaned back with his arms crossed over his chest. "Is that an interest of yours?"

"It was a gut. You only have to take one class in science."

"What's a gut?"

"You know. Just an easy class."

"I see. But what does 'gut' mean? Is it an acronym?"

"Is it a what?"

"What does gut mean?"

"It doesn't mean anything. It's just a gut. They taught it from a high school textbook."

"And that's why you took it?"

"Are you a doctor?"

"You seem surprised."

"I've seen you in the dining hall."

"That's because I eat there."

"None of the other doctors eat in there."

"Four years of medical school. Five years of residency. Fifteen years at McLean Hospital in Boston. Widworth since 1971. I'm fairly certain I'm a doctor."

"So you know about dreams," I said as I closed the book again and set it on the table.

"Dreams?"

"I have the same dream every night."

"You're thinking of Freud."

"Yeah. Freud."

"What happens in your dream?"

"I can't find my shoes," I said. "My cleats actually. I'm in the stands at Yale Field, and there's a game going on. A baseball game. I'm in my uniform, only I'm not in the dugout. I'm sitting in the first row with my feet up on the railing, and I don't have my cleats on. Then our coach comes out of the dugout, and he turns to me, and he tells me he wants me to hit, so I start looking for my cleats, only I never find them. That's it. That's the whole dream. I never find the cleats. I just keep looking while the game goes on without me."

"Interesting," said Nafziger.

"What do you think it means?"

"I have no idea."

"I thought you were a doctor. How can you have no idea?"

"Because I'm not clairvoyant."

"I thought you knew about dreams."

"It could be anything really," he said, leaning forward as he clasped his hands together on the tabletop. "Indigestion. Pressure on the inner wall of your bladder."

"You think I'm having this dream because I need to take a piss?"

"Possibly."

"Well, can you give me something for it?"

"Something to prevent the dream or something to prevent you from urinating?"

"Something so I can sleep."

"Have you considered the possibility that your dream is nothing more than a manifestation of anxiety?"

"I just need something to help me sleep."

"Why stop there? What if I could give you a pill for everything that was wrong with you? We could treat your whole life like a disease that required constant care and medication."

"What kind of a doctor are you anyway?"

"Perhaps you should explore what you're so worried about. There's no reason to suffer before it's necessary."

"I'm worried about not sleeping."

"The problem with pharmaceuticals is that they often deprive us the precious opportunity of doing the hard work of living."

"Is that a no?"

"Life is not a disease, Mr. Chase," he said as he craned his neck to get a better look at the spine of my book. "It's more like a daily assault on your confidence. *The Portrait of a Lady*. Interesting choice."

"I'm working my way up to *Ulysses*."

"James Joyce's *Ulysses*?"

"Yeah," I said, since I wasn't sure if there was another one.

"Why are you working your way up to *Ulysses*?"

"I don't know. It's stupid, I guess. Somebody once told me it was the best book ever written."

I opened the book back up to the page I was on.

"Then why aren't you reading *Ulysses*?" he said.

"It's too long."

"Yet you still want to give it a go?"

"I figure if somebody brings it up again, at least I'll know what they're talking about."

"Who brought it up before?"

And that's when it occurred to me that maybe this wasn't really a conversation. It kind of felt like he was trying to get inside my head, so I smiled to let him know I was on to him. Then I went back to reading.

"What does *The Portrait of a Lady* have to do with *Ulysses*?"

"It's long," I said, without looking up.

"It's long? Do you even like it?"

"Not really."

"I tell you what. I'll bring in *A Portrait of the Artist as a Young Man*. It's a better place to start if you want to read *Ulysses*. It's by Joyce, and you still get a portrait of something."

"How long is it?" I said, looking at him again.

"It's actually quite short."

"No… I need something long."

"Why?"

"I've never read anything this long before," I said, shaking *The Portrait of a Lady* at him. "That's why I picked it. It's long. *Ulysses* is like seven hundred pages long."

"You chose to read *The Portrait of a Lady* simply because it's long?"

"I'm trying to get used to it."

"For *Ulysses*."

"Yeah."

"Like a prizefighter at altitude."

"Like a what?"

"How did you manage not to read anything long at Yale?"

"Nobody made me."

"And you didn't think it was a good idea to make yourself?"

"I guess not."

"Then why are you doing it now?"

But before I could say anything else, this other doctor appeared in the library doorway behind Nafziger. His name was David Irving. David Irving was the doctor I thought ran the place when I first got there. Besides Nafziger, no one else seemed to like him. The staff called him Diamond Dave. The nurse who handed me the tiny paper cup of little green pills every morning told me Diamond Dave made a small fortune consulting for biotech companies that developed drugs for wing nuts. He drove an expensive car. He wore expensive suits, and the face of his Rolex was all covered in diamonds. There was just something not quite right about the guy. He wouldn't make eye contact, but it was more like you weren't worth looking at, and he always came and went in a hurry like there was something far more important to be doing somewhere else, but the thing that made me avoid him was how shitty he treated the people he did bother to look at. Widworth was a revolving door of fired psych techs and crying nurses, and it made me wonder what he might do if he ever figured out who I really was or what I was actually doing there.

"I need to talk to you," said Diamond Dave.

"Please do," said Nafziger.

"In private."

"I guess I'll be leaving you to your endurance training, Spencer," said Nafziger as he stood. "I'm glad to see you're putting the library to good use. When you get to be my age, you look back on the idealism of your youth with a certain sense of embarrassment. I'll bring in *A Portrait of the Artist as a Young Man*. It'll be in my office if you want it. I think it's a better place to start if *Ulysses* is what you're after."

# Chapter 11

*Summer 1989*

I told Ross Carp I could stay another week. He told me to clean the shit out of my desk and get the fuck out, so I bailed on my August rent and got on a flight to San Diego. I was already sketched by random turbulence by the time we were somewhere over Oklahoma, but that's where I really learned what high pressure and hot air can do to a man-made object at thirty-five thousand feet. We bounced straight up. Then, we came crashing back down. I actually popped out of my seat because my seat belt wasn't buckled. Then the plane jolted sideways and shook before it was yanked straight down what felt like a thousand feet. Then we did it again. And again. It was a good thirty seconds of a plane full of people shitting their pants, and all I could think about was this class—Mathematics in the Real World—where we explored the unraveling of complex systems, one of which was a DC-10 engineered with three separate power systems and three separate hydraulic fluid reservoirs, a plane so redundant that the airline industry deemed a triple-hydraulic system failure impossible—until the rear engine of a DC-10 exploded at altitude and sent shrapnel flying into the fuselage, unceremoniously severing all three redundant hydraulic systems simultaneously, rendering the plane uncontrollable. I broke out into hives.

The guy next to me looked like a suburban father decked out in a green rugby jersey tucked into Wrangler blue jeans. He turned out to be a born-again Christian, and when he noticed my hives, he produced a tiny hymnal and stuck it on the tray table in front of me. I suppose this was his way of helping me out, but he leaned into my space and strong-armed me into singing hymns with him. I just let him do it, but I didn't know any of the words and the print was too tiny to read. I just mouthed whatever to get him to stop pestering me. I wasn't sure what was worse—the wind shear or the Christianity. Then we had to land. You weave through skyscrapers to get to the runway in San Diego, and no one would have called our touchdown graceful. All I know is I was happy to be driving back to New Haven when it was over.

John Henry was waiting for me at the curb in the brand-new two-toned, black and gray Chevy Blazer his parents bought him for our drive. They'd even installed a phone between the seats. He looked tan and well-fed for a change, and his hair hadn't been cut all summer, so it was all thick and dark and longer than usual, parted just off dead center with the strands in front curled around his face sort of like the horns of a ram. This was his natural, healthy state. It really was amazing what the East Coast winters did to him, turning him all scrawny and pale and sickly with flat, lifeless hair.

I could see boats moored in the harbor next to the airport as we merged into traffic headed for the freeway. John Henry pointed toward the zoo just up the hill as he rolled down the window so we could enjoy the usual sunny and seventy-two. No humidity. No need for a freezable thing under my pillow, and when we reached La Jolla, it was just massive house after massive house built into the hillsides that overlooked the ocean.

My first night we were all the way downstairs waiting for Yolanda the live-in housekeeper/nanny/cook to finish dinner. I was trying to help John Henry understand the significance of what awaited us in Dallas, but I was having to do it using a sort of pidgin code and awkward hand signals because his little sisters wouldn't leave us alone. They were twins and six, and you could barely tell them apart. They both had long, dark hair, knotted and frayed from all the rolling around on the ground they did, and about the only real difference between the two was Marcie's forever chapped lips and Maggie's constantly runny nose.

The room was covered in a deep white shag carpet and powder blue beanbags. It was like the entire downstairs had been childproofed, but you could tell the parents never went down there because there was crayon scribble all over the walls and dollhouse shit everywhere. Marcie was wrapped around John Henry's legs while Maggie bounced around behind him, and their little girl warbling made it difficult for me to articulate the magnificence of what awaited in Dallas. Between my pidgin code and hand signals, it just sounded like a pervy trip to fuck strangers.

"I don't know what to say," said John Henry. "I just don't like the guy."

"You don't even know him."

"Does anyone though? Who are his friends? When does he come and go? He's more like a vampire."

"You're just pissed he never remembers your name."

"The last time I saw him he was tripping on ecstasy."

"What's tripping on ecstasy, John Henry?" said Marcie.

"It means you're really happy."

John Henry collapsed into a beanbag so Marcie could crawl up into his lap while Maggie marched over to me and placed three tiny blown glass bunnies into the palm of my hand.

"These are my pretties," she said. "Don't break them."

Then she turned and jumped onto the beanbag with her brother and sister. You could tell this was not the first time the three of them had shared that beanbag. They were peas in a pod, but the beanbag was enormous, so it made them all appear smaller than they actually were, like something out of *Alice in Wonderland*, like we were already through the looking glass.

"If I pull it off, we live rent free," I said, not sure what to do with the pretties.

"You bet on this?"

"It was his idea."

"Rent free where?"

"Wherever we want... off campus. He said we could both come."

"I don't want to live off campus."

"For free?"

"We're living in Berkeley," he said, sort of stunned that was even open for debate.

"We don't have to play by their rules."

"What?" he said. "What rules? What are you talking about?"

I couldn't remember exactly what Vandershar had said, and I could tell John Henry was now connecting dots that would lead to a string of questions I would never be able to answer, so I tried to knock him out of his rhythm.

"You're not listening," I said with some urgency. "These girls like to party."

"We like to party," said Marcie.

"Kiss party!"

Then the girls doused John Henry with little girl kisses.

"Dallas is not on the way to New Haven," he said. "It's like a five-hundred-mile detour."

"All we have to do is show up."

"When?"

"Friday."

"We're not leaving until Sunday."

"It'll be over by then. Sunday is too late."

"Are you leaving us?" said Maggie.

"Don't leave us, John Henry."

He looked at me with the girls still crawling all over him.

"I don't know," he said. "You really want to do this?"

"We *need* to do this."

"I'll have to think about it."

The house was built on stilts into the side of a hill next to the Pacific Ocean. It was all weird and formal at dinner that first night with candlesticks and good china. One wall of the dining room was nothing but enormous windows all cranked wide open. The candles would flicker, and you could hear the sound of waves crashing into the rocks and sea lions yelping somewhere off in the distance. Pretty soon Yolanda brought out a huge, shallow bowl of fish-smelling something, and the twins stood in their chairs and yelled, "Hola, Yola!" They were so close to the open windows I wanted to run around the table to catch them before they tumbled out of sight, but I was paralyzed by the stink in that bowl. The rice was all purple from squid ink, and I could see other squid parts floating around, crustaceans too, all looking at me with beady little eyes and feelers, and legs and claws and tails, and the smell, like something you might take out and dump in the garbage.

"Girls, sit," said Mrs. Cole. "Don't do that."

John Henry's mom didn't weigh a hundred pounds. She also never blinked. Her eyes were pegged wide open and lit from behind with batshit crazy.

"So you're the great Spencer Mazio," said Mr. Cole from the other end of the table, unfurling a napkin.

"I'm sorry?" I said.

"My son has told us a lot about you, and thank you for venturing far and wide to join us." He lifted his glass to make a toast. "Better you than me on that drive."

"Dad," said John Henry like he was trying to intervene, only it wasn't clear to me yet what needed stopping.

"What?"

John Henry's dad had to be at least six inches taller than John Henry. He did triathlons and listened to not a word anyone said.

"Girls, enough," said Mrs. Cole. "Where do your napkins go?"

"Spencer," said Maggie. "Did you have a little brother that died? Because John Henry said you had a little brother that died."

"Maggie," said Mrs. Cole.

"It's okay," I said.

"No, it's not," she said. "That is not appropriate conversation for the dinner table."

"His name was Nathan," I said, sort of lowering my voice as if only Maggie could hear me.

"What happened to him?" said Maggie, now whispering with me.

"He was sick," I said. "He was very sick."

"What'd he have?" said Marcie in the same hushed tone.

"It's called meningitis," I said.

"Did he catch it?" said Maggie at full volume. "Can you catch it from germs? Mommy doesn't let us touch anything with germs."

"Maggie," said Mrs. Cole. "That's enough. Stop it. Right now. I mean it."

"Anybody want a peanut?" said Marcie.

"Are you tripping on ecstasy, Daddy?" said Maggie.

"Am I tripping on what?" said Mr. Cole.

"Ecstasy," she said. "I'm tripping on ecstasy."

"And what do you mean by that?"

"John Henry says if you're really happy, you're tripping on ecstasy. Spencer has a friend named Jonathon who's tripping on ecstasy all the time. John Henry said so."

"He also likes girls," said Maggie.

"Yeah," said Marcie. "Lots of 'em."

"Spencer does too," said Maggie with a monumental smile on her face.

Mr. Cole dumped a spoonful of fish parts onto his plate and looked at me funny.

"John Henry tells me you spent the summer working in the insurance industry," he said.

"It was actually kind of a mistake the way it worked out," I said. "The job was supposed to be at Morgan Stanley."

"Ah... investment banking," he said. "My company just raised seventy-five million dollars in a follow-on Goldman ran. The only thing I saw a banker do was change a semicolon to a comma."

He ate a shrimp.

"And what is it that you do, Mr. Cole?" I said.

"I'm the general counsel of a biotech. We're developing therapeutics for cardiovascular disease," he said as he chewed. "But I suppose you could do worse than investment banking. That was a five-million-dollar comma. I'm spending a fortune on Yale, and my son appears bent on life as a pauper."

"What's a pauper?" said Marcie.

"It's a very poor, pathetic person," said Mrs. Cole.

"Why do you want to be a pauper, John Henry?" said Marcie.

"I don't want to be a pauper," he said. "I want to be a writer."

"You're going to law school," said Mr. Cole.

I remember this one time I found John Henry staring at a pencil sketch hanging in the coatroom of the Berkeley College dining hall. It was a technical sketch of a windmill that showed all its parts and how they worked. I looked at it for a while too, but mostly to figure out why the fuck anybody would give a shit about a windmill. John Henry wrote this whole story about an old windmill lamenting how the world had left it behind and how technology made it lonely. It won some award from the Yale English department.

"Are you gonna write books, John Henry?" said Maggie.

"No," he said. "I want to be the kind of writer who writes for newspapers."

"Why would you want to do that, John Henry?"

"Because it's important to tell the truth when other people do bad things."

"Maggie," said Mrs. Cole. "Use your fork."

"So now you're the next Bob Woodward," said Mr. Cole.

"You mean like when Daddy wouldn't pay Rosalio?" said Maggie. "You said that was bad."

"Rosalio was the gardener," said John Henry, looking at me.

"What about when Mommy gave Gigi away because she wouldn't stop peeing on the carpet?" said Marcie. "Would you write about that, John Henry?"

"Girls, that's enough," said Mr. Cole. "Why you would want to write about the things other people do is beyond me. The credit belongs to the man in the arena."

I started to move the paella around my plate to make it look like I was eating it. I spread it thin in spots, buried a bit underneath the grilled veggies. It was sort of the opposite of packing a lot of luggage in the trunk of your car.

"So John Henry tells me you play baseball," said Mr. Cole to kill off the silence, only he didn't let me answer. "I played split end at Stanford."

"My dad's a football coach," I said, but he wasn't listening.

"Jim Plunkett was my quarterback."

"Dad," said John Henry. "Seriously?"

"What?"

"You played with him for one year."

"We won the Rose Bowl that year."

"I'm sure Spencer is not interested in any of that," said Mrs. Cole.

"John Henry could've been a ballplayer," said Mr. Cole. "He just never wanted it. Did you? He was a good second baseman... but he quit. Didn't help that he never grew. You can thank your mother for that."

I packed and unpacked the paella—all the way through Mr. Cole's monologue about the chamber music society and how they were hoping to work out funding for it or something like that. Then he started in about how great La Jolla was and how it had its own zip code, and then he threw his napkin on the table and asked the girls if they wanted to play some music while Yolanda served us funky green ice cream.

"They're not playing tonight," said Mrs. Cole.

"Why not?" said Mr. Cole.

"Because it's almost eight o'clock," she said.

"I think I'm capable of knowing when they should and should not play."

"Daddy's our teacher now," said Maggie.

"Daddy fired Mrs. Mortimer because me and Maggie got too good," said Marcie.

"I did not *fire* Mrs. Mortimer."

"That's what Mom said," said Maggie.

"Mom said you had to fire her," said Marcie. "Mom said you had to fire her because me and Maggie got too good. And you said you were the only one that could teach us."

"Maggie and *I*," said Mrs. Cole. "Maggie and *I*."

"Come on, girls," said Mr. Cole as he stood. "Go get ready."

The girls scampered off while Mrs. Cole sat there seething. She didn't move while we cleared the table around her. I think she was doing some sort of breathing exercise. I asked Yolanda what to do with the leftover asparagus about five times before I realized she didn't speak a word of English, so I went for the refrigerator and found myself staring at all these Cole family Christmas cards stuck to the door beneath bunny-shaped magnets: *Season's Greetings from Rome! We Wish You a Merry Christmas from a Winter Wonderland!* The one from the year before read *Happy Holidays from Tokyo!* with all the Coles decked out in traditional Japanese attire. John Henry and Mr. Cole were full-on samurai warriors while the girls and Mrs. Cole wore tiny kimonos and were covered in heavy white makeup, and they were all standing in front of a white pagoda with a blue tile roof. John Henry looked miserable.

"We're ready," said Mr. Cole. "And throw away the leftovers. My wife thinks they harbor bacteria."

I could hear Marcie warming up on the piano as I dumped the asparagus in the garbage. The light in the living room was dim, with only a floor lamp behind the piano so Marcie could see her sheet music. There was an eerie vibe. I sat down next to John Henry on a long, expensive-looking blue leather couch. Then Maggie showed up with a violin. I didn't know what to expect really. "Mary Had a Little Lamb"? "Twinkle, Twinkle, Little Star"? How good can you be at anything when you're six?

Mr. Cole stood and said something about a sonata in something minor by Beethoven before he started to direct traffic like a symphony conductor without a baton, and then it was like time stopped.

"Yes," he said as they got going. "Excellent. Yes."

He wouldn't shut up, but the music eventually shoved Jim Plunkett's split end out of the way. If only you could have seen their faces, those tiny determined faces, experiencing something I couldn't even understand, something otherworldly—unencumbered by all the bullshit that swirled in that house, oblivious to even our ears—and it was so unexpected all I could do was sit back and smile because I think for the first time in my life I could hear what it sounded like to be happy, but then Maggie sneezed, and it all came to a grinding halt.

"I thought you were taking her to see an allergist," said Mr. Cole, looking mildly irritated and in the general direction of Mrs. Cole, who was now standing in the doorway to the dining room with her arms folded across her chest and affirmatively pissed off.

"It's next Tuesday," she said.

"I've been asking you to take care of this for weeks," he said. "They have a recital in eight days."

"She's allergic to dust mites," said Mrs. Cole. "What else do you want me to do? Her appointment is next Tuesday."

"I don't want shots, Daddy," said Maggie as she wiped her nose into her sleeve.

"What shots?" he said.

"Allergy shots," said Marcie. "John Henry told us all about it."

"What did you say to her?" said Mr. Cole.

"I told her about the shots," said John Henry.

"Why?"

"Because she's entitled to know."

"Well, don't just stand there," said Mr. Cole. "Get her something to blow her nose into that's not her shirt."

John Henry grabbed a silk pillow off the couch and threw it to her.

"Blow your nose into that, Maggie," he said. "You shouldn't use your shirt."

"This is the fifth night in a row you've had them playing," said Mrs. Cole. "She's exhausted. They're six. It's eight o'clock at night. We agreed you wouldn't do this."

"Wouldn't do what?" said Mr. Cole, trying to get the pillow away from Maggie before she actually blew her nose into it.

"Don't be an ass," said Mrs. Cole. "They shouldn't be playing. They need to go to bed."

"We're the M&M Girls!" screamed Marcie as she leaped off the piano bench and lifted both hands high above her head like she'd stuck the landing of some impossible dismount.

"Maggie," said Mr. Cole. "Give me the pillow. John Henry wasn't serious." Then he looked at Marcie. "You're what? What did you just say?"

"We're the M&M Girls."

"What does that mean? What is she talking about?"

"Spencer says we're the M&M Girls," said Marcie. "Roger Maris and Mickey Mouse were the M&M Boys, so we're the M&M Girls."

"Mickey Mantle," said John Henry.

"We're the M&M Girls!" they shouted together as they broke down into giggles.

"You're not the M&M Girls," said Mr. Cole. "Stop saying that."

"We have discussed this fifty times," said Mrs. Cole. "You agreed. You agreed you wouldn't do this."

"Are you kidding me?" said Mr. Cole. "Are we really going to do this right now?"

"Do what?"

"You're the one who wanted this," he said.

"You can't parade them out whenever you feel like it."

"I find that amazing given that you have them performing at every one of your little functions like they're a carnival act."

"Everyone agrees with me on this."

"Everyone?" he said. "Who's everyone? Have you formed a committee to raise our children too? Because I'd love to be on it. Do you think you can pull some strings and get me on it?"

"I doubt it," she said. "No one can stand you."

"No yelling, Daddy," said Maggie. "You promised."

"I'm not yelling, sweetie. Someone has to point out to your mother that she's a hypocrite."

"Alright," said John Henry. "That's enough. That's the end." He looked at the twins: "Wonder Twin powers."

"Activate!" screamed the girls.

They bolted down the stairs and out of sight.

"Where are they going?" said Mr. Cole.

"To the Hall of Justice," said John Henry as he stood. "Tonight's rehearsal is over."

The Hall of Justice turned out to be the space between their beds. They'd pull a blanket over the top and make a fort just like Nathan and I used to. John Henry and I climbed under there with a flashlight and sat with them as they played a game of Uno while their parents bombarded each other with *fuck yous* until doors started slamming and finally we heard a car start.

"I think Tolstoy was wrong," said John Henry.

"About what?" I said, since I had no idea what Tolstoy had to say about anything.

"I don't think there are any happy families."

# Chapter 12

*Summer 1992*

The West Wing of Widworth (home of the wing nuts) and the East Wing of Widworth (where my grandmother lived) had similar floor plans, but they were really nothing alike. There were the doors for starters. Basically, there were no doors anywhere in the West Wing while the East Wing was nothing but closed doors for about as far as you could see. The color schemes were different too—both pastel, but the West Wing was anchored in a Pepto Bismol puke while the East Wing's primary color reminded me of the seafoam green carpet from our living room back in New Brunswick. Then there were the dining halls. They looked the same—cafeteria-style with simple rectangular tables that sat about fifty and a TV tuned to CNN up out of reach near the ceiling—but they were really nothing alike either. The assisted-living dining hall was generally somber and clean and usually half empty, while the West Wing dining hall was always raucous and loud with spilled spaghetti and lumps of melting ice cream all over the floor.

My grandmother doddered ahead of me one morning as we got to the East Wing cafeteria for breakfast to find her usual table over by the TV, but I found myself mesmerized by a tray of cantaloupe wedges that sat unmolested on the buffet. I'd escalated my chemical arms race by getting Kyong to up my daily dose of little green pills to forty milligrams not long after Alan and Leonard visited me in the library, so I was feeling pretty good standing there in front of all that creamy orange fruit, but as I stared at it, I started remembering things, and an odd feeling of sadness hit me—this deep sadness. I looked back at Gram, who now appeared confused trying to pull a chair out.

Papa's deterioration had been physical. He was in pain all the time even though he never complained, but his arthritis eventually got so bad he never wanted to get out of bed. That was the killer. It was all downhill after that—one thing after another until finally he got pneumonia. I wanted to be there with him. I made sure I was there when it happened, like me being there would somehow make it less awful. It was the smell I remember most, not even the smell of death. It was the smell of dying—this acrid body odor that only comes at the end when you've been lying there immobile in your own sweat for days. His lungs filled with water, and he died with his eyes wide open.

Gram kept fumbling with the chair, and I kept heading down a hole.

The signs were there even before I moved her in to Widworth, cognitive lapses I think I knew were the beginning—forgotten house keys, uncertainty about the route home. I made up excuses not to call and reasons not to make the trip, but I knew what I was doing. I didn't want to watch it happen again. I mean, how many people do you have to watch die in a lifetime?

She used to pepper cantaloupe wedges while David Letterman's morning show blared on a tiny nine-inch color TV next to the range. She always said the pepper made the cantaloupe taste sweeter. I never believed her, so I never took a bite, but the idea of peppered cantaloupe made me feel a little better, so instead of her usual Raisin Bran, I tore open a tiny packet of pepper and sprinkled it all over a cantaloupe wedge. I even cut it the way she used to (thanks to the East Wing stainless steel silverware), scoring it to make perfect bite-size cubes before I ran the knife along the inside of the rind so all the cubes fell free onto her plate.

"Here's your fork," I said, placing it gently in her hand.

"Oh, that's very nice of you. You're so good to me."

She took a bite, but after a couple chews, she stopped and didn't seem to know what to do.

"I put pepper on it," I said.

She let the semi-chewed cube fall out of her mouth onto the plate.

"But that's the way you like it."

"Oh, like hell it is."

Then she went right back to watching CNN like nothing had happened. I didn't push it any further. I just got up and poured her a bowl of Raisin Bran, but I couldn't stop thinking about it all—that cantaloupe, especially, and her tiny kitchen—that little television, the yellowing appliances straight out of a catalog from the 1950s, the oval green Boltaflex table and the corkboard above it, covered with my childhood doodles of the "fis" I'd caught with Papa and funny cartoons she'd cut from the pages of magazines and newspapers. I remembered the color of her china (a dull yellow like Dijon mustard) and the shape of her silverware (all modern and angular). I remembered every detail while she remembered nothing. What did it mean to remember nothing? What does it even feel like? She had no idea who I was, but she remembered exactly where she wanted to sit at breakfast every morning. How does that work? I mean, if you can't remember who you are, then what are you? Who can you trust? It's like everyone is a stranger all the time. I didn't want her to be alone like that anymore, so I did my best to help her remember.

I tried to remind her of all my time in Widworth, even the time she left me in jail. I went on and on about our Sundays—how she would do the *New York Times* crossword before we walked to church, and how Papa would always stay behind to mow the lawn, and how the ceiling of that cavernous Methodist church leaked way in the back, so an usher was always stationed there with an umbrella on rainy days. We walked everywhere—to the post office, to the ShopRite, to the dime store all the way into town, so I asked her why she never learned to drive, but she couldn't remember. I asked her why her ears weren't pierced even though she always wore earrings, but she didn't have an answer for that either. I reminded her how she would sit on the bench at the park and watch Papa throw me stiff-armed pitches from a bucket of tattered baseballs until it was dark, but she remembered none of it, so I rummaged through her room, looking for something, anything that might remind her of me, that might remind her of anyone, just something so she could claw back at least a little something of herself.

Her room was clean, but more sterile than taken care of, and there was nothing hanging on the seafoam green walls, no pictures anywhere. No stuff. Gram had always kept everything. Her creaking white house was packed with all kinds of shit. Boxes filled the basement and attic—newspaper clippings, report cards, a thousand trophies, recruiting letters—a shrine to my mom's basketball career packed away and just waiting to spring back to life—but there were also yearbooks and magazines, photo albums and old stuffed animals, books (tons of books), an old family Bible, old family china, random heirlooms, letters typed on wispy white typing paper, just a lifetime's worth of stuff—and the walls of that house were covered with photographs of family that went so far back some of them were actually made of tin, and even though I didn't know most of those people, I was always aware that they were there, that I was somehow connected to them and that every single thing in that house meant something, but it was all gone now, and I felt responsible. Some lady was in charge of selling the house. It never occurred to me that I was the only one left who could save what was inside it. An entire family history turned to junk somebody tossed in a dumpster the moment I moved her out. It shouldn't be so easy to erase something like that... but it is.

The only thing I found, besides some clip-on earrings, was a small photo album stashed at the bottom of her sock drawer. There were a handful of pictures in it. Mostly it was filled with random notes and poems and letters tucked into cellophane pockets, some of them in her handwriting, some of them typed on that same wispy typing paper. I sat down on the wooden chair next to the dresser and unfolded the piece of paper I found tucked inside the front cover. It was a poem she'd typed, with the few typos corrected in her own handwriting.

> *Music, when soft voices die,*
> *Vibrates in the memory—*
> *Odours, when sweet violets sicken,*
> *Live within the sense they quicken.*
>
> *Rose leaves, when the rose is dead,*
> *Are heaped for the beloved's bed;*
> *And so thy thoughts, when thou art gone,*
> *Love itself shall slumber on.*

And as I flipped the pages, I realized that this album was the one thing she'd brought with her to remind her of the life she'd lived and the people she loved.

The letter Papa wrote to her on her sixty-fifth birthday:

> *I see your face more clearly now. Your heart and soul...
> and then somehow I surely know that I have been the
> luckiest man on this Earth. I hear your voice more
> clearly, too, the laughter and the joy that you so freely
> give to all that need compassion and a loving deed, or
> just a listening ear. I've known your sadness and your
> sorrow. I've shared your passion and your love. I've had
> your strength from which to borrow. And now I thank
> the stars above. I feel your love more deeply now. I
> sense your touch and know that I have had the best
> this orb can offer. That I will cherish until I die.*
>
> *Bud*

The poem taped next to a photo of my mom (around age ten) holding a stringer of fish:

> *"A daughter!" they say with a trace of sneer.*
> *"No sons?" they exclaim with a crocodile tear.*
> *Well, that's as I want it.*
> *I have no regrets.*
> *Do daughters tear clothes? Or bring in stray pets?*
> *Or flaunt blackened eyes for their parents to praise?*
> *Or wear out their shoes in a matter of days?*
> *Or track in the mud from the murkiest of water?*
> *If you think that they don't*
> *Then you don't know my daughter.*

And then the handwritten notes scrawled next to a picture of me in braces:

> *The Spencer Summers.*
> *The memory pictures tumble about*
> *Impossible to sort them out.*
> *Mosquitos and squirrels.*
> *Lemonade, yellow cake.*
> *Tapeball.*
> *Gram with her everlasting cure-all for Papa… orange juice.*
> *A boy.*
> *Half-man.*
> *And then he's gone,*
> *I pray he comes back again.*

I looked up to find her when I was done reading, but she wasn't paying attention. She was seated on the bed brushing her hair.

"I came back, Gram."

"Oh?"

"It's me," I said, pointing to the photograph. "This is me."

But it meant nothing to her.

Every day I came to see her first thing in the morning, and every day we started over. The same confusion. The same wariness. The same conversation about her socks, but she hadn't really deteriorated that much physically. She could still get around, and she could still dress herself, so this routine actually gave me hope that maybe she was still in there somewhere, that I might still find the Gram who sat on the front porch with her friend Helen and watched me and the neighbor kids play baseball with a novelty Red Sox bat and a ball made of tape, a pitcher of lemonade between them, their stockings rolled down and their pant legs rolled up, the two of them laughing on a random summer day.

Then there was the matter of her teeth. She didn't have any. She wore dentures, and she was in the habit of spitting them out without warning, so I was eternally on the lookout for her uppers and lowers. It also turned out my grandmother was a sundowner—a psychological phenomenon that basically means you turn into an asshole when the sun goes down. It was true, unfortunately. She was hard to be around after dark, and no one wanted to tangle with her to get the dentures out of her mouth at bedtime, so every night after dinner I'd head back over to the East Wing to engage in the almost impossible task of getting my grandmother's teeth into a glass of Polident. It's dangerous business messing with the teeth of a sundowner, so I sometimes had to sit there until we finally reached that moment when she voluntarily pushed her teeth out of her mouth because, for whatever reason, she didn't want them in there anymore.

When there was nothing left in that tiny album to read, I started to tell her stories—her stories mostly—as if reminding her how she waged war against Sears, Roebuck and Company over a defective vacuum cleaner and their shitty customer service would somehow bring her back, but nothing worked, and it seemed like the more I said, the lonelier she got, even with me right there in the room with her. I couldn't understand why no one was helping her. They weren't mistreating her. They kept her fed and attended to and all that. It's just that they weren't doing anything to make her better, and if they weren't doing anything to make her better, what was the point? So I finally went to see Nafziger. I wasn't exactly sure what I was going to say or how I would explain to him who I was or what I was really doing there, but it didn't matter anyway. Nafziger wasn't in his office. It was just Diamond Dave at the nurses' station, bitching out a Filipino lab tech.

"Does she have any idea how important this is?" he said.

He looked disgusted. The nurse he was talking to was short and stocky with a meaty neck and a head the shape of a charcoal briquette. She was standing while the lab tech he was berating (much younger, with a head that looked more like a Q-tip) was seated on the other side of the station.

"Does she speak English?" he said. "She can't speak English, can she?"

"She speak English," said the Charcoal Briquette.

"Then why am I not hearing it?"

"You upsetting her."

He looked at the Q-tip.

"English?" he said. "Speak English?"

"She say she can't find some these patients," said the Charcoal Briquette.

"What?" He said it like it was the dumbest thing he'd ever heard. "What'd you say?"

"She say she can't find some these patients. They not in beds."

"Patients?" he said. "What is she going to do with the patients once she finds them? She's here to type. She's a data processor. I just want her to enter the data from the case report forms. She can type, can't she?" The Q-tip was sobbing now. "Can you get her to shut up? We're not getting to the bottom of this if she can't shut up."

It didn't matter how good I was feeling or how many milligrams of that little green shit I had in my system, Diamond Dave always made my skin crawl, so I slid into Nafziger's office to get away from him.

The office wasn't much really—a simple wooden desk, two weathered red leather chairs, ugly beige carpet, a bookcase, and paper everywhere, stacks and stacks of paper, on the desk, on the floor, on the chairs, some of it a foot high, all of it teetering and degenerating into piles all over the place.

The wall next to the desk was covered with framed photographs, all radiating outward from the one in the middle, which happened to be larger than the rest. It was like he'd started hanging them the day he got there and never stopped. The one in the middle was taken on the front steps of Widworth: a young Nafziger looking like a proud father with his arm around a very young Diamond Dave. The rest seemed to be Nafziger's wife and kids and what looked like a never-ending supply of grandkids. There were several of Diamond Dave too, and his perfectly perfect family: pretty blond wife, happy kids—one boy, one girl—an elderly golden retriever making an appearance in one of them.

There was also a series of old black-and-white photos below the rest—a group of soldiers crouched low in front of an old bomber, arms up on each other's shoulders, the soldier on the far left holding a wrench and looking a lot like Nafziger fifty years ago. I could tell from the horse teeth. The rest of the black and whites were World War II fighter planes with pinup girls painted on the cowlings. Below the black and whites, almost near the floor, were two framed pencil sketches. The first was a bunch of soldiers, dirt flying as they dug a hole with shovels, and the word "Lymington" written at the bottom. The other had the Eiffel Tower in the background and a French girl in a short dress in the foreground. That one said: "The Terrible Battle of Paris."

There was also a bookcase next to the door. It didn't have any books in it though. It was filled with crap instead—mugs and coins and fountain pens, old keys and pocket knives. It was this massive collection of nothing. I grabbed a metallic blue pocket knife and opened the blade.

"Mr. Chase," said Nafziger as he hurried into his office.

"Is that you?" I said, pointing the blade at the young soldier with the horse teeth.

"I was an airplane mechanic in the 81st Fighter Squadron, 50th Fighter Group."

"You were in the Air Force?"

"I was in the Army."

"You just said airplane mechanic."

"The Air Force was part of the Army in those days. My company stormed the beach at Normandy two days after we had complete control over it. I was in Paris the day we liberated it from the Germans though. Now that was something. Then the war ended. We won in case you didn't know."

"Did you draw these?"

"I did."

"What about the engines?"

"The cover of an engine is called a cowling."

"So you painted those too?"

"It was a long time ago."

"So how'd you get to be a shrink?"

"When the war ended, the field of psychiatry was burgeoning. The best and the brightest were all flocking to explore the repressed memories of the masses. An unconscionable waste of talent as it turned out."

"Why's that?"

"As a clinical tool, psychoanalysis is useless."

"Then why do I have to go to group therapy twice a week?"

"Therapy is different," he said. "You can think yourself into any number of terrible places, but if you give it a chance, you can also think your way back out. Conversation... art... music... all useful in this regard. Psychoanalysis is something different altogether. Take this dream you've been having." He started to empty his briefcase onto his desk. "Freud would tell you it's a manifestation of an unspeakable memory your subconscious dredged up, and that a tiny censor in your head hacked it all to pieces to disguise whatever it is that's so unspeakable. Psychoanalysis is intended to help you put all the unspeakable pieces back together. Does that sound reasonable to you?"

"Not really."

"Good. It took me fifteen years to figure that out. I was treating patients with underdeveloped prefrontal lobes and an increased sensitivity to dopamine as if their fathers had caused the problem. We opened Widworth to get away from all that."

"You and Dr. Irving," I said, pointing to the picture in the center of the wall.

"David took quite a risk to come with me from McLean, but then David was always the entrepreneur. He's the one who gets the bills paid." Nafziger looked at the open blade in my hand. "Titanium alloy," he said. "Harder than steel, but lighter. Amazing stuff."

That's when Diamond Dave appeared.

"Where have you been?" he said. Then he saw me with the knife. "What is this?"

"*This* is Spencer Chase," said Dr. Nafziger.

"It really becomes a little hard to understand after a while."

"Nothing wrong with looking," said Nafziger.

"It's a knife, not a Polaroid," said Diamond Dave. "Is it too much to ask that you hang a door here? It's not 1973 anymore."

"Trust is the foundation of any relationship," said Nafziger. "We're not running a prison."

The Dread jumped me as Nafziger came around the desk to trade me a paperback book for the titanium alloy pocket knife. I stood frozen as I looked at the cover—a picture of a queer-looking guy and the words *A Portrait of the Artist as a Young Man* across the top. Nafziger put the knife back on the bookshelf, then handed a clipped stack of paper about half an inch thick to Diamond Dave.

"No dystonia," said Diamond Dave. "No akathisia. No tardive dyskinesia."

"I'm aware," said Nafziger cheerfully. "I read it."

"That's not exactly the response I was expecting."

"What about the agranulocytosis?"

"It's statistically insignificant," said Diamond Dave.

"Tell that to the people who get it."

Diamond Dave looked right at me.

"You can go now," he said.

But I couldn't move. I stood there terrified for no apparent reason, clutching that paperback copy of *A Portrait of the Artist as a Young Man* as if my life depended on it.

"Can he hear me?"

"Spencer?" said Nafziger.

The Dread plowed over the top of whatever drug substance remained active inside me. I could feel myself leaving my own body again, so I didn't say a word. I moved toward the door instead. I don't think I was even consciously trying to move, but I was moving anyway, and then I was gone, in the hallway without so much as a goodbye, past the nurses' station, past the Q-tip and Charcoal Briquette, past the open door to the library, past Alan as he trolled the hall, past Kyong on his afternoon rounds, down the stairs and past the Admitting Nurse at the front desk, out the front door and into the parking lot where the hot, humid air filled my lungs and finally reminded me I was still breathing.

# Chapter 13

I didn't really have to say much more about Dallas after that first night at John Henry's. His parents did all the work for me. Their pissing match lasted the whole time I was there. The screaming would erupt. Then they'd go silent and neither one of them would say a word to the other for a day or two until something else would set one off and the screaming would start all over again. The whole thing reminded me of our neighbors in Paterson. (Their Rottweiler incessantly shit on our front lawn. Troy broke into their house and stole a bunch of jewelry. They built an eight-foot fence on the property line.) And while John Henry had mastered the art of managing his parents—diffusing their insanity, de-escalating their hostility—there we were, backing out of the driveway three days early. Even he couldn't take it anymore.

His mom leaned in the driver's side window and rehashed (for about the fiftieth time) the first leg of a make-believe journey she'd planned that was supposed to end with a side trip to an artists' colony in Santa Fe. If she knew the actual plan was to drive straight into the desert so I could fuck strangers two at a time with nothing but a scrap of Waldorf Astoria stationery to guide us, she would've locked John Henry up and thrown away the key. As it was, she'd installed the phone between the front seats just to keep tabs on us. When she was done, John Henry put the Blazer in reverse, but he paused to watch his parents struggle to herd the twins together for the long march back to the house, and he wouldn't take his foot off the brake until the girls finally turned and he was able to squeeze in one last goodbye. Then he backed the car out of the driveway.

"I don't think your parents like me too much," I said.

"I wouldn't take it personally."

It was still early, and I wasn't fully awake yet, but as we accelerated onto I-8 heading east, I felt the Dread stir for the first time in a week—just a hint of doubt really, a little jolt of uncertainty—so I opened the glove compartment to find some music to take my mind off Vandershar and whatever potential embarrassment awaited me in Dallas. That's when I discovered the next three thousand miles would be spent suffering with nothing but The Pet Shop Boys and everything The Smiths had ever recorded. I leaned the seat back and closed my eyes in an attempt to calm down, but I passed out before I could manage it, and that's when I had the dream for the first time.

I'm in the first row with my feet up on the railing in my home whites, the blue of my stirrups dangling. I'm perfectly content to sit there and do nothing. Then Canelli comes out of the dugout and whines at me to get ready to hit, so now I have to find my cleats. I look underneath my seat. I rifle through my bag. I look under the seats behind me. I look and I look as worried thoughts of disappointing everyone imaginable zip past me only to circle back around and worry me again as they head the other way, but I never find the cleats, and the game never stops. It just goes on without me until I wake up in a nervous sweat, only this time when I woke up, John Henry was singing like a fairy.

"This is the guy you say is a genius?" I said, struggling to get the seat back upright.

"It's ironic."

"Does that mean it sucks?"

"He's a poet."

I turned The Smiths down, but I still couldn't slow the churn in my brain.

"You think we can make it the whole way in a day?" he said.

"The whole way where?"

"To Dallas." He smiled like there was no place he'd rather be. "You want to go for it? I think it might be possible."

I'd only been asleep a couple hours, but it might as well have been days. The road to Dallas had been an irritating detour for John Henry when we got in the car. I was the one heading into the desert to get laid, but while I was out, the trip had somehow transformed into an adventure for him, while for me it had morphed into something more like a risky game I wasn't sure I even wanted a part of.

"How come you never told me you played baseball?" I said to get my mind somewhere else.

"I quit. There's nothing to tell."

"Were you any good?"

"I was okay. That's not why I quit though."

"Then what was it?"

I punched The Smiths out of the CD player, which automatically switched us to radio, but we were now in the middle of nowhere so the reception was terrible. John Henry reached over and turned it off.

"What'd your dad do during games?" he said.

"What do you mean?"

"Like was he a screamer? Did he pace? Or did he just sit there like a normal human being?"

"He didn't really do anything."

"What do you mean? He had to do something."

"He wasn't there."

"He didn't go to your games?"

"No."

"Like ever?"

"Not really."

John Henry paused for a second and seemed to consider that before he went on with his story.

"Well... my dad would taunt other kids," he said. "He'd sit right behind the plate... the same place every game. But he never raised his voice. He didn't yell. He wasn't trying to intimidate anyone. He was really just trying to let everyone know he was the smartest person there, so he'd watch a kid, you know, analyze a swing or two, and when he finally decided where the flaw was... he'd just start talking."

"To who?"

"The kid... the parents... anyone who'd listen. Like if a kid was stepping in the bucket, he'd tell him. He'd be like, 'You're in the bucket on every pitch, kid. You'll never hit a curveball like that.' Totally matter of fact like he was doing the kid a favor, but then he'd say 'he's in the bucket' like five thousand more times to make sure everybody heard him."

"What'd the other parents say?"

"They couldn't stand him. It was so embarrassing. No one would sit near him. My mom wouldn't even sit near him. Who wants to hear that the whole game? He actually got in a fight with another dad once. He kept telling this guy's kid to get a smaller bat. And then on the way home, I got to hear how much *I* sucked and what *I* fucked up. Then they'd start to bicker and pretty soon it was a screaming fight. When I finally couldn't stand the ride home, that's when—"

But I wasn't really listening anymore. I was lost in my own head, thinking about my own Little League experience, thinking about how my mom signed me up not long after our night at Mount Sinai, and how I didn't even want to play. The idea of playing with kids I didn't know for a coach I'd never met was terrifying. She dropped me at the park the first day of practice anyway and just drove away. I wasn't even sure where to go. It was just two flea-bitten diamonds that sat back to back with a snack stand in between, and there were about eight different teams out there practicing, but then I saw the kids wearing the same orange T-shirt I had on in the right field corner of the smaller field and something magnetically dragged me over there. I didn't say a word to anyone. I just stood there fighting off the urge to scratch a hole through my chest when somebody I'd never seen in my life handed me a bat and told me it was my turn to hit. It was purple and made of aluminum, and it felt oddly natural in my hands, but I was still nervous holding it. Then an out-of-shape dad in glasses tossed a ball at me underhanded, and I swung as hard as I could, and for just that second, it was like the nerves flew right out of me. I smashed the ball all the way back into the infield where it hit some kid in a red T-shirt right in the back. It was the weirdest thing—they all seemed to love me for it, even the adults, even the adults coaching the other teams, like I was suddenly the most important person there, even though the kid in the red T-shirt was crying.

"Maybe you were lucky," said John Henry.

"About what?" I said.

"That your dad stayed away."

"Yeah," I said. "Maybe."

"I do miss it though. Just being out there. You know, just hanging in the dugout, but who wants to listen to their dad talk shit to some kid who can't hit a curveball?"

"Who won the fight?"

"The concrete was sandy and they were both in loafers. It was pretty pathetic really. A couple of moms had to separate them. Nothing happened."

The phone rang in the space between the seats, and I nearly jumped out of my skin.

"Where are you?" said Mrs. Cole through the speaker.

"I'm in the driver's seat," said John Henry. "Spencer here is in the passenger seat—"

"Very funny. You know that's not what I meant."

"Just past Phoenix," he said, when in fact we were at least a hundred miles away from civilization of any kind.

"You're making good time. How fast are you driving?"

"We've been averaging about ninety-five miles an hour, but I think we can push it a little harder."

"Do not get a speeding ticket."

"We're fine, Mom."

"Call me when you get to Albuquerque."

I wondered what my mom would be doing if she were still alive. Would she be worried about my every move? Would she keep me from getting on a plane or force me to drive cross-country even though I didn't want to? Would she know where I was at all?

She showed up one morning at my Little League field. She hadn't come to many of my games either. She was usually too busy dealing with Nathan or my idiot brothers, but when I took my spot at third base that morning, there she was, on the other side of the short chain-link fence with Nathan right beside her. I was so nervous I struck out my first three times up, and I couldn't stop looking over at her when I was in the field, wondering if she was disappointed, praying that nobody would hit a baseball at me. The Dread was unbearable, humming in my head, taking my breath away, but before my last at bat, I stepped out of the box and closed my eyes and tried to forget everything until the only thought left was of me bombing the next pitch over the left field fence. Then I stepped back into the box and did exactly that. I hit an absolute laser beam over the scoreboard, and as I rounded third base my mom was laughing and crying at the same time. I'd never seen her like that, like she couldn't believe she was allowed to be that happy, and I just wanted to keep circling the bases so she could be that happy forever.

She let Nathan stay with me after the game—just the two of us. She'd never done anything like that before either. Nathan jumped from picnic table to picnic table pestering the other moms for loose change to buy watermelon Jolly Ranchers, and every time he hit one up, he'd introduce me as his big brother— the one who'd just homered over the scoreboard—and I'd stand there in my dirty uniform like a little celebrity while these women fished through purses and random dads congratulated me for blasting a baseball farther than any one of their own sons could ever dream to. I never really understood that day. I mean, why did she let it happen? Maybe she wanted Nathan to feel normal. Maybe she wanted me to feel normal. Maybe she already knew what was coming.

We kept driving without saying anything for a long time after that, deeper and deeper into the desert, only now I had both the Dread of Dallas and thoughts of home reverberating in my head. I struggle most when it all swirls together, so I got more and more uncomfortable sitting there, squirming in my seat while Morrissey droned on about the misery of the world. I wanted to say something, like I needed to tell him the truth about Nathan to pull out of it, but I couldn't because you never know what someone will do with the truth.

"You know," he said at some point when the monotony of New Mexico seemed never-ending, "I've always thought Polk was a pretty underrated president, but this kind of makes you wonder why we fought the Mexican War."

"What Mexican War?"

I said it almost as an afterthought, trying to sound as normal as possible while I adjusted myself in the seat for the eight-hundredth time.

He looked at me funny.

"*The* Mexican War. We only fought the Mexicans once."

"We did not fight a war against Mexicans."

"You're serious. You've never heard of the Mexican War. The front cover of my fifth grade history book was a picture of Zachary Taylor leading a charge up the Rio Grande. Manifest destiny? The Alamo?"

"I thought we lost at the Alamo."

"We did, but we won the war. That's how we got all this."

He waved at the landscape again with the sky now dark ahead of us. I didn't have the heart to tell him I'd never heard of any President Polk either. My mom died about a year after Nathan. Her cancer was in her bones by then and she didn't want any more drugs. A couple months later, my dad quit his job and moved us out of New Brunswick, only he didn't really have a plan. We just moved, like he had to get out of there, like it would kill him to be there for even one more day, but then we moved again, and again, each neighborhood shittier, each high school football program worse than the last, like he was on some kind of self-immolation tour, and the whole time, I bounced from one school to the next: New Brunswick to Elizabeth, Elizabeth to Paterson, Paterson to Passaic, Passaic to Bloomfield, Bloomfield to Newark, until finally Gram put an end to it and insisted I finish high school in Widworth. I'd leave one school right in the middle of the year only to start somewhere else. Nothing ever matched. No one was ever doing the same thing. It's no wonder I don't know shit about anything.

John Henry finally reached over and turned the music off again.

"You okay?" he said.

"Yeah... why?"

"You keep talking to yourself."

"No, I don't."

"You just said: 'I don't know shit about anything.'"

"My legs are killing me," I said since I couldn't stop my knee from bouncing up and down.

"You want to stop?"

"Where?"

There was nothing but dirt in every direction, so I'm not exactly sure where he thought we would pull off the road.

"We don't have to do this," he said.

"We might as well give it a shot. We're halfway there."

"I'm not talking about one day to Dallas."

"Then what are you talking about?"

"Have you even given this any thought?"

"Given what any thought?"

"I don't know," he said. "The logistics of it."

"The logistics of what? A three-way?"

"Well, yeah."

"That's what you think of when you think of a three-way? The logistics?"

"So how's it work then?"

"Well, I'm not an expert, but there's two of them and one of me, and we all fuck each other, so even if there's only five ways to fuck, that means we'll have a hundred and twenty-five different fuck combinations to choose from, so I can't really tell you for sure which route we'll take... and that doesn't even include what they might be doing to me. Maybe they both just suck dick. I don't know. It doesn't matter. Once the three of us are alone in a room together, I win."

"But how do you get them in the room with you?" he said like I was an idiot. "Vandershar's not helping you. He's probably lying about Antibes. These girls aren't waiting for you in threewayfuckland. At some point, you have to suggest to one of them that you're not so much interested in her as you are interested in her *and* her friend. You don't think they might find that a little insulting?"

"You sound like a truancy officer."

"Even if they don't, they're gonna know Vandershar told you about Antibes. The whole thing has the potential to go completely sideways."

"It does not."

"What about condoms?"

"You think I want the Clap again?"

"There's two of them."

"I realize that. That's what makes it a three-way."

"You're just gonna take your dick out of one and stick it in the other?"

"Well, I'm not gonna leave it there."

"She might object."

"Which one?"

"What do you mean, 'Which one?' The second one."

"Why would she object at that point? It's already on."

"The condom?"

"No. The three-way."

"It just doesn't sound particularly sanitary is all I'm saying."

"Sanitary?"

"Yeah... it's not sanitary."

"No one cares about this shit."

"The only good advice my dad ever gave me is everything matters. Every detail. You either know what you're doing or you don't."

"Did this just occur to you?"

"No. It occurred to me about two hundred miles ago, but you were asleep."

"Nobody choreographs a three-way."

I turned the music back on to shut him up, but we were suddenly eating up that formerly Mexican desert like it was nothing, miles flying by in the darkness, like fear somehow warps time and brings everything you're afraid of closer, like uncertainty rushes toward you faster than you can run away from it. The truth is I had no idea how I was getting those girls into a room with me, and I'd avoided thinking about it after I'd made the bet because I knew Vandershar was right. I was a neon bug zapper, and now I needed two of them to fly into the light holding hands. We stopped in El Paso, but only long enough to fill the tank and clean the dead bugs off the windshield. Then we barreled off down the interstate again. It wasn't until we reached the outskirts of Abilene that John Henry finally called it quits and pulled off the road to find us a motel. I didn't sleep though. I just lay there staring at the ceiling thinking through every way Dallas could possibly go wrong.

We rolled into a gas station in Fort Worth at about eleven the next morning, me clutching the crumpled piece of Waldorf Astoria stationery that had the girl's phone number on it. The idea of calling a stranger physically repulsed me, so I stopped and turned back to look at John Henry as if he might help me in some way, but the space between me and the car seemed to get wider. I turned back to the pay phone, and that's when it happened. It's hard to explain really. Maybe I was just sleep deprived, but I swear to you, I split in two for a second. I somehow broke apart. One of me was hovering about ten feet above the other, looking down, suddenly free from my thoughts, just watching the other me, waiting to see if I'd make that phone call, and then just like that, I was back on the ground inside the other me face-to-face with the pay phone with no way to turn back. I picked up the receiver and willed myself to dial those seven digits as if dialing the phone number of a girl you didn't know was the bravest thing anyone had ever done.

The dad answered, and I immediately forgot her name.

"Is Jonathon there?" I said after a moment of silence.

"I'm sorry, who?"

He sounded not so much from Texas as from a farm somewhere in Iowa.

"Jonathon," I said. "Jonathon Vandershar?"

"Vandershar, you say?"

"Yes, sir."

"I've never heard of no Jonathon Vandershar."

"He's friends with your daughter. Is she there?"

"My daughter's headed down to South Padre. She'll be there a week."

"South Padre?"

"South Padre Island. A whole bunch of 'em started down there this morning. Maybe your friend is with 'em?"

"How far is that?"

"South Padre? Oh, I don't know. Nine hours maybe. Give or take."

"Nine? Did you say nine hours?"

"It's all the way down on the Gulf."

I set the receiver on the cradle and then looked back at the car. I now had twelve hundred miles' worth of *I told you so* coming, and even though there were no more phone calls to make, I still felt unstable. Vandershar was still out there somewhere laughing at me. So I punched the side of the pay phone.

# Chapter 14

We took off headed east again, but my hand was swollen like an inflated rubber glove. We didn't even make it out of Dallas before John Henry pulled off to find an emergency room. We generally tried to avoid the emergency room when I was a kid. It was a place to sit uncomfortably for hours around sick people, so to do that with a little brother who had a compromised immune system was usually pretty unhelpful, but now I didn't really have a choice. John Henry finally found one (after stopping twice for directions), but it wasn't connected to a hospital. It was wedged into the corner of a strip mall out near the Cotton Bowl, and it was teeming with broken bones, lacerations, ringing phones, and a Thai family all sniffling and coughing in the corner.

The check-in desk was run by a prickly woman who looked like she was from the future. She had short, white-frosted hair, sharp features and a long nose, and she had no time for John

Henry's good mood. There was a ton of hustle-bustle, and it was loud with all the people, but she had that place running like an assembly line.

"Is it me or does she look like Snow Miser?"

He said it under his breath, but it didn't matter since she never would have heard him anyway. She was doing about ten things simultaneously, and she processed the woman in front of us (deep cut to left index finger, self-inflicted with a kitchen knife) without ever letting the phone leave her ear.

"The cartoon?" I said.

"Claymation."

"What?"

"It's not animation. It's claymation."

I just looked at him like who fucking cares.

"No one draws the Misers," he said. "The characters are made of clay. You know... stop motion."

"Snow Miser is a guy."

I couldn't find my dad to get my insurance information, so I think Snow Miser might have made us sit there extra long just to see if we would leave. John Henry took the news of Vandershar's disappearance with a smile. He didn't give me any shit about it at all. Instead, he brought the map his mother had given him to guide our trip into the waiting room so he could revise our route. Before long he had this thing all spread out on the ground as he plotted our new course back to New Haven, entertaining half a dozen little kids who'd probably all been dragged there by hypochondriac mothers.

"Can you put that away?" said Snow Miser, holding the phone away from her ear just long enough to get John Henry's attention.

"I need a highlighter," he said, like the two of them were now collaborating. Then he folded the map in half to make it a little less unwieldy. "Anything but yellow."

Snow Miser put the phone back to her ear and held up a green highlighter.

"I think she likes me," he said as he returned with the fluorescent green marker.

John Henry's mom had traced our intended path with a yellow highlighter and written in black pen all the places of interest where we were supposed to stop: Petroglyph National Monument—Albuquerque, New Mexico; Fantastic Caverns—Springfield, Missouri; Louisville Slugger Museum—Louisville, Kentucky, and on and on and on. Of course, we were nowhere near any of that shit, so John Henry began to busily mark up our new route with the green highlighter he'd borrowed from Snow Miser.

It was hard not to feel better around John Henry. He always had all this energy—this forward momentum—and the emergency room itself was surprisingly full of life, so despite my throbbing hand, I was momentarily out of my funk, watching all the kids gathered around this map like John Henry was the pied piper.

"If we average seventy miles an hour for six hundred eighty miles, how long is that?" he asked, studying something right there in the heart of the country.

"Seriously?"

"About ten hours?" he said, still not sure.

"Very good."

A plump firecracker of a nurse with red hair and purple scrubs poked her head out the door and called my name.

"You've got to be kidding me," said John Henry.

"What?" I said.

"It's Heat Miser."

He packed up his map (much to the chagrin of all the tiny people gathered around it) and we headed for Heat Miser, who now stood solidly in the doorway like a roadblock.

"You can't come back unless you're family," she said.

"We don't look alike?" said John Henry.

"You look nothing alike, and he's a foot taller than you."

"We both have brown eyes."

She shook her head and rolled her own eyes like she had no time for humor, but then she turned to take us both back anyway.

"You're on a roll," I said.

"Now *that* would be a three-way."

"With the Misers?" I followed him through the door. "Aren't the Misers brothers?"

"I'm talking about the nurses."

Heat Miser took me in for X-rays, and then John Henry and I sat for another eternity in a tiny exam room with a little curtain for a door before a doctor who looked like he'd been up all night came in to tell me I'd broken the middle finger of my right hand just below the knuckle. Half an hour later, we were still waiting for him to come back and stick a cast on me.

The curtain was open, and we could see into the room on the other side of the hall, which was inhabited by an incredibly scrawny meth-head-looking dude covered in mud. He was alone and his nose was bleeding. The whole time we sat there he had to keep his head tilted back with this bloody rag jammed up his nose, and still it wouldn't stop.

"That ever happened before?" said John Henry, loud enough to be heard across the hall.

"Not like this," said the meth-head through the bloody rag.

"What happened?"

"Just started bleeding."

"This has to be the worst job imaginable," said John Henry.

"What is?" I said.

"Emergency room doctor."

"Why's that?"

"How can you ever be prepared? That guy has an uncontrollable... undiagnosable nose bleed. You need X-rays and a cast. The next guy's gonna come in here... maybe he has a hernia or a contagious skin condition no one's ever heard of, or maybe an ambulance rolls up, and they bring in a girl they just cut out of a car and her life depends on what you do in the next fifteen minutes. There's gunshot wounds. Stab wounds. Strep throat. *Staph*. Whatever that Thai family in the waiting room's got. Maybe you have to remove a foreign object from somebody's ass. It's nuts. You have no idea what's gonna walk in here."

I was oddly calm now, but then there's always a calm that comes to me after meaningless failure, when it's finally over, and that's maybe when I think the clearest. Right then, staring at my hand, I wasn't thinking about a three-way anymore or even some emergency room doctor extracting a foreign object from an unknown ass. All I could really think about was John Henry's little sisters and his parents clumsily leading them up the stairs as we backed out of their driveway.

"I'm sorry I made you do this."

He was now inspecting a poster of the human circulatory system. He was always checking out shit like that, like he never wanted to waste an opportunity, and then he'd store the information in some vast database for later use.

"You didn't know Vandershar would leave without you," he said, without looking away from the poster. "I mean, it was fairly predictable. Let's be honest. But how could you really know?"

"I shouldn't've made you leave early."

He looked at me.

"You didn't make me leave early. It was time to go."

"No. It wasn't. You should still be there."

"You mean with the girls? Little kids are resilient. They'll be okay."

I kept looking at my hand.

"How'd they learn to play music like that?" I said.

"I don't know." He looked back at the poster. "At some point, I'm sure my dad'll take credit for it, but he really didn't do anything. I'm not sure they *learned* anything to be honest."

"How's that possible?"

He turned to face me again.

"I think music is like another language for them, but it was already in their heads, you know, like they could already speak it."

"So one day Marcie just sat down at a piano and that was it?"

"Pretty much. I mean, it wasn't instantaneous, but it was obvious they were both different like that."

I couldn't look at him. I kept looking at my hand, thinking about the moment his sisters began to play, thinking how stunned I was that you could be that good at something when you're only six. I felt kind of envious. I mean, how lucky can you be? How lucky can you be to just sit down at a piano one day and see your own future?

"My little brother didn't die from meningitis," I said.

"I thought he was sick," said John Henry.

"Yeah... but that's not how he died."

"Then what happened?"

I felt hollow, and I kept staring at my hand worried I'd never be able to look John Henry in the eye again.

"My dad kept a loaded gun on a bookshelf in our spare bedroom," I said. "Troy told Nathan there was a present for him up there. It was his birthday... so he climbed onto a chair, and he reached over his head, but the only thing up there was that gun, and when he pulled it over the edge... it went off... in his face."

"Jesus, Spencer. I had no idea."

"I just stood there. I stood there and let it happen."

"You didn't know."

"My dad used to keep that gun in his nightstand," I said. I just felt like I couldn't stop. I didn't want to stop. I needed him to know. It was almost like John Henry was my last chance. "It was right next to his bed, but Troy found it there, so my mom made my dad move it, only I saw where he put it... so I told them. I told those two stupid fucks where that gun was because I thought they might like me better."

"You're not responsible for what they did."

"I should've stopped them."

"You were a little kid."

"I was afraid."

"You were ten."

I was holding back tears, but I wanted to remember. I wanted to remember my little brother.

"I used to miss him, but it doesn't really get any better... missing him. It gets worse, so sometimes I try not to think about him at all... but I want to miss him, you know. I just don't know how."

We sat there not saying anything for a minute, me still looking at my hand, John Henry not sure what to do, but in the end, I think he did the only thing that mattered. My thoughts were accelerating again, bouncing all over the place, but it was suddenly like they had somewhere else to go.

"He loved baseball," I said.

"Did he ever play?"

"No. He wanted to. He never got the chance."

"He wanted to be like you."

"No," I said. "It was the other way around. He was fearless. No matter what they told him. No matter what they did. He was never scared. You know how many fucking needles they stuck in him? They gave him a spinal tap when he was five. He was fucking five, and he didn't flinch. He never said a word. He was afraid of nothing. I can't even make a phone call."

# Chapter 15

*Summer 1992*

T he song Methodists sing at the end of every service is so simple it's impossible to forget. I must have heard it eighty-five million times, so I figured if I'd heard it eighty-five million times, then my grandmother had heard it eight hundred and eighty-five million times. If Gram was going to remember anything, it would be that song, so I was singing it. Unfortunately, she wasn't paying any attention. She was sitting in the chair next to the dresser, staring at the seafoam green wall and missing the whole performance.

> *Trust in the Lord with all thine heart,*
> *and lean not unto thine own understanding.*

I got Kyong to up my dose of little green pills to sixty milligrams a day after the episode in Dr. Nafziger's office, so I was feeling pretty uninhibited, but I was also having a little trouble maintaining focus, and not just because of the dope. There was a nurse bent over Gram's mattress struggling to pull the top sheet tight. She was short, which made the sheet-pulling task more difficult, and her baby blue scrubs were snug, so I could see the curviness of her frame. The Sheet Changer looked over her shoulder and smiled, and it occurred to me that my mangled vocals were amusing her, but I didn't really care. Her ass was right there in front of me, so I kept going.

> *Acknowledge Him in all thine ways.*
> *And He shall direct thy path.*
> *Trust in the Lord with all thine heart,*
> *and lean not unto thine own understanding.*
> *Acknowledge Him in all thine ways.*
> *And he shall direct thy path.*
> *Trust in the Lord—*

It was unconscious, monotonous, as I stared at this nurse's ass the same way Gram was staring at the seafoam green wall, and then I realized my dick wasn't working. Through the haze of sixty milligrams, I could tell nothing was happening. It was numb, so I jammed a hand into a pocket to figure out what was going on down there, doing my best to make it look like I was just shifting things around, but it was pretty obvious my dick was useless. The Sheet Changer finally got the sheet tight, and when she did, she stood, giggling as she turned to face the source of the ridiculousness, but she caught me mid-fishing expedition, and I'm not sure which one of us was more horrified. She left the room in a hurry after that, and only then did I realize my grandmother no longer had any teeth in her mouth.

"Where are your dentures?"

She was still staring at the wall.

"Gram. Where are your dentures?"

I got down on the floor to look.

"I brought the paper," I said, crawling toward her bed. "*New York Times.*"

"Oh?"

"I was thinking we could do the crossword."

"Now why would I do that?"

"Gram, you did the *New York Times* crossword puzzle every Sunday for like fifty years."

My head was now under her bed.

"I don't know what you're talking about. What did you say your name was?"

"Spencer."

"You look like Patrick."

"Patrick was your brother," I said. "He's the one who fought in the war. I'm the one who lived with you."

"Oh?"

I found her teeth perched in the potted plant near the bathroom door. I cleaned them in the sink, then dunked them in Listerine. Once they were dry, I ran a strip of Poligrip along the gum edges. That's when the real fun started. She would fight me to keep them out of her mouth, so I developed a one-handed technique that enabled me to use my free hand to defend while I gently pushed her dentures into place, but you couldn't rush it. It usually took a while.

"Come on," I said, picking up the newspaper again when her teeth were safely back where they belonged. "Twelve down. Chester Arthur's middle name?"

"Oh, how would I know that?"

She was now preoccupied by something on her pant leg.

"I have no idea. Let's try a different one. How about... six across. A place for a crick. Four letters."

I tried to figure it out by taking a look at six down, but if you gave me ten thousand years to do a *New York Times* crossword puzzle, I still wouldn't finish it.

"Crick," I said, wondering aloud. "Four letters."

"Your neck," she said, without looking up.

"What? What'd you just say?"

"Your neck. Your neck is a place for a crick. Four letters."

"Neck. That might be right."

"Of course it's right."

"Well, don't get cocky. We have like a hundred and twenty more of these. Seven across. Old-fashioned letter opener. Five letters."

"Steam," she said as she stood from the chair without missing a beat.

"S-T-E-A-M. Jesus Christ. That works. Okay. Now we're talking. Ten across. George Gershwin's brother."

"Ira," she said, stepping confidently to the dresser for her hair brush.

"Seriously? You remember George Gershwin's brother, Ira, but you don't remember me?"

"They made such beautiful music."

"They did?"

"Erin used to dance to it."

"Wait... what'd you just say?"

"She was a wonderful dancer."

"Who was?"

"I was so sad when she quit the ballet."

"Who quit ballet, Gram?"

"She was such a tomboy... always with her sports."

Gram began to brush her hair as she looked into the mirror above the dresser.

I was stoned enough to wonder if I was hearing her correctly, so I tried to run the last few beats of our dialogue back in my head.

"Who was a tomboy?" I said.

"You know she played basketball in college."

"Who did?"

"Erin."

"Erin was my mom."

Gram stopped with the brush and turned to face me.

"Well, she married an asshole. What was his name? I told her not to marry him. You're one of her kids?"

"I'm Spencer, Gram. I lived with you in the summers."

"Spencer?"

She looked right at me like she knew something had just happened—something incredible and devastating at the same time. She even started to say something, like she knew who I was, but then she stopped, and I could see her confused and afraid again as she receded back into her own mind just as fast.

"Your grandson," I said, trying to keep her there with me.

She put both palms on the dresser like she'd lost her balance, and I could tell the moment was gone.

"Don't be like me," she said. "Don't you ever get old."

# Chapter 16

*Summer/Fall 1989*

John Henry finished recalibrating our trip from Dallas to New Haven while we waited for my cast to cure in the exam room. Instead of interstates and safety, the new route took on more of an S curve through Mississippi, Tennessee, Maryland, and Pennsylvania, and safety had nothing to do with it. We wound our way up remote country roads and cut through dense forests, using the extra three days Vandershar provided by ditching us in Dallas to explore every last inch of Vicksburg, Shiloh, Antietam, and Gettysburg. We didn't even bother with the battlefield tour guides. John Henry didn't need them. We'd blow right past whatever touristy group was milling around, so he could lead me all over hell and back on foot even though we were both sniffling our way through the beginnings of the crud we'd picked up from the Thai family in the Cotton Bowl emergency room. John Henry just talked battlefield strategy, and I listened—ironclads and sunken roads, cornfields and old bridges, generals and tactics, the persistent preeminence of cavalry in the art of war, and what it all meant in the grand scheme of things. For three days, my mind centered on nothing but what was right there, what was right in front of me, and I maintained a pleasant calm as we cruised the backcountry and hiked old trails lined with cannons and statues and the signposts of war, but when we finally reached the Devil's Den, a massive rock-strewn hall of mirrors at Gettysburg, I realized I just wasn't paying attention anymore. Staring at a plaque that memorialized a nightmare called the "slaughter pen," commemorating men no older than me who'd been terrified on that very spot before they fought and died anyway, I realized I just wanted the trip to be over.

You could tell John Henry was affected by the place, even more so than by any of the other slaughter pens we'd visited. He got real quiet, and he stopped right in the middle of that boulder maze to take it all in, and it was almost like he was seeing something, you know, hearing what it was like... so I tried. I tried to see it too. I tried to hear whatever he was hearing, but all I could see were thick-ankled tourists in polyester shorts and bright white sneakers, and all I could hear was their shuffling along the dirt trail between the boulders, cameras dangling at their sides as they trampled the ground where the 6th New Jersey regiment was sliced to pieces in defense of the Union. I was bored out of my fucking mind, and I felt terrible about it. I didn't want to disappoint him, so I stood there doing my best to express a reverent awe while the Dread oozed back into my gut.

When we got back to campus, we moved into our room on the fourth floor of entryway F in the North Court of Berkeley College—a building that was basically the electrical substation of college dorms. It looked like all the other Gothic buildings around it, and it was right there in the middle of campus. You couldn't miss it, but hardly anyone ever noticed it because there was really no reason ever to be there. Everything you needed—like the dining hall or the laundry room or the dean's office—was in South Court or the tunnel that connected the two. My hand was in that cast, and the Thai family crud was still lingering, so moving in up those four flights of marble stairs was sort of miserable. Our suite wasn't bad though. It had a decent-sized common room with wood floors and a fireplace we weren't allowed to use at the far end, but the bedroom was so narrow the bunk beds actually covered half the window, so if the window hadn't opened out, it wouldn't have opened at all. Vandershar, of course, was nowhere to be found, so over the coming weeks, the shadow world in which he existed, where nothing mattered and no one cared, lost shape in my head until finally it vanished altogether, and I was left wondering once again if it was even real.

At some point, John Henry's mom called. It turns out we stayed at all the wrong Holiday Inns and lied about the location of a Howard Johnson's in Tennessee, details not overlooked by Mrs. Cole when she inspected her credit card bill and figured out where we'd actually been, but instead of blaming me for our monumental detour, John Henry told her the whole thing was his idea. When would he ever again have the chance to see so many Civil War battlefields in a single summer? She railed on him anyway, and as I listened to her incoherent raving, I realized that John Henry had willingly allowed me to see the unhappiness of his own family. He wasn't afraid of what I might do with the truth, and it was like our shared unhappiness somehow connected us and made us stronger. The Dread retreated before he'd even hung up the phone, and it seemed to become more manageable after that—at least inside our dorm room where it was usually just him and me.

Unfortunately, my freshman roommate, Derek, turned out to be our next door neighbor. Living next to Derek was only slightly less awful than living with Derek, so my zone of comfort really didn't extend much past the threshold of our doorway. I remember waiting for him to get there that first day of school freshman year, thinking I was about to meet this friend I would know forever. Instead, I got to meet Derek. He rowed crew and looked like a rodent with one of those down-turned little rodent mouths. His hair was always messed up too, but messed up like he wanted it that way, and he wore those brown leather lace-up shoes they must hand out at Choate or Hotchkiss or wherever he went to boarding school. He dismissed me almost immediately. I was a recruited athlete from a public high school, and he didn't think I belonged there. The one good thing about Derek was his girlfriend, Molly. She was tiny with perfect olive skin that made her look tan even in the middle of winter. She was from Choate or Hotchkiss too, only instead of the brown leather lace-up shoes, she always seemed to be wearing Birkenstocks.

They were bickering in front of his door one night as John Henry and I headed out for dinner.

"I don't see why you have to get up at four in the morning," she said as I stepped into the entryway. She was wearing a pair of shorts that were slightly distracting. "You don't have a race until March."

"You don't understand commitment," said Derek as he unlocked his door.

"You row in a tank for ten thousand hours, then you have like three races," she said. "It's stupid."

"There's six boats in a race, and there's more than three races."

"It's still stupid."

Derek finally noticed me as John Henry pulled the door shut behind us.

"You're from New York, right?" he said.

I was still distracted by Molly's ass.

"Hey," said Derek. "I'm talking to you."

"What?" I said, finally looking up.

"Remind me where you're from."

"Outside the City," I said.

"Yeah, I know that. How far outside?"

"Newark."

"Newark?" he said. "Why does everyone from New Jersey say they're from outside the City? You're not from outside the City. You're from inside New Jersey." Then he looked at Molly. "You're coming with me."

"Yeah, like I really want to spend my weekend in Albany."

"What's in Albany?" said John Henry.

"My brother's running for congress," said Derek. "I'm helping with his campaign, but we can only use actual New Yorkers. The Republicans sent a bunch of carpetbaggers up there, and we're killing them with it in the press."

"I have a brother in New York," I said, since I had no idea what a carpetbagger was.

"Does he vote?" said Derek.

"I don't think so."

"Why not?"

"He's on Riker's Island."

Molly giggled.

"Your brother's in prison?" said Derek.

"I didn't mean to laugh," she said. "It's not funny your brother's in jail. It's just funny... what you said."

"What'd he do?" said Derek.

"He robbed a bakery."

"A bakery?" said Derek. "What he get? A glazed donut?"

"He's an idiot," I said.

"Does that run in your family?"

"Derek," said Molly.

I just stood there like an idiot.

"Does it run in yours?" said John Henry.

"What's that supposed to mean?" said Derek.

"What exactly is your brother entrusting you to do with his campaign?"

"Voter contact. I work for the field director."

"So they actually let you talk to people?"

"I run voter contact."

"It's just that you're really unlikable," said John Henry. "You're like one of the least likable people I've ever met. Who would vote for your brother after they meet you?"

Derek opened his door as Molly looked back hesitantly like she wanted to say something, but nothing came out of her mouth, and then Derek grabbed her by the wrist and yanked her inside.

"I can't believe she's with him," said John Henry. "What about that guy is appealing?"

I didn't say anything. I just wanted to get away from Derek. In addition to everything else that plagues me, I think I developed a mild form of post-traumatic stress disorder after two semesters with that guy—being reminded over and over that I was an idiot—so I had a ringing in my ears like an improvised explosive device had just detonated in my general vicinity as we headed down the stairs to the tunnel that connected the North Court to the South Court.

John Henry and I spent an inordinate amount of time down there, mostly trudging to and from the dining hall. The tunnel walls were covered in enthusiastic murals of knights and unicorns and X-Men, and there was always this hive of activity that caught my attention in a well-lit room at the north end, right at the bottom of our stairwell, so when we reached the landing that night, I left the thought of Derek behind and peered through the small window in the door.

It looked like a Dungeons & Dragons convention inside. The room was perfectly square and bigger than you might expect. (It never ceased to amaze me how much real estate existed below ground at Yale—tunnels and catacombs all over the place.) When I opened the door, the smell of skunked beer hit me square in the face. There were about thirty Tunnel Dwellers inside, most of them seated at square card tables, but they weren't playing board games. There wasn't a Dungeon Master in sight. They were playing Texas Hold'em, and in the far back corner, another group had gathered around a midsize pool table. I couldn't really believe what I was seeing. They were all hopeless gamblers, as pitiful as any of the losers I ever saw in Bobo's, and about the only time I ever saw any of them come up out of the basement was to take the train down to Bridgeport to bet on jai alai.

John Henry and I wormed our way back to the pool table— each of us wondering in our own way how we might make use of the scene. We stopped to watch this impossibly scrawny kid in a size small powder blue T-shirt and a bearded doofus wearing a magenta Members Only jacket zipped all the way to the top engaged in a game of straight pool that had been going on for two days. The scrawny kid's name was Ernie Rickman. Ernie loved to tell a story about himself heroically strapping a half-yard beer glass to his back and smuggling it out of a New Haven bar called Richter's, but the story took forever, and Ernie never told it well, so hardly anybody ever listened. The bearded doofus was this law student named Wayne. I don't think I ever knew Wayne's last name.

"It's a rip off is what it is," said Ernie, only it sounded like he said it through his nose.

"It was a mistake," said Wayne.

"How hard is it to calculate the vig?"

The bookie who flicked cigarette butts at my head from the pay phone in the Bobo's bathroom wasn't good at math either. I noticed him squirreled away one night in a booth back near the kitchen. He was struggling to calculate implied probabilities so he could set odds to maximize his profit on a Tyson fight. I offered to help him, thinking maybe he would stop flicking cigarette butts at me if I did. He ended up paying me fifty bucks a week just to double-check his math. He ran all kinds of games, but simple moneyline betting on football and basketball was the easiest. The idea there is to set a line that gets about the same amount of money on both sides. The losers pay the winners, but the odds are always -110, which means you have to bet $11 to win $10. The bookie keeps that extra ten percent as profit. We called it "juice" in Bobo's, but they called it "vig" just about everywhere else.

"It's twenty bucks," said Wayne.

"It was the second time," said Ernie.

"You really want to mess with this guy over twenty dollars?"

"You don't get it," said Ernie, lining up his shot. "He's doing it to all of us."

"Then why is no one else complaining?"

"He says it's a mistake and figures nobody's gonna say shit about a few dollars, but it adds up."

"I think he just made a mistake."

"It was not a mistake," said Ernie, now irritated and looking up from his shot.

"What are you looking to bet on?" I said.

Ernie looked at me from behind his pool cue.

"Who the fuck are you?" he said through his nose.

"What are you doing?" said John Henry.

"What does it look like I'm doing?"

"It looks like you're committing a felony."

It wasn't that I needed money. I mean, I always needed money, but it was more than that. I knew how to run a book. I knew what I was doing, and I was tired of feeling stupid. John Henry never really cared what other people thought, but he always considered the consequences—what would happen, what could go wrong, who would be responsible? I'm the opposite. I worry endlessly about what other people think, but I pay zero attention to what might happen when I actually do something hazardous—as long as I don't look like an idiot doing it. John Henry begged me not to book bets in the basement. He even read me the subsection of the Yale code of conduct relevant to criminal behavior, but there was no way he was talking me out of it. Running that book let me push the zone of comfort all the way down the entryway stairs and into the basement. For the first time ever, it felt like I was gaining ground, moving the enemy—finally winning the war against the Dread. It's that simple. That's why I became the bookie to the nerd herd in the basement of Berkeley College.

# Chapter 17

Molly would make her way from Derek's room to the shower just about every morning in nothing but boxer shorts and a tank top. The bathrooms were all coed, so John Henry's day almost always started with a hurried trip down the hall so he could make conversation with Molly before she slid into the shower with her boxer shorts and tank top draped over the stainless steel swinging door. My day usually started a couple hours later with a dump in the stall next to one of the lesbians who lived down the hall, me and her shitting side by side at the pinnacle of higher education.

Then John Henry walked on to the baseball team. He didn't even tell anyone he was doing it. He just showed up one day with a pair of spikes and a smile. The dynamic was different with all the Assholes gone. It was actually more uncertain in a way since no one really knew what to expect or who would start or who would even make the team, but Canelli also seemed more muted, less interested. He liked to say he could get his teams so pissed off at him that they'd just go kick the shit out of whoever they were playing. It never really worked out that way though. Canelli thought that team of Assholes would win the EIBL and take its chances against Maine in the Northeast Regional of the College World Series. He actually thought that team had the pitching to get all the way to Omaha, so he spent a considerable amount of time pissing everyone off, but in the end, we did none of that. We went 18–16 and finished third in the EIBL behind Princeton and Navy, and when the season was over, you could tell Canelli knew his last best chance was behind him.

There were actually five who tried out that day. John Henry and four freshmen I'd never seen before. These were guys Canelli had not really recruited, but who'd managed to get themselves into Yale anyway. They were all wearing gray sweatpants and a random array of colorful T-shirts that made them easy to find on the field. Canelli sprinkled them into our usual practice groups to work with the infielders or outfielders or pitchers, depending on what they claimed they were able to do. I took my seat behind the dugout on the third base side since I couldn't play with my forearm still encased in fiberglass. Then I watched John Henry take up position at second base. He didn't look worried at all—even after Janice ripped a wicked in-between hop at him. John Henry stayed in front of it and knocked it down with his chest, and as Janice pinged fungo after fungo in John Henry's direction a picture of him as a player emerged. He was rusty for sure, but he wasn't bad. His footwork around second base wasn't great. He needed work turning double plays, but he could field a ground ball even if he didn't have a great arm.

Then Canelli rounded the five tryouts together so Puzzo could herd them over to the jayvee field behind the right field fence for batting practice. I watched that from the right field foul pole.

They stuck the one who pitched on the mound to throw the other four live batting practice. There wasn't even a catcher. This kid was just throwing pitches from in front of the mound with no target and no screen to protect him from line drives. The other four had it no better. They had to hit against a background that was nearly hitter proof. The jayvee field was nothing but a diamond and a backstop and then an outfield that went on fenceless for a couple hundred yards until finally there was a row of maple trees way off in the distance, but the leaves were already turning and the trees ran away from the hitter at a diagonal, which somehow made for the perfect camouflage. It was easy to see nothing but trees as the baseball made its way to the plate.

It didn't seem to matter. John Henry hit a hard line drive into left field on the first pitch he saw, but I could see the problem immediately. He hit off his front foot. All that unsolicited swing analysis, and John Henry's dad never bothered to show him how to hit a baseball. There was nothing Canelli had less interest in than a front-foot hitter. Canelli's way was the only way. You stayed balanced and spun off your back foot to generate power. Canelli and Puzzo had reduced hitting to a sequence of five key positions that every hitter had to replicate on time in order to be successful, and lunging out onto your front foot to hit the baseball in front of home plate was not one of them. John Henry never did hit another pitch as hard as that first one, but it didn't matter. Canelli lost interest the moment he saw the flaw. He finally muttered something to Puzzo and just walked away.

John Henry was still upbeat at dinner that night. The whole time he was loading a pile of London broil onto his plate, he was going on and on about how great the day had gone and how much fun he'd had, even though I was pretty sure he had no shot at making the team. After dinner, he left me in the basement with the Tunnel Dwellers where I recorded a week's worth of

NFL action before I made my way back up to the room. Our door wasn't shut ten seconds behind me when I heard a knock. I figured it was the manlier of the two lesbians there to complain again about toothpaste spit in the sink, but when I peered one-eyed through the peep hole, all I could see was the top of Molly's head. Derek always had to be in bed by nine because he had to get up at four-thirty in the morning to pull an oar in a Payne Whitney crew tank. Molly was tired of turning in early, so there she was in her pajamas holding a Scrabble box.

Scrabble is easily the worst game ever invented. It's boring and humiliating at the same time. I'll admit there was a mathematical allure at first—the probability of certain letters appearing, the odds of plopping a "z" down on a triple word score—but none of that means shit if you don't know the words or how to spell them. John Henry thought it was the greatest thing ever—Scrabble into the wee hours of the morning with the girl next door. For me it was agony. I'm not a strong speller. I can't spell. It's not a crime, so I hid behind my injury at first. My hand didn't heal right. A piece of knuckle had drifted away to a place where no knuckle should ever be, so I needed surgery to put it back where it belonged, and when that didn't work, they actually had to stick a pin in it to keep it in place. I was in and out of casts for months. I missed all of fall practice because of it, but it only got me out of two miserable games of Scrabble. John Henry always kept score as the two of them battled to be the greatest wordsmith of all time. My best score would have been "xray" on a triple word, except "xray" is spelled "X-ray," and John Henry fell all over himself explaining that you can't use hyphenated words. I never know where the hyphens go. Fuck hyphens. The only other clever thing I did was create the word "midget" by adding a "t" to the end of the already-on-the-board word "midge." I didn't even know what a "midge" was. It turns out to be a small, swarming fly, according to *Webster's*.

So I was sitting there one night bored out of my mind, waiting for John Henry to wow us with another six-letter word, with one eye on *SportsCenter* and the other on a meaningless jumble of vowels and consonants, when Molly threw a wood tile at my head.

"How come you're so quiet?" she said.

"I'm not."

"You lived with Derek for a year," she said. "You're quiet."

"I didn't have anything to say to Derek."

"Well, what about me?" she said with a funny little smile.

"What about you?"

"Don't you have anything to say to me?"

She perked up and waited, her eyes now locked on mine.

"What do you want me to say?"

"I don't know. That's up to you."

So I thought about it for a second, and then I said the only thing I could think of that might amuse her.

"My other brother is in prison too."

"What?" Now she looked concerned. "Why?"

"He got busted selling coke."

She looked almost sick.

"It doesn't sound like it was very easy growing up where you did."

"Queue," said John Henry. "Q-U-E-U-E. Triple word score. That's forty-two big ones!"

The next day as I left for class Molly was waiting in the entryway, fidgeting with the straps of her backpack as I got closer.

"Where you headed?" she asked.

"Statistics."

"I'll walk down with you."

It was oddly quiet as we descended, and by the time we were halfway down it was apparent we were alone, and that's when

I felt her hand on my shoulder. I turned to find her a couple steps behind me, so we were about the same height, and she was looking at me like she was trying to decide whether to say something, only she didn't. She just leaned in and kissed me instead. To this day, I don't know what prompted her to do this, but the look in her eyes as she pulled away—the brazen absurdity of what she'd just done and the reality that there was no turning back—made me want to join her on whatever brazenly absurd journey she'd just embarked upon.

We spent the next month sneaking around, meeting clandestinely with her Timothy Dwight roommate sworn to secrecy. There wasn't a minute in the day I didn't think about her, and even though I was still anxious, this was a different kind of anxious, more hopeful, more in the front of my mind, not the Dread lurking in the shadows.

Then she persuaded me to smoke some weed one night in her dorm room. Molly loved weed. Derek did not, so this one weekend she told Derek she was headed home to Syracuse and instead she holed up with me in her TD suite. It was just me and her and a Ziploc bag of pot. We watched old movies in a cloud of fetid smoke, and she indoctrinated me into the world of tantric intimacy—even though she never told me what *tantric* meant. *Webster's* says it has to do with doctrines or principles of Hindu or Buddhist tantras like meditation. I'm pretty sure it has nothing to do with any of that. It's more like learning how to breathe while slow-fucking yourself into a pretzel.

You'd think weed would calm me down, but it's somehow the opposite. We risked getting caught by making a Park Street Sub run in the dead of night after a particularly lengthy session of tantric sex, but on the way back, it was like the pot released the Dread. Without warning, my heart wanted out of my chest. I couldn't breathe. I hid at the bottom of the moat that surrounds

Morse College so she wouldn't see me losing my shit. I wanted her to leave Derek, and then on the stone wall of that moat, like one of those old movies, my mind projected the two of them larger than life. His hands were all over her. His tongue was in her mouth. I watched him reach up under her skirt. My skin crawled. I did my best to laugh it off when she finally found me, like I'd been hiding from passersby so we wouldn't get found out, but the paranoia ate at my insides all night. She'd be with him again in the morning, letting him touch her, letting him kiss her, letting him slow-fuck her into a pretzel just the same. She wouldn't stop him. She wouldn't say a thing, and I just couldn't understand, but when she woke up and rolled over in the morning light with her hair all mangled and looking at me the way she did, I froze and said nothing.

"I'm so fucking addicted to you," she said.

Then she got out of bed.

I think it was the way she said it that ruined everything— almost regretful like I was something to quit—and before she'd even slipped on her slippers, I knew she was never leaving Derek, at least not for me. I started to avoid her after that. It was unconscious at first, but pretty soon I was affirmatively ducking late-night Scrabble, and then I went cold turkey and stopped meeting her in front of Naples for our usual midday sneak around. I never told her why either. I just knew I had to get away from her, so I'd blow past her in the entryway and hardly say hello. I even ate dinner in Calhoun for a while so I wouldn't have to see her in the Berkeley College dining hall. She finally left me this psychotic message, a pleading, sobbing message on our answering machine begging me to talk to her—only John Henry heard it first. I never did talk to her. I never did tell her why, and the only good thing that really came from any of it was a merciful end to late-night Scrabble.

# Chapter 18

Eventually, I settled into a routine. My spring semester schedule was pretty basic. On Monday, Wednesday, and Friday, I'd head up Science Hill for Linear Algebra and then back to Linsly-Chit for this class John Henry talked me into since Yale made you take two courses in the Humanities. Then I'd head over to SSS for Statistics 120a. On Tuesday and Thursday, I woke up early for Italian. Then it was back up Science Hill for Astronomy 120. Monday, Wednesday, Friday. Tuesday, Thursday. Breakfast. Lunch. Dinner. Tunnel. After a while, it just reminded me of this mechanical maze that hung on the office wall of a doctor Nathan used to see when we were kids, chutes and slides and corkscrews made out of heavy wire, almost like coat hanger, and there was a little steel ball that rattled around in it, and sometimes the ball would go this way, and sometimes the ball would go that way, but it always ended up back at this lift that looked like a bicycle chain, and the bicycle chain would take the ball back up to the top where it would start all over again. Nathan loved to watch this ball make its way to the bottom, and he would try to guess which way the ball would fall the next time down, but then I realized that every time the ball fell one way, it flipped a little mechanical switch to make it go another way the next time down. That kind of ruined it, I guess. There was nothing to look forward to after that.

Most of the Tunnel Dwellers paid me on time (I was making about $500 a month), but Wayne the Law Student was pretty much penniless as far as I could tell. He got so far behind halfway into that first NFL season, he had to cough up his Nintendo game console to call it even. That's when I got hooked on a game called *R.B.I. Baseball.* I'd cave it up in the safety of our dorm room and do nothing but play this video game for hours. I perfected John Tudor's slider. I invented Vince Coleman's steal of home. I discovered Reggie Jackson's superhuman strength. In the real world, baseball is about failure. You don't escape the strikeouts and errors. But in the virtual world of *R.B.I.*, I was almost infallible. So when the phone rang one morning as I flirted with a no-hitter courtesy of a California Angel named Mike Witt, I let the call go to our answering machine because what I was doing was far more important.

"Hey, man. I'm in town. Where you been? We need to hang out."

It was Vandershar. I jumped at the sound of his voice and grabbed the phone before he could hang up. I don't know why, but I was relieved to hear from him. I just felt a sudden overwhelming desire to get off the couch. I didn't say a word about Dallas. Instead, I told him about a party in the Moose Room, and we agreed to meet in front of Sterling Memorial Library at eight. Then I grabbed my backpack and headed out the door to a discussion section I was already late to.

It was a gray gloomy morning as I made my way through Cross Campus quad. I dodged some dope juggling bowling pins in his pajamas before darting into Harkness Hall. The section met in a small wood-paneled room. It was crowded with gray hooded sweatshirts and irritated faces when I opened the door. I took a seat up near the front and nodded to John Henry who was way in the back near the corner. It was English 291: The American Novel Since 1945, but for me it was more like Reading 291: Endless Reading. I'd actually been ditching the discussion section for a while because it was impossible to keep up, so I think John Henry was a little surprised to see me.

Our section leader was an attentive graduate student named Francine. She looked about thirty-five with all this wiry black and gray hair. We were supposed to be reading *The Catcher in the Rye*, but I'd only managed to get about thirty pages into it. They all hated it. It seemed like they hated everything.

This one girl named Belinda Pitt was the worst. She always wore these wild, draping gypsy clothes, and she was so humongous that when she bent over it was like staring straight up the ass of a rhinoceros. I couldn't understand why she was even in the class since she despised every book on the reading list, until I realized that was sort of the point. It was like open season on everything all the time.

"Why can't Phoebe just take care of herself?" said Belinda as I wedged myself into an uncomfortably tiny desk.

It wasn't really a question.

"Is she not too young?" said Francine.

"That's not why," said Belinda. "The whole thing is symbolic of the need for men... white men... to have complete control over everything. Like it's their job to protect everyone."

"You think that was the author's intent?"

"Does it matter?" said Belinda. "It was his perspective. It's irrelevant what he intended. Did he intend to write a sexist book about white privilege? Who cares? That's what he did because how could he possibly do anything else?"

"Be specific."

"Well, on top of the women in this book having no agency whatsoever, except for maybe a prostitute, Holden's lucky his parents could afford to put him in an institution. His socio-economic status ensures that he'll find the help he needs to keep him off the streets. He's a lazy brat, but you know he won't fail. There's an entire infrastructure around him that will never let him fail... whether he applies himself or not. This book is completely un-self-aware. The fencing team? Are you kidding me?"

"Mr. Mazio, nice of you to join us today," said Francine. "What do *you* think about all this?"

I was hardly into my seat, and I had no idea how she knew my name. I started to flip through the pages, hoping maybe she'd move on, but when I looked up, she was staring like she expected me to say something. They were all staring like that, except I had nothing to say, and those few seconds felt like a lifetime as the air somehow leaked from my lungs and I slid backwards into my own head. I just sat there feeling smaller and smaller until finally there was nothing left of me.

"I thought it was just a story about a kid afraid of dying?" said John Henry from the back of the room.

"He's not afraid of dying," said Belinda, turning to take John Henry head-on. "Where do you get that? He might be obsessed with dying... but the only way to control death is to become the killer. Isn't that what white men have been doing for a thousand years?"

"I wouldn't know," said John Henry. "I've only been around for the last nineteen."

She kept looking at him like she was trying to figure out how to pick him apart, like she wanted to reduce him to rubble even though she didn't even know him, but she finally just turned back around like he wasn't worth it.

"This book says nothing to me," she said.

"That doesn't make it invalid," said John Henry, like a little dog who wouldn't let go of a chew toy. "It's not supposed to be didactic."

"I didn't say it was," said Belinda, her back still turned to him.

"I'm just saying it's still useful. Even if you don't like it... it can still be useful."

"Useful?" she said, turning to face him again. "Useful for what?"

I just sat there the whole time with my head down until it was over.

"Did she make that shit up?" I said when we were back outside on the street. "He doesn't kill anybody, does he?"

"You didn't read it, did you?"

"How'm I supposed to read an entire book in a week?"

"You played *R.B.I.* until four in the morning."

"I had the National League All-Stars."

"How do you expect to defend yourself if you never know what anybody's talking about?"

"Defend myself from what?" I said. "I didn't do anything."

He didn't hear me though. A circular saw five feet in diameter was slicing through Elm Street as we made our way toward Linsly-Chit. About half a dozen men in orange jumpers were wandering around watching it do its thing. It made this deafening, high-pitched, grinding circular saw noise that you heard all the time in New Haven. It was like a demilitarized zone in every direction—old furniture and garbage stacked in front yards and trash spilling into gutters—block after block of red brick housing projects and old wood-frame houses rotting off their foundations, and always some monstrous circular saw ripping something up somewhere as if it made a difference. But when we got to where he could hear me again, he wasn't listening anyway. There was a blond girl about a hundred yards in front of us, and he was just about running to get a better look at her.

She took a left onto Chapel Street, but by the time we got to the corner, she was nowhere in sight. There was a string of decent retail storefronts on Chapel, but only about a block's worth—boutiques and bookstores and art galleries. It almost made you forget you were in New Haven, but only for that one block. John Henry peered through the windows shop by shop as we made our way until he finally found her in a lingerie store about halfway down the street. She was standing next to a headless mannequin in purple satin panties and a matching push-up bra.

"Check out her calves," he said with his nose pressed up against the glass and all this women's underwear about three feet from his face.

She was wearing baggy jeans and sandals, but the jeans were rolled up so you could see her calves. They were smooth and athletic, and a tan line circled her left ankle where an anklet used to be. You could tell she'd just been somewhere warm, somewhere sunny, somewhere better than New Haven, and it made me think of all those girls on the beach in Juan-les-Pins happily done with morning class, indifferent to the stares.

John Henry pushed through the front door like it was nothing as a little bell jingled on the inside to announce his arrival. I couldn't make myself go in—not because it was a store full of bras and panties, but because I knew I had nothing to say to her. I knew I'd just stand there like a bug zapper, so I stood outside in front of all that women's underwear instead, nodding at passersby for what seemed like an eternity until finally John Henry pushed his way back out the same door holding a bright red shopping bag full of boxer shorts. He was glowing like he'd just won the lottery. We turned to head back toward campus, but I took another look through the window. I wished I'd gone in, and I lingered for a beat, thinking maybe she'd reappear, thinking maybe I'd lock her in some really unforgettable eye contact, but I would never get that lucky, and as we walked away, I was already trying to remember exactly what she looked like.

# Chapter 19

Vandershar was supposed to meet us at eight, so we were still standing in front of Sterling at eight thirty. The entrance to the library looked like a European cathedral, and there was this demonstration going on out front—picket signs and bullhorns with a fair amount of debris as they wound it down. I was taking long, slow swigs from a bottle of Southern Comfort while we waited. Then Vandershar appeared out of the darkness.

"There he is," he said as he took the bottle from me. Then he looked at John Henry. "Hey, buddy. Didn't expect to see you."

"I didn't expect to see you either."

"What's with the cast?" he said as he slapped my forearm.

"Don't ask."

"What's all this then?" he said, looking at the wake of trash and demonstration paraphernalia.

"Something to do with Indians," I said.

"It's the Association of Native Americans at Yale," said John Henry.

"Indians," said Vandershar. "What are they doing?"

"Raising awareness."

"Awareness for what?" Vandershar took a swig.

"Wounded Knee," said John Henry. "The Trail of Tears. A couple hundred years of genocide and murder."

"Please," said Vandershar. "They were killing each other for a thousand years before we got here."

It started to rain.

We didn't take two steps toward Pierson College before it was coming down in buckets. We finally ducked under the entrance to Saybrook to keep from getting soaked, and while we hunkered down, Vandershar and I polished off the SoCo, so I finally started to feel the warmth of my buzz.

The Moose Room entryway in Pierson College was packed, so we wormed and shoved our way up to the third floor. The slate floor inside was wet, and it seemed like the water from outside had been tracked all the way to the keg, but in fact there was something backed up or leaking in the second floor bathroom so the water was actually moving in the opposite direction. Geniuses everywhere and all anybody could ever think to do on the weekend was stick a keg in a shower stall.

"This is the Moose Room?" said Vandershar, yelling to be heard over the noise.

"There's a stuffed moose head in that room over there," I said.

"I thought it was a bar."

"How can you not know what the Moose Room is?" said John Henry. "Do you even go to school here?"

"The keg is in the toilet," said Vandershar. "What do I do if I have to take a piss?"

It was pouring outside and about a thousand degrees inside, so the entryway was all sweaty and hot and clogged like a river full of writhing salmon, hurdling over one another in a heated, horny mess. Then somebody spilled a beer on Vandershar's shoes.

"Is this what you do every weekend?" he said.

"Sometimes there's a fraternity party."

"What's the difference?"

"We do this in a basement."

I saw Larry, Norman, and Billy pushing through the crowd toward us, all double-fisted with red keg cups full of Natural Light.

"Gentlemen," said Larry.

Then he handed Vandershar a beer.

"Oh, Larry, you shouldn't have." Jonathon looked at it like it was a cup of formaldehyde. "You really shouldn't have."

"I think my tattoo's infected," said Norman as he handed me a beer.

"You need to leave it alone," said John Henry. "He said it would feel like a sunburn."

"How would you know?" said Larry.

"We all got tattoos," I said to Vandershar, pushing up my sleeve to show him the cartoon bulldog on my shoulder.

"Why?" he said.

"John Henry made the baseball team."

It wasn't just that all the Assholes had graduated. We lost other players too. We lost them every year, mostly recruits who couldn't take Canelli—some of them good players he just wrecked. Baseball is a game of failure. The failure rate of the very best hitter is seventy percent. Errors happen all the time. Guys get picked off. Pitchers don't throw strikes every pitch. Hitters swing and miss. Canelli refused to accept any of this. It was like he'd devoted his entire life to a game he didn't understand, so his expectations were ridiculous. Every walk was a disaster. Every strikeout was a pathetic failure. Every error was a catastrophe, and it would have been laughable if the stakes hadn't seemed so high—if a head coach didn't wield some strange power—but the more you fucked up, the more he buried you in sarcasm, or he'd just stop talking to you altogether, never a teaching moment either, never anything positive that came from all the "pissing us off," just a downward spiral some guys never pulled out of, so every year we needed bullpen catchers and fly ball shaggers and someone to get the foul balls that ended up on the wrong side of the fence. That's how John Henry made the baseball team.

Larry did the artwork. The tattoo guy was bald with tattoos all over his head. I think they were supposed to be reptile scales, but it looked more like green chain mail. We asked him a bunch of questions about the needles and if they were new and how he cleaned them. He just laughed and said he should be the one worried about us.

John Henry went first. He climbed onto an old dentist chair and pulled his pants down to his hip. Then the bald guy rubbed some Mennen Speed Stick all over the spot where John Henry pointed and shaved it clean with a razor. After that he fired up a needle that looked like it was powered by a mouse on a treadmill. Larry said something about a Dr. Mengele as the needle hit John Henry's hip, and then John Henry turned a milky shade of green. That was it for his blood sugar. He looked like he was about to pass out. The bald tattoo guy wouldn't work on him after that. John Henry had hypoglycemia, which is sort of like the opposite of diabetes, except nobody knows what the fuck to do with you when it strikes. Papa had it too, so Gram always kept a can of orange juice and a pack of saltines in her purse just in case. I was constantly hunting down Wheat Thins just so John Henry wouldn't pass out. This time, I had to wait in about three feet of smoke at the dive bar next door before the bartender would give me a can of Tropicana.

The whole thing took about three hours. Billy got a swinging bulldog on his hip. I got a swinging bulldog on my shoulder. Larry got a throwing bulldog on his ankle. Norman got the same thing as Larry. And John Henry got the little green dot the needle made right before the bald guy told him to get the fuck out of the chair.

Vandershar appeared horrified as he sized up the cartoon bulldog on my shoulder. Then he looked past me at the salmon pushing and shoving for the keg and the salmon spilling out of the Moose Room. Then he stepped around me to mull the salmon hurdling their way up the stairs.

"I should've made you run naked to Naples," he said, only he said it just to me, like we were having our own separate conversation.

"Yeah... right," I said.

"It definitely would've been more entertaining than this."

"You weren't there."

"Where?"

"In Dallas."

"What do you mean I wasn't there. You didn't show up."

"I showed up," I said. "I called the number you gave me. The dad said he never heard of you."

"Maybe I didn't make my usual impression, but I definitely met him. I fucked his daughter right there in his kitchen."

"That's not what he said."

"He didn't say I fucked his daughter in the kitchen?"

"He said you went to South Padre."

"We did. I told you."

"No. You told me be there by Friday."

"We left on Friday."

"Yeah, no fucking kidding."

"So you were there," he said, sort of impressed.

"How do you think I broke my hand?"

"I have no idea how you broke your hand."

"I punched the pay phone after talking to the dad."

"How would I have known that?"

"I didn't lose the bet."

"Relax," he said. "I'm still good for it."

"Good for what?"

"The apartment... off campus. We'll still get it. You can't live here."

"I don't understand why you bought the boxer shorts," said Larry.

"What'd you want me to do?" said John Henry.

"Did you even talk to her?" said Norman.

"That's why I went in to buy the boxer shorts."

"So you could talk to her?" said Larry.

"She worked there."

"But you didn't have to buy anything," said Norman.

"It seemed like the thing to do at the time."

"She thinks you're gay for sure," said Billy.

"She does not think I'm gay."

"You walked into a lingerie store and bought silk boxer shorts," said Larry.

"Two pairs," said Norman.

"That's not particularly heterosexual behavior."

Vandershar leaned over so only I could hear him again.

"You don't belong here."

I took a look around, and it struck me how few of the people in that entryway I actually knew, how many of them I had seen in passing—in Commons, on the Cross Campus quad, in class— and still I didn't really know a single one of them.

"Come on," he said as he gave me a shove.

"Where we going?"

"It's time to see what you can do on your own."

Across the entryway was a girl leaning against the far wall by herself. I'd never seen her before. She had dull brown hair and a snaggletoothed smile, and as we got closer I could see she was wearing a dark blue Yale Track jacket.

"All alone?" said Vandershar as we got close enough for her to hear us.

"My boyfriend just left," she said.

"Interesting strategy."

"He has to get up early."

"What about you?"

"I don't have to get up early."

"I'm Jonathon."

"Claire," she said, but she barely looked at him.

"Claire?"

"Is that a problem?"

"It's kind of a fat girl's name, isn't it?"

"Very funny."

"Where you from... Claire?"

"Provo," she said.

"Provo, Spain?"

"Provo, Utah." She rolled her eyes like we could not have been annoying her more. "There is no Provo, Spain."

"There was one?"

"What is wrong with you?"

"You run track?" he said.

"Did you figure that out all by yourself?"

"Not really. It's right there... on your jacket."

"Yeah. No shit, Sherlock."

"So what's your thing?" he said.

"My thing?"

"What event do you do in track?"

"The heptathlon."

"Does that mean you were born with a dick?"

"That's a hermaphrodite."

"Ah… right. Then what's the heptathlon?"

"It's basically the decathlon without the pole vault."

"So you throw the javelin?"

"I do," she said, looking beyond us into the mass of salmon.

"What's your best event?"

"Long jump," she said. Then she looked at me. "You know, I know who you are. My roommate's best friend is Molly Blair."

"This is Spencer," said Vandershar. "Who's Molly Blair?"

"We all thought Derek was an asshole," she said. "You turned out to be worse."

"Derek Hinkle?" said Vandershar. "Derek Hinkle and Molly Blair? I went to Choate with those two. Nobody is a bigger asshole than Derek Hinkle. That's impossible."

"How is Molly?" I said like an asshole.

"She's great," said Claire. "I'll tell her you asked."

"So what's your longest jump then?" said Vandershar.

"Sixteen, eight and three quarters."

"That means absolutely nothing to me. Is that any good?"

"I finished fourth in the Ivies last year, but two of the girls ahead of me graduated. My goal this year is seventeen feet. I compete individually in the long jump too."

"They used to make us run three miles in thirty minutes at Choate," he said. "I never made it. I never made the thirty minutes come to think of it."

"That is so impressive," she said.

"Spencer here is the athlete."

"I know," she said. "I've heard all about him."

"That reminds me," said Vandershar. "I need to be going. There's an eleven-thirty from New Haven to Grand Central I can still catch. Claire, it was an absolute pleasure." He leaned in again so only I could hear him. "Good luck with this one. Let me know how it goes... and get on the apartment thing."

He swatted me on the back and left me there. I didn't say anything for a second. Neither did Claire. She took a sip from her red keg cup and avoided eye contact while I did my best fluorescent bug zapper impersonation.

"So," I said. "Provo."

"Yep."

"You have any brothers or sisters?"

"Do I have any brothers or sisters? What the fuck do you care?"

I pretended to drink from my own red keg cup even though it was empty.

"I have a brother," she said. "He goes to BYU."

"You think it's still raining?"

"What happened to your hand?"

"I broke it."

"How?"

"I hit a pay phone."

"Well, that was stupid. Why would you hit a pay phone?"

"I don't know," I said, looking at it. "Don't you ever feel like punching something?"

She smiled when I said that, and I could see that crooked front tooth.

"This is so lame," she said, looking over my shoulder again.

"You want to go?"

"Yeah, right."

"What?"

"You think I'm going home with you?"

"No. What college are you in?"

"You're not coming home with me either."

"I just meant I'd walk you there."

"TD," she said.

Then she slugged what was left of her beer.

"You shouldn't walk to TD alone."

She tossed her keg cup on the ground.

"Fine," she said. "You can walk me to the front gate."

Timothy Dwight College was about eighteen million miles away from the Moose Room and probably the last place on Earth I wanted to walk in the rain, but I needed Vandershar to know I left with her, so I gave the guys a nod as we headed down the slate stairs to find the rain coming down in sheets.

We decided to make a break for Demery's to wait it out. About halfway there, I realized she was racing me to the front door. As I pulled a little closer, she cut me off to keep me from passing her, but I reeled her in about fifty yards out and blew by her as we darted across Elm Street.

"You're such a shit," she said. Then she hit me in the back of the head as we went inside. "I want some pizza. I start training hardcore on Monday."

"Training for what?"

"Penn Relays."

"What are Penn Relays?"

"You've never heard of Penn Relays? It's like the biggest track meet of the year. There'll be like five thousand people there."

"Where?"

"Where? At Penn, stupid. That's why they're called the Penn Relays."

She wouldn't shut up after that. She just kept talking—mostly about herself. She'd stop only long enough to take bites out of her massive slice of greasy pizza. Then she was right back at it with her mouth full, talking all the way through the line into the bar, talking as I paid her cover, talking while we downed a couple Alabama slammers.

"I thought Mormons didn't drink," I said. I had to raise my voice to be heard over the crowd.

"I'm not a very good Mormon."

"How far can you throw a javelin?"

"What the fuck does that have to do with me not being a very good Mormon?"

"I don't know."

"Who cares how far I can throw a javelin? The heptathlon is bullshit my coach makes me do. I'm here to win an Ivy League championship in the long jump."

The bartender put another round in front of us.

"You think maybe you've had enough?"

"You think maybe you're a pussy?"

She raised her slammer toward the ceiling and spilled about half of it on my arm in the process.

"To the long jump, motherfucker!"

"To the long jump," I said, raising my translucent plastic cup, but she failed to recognize my lack of enthusiasm since she was already on to the next thing in her head.

"You know, Molly still talks about you."

"Really? What's she say?"

"She says you weren't very good in the sack." She said it so matter-of-factly that it sounded more like well-settled knowledge that had been circulated and discussed, debated and verified by hundreds of people, most of whom I'd never heard of. "She said you were always in a hurry."

"She seemed to be enjoying it at the time."

"That's after she schooled you up in the ways of the tantra." She took another slug of Alabama slammer. "She did say you have a big dick though."

"She should've dumped Derek."

"You're the one who blew it."

"I didn't do shit."

"Is that right?"

"She wouldn't dump Derek."

"Did she hurt your feelings? Did she make you sad?"

I wasn't sure what else to say since whatever I said seemed to make it worse.

"I shouldn't even be talking to you," she said.

"Why not?"

"You're on the blacklist."

"What's the blacklist?"

"You don't think we keep track of you motherfuckers?"

"What motherfuckers?"

"The misogynists."

"Misogynists? Why am *I* on it?"

"Are you kidding?"

"She wouldn't dump Derek."

"So?"

"What was I supposed to do?"

"You could've taken it like a man for starters."

Then she downed what was left of her slammer.

I couldn't stand her, and I wanted to get out of there. The rain had stopped and it was a good time to go, so I suggested we leave. She told me to shut the fuck up and ordered another round. By the time we finally got back out onto the street, she was hammered and it was pouring again.

"What college are *you* in?" she said, the rain coming down in big fat drops.

"Berkeley."

She bolted down Elm Street before I could say another word. I raced to catch her again, but this time she beat me to the front gate of South Court. I had to explain to her that I lived in North Court. She didn't even know there was a North Court, and then she insisted on seeing the tunnel, so I took her down there even though I didn't really want to. We had to stop and check out every room, every mural. She challenged me to a pull-up contest in the gym. It was barely a gym at all really—just an old squash court and a bunch of medieval-looking torture devices that passed as gym equipment. I won, which only irritated her. I finally got her upstairs, but then she started to rifle through all our shit like it was a scavenger hunt—flipping through paper and pictures and turning over books and leafing through the mail and being generally annoying, until finally she stumbled onto Nintendo.

"I want to play," she said.

"No, you don't. It's late. We need to get you back to TD."

"Shut up and turn this on."

So against my will, I popped in *R.B.I.*

"I'm so gonna kick your ass at this," she said.

I showed her the basics. She picked the '84 Tigers. I played with the '85 Cardinals. I even let her score in the top of the first inning, but she wouldn't shut up. She babbled in between pitches. She screamed randomly when anything happened. She bitched when it didn't go her way, but I actually had to take John Tudor out of the game after only three innings because she'd somehow programmed herself to mash his slider. And that's when it hit me. I stopped paying attention to her altogether and instead began to focus on the game itself. It occurred to me that the computer could hit John Tudor's slider too. When I played the machine, just me against the computer, John Tudor would dominate for about three innings, and then the machine would start to get to him. I figured it just knew what was coming based on the buttons I pressed, but what if it was predicting outcomes like she was? What if it was all algorithms—probabilities, odds, and math, pumped up with real-time data? I started to see the game as something that unfolded pitch by pitch, with the odds of outcomes shifting every time the count changed.

"Fuck," she said as Vince Coleman ripped a Jack Morris fastball into the gap in left center. "Why is he so fast?"

"It's Vince Coleman."

"That's bullshit. That's not even realistic. It's not humanly possible to run that fast. Fuck. Fuck. Fuck!"

Vince Coleman slid into third with a triple, and then I had him steal home on the next pitch, but it wasn't until Jack Clark bombed a three-run homer over the wall in left field that she finally pulled the power cord out of the wall and the screen went black.

"What the fuck?" I said.

She just laughed with that snaggletoothed smile, and then looked at me funny, her head kind of cocked to one side.

"You really aren't very good at this, are you?"

"Then why am I kicking your ass?" I said.

"Not the game, dumbass."

I wasn't sure what she was talking about, so I just sat there.

"How many girls have you been with? And I don't mean here. I mean total."

I decided in that split second to let her have my number right between the eyes.

"Seventeen," I said.

"How is that even possible? How much longer were you gonna make me sit here and play this?"

"I thought you wanted to play."

"Could you be any more ridiculous?"

"So you don't want to play?"

"I want to fuck, stupid. It's my last night out. You think I came here to play a video game?"

It occurred to me that fucking her might be the only way to shut her up. She certainly wasn't going to tell anyone, so I slid toward her, but my momentum pushed us both uncomfortably onto the floor next to the couch. I heard one of the remote controls crack underneath her, and for some reason, Vandershar's tiny room in Welch Hall popped into my head. If anyone ever deserved to have their head fucked out a window and into the driving rain, it was this girl. I told her not to move. Then I rushed into the bedroom to push the bunk away from the wall—far enough that the bed covered the entire window, which I cranked wide open.

We peeled off wet clothes after that. She did most of the work. My cast didn't help, but she seemed to like to do all the work anyway. She started to drag me down onto the bottom bunk, which would have ruined everything, so I had to tell her that the top bunk was mine. We then proceeded to engage in a mortal struggle for position—me trying to flip her doggie so I could maneuver her head out the window, her trying to climb on top so she could ride me like a pony. I needed her head at the far end of the bed where the window was, so I attempted a move I can only describe as Greco-Roman, but I couldn't get any leverage because of the stupid cast and she was strong as an ox besides. I just gave up. She mounted me with her feet flat on the mattress and fucked me from the squatting position like an All-Star catcher. All I could think about the whole time was Thurman Munson. Her head was cocked back, eyes fixed on the ceiling about eight inches from her face, and that's the way it stayed until she wore herself out and fell off me in a sweaty heap. I could feel the rain falling on my feet. At least I outlasted her. When she finally fell asleep, I crawled down into my own bed just to get away from her, and I didn't wake up until I heard the sound of her falling into the bedpost as she tried to pull on wet jeans the next morning.

"I can't believe I did this." She was wringing out her shirt. "I have a boyfriend. I don't know why I even talked to you."

I closed my eyes and let my head fall back onto the pillow, but she wouldn't shut up.

"I can't believe I did this."

"Why don't you just go?"

"I never do this."

"Do you have to narrate?"

"You're gonna tell everyone we did this, aren't you?"

"That really doesn't sound like you leaving."

"You're such an asshole."

I didn't know what else to say, so I closed my eyes for a second, and by the time I sat up, she wasn't in the bedroom anymore.

"Fuck you!" she screamed.

Then I heard the front door slam shut behind her as John Henry's head poked up from the couch.

"Well, that went well," he said.

According to my *Webster's Pocket Dictionary*, a "misogynist" is a person who (a) dislikes, and/or (b) has contempt for, women—but I don't think I dislike women any more than I dislike anyone else, and I'm not sure I've ever really had contempt for anyone besides my idiot brothers and Derek, so it was hard to understand Claire's blacklist or what I was doing on it, and the more I thought about it, the more I realized she had in her head a completely different version of me. I started to wonder how many other versions of me were running around out there. I mean, how bad did it get? And when I realized the number was only limited by the number of people on the planet, I started to think maybe Vandershar was right. There was a not insubstantial subset of people at Yale who really didn't know me, and even more I'd never met, all of whom wanted nothing to do with me—and not even me really, but the idea of me—their version of me. How was I supposed to defend myself from that?

# Chapter 20

*Spring/Summer 1990*

I called Vandershar about five minutes later and told him I fucked Claire's head out the window. It was just a better story. He thought it was hilarious. I left out the part about the blacklist though. I never told anyone about the blacklist, but I kept thinking about it. I kept thinking about Derek too, and Belinda Pitt, and all those salmon, even the guy juggling bowling pins on the Cross Campus quad. Vandershar was right about every single one of them, and it gnawed at me as I went about my business, sitting in classrooms, sharing dining hall lines—constantly surrounded by these people who wanted nothing to do with me—so I started to avoid the usual Yale weekends. I'd lay low in our dorm room and wait for opportunities to hang with Vandershar instead.

At first, I mostly watched him. I studied him to be honest. I also did a mountain of blow with him. The first time was in the bathroom at the 21 Club. It burned a little going up, and it tasted medicinal as it dissolved in the back of my throat, but I did more of it anyway since it made me feel like a fucking genius. We'd get all wired, and I'd try to mimic Jonathon even though it was basically impossible. He was a chameleon. He could adapt to any situation. He was comfortable anywhere, and people just wanted to be around him. He'd pretend he didn't like it when they knew who he was, but I could always tell it irritated him when they didn't.

What struck me most though, after watching him do his thing for hours on end, was that he never really tried to persuade anyone of anything. It was like he agreed with you no matter what—unless he wanted rid of you. It's disarming to have someone agree with everything you say, and then he'd ask questions to get you talking about yourself, to get inside your head, and once he was there, once he knew a little bit about you and understood what you wanted, he reinforced those wants, and once he figured out what you were afraid of, he played those fears against you, until finally it was like he could weaponize you for his own amusement. If other people are just there to be manipulated, you're suddenly immune from their bullshit.

We pretty much rampaged through the tri-state area for the rest of the semester, leaving a trail of nameless female faces and credit card receipts in our wake. We'd head out to Atlantic City and piss his money away playing blackjack and craps, tipping big-titted cocktail waitresses twenty bucks a drink while we waited for their shifts to end. We saw Bon Jovi at the Meadowlands. We went backstage at Madison Square Garden to meet INXS. We'd hold court at Building while A Tribe Called Quest did its thing in the background. And we developed a point system to keep track of all the debauchery. It was like these nights became the sole purpose of our existence, and if the night didn't end with a score, it was a failure, only I was never really sure if it was about the hookup or the story about the hookup, like we were in some depraved competition that had no end.

But it wasn't until we hit this shithole up Whalley Avenue in New Haven to see a band no one had ever heard of that I finally transformed into something else altogether. We'd all piled into John Henry's Blazer, but we were late thanks to Jonathon, so there was already a mob out front and a long line to get in when we got there. The venue was tucked into a strip mall that had its own parking lot, but the lot was already full, so John Henry had to park a few blocks away. Vandershar and I hung back at the car to blast our way through the last of his cocaine before the show started. I was so wired by the time we caught up to everyone I felt like I could climb the Empire State Building.

It was pretty dark already, and there was a crowd of about fifty or sixty townies out front, all agitated that they weren't inside. I stumbled into John Henry at the outer edge of this horde. He was engaged in what appeared to be a harmless conversation with a little dude who looked like a roadie—only as I got closer I realized the conversation wasn't so harmless. I had no idea what they were talking about, but I could tell by the roadie's body language that something was up. He went from casual to upright, and then he dropped one foot behind the other like he was ready to throw a punch, only before I could do anything about it, this greasy-haired giant in an untucked plaid flannel shirt joined the conversation.

I didn't hear a word that guy said either. I just remember the clarity of my own thoughts as I watched him. The certainty, you know. How right I was—almost like I could see into the future. The Giant did exactly what I expected him to do. He stuck a finger in John Henry's chest, and then John Henry did exactly what I thought he would do. He smiled and started babbling, but the Giant had no interest in being appeased. I was right about that too. He only got more aggressive. All the talking in the world wasn't going to do shit, so I surveyed the crowd one more time to make sure my plan was sound. But it wasn't just sound. It was genius. The plan was basically this: swing as hard as I could and drop their biggest guy with one punch. That was it. That was my stroke of coke-addled genius. I was absolutely certain if I put their biggest guy on the ground, the rest of them would leave us the fuck alone. I actually felt superhuman standing over him once he was down, but leaving us the fuck alone was the last thing on anyone's mind.

They didn't even care that I was the one who threw the punch. They came at us like we were all one and the same, just this wave of untucked plaid flannel shirts and long greasy hair washing over us. We scattered. I had to do figure eights in the parking lot to avoid getting torn to pieces. I don't know how long I dodged them, but it was long enough for me to run the coke right out of my system because pretty soon all that superhuman confidence was gone, and then there was no one chasing me. I stopped to figure out what the fuck had happened, and that's when I realized they had John Henry. He was on the ground, and I could see by the yellowy parking lot lights that they were beating the fuck out of him. I just stood there. That's what I remember most—the standing there, you know, like a coward doing nothing as the Dread took hold again. I woke up in a Yale New Haven Hospital bed a few hours later with a fractured orbital bone and twenty-six stitches to close a stab wound in my right shoulder.

I couldn't throw for two months, and I missed the last ten games of our sophomore season because of it. John Henry begged me to come home with him for the summer, but I blew him off and went to Greenwich instead. It still took Jonathon weeks to get me out on the water. I just didn't want to do anything, and I couldn't understand why he didn't feel the same. I mean, he was right. He was right about everything. No matter where you looked there was someone ready to hate you. He finally grabbed a couple rods from the boathouse and shoved me onto a Sea Ray—mostly just to get me out of the way of the help, who were busily setting up for the Vandershar Fourth of July party. We spent the rest of the day slaughtering bluefish by the dozen. We'd gaff these things and throw them back into the water bleeding until this semi-living chum slick brought about a dozen sharks to the boat. We hooked one of those too, only when we got it close enough, I tossed an M-80 down its throat, and we watched its head blow to smithereens about a foot below the surface.

The next day was the party. The Vandershar estate was this massive compound that looked like the picture of Versailles on the cover of my fifth grade history book. They'd rigged the tennis courts with fireworks for a party about half of Greenwich was invited to. There were men in chef's hats slicing through slabs of roast beef and little kids running all over the place with sparklers. At some point I found myself in front of a table loaded down with these monumental wheels of cheese, one stacked on top of another like the whole thing was a piece of art. There were also a bunch of silver cheese-covered platters with tiny forks and toothpicks, and something I think came out of a goat.

"So how do you know Jonathon?" said this blond girl who slid up next to me as I fumbled to cut a sliver of blue cheese from a crumbly wedge.

"Vandershar?"

"I saw you with him earlier. Do you go to Yale too?"

She was packed into a tight red dress that had her tits all crammed together.

"Yeah," I said, popping the blue cheese into my mouth.

"Do you like it?"

"Not really."

It tasted like mold.

"Yale," she said. "Not the cheese."

I spit the mold into a cocktail napkin.

"It's okay."

"Okay?" said Jonathon, arriving out of nowhere. "He does not think it's okay."

"You don't?" she said. "Why?"

"Julia Dwyer," said Jonathon. "Look at you. All grown up." Then he looked at me. "I used to hang out with Julia's brother when we were little. Is he here?"

"No," she said. "He's away for the summer."

"Too bad."

"So why don't you like Yale?" she said.

"Spencer doesn't like much of anything."

"How can you not like anything?"

"*Je crains que le pauvre monsieur Mazio soit devenu un peu d'un misanthrope*," said Vandershar as he popped some mold into his mouth.

"*C'est si triste*," said Julia with a smile. "*Pourquoi*?"

"Show her your scar," he said.

I pushed my sleeve up so she could see my shoulder.

"Is that a tattoo?" she said.

"It was," I said.

"Tell her what happened."

"I got stabbed."

"Great story, Spencer."

I just stood there.

"We need more champagne," he said. Then he shook his head in disappointment. "Try not to let Spencer bore you to death."

Julia never took her eyes off Jonathon as he slid through the crowd to reach over the bar and grab a bottle of Dom from a stainless steel bowl of ice that had about fifteen other bottles in it.

"So who stabbed you?" she said, still looking at him as he made his way back toward us.

"I don't know."

"Why'd they do it?"

"It wasn't me they were trying to stab."

"Quick," said Jonathon. "Drink it. It's the antidote to Spencer's nasty disposition." Then he handed me a glass. "Here, have some mildew to wash down the mold."

"Yummy," she said as she took a sip.

"Are your parents here?" said Jonathon.

"Somewhere."

"Do they know you're drinking?"

"Yeah... it's no big deal."

"Julia's dad runs trading at Goldman. We do not want him mad at us."

"Let me take a picture of you guys," she said.

Vandershar's little sister, Stephanie, made the staff spread disposable box cameras all over the house so the guests could take pictures of the party. She was compiling some sort of record of her life for a school project, so the idea was for the guests to take photos, then leave the cameras for Stephanie so she could develop all the film. Their Honduran gardener originally came back with all the little box cameras they had at the local pharmacy, but Stephanie went apeshit and made him go back out three more times before he'd finally amassed enough to satisfy her.

Julia snapped a shot of me and Jonathon, but the flash didn't go off.

"You like taking pictures?" he said.

"Yeah." She was trying to figure out what went wrong. "Not with these though."

"My sister doesn't always make rational decisions. Here, let me see it." She handed the box to him. "What kind of camera do you normally use?"

"I think it's a Nikon," she said.

"F-401?"

"Is that a good one?"

"401... 402. Whatever it takes."

"It's my dad's. He lets me use it."

"Then I'm sure it's a good one. Here." He handed the box camera back to her. "Wait for the light on the back to come on."

Julia stared down at the back of the box, waiting for the little orange light while Vandershar put his arm around me.

"Okay, I think it's working," she said. "Let me try it again."

So she took another picture—just me and Vandershar and a thousand pounds of moldy cheese, only this time the flash went off.

"I like to take pictures too," he said.

"Of what?"

"People mostly. You want to see some?"

"Now?"

"Yeah, why not?"

"People doing what?" She downed her champagne.

"Nothing special."

"Then why would I want to see them?"

"Because most of what we do is nothing special." He filled her glass again. "The best art is beauty found in the mundane."

"Where are they?"

"Upstairs."

She gave him a funny look like she suddenly didn't trust him, but then she looked around to see if anybody was watching.

"In your room?"

I turned for a piece of bread hoping to get the putrid taste of that horrible cheese out of my mouth.

"What are you doing?" he said, looking back at me.

"That shit is awful."

"Shut up and grab another bottle. You're coming with us."

We slipped through the crowd and up the stairs then down a long dark hallway to Jonathon's bedroom, which looked about the same as it probably did when he was twelve: built-in desk and bookcase, white shutters, lacrosse player-covered wallpaper. He reached under his bed and pulled out a black leather portfolio, then flopped it down in front of us. It had a million photographs in it, from all over the world, all beneath clear plastic pages—shots of street vendors and taxi cab drivers and strangers walking down the street in just about every city you could imagine.

"Jonathon, these are amazing."

"That's because these people are real."

I thought he was bullshitting her, but the way he was looking at this one picture, you could tell he remembered the very moment he took it. It was a girl seated sidesaddle on a towel at the beach. She was topless and in the process of pulling her hair into a mess at the top of her head so she could run a pencil through it.

"That's Imke," he said.

"She's so pretty," said Julia.

"That photograph is the truth. You know what I mean? That's exactly who she is."

"I could never do that."

"Do what?"

Then the fireworks started to go off.

"Come on," he said as he grabbed his camera. "We can watch from my parents' room."

The master bedroom was bigger than our Berkeley College suite. There was a king-size canopy bed at one end and a fireplace and chairs at the other. Jonathon pushed open the drapes at the foot of the bed and gave the French doors a shove as a shell exploded over the pool, and then we sat down at a round wrought iron table on the balcony.

"So is Yale hard?" she asked me.

Jonathon filled her glass again.

"Why do you care so much about Yale?"

"Her dad was in Branford," said Jonathon, now fucking around with something on his camera.

"Where do you go?" I said.

She was in the middle of another gulp of champagne, so I had to wait for the answer.

"Lauralton Hall."

"Where's that?"

Vandershar snapped a shot of her.

"Milford," she said. "Jonathon, stop."

"Milford?"

"What?" said Vandershar. "I thought you liked pictures."

"Not of me."

"Why not?"

"I always look fat."

"Don't be ridiculous. Go stand by the railing."

"Why?"

"The light is interesting when the fireworks go off. Go stand by the railing."

She took another sip, and then, with a not entirely persuaded look, she got up and went to the wrought iron railing overlooking the pool, where she turned, looked right at him, and smiled.

"No," he said. "Do not look at the camera."

"Why not?"

"Because I don't want that."

"Well, don't be mad at me."

"I just want you to relax," he said. "Don't pay attention to the camera. I've only got six shots left."

"It's kind of hard when you're right there."

"Pretend I'm not. Enjoy the fireworks. How hard is that? I want to get you in silhouette."

She put her hand on the railing and looked right at him again, only this time with a buzzed little smirk.

"We're gonna lose the light."

She stuck her middle finger out at him.

"There," he said, taking a picture of it. "That's good. That's honesty."

She giggled and turned back to look up at the fireworks.

"What am I gonna do with you?"

"You could trust me for starters," he said. "These are gonna look great."

"You're wasting your time."

He stopped with the camera and looked right at her. Then he waited. He waited for her to turn and look back over her shoulder.

"What?" she said.

"You have no idea how beautiful you are, do you?"

Her face lit up as a shell exploded in the night sky. Then the fireworks went crazy behind her. They just kept staring at each other. She had this look on her face like he'd said the only thing that had ever really mattered, and he had this look like he meant it.

He went back to fucking around with the knobs on his camera when it got dark again, only she let go of the railing and turned to face him. Then she reached up behind her neck and took hold of the zipper on the back of her dress.

Another rocket whistled into the air.

"Don't move," he said, without looking up. "This is gonna be a good one."

She slid the dress off her shoulders anyway, and that's when Jonathon finally peered out from behind his camera.

She was still smiling as she pulled the dress down to her waist and pushed it over her hips. It fell to the ground, and she stepped free of it to walk right past him. She brushed his cheek with the palm of her right hand as that rocket exploded in the thick cloud of smoke over the pool while the car alarms blared somewhere off in the distance. Then he took another shot of her as she disappeared back through the French doors.

# Chapter 21

*Summer 1992*

It didn't look like anyone had touched the Widworth rec room in about twenty years. It was all circa 1970. The furniture was brown and yellow and orange and ugly: hideous couches and uncomfortable egg-shaped lunar lander chairs. There were also a few tables and benches and a row of locked cabinets against one wall where they kept the paint and clay and all the other crap they made us fuck around with. An ancient Zenith TV with the world's oldest remote hung up near the ceiling, and in the middle of the room sat a shabby midsize pool table. I never really understood why anybody would put a pool table in a lunatic asylum, but there it was, and Leonard was now following me around it, fascinated by the clickety-clack of the pool balls. They were actually both in there with me—Leonard in my shadow and Alan playing chess against himself in the corner.

Kyong cut me off at eighty milligrams. At that dose, the little green pills weren't even little green pills anymore. Eighty milligrams of that shit comes in an orange capsule that looks more like something you'd feed to a horse. It took about three days' worth of horse pills for a chemical fog to rise in my head, so even though the Dread was nowhere in sight, I pretty much felt dull and stupid all the time.

"Board games are fascinating really," said Alan. "Did you know when the French were invading Madagascar, the Queen's strategy relied on the results of a board game called Fanorona?"

"What queen?" I said through the fog.

"The Queen of Madagascar," he said. "France never had a queen that did anything."

"The white ball, Leonard," I said. "You have to hit the white ball first."

Leonard drilled the cue ball directly into a corner pocket with a short violent stab that ripped a hole in the felt.

"No. You don't hit it straight in."

"He's an idiot," said Alan. "Without the savant."

"Leonard," I said. I could barely keep my eyes open. "That's not how you hold it."

Leonard was manic now, hopping around the table, taking short stabs at anything round, and giggling like an idiot the whole time.

"You're gonna rip another hole in the felt," I said.

"Like he gives a shit," said Alan.

"I'm trying to help him."

"Help him what? He's not gonna remember a word you say."

Leonard took another wild stab.

"He's lucky if you ask me." Alan didn't look up from the chess board. "How liberating it must be to live unburdened by your own thoughts. Stop feeling sorry for him. We're the ones who are fucked."

I looked at Alan as Leonard danced around with the pool cue, but I felt like I was behind glass, like there was something physically separating me from Alan and his words.

"I've been watching you," he said. "Thinking about your situation."

I wanted to say something, but I couldn't make anything come out of my mouth.

"You wouldn't be here anymore if you were just another pussy suffering from some bullshit like depression. They run those twats in and out of here. A month max. No... I think you and I are more alike than you think. The difference is I'm not afraid anymore. You're the one who's still suffering. I can see it. I know what it feels like when they have you. I've seen it in your face."

I just stood there in the fog, straining to understand him from the other side of the glass.

"I used to be afraid too," he said. "They were the ones who told me to do it, you know. They wanted me to do it with my hands. It was actually quite sporting of me to shoot that bitch. A bullet has a cauterizing effect when it goes through, but I wouldn't do it at all now... and you know why? Because I'm not afraid of them anymore. Don't you see? That's the difference."

Duddle blew into the room and knocked over a steel trash can with his size-thirteen feet.

"It's time to do your vitals," he said.

"We're playing pool," said Leonard.

"Not anymore," said Duddle. "Get over here."

Then this other psych tech toting a portable triage center showed up behind Duddle. His name was Scott, and he looked a little like Shaggy from *Scooby-Doo*. Duddle hated Scott because Scott didn't give a shit about anything. Scott just went about his business like he could take his job or leave it.

"Where were you this morning?" said Duddle to Alan as he yanked the triage center away from Scott. "You forget where group was again?"

"It's a group of retards," said Alan. "Why would I want to be a part of that?"

"What's your excuse?" said Duddle, looking at me.

"I had to run my car."

"Leonard, get over here and give me your arm," said Duddle.

"Your car?" said Alan.

"Leonard," said Duddle.

"They let you out to run your car?" said Alan.

"So the battery doesn't die," I said.

"Pick another time to turn your car on," said Duddle. "You make me look like an ass when I don't know where you are."

"Leonard, come on," said Scott, halfheartedly chasing Leonard around the pool table.

Duddle kept fumbling with the triage center while Leonard circled the table, grinning ear to ear like it was the greatest day of his life.

"I'm responsible for you," said Duddle. "You can't just come and go as you please. Scott, can you get him over here? What the fuck."

"Leonard, stop," said Scott.

Leonard turned the corner one last time. He was looking right at me, still beaming, still basking in a moment of pure joy, and for that brief instant it really did seem like Leonard was the luckiest person in the world. Then Duddle stuck an arm out like a clothesline and nearly took Leonard's head off with it. It was like time stopped with Leonard about a foot above the pool table and completely horizontal before he hit the ground screaming like a madman.

"Put the cuff on him," said Duddle as he climbed on top of Leonard.

"Jesus," said Scott. "Was that really necessary?"

Duddle grabbed Leonard's shoulders. Then he climbed on top of him to stop him from squirming.

"I'm sure that's great for his blood pressure," said Alan as he made his way to the door.

"It's been six hours," said Duddle. "Put the fucking cuff on him."

Scott just stood there.

"What the fuck are you looking at, Scott? Put the cuff on him!"

I wanted to stop him. I felt an urge to grab Duddle by the neck and pull him away, but I just stood there thinking about it instead, thoughts passing slowly through my head—the things I wanted to do, the things I could do, the things I'd done before—all while Duddle manhandled Leonard on the floor right in front of me. In the end, I just watched him do whatever he wanted from behind a make-believe pane of glass until Scott finally shook his own head and rushed around to Duddle's side to slide the blood pressure cuff over Leonard's arm. Alan disappeared out the door behind us, and the moment they had a number to scrawl onto a chart, they let Leonard loose, and he ran screaming from the rec room too. It was just me in there after that. I was the only wing nut left, so they put the blood pressure cuff on me, only when they pumped it all full of air, my blood pressure turned out to be 110/70—perfectly normal—like nothing had happened at all.

# Chapter 22

*Fall 1990 – Spring/Summer 1991 – Fall/Spring 1992*

We rented a two-bedroom apartment on the eighth floor of a twelve-story building five blocks from campus. It was about as nice as you could get in New Haven, and it still looked like a tenement. I liked it because it had a doorman. John Henry spent a week trying to convince me not to move off campus, but he eventually gave up, pulled his name out of the Berkeley College room draw, and came with me. It was about a thousand square feet. We had two bedrooms to go with two bathrooms, the kitchen, a common room, a dining area, and this thick oxblood-red shag carpet. Vandershar also pissed away about seven thousand dollars one weekend filling the place with furniture, so we had two black leather couches and a bar to go with two twenty-seven-inch Sony televisions. The bar went where a dining table was supposed to go, and the televisions sat side by side in front of the couches. When he was finished, the place looked more like an Atlantic City sportsbook than a college dorm room, except for the kitchen. The kitchen was still coated in a wood finish stick-on material that looked more like the inside of an RV.

Vandershar also paid half the rent to never be there, but the truth is John Henry was never there either. He was writing for *The Yale Herald* by then, and he spent our entire junior year in libraries researching and writing essay after essay about Timothy Dwight, George Berkeley, John Davenport and his servant boy, not to mention all the other heavy hitters who had their names carved into all the buildings at Yale. In the few moments when he was around, he'd test out his material on me as if I might have something constructive to offer. He'd quote John C. Calhoun, former vice president of the United States, with something like:

> *The proposition to which I allude has become an axiom in the minds of a vast majority on both sides of the Atlantic, and is repeated daily from tongue to tongue as an established and incontrovertible truth; it is that "All men are born free and equal"... As understood, there is not a word of truth in it... It is utterly untrue.*

But I wouldn't say shit because I was too busy slaughtering the American League All-Star team with the California Angels.

I must have logged another ten thousand hours of *R.B.I.* holed up in exile with nothing but a cracked Nintendo remote to remind me I wasn't welcome anywhere else, and even though I'd arranged it so I only had class on Tuesdays and Thursdays, our building was just far enough from campus to make a morning walk in the middle of winter miserable, so I missed a fuck ton of Differential Geometry too. I'd stay up late doodling flow charts and tinkering with algorithms that predicted the outcomes of baseball games pitch by pitch. (What are the odds the next pitch is a fastball? What are the odds the next pitch results in a double?) Then I'd sleep in, getting up just in time to watch *The Price Is Right* and *Days of Our Lives* back to back. I survived on beef stew out of cans and mac and cheese out of boxes. I didn't really even head down to the City that much. It was the same clubs, the same casinos, the same stories, until finally I just wasn't motivated to get to the train station anymore. That whole year was an unmemorable homage to time wasted, a complete blur, until Canelli left John Henry and Norman behind at Dartmouth.

I was finally healthy again and hitting home runs, but it was never enough to push us over .500. We hovered right there the whole year, beating teams we probably shouldn't have beat, then losing to ones we probably should have. The bus ride to Dartmouth always sucked. Our Peter Pan travel coach wasn't bad. The seats were new and vaguely comfortable, but no one wants to sit on a bus for four hours, and we always stayed at this creepy ski resort that was otherwise deserted because there wasn't any snow. It reminded me of *The Shining*. Our rooms were all scattered too, which sort of added to the creepiness. I stayed with Billy on that trip, but I didn't sleep well, worried he might murder me with an axe, I guess, so I was up early and on the bus before anyone else was even done with breakfast. I just remember sitting toward the back and staring out at a chairlift winding its way up a snowless ski run thinking how it might have been nice to go to a place like Dartmouth—in the middle of nowhere with no one else around. Pretty soon the bus was filled with teammates, and the driver fired up the engine, but as he put the thing into gear and we lurched forward, Larry popped out of his seat and marched down the center aisle to find Canelli who was right behind the driver.

"John Henry and Norman aren't on the bus," he said.

"I know that," said Canelli. "Sit down. We're leaving."

"We're not even coming back here."

"They should have thought of that before they made us late."

"How are they supposed to get home?"

"That's not my problem. They don't want to be here. Fine with me."

"Wait," said Larry, leaning forward so the bus driver could hear him. "Stop." Then he turned back to Canelli. "Just let me go grab 'em. It'll take like five minutes."

So then Canelli leaned forward.

"Let's go."

"Fuck that," said Larry. "Open the door."

"We're leaving," said Canelli to the driver. Then he looked up at Larry. "Sit down."

"What are you doing?"

"They're late," said Canelli.

"So what?"

It was like Canelli'd been waiting for this moment. John Henry and Norman were a constant reminder of our mediocrity, and it bugged Canelli that they were content to hold clipboards and clean up after everybody. It would have blown his mind to think they showed up day after day for reasons that had little to do with winning. He hardly ever spoke to either of them. They never played, and on the morning that the alarm clock in their shared room at an empty ski resort in Hanover failed to function, Canelli took the opportunity to make it clear to all exactly what he thought of them. We left. We pulled away and drove to Dartmouth in silence.

It felt like any other game day once we got there—the air was crisp and the outfield grass was wet. We went three up, three down in the top of the first inning. I stood on Dartmouth's ashy gray infield waiting for Larry to throw his last warm-up toss in the bottom of the first, only it felt sort of pointless. I didn't even want to be there, but before Dartmouth's leadoff hitter could even step into the box, a yellow cab pulled up. The back door opened, and

Norman got out with his hat on backwards, laughing, with John Henry right behind him, and while they did their best not to give a shit, nothing was ever really the same after that. Canelli ignored them, of course, but it was like it was Canelli who suddenly didn't matter, like it wasn't his team anymore. Larry struck out the first three batters he faced, and when it was our turn to hit again in the top of the second, I led off with a mammoth home run that unleashed a torrent of pent-up anger and filth from our dugout that would have embarrassed even the Throaty Fatboy at the end of Cornell's bench. Dartmouth didn't stand a chance, but neither did Canelli. For that one day, we became the team we could have been all along, but we were so obnoxious it was sort of horrifying, and as I rounded the bases in the top of the second, I wondered if Canelli thought he finally had us so pissed off we could beat anybody, because if he did, how could he possibly have thought it was worth it?

My exile resumed when we got back to New Haven, except now the year was almost over. A year that had plodded on and seemed to take forever was now accelerating uncomfortably, and it felt like every day I was losing ground. Fitz didn't just emerge from his basement with a foreign currency trading algorithm. He worked at Lehman for five years and learned what he needed to learn and met who he needed to meet there, so as another summer barreled down on me and the Dread took firm root again, I asked Vandershar to help me get an internship somewhere on Wall Street—something to replace Empire Life & Annuity on my resume. He told me internships were for losers and invited me to Europe instead. It was his dad's fiftieth birthday, and the Vandershars were going to spend a quiet few days on the Italian Riviera before meeting an entourage of family and friends in Rimini where a chartered yacht sat ready to take a group of fifty to Croatia. He told me he'd handle Goldman when the time came.

We flew first class from JFK to Milan where a driver awaited to take us to our hotel. Vandershar bitched the whole time about how he didn't want to go to Croatia. He didn't want to spend a week trapped on a yacht with aunts and uncles and cousins he couldn't stand. We didn't get to the hotel until about midnight. The suite had four bedrooms, four bathrooms with gold fixtures and elaborate gold molding, and a tiny kitchen. The floors were a dark wood with expensive-looking rugs and there was ornate furniture everywhere. Neither of us was tired, so we unpacked and headed down the hill into the *piazzetta* of a small "fishing village" loaded with cafés and American tourists, only there was a strange lightness to the place, like it wasn't even real, like it wasn't to be taken seriously, almost like an amusement park.

I'm not even sure what time I finally got up the next day. I wandered out into the living room where the French doors to the balcony were already open and the white silk curtains were billowing in the breeze, and I could see what had been hidden in darkness the night before. The whole town seemed vertical, rising up from a small yacht-filled harbor into wooded hills, and the buildings were all colored like the sherbets Papa and I used to eat when I was a kid—orange Creamsicle stacked on top of pink lemonade stacked on top of pomegranate sunrise stacked on top of lemon meringue. I didn't notice Vandershar's dad sitting on the balcony sipping an espresso until I was already out there taking in the view. He was reading a newspaper and wearing bright orange swim trunks and a white linen shirt unbuttoned to his navel. He was the tan, aged version of Jonathon with a gently receding hairline and a slightly puffy face. There was no six-pack though. His days with a six-pack were long gone.

"Who are you?" he said.

I'd already spent half a summer under his roof, and I'd met him three times, but he still had no idea who I was.

"Uh… Spencer. I came with Jonathon."

"What time did you get in?"

"I don't know. It was late."

He looked around.

"Did you just get up?"

"Yeah."

"Espresso?"

"I'm good."

"It's no trouble."

"Okay, then."

So he went into the kitchen and made me an espresso.

"How do you know Jonathon?"

"I go to Yale," I said. "We're roommates."

"I didn't know Jonathon had roommates."

"There's two of us actually."

"You like sugar?"

"Sure."

He put the espresso down in front of me.

"Welcome to Portofino," he said. Then he headed back into the suite. "When Lord Fauntleroy gets up, tell him you can meet me for lunch. He knows where to go."

We met his dad at a little café about an hour later. It was so close to the water you could hear all the boat sounds coming from the harbor.

"Where's Mom?" said Jonathon as he unfurled a napkin.

"Your sister whined nonstop about having to spend her whole summer in the sun, so I sent them to Paris for a few days. They'll meet us in Rimini."

Our waitress wasn't much older than me and Jonathon. She had this jet-black, thick, curly hair and dark, almond-shaped eyes.

"*Che fai, bella ragazza?*" said Jonathon's dad, leaning back to get a better look at her.

My Italian was pretty useless, but I did know this phrase roughly translated into *What's up, beautiful girl?* She blushed, but her smile was kind of receptive, so he kept at it.

"Are you from here?" he said.

"Yes."

"You should be in Milan. Paris. Look at you."

"What would you like?" she said in perfect English.

"Is that a trick question?"

She didn't seem to understand, so she just looked at him quizzically.

"Dad," said Jonathon. "I think she just wants to take our order."

After lunch we got in a wood-paneled speed boat with our own private driver who took us around a point to a cove with a cramped sandy beach that sat right in front of an old abbey, but Vandershar's dad couldn't sit still for even five minutes. He was like a shark that couldn't breathe if it stopped moving, so he got up from his lounge almost immediately and started cruising the beach. He'd stop and talk to anyone really, kick a soccer ball, throw a Frisbee, but he lingered around the girls the longest. He'd casually start a conversation. Then he'd test the waters by slipping in an inappropriate comment about cleavage or the cut of a bikini, and occasionally, if the opportunity presented itself, he'd touch a bare shoulder. He might have been the horniest dude I've ever seen. It was like he was in a race against time, and the only thing worth doing with the few years of virility he had left was fucking girls half his age. I don't know. I just know it was creepy as fuck watching him hit on girls so young their parents were somewhere on the beach with us.

His charm wasn't working that day though, and it irritated him that all Jonathon and I had to do to get the attention of a seventeen-year-old girl was sit there, so he made us get up a couple hours after we got there to head to some other private beach, but this one was rocky and kind of uncomfortable to cruise, and it wasn't nearly as crowded or target-rich, so Vandershar's dad didn't stay there even fifteen minutes. He took the boat back and left us with a couple striped towels and a forty-five-minute hike through the hills to get back to the hotel. This was when I realized how bored Vandershar was by it all. While his dad had checked out every ass from Portofino to Punta del Vessinaro, Vandershar barely looked out from beneath the ridiculous white bucket hat he wore the whole time with the name "Lester Lanin" stitched into the brim in bright yellow cursive. He hardly acknowledged his dad's departure. They barely spoke the whole time, and I never once saw them have an actual conversation that amounted to anything, but an empty, rocky beach was no more appealing with his dad gone, so after doing nothing for another half hour or so, we decided to head back to the hotel too. It was a decent hike along a hilly dirt path underneath the shade of a wooded canopy, so it wasn't nearly as hot as it had been down near the water.

"We need a vacation from this vacation," said Jonathon.

"What do you mean?"

"This place sucks. There's too many Americans."

"What about Croatia?"

"That'll be worse. Too many Vandershars."

He put the key in the door when we reached the suite, and when he opened it, we had a full view of the living room. The French doors out to the balcony were still wide open and that pleasant breeze was still blowing through the white silk drapes, but there was his dad reclined on the couch with those orange swim trunks now down around his ankles and the hotel concierge wrapped around his cock. She was on her knees in front of him with his dick in her mouth. She stopped the moment we entered and covered herself before reaching for her wadded blouse on the floor. She was a little older than the other girls his dad had hit on that day, probably mid-thirties, and now her dark hair was sort of mangled from the quickie they were slipping in during her afternoon break. Vandershar was totally unfazed. He didn't say a word. He went for the fridge as she pulled herself together, and then he popped open a Diet Coke as his dad pulled his shorts up.

"*Mi dispiacci*," she said. "I should go now."

"It's fine," said Vandershar's dad.

"Was that complimentary?" said Jonathon.

"*Sono cosi imbarazzato*," she said, brushing past me out the door.

"This is the nicest place," said Jonathon as the door shut.

Then he turned his sights on his dad who was remarkably unembarrassed.

"We're not going to Rimini," said Jonathon.

"How do you expect to get to Croatia?"

"We're not going to Croatia either."

The next thing I knew we were on a filthy Italian train headed to the southern tip of Italy and an empty town called Brindisi. It was a place that seemed to exist for no other purpose than to collect tourists at dawn before the ferries embarked for Corfu at dusk. The train and ferry schedules were designed to leave you marooned in Brindisi for the day, propping up the local economy, so I spent most of my time watching Vandershar from a concrete bench. He roamed the piazza chatting up locals and taking pictures as the town square filled with the youth of the world. He would just come alive in the middle of strangers and then somehow transcend them all to become the center of their attention.

In the baking heat of midday, still in that ridiculous Lester Lanin bucket hat, he stopped next to a pushcart loaded down with gelato and started buying it from a short, squat Italian dude with a brazen comb-over and a white apron, only he wasn't buying it for himself. He was buying it for everyone, just handing it out to anyone who wanted it. He bought gelato until there was no more gelato to buy, and as he did, he introduced himself to pretty girls from far off places. He tried languages he didn't know and shook hands with the alpha dogs who were all now somehow in his service, the whole time laughing and smiling. It was like he made a point to put a smile on every face in Brindisi, so by the time we got on the boat to Corfu, every single one of those weary travelers knew exactly who he was, and I finally realized that that had been the point all along. None of the rich Americans in Portofino, and certainly no one on the boat from Rimini to Croatia, would give a shit what his name was, but here, in Brindisi, he wasn't just fake American Royalty. He was a real International Playboy, and the name Vandershar meant everything. These people wanted to know him. They wanted to exist within his orbit. His name, and what it represented, was the reason for his ease around strangers. It was the source of his confidence. The secret to his lack of Dread. People listened to him because of that name, and he was so used to the listening, it never even occurred to him that one day the listening might stop. But that kind of confidence—that kind of credibility—was out of my reach. It was inherited. It was pure luck, and luck was something I'd never had. In my mind, I was the unluckiest motherfucker who ever lived, so I thought right there, *Fuck that. I'll make my own luck.*

We slept on the deck of the ferry and woke up in Corfu. It was absolute mayhem from the moment we got off the boat. We were greeted by girls wearing nearly nothing as they passed out 7:00 a.m. ouzo shots for the drive to a place known as the Pink Palace—a semi-decayed, sprawling, pseudo-youth hostel/ resort on the beach in Corfu—and when we finally got to the

Palace itself, we were thrown into a frenzied Greek dance that involved more ouzo and a fuck ton of broken plates. I must have destroyed a hundred plates. The party never stopped. It didn't even slow down. It was a factory, a never-ending assembly line of debauchery that started when the ferry arrived and ended only when the SUVs took you away, but Vandershar left an indelible mark on that place. He footed every bill. He delivered a remarkable impersonation of David Bowie when the karaoke mic got shoved in his face. He made a legendary run in two-man coed beach volleyball with a six-foot Hungarian, and he was with a different girl every night (the Hungarian included). His point total dwarfed mine. I managed a single smoker on the beach from some German girl who spoke absolutely no English. My attempts at anything more were strictly *verboten*. When the week was over, I'm also pretty sure Vandershar offered to buy the place from the thirtysomething American running it—an offer that was declined with a smile. We weren't gone even fifteen minutes before the gears of that assembly line began to grind again.

When we got back to New Haven that fall, I pestered Vandershar relentlessly about Goldman. He was around more that semester because he had to take some class that met five days a week to finish up his philosophy major. We spent a lot of time in this new place that opened in what had been an old parking garage a couple blocks from our building. It was called Bar, and the entrance was a heavy, sectioned garage door that slid straight up. The walls were brick and the floors concrete, and there was this huge purple felt-covered pool table right there in the front room surrounded by little round lacquered tables and a dark pulsing club in the back. It had an urban feel that Vandershar liked—not to mention an eight dollar cover that kept most of Yale away.

I'd convinced myself that a job at Goldman was where my luck would begin. Yale was worthless. Vandershar was right about that too. I would have been looking for jobs in the classified ads if it hadn't been for Jonathon, so as we played game after game of eight ball on that oversize purple table in the front room at Bar, I'd ask him about the bankers his dad knew and the strings he could pull to get me where I needed to be. Vandershar finally told me to shut the fuck up, and then he explained how his dad now owed me since I knew about the over-attentive concierge in Portofino. It was like having people know and then buying their silence was part of the deal, but by the time the spring semester rolled around, Vandershar was nowhere to be found again, and I was left not entirely sure if he, or his dad, could be counted on.

I was leaning on my pool cue, waiting for this Euro-looking dude in black leather pants and a white silk shirt buttoned all the way to the top to take his shot. It was just me, John Henry, and Billy in Bar that night. They were sitting at the little round table behind me, waiting for me to be done so we could eat. The guy I was playing had hardly even acknowledged me, and he kept flipping all this long, shiny black hair over his shoulder, until finally the waify girl at the table next to him pulled something out of her own hair and shot it at him like a rubber band. He used it to pull all that hair back into a shiny black ponytail. It reminded me of the ass of a racehorse named Hansel I wanted to bet on in the Preakness the year before in Atlantic City. I got stuck in an elevator at Caesar's, stopping at every floor to pick up blue-haired ladies holding cups filled with quarters. By the time we reached the lobby, the race was over. That elevator ride cost me eight hundred dollars.

"I just kept going back and forth in my head," said Billy. "While I'm sitting there. Like right in the middle of the interview I'm thinking, *Am I really doing this? Is this really what I want to do?*"

"Have you seen the loft space yet?" said John Henry.

"No," said Billy. Then he spit some dip into an empty beer mug. "I'll see it tomorrow."

"It's pretty sweet," said John Henry as Billy stared wistfully out the open garage door. "I'm gonna need reinforcements."

"The fucker today wanted to know how many manhole covers I thought there were in New York."

"The city or the state?"

"I don't know. I didn't even fucking ask."

"They just want to see if you can think on your feet."

"Well, I sat there... in my new suit. I mean just stop right there. Can you even picture me in a suit? Every day?"

"No. Not really."

He spit into the beer mug again.

"So I sat there, and I estimated the number of city blocks in Manhattan, and the number of avenues running north and south, and the number of manholes per block... all out loud too like a total pussy, and the whole time, I'm thinking: *Don't give him a number*, you know. *Don't do it*. Just get up and leave. But I fucking sat there and went through the motions anyway and told him I thought there were about three hundred thousand manhole covers in New York City. And you know why? Because I'm already on the fuckin' treadmill."

He spit into the beer mug again.

"How many you have left?"

Billy didn't answer though. He nodded at me instead.

"He do any yet?" he said.

"He's only got two."

"Who'd he get?"

"Prudential... and Goldman."

"How'd he get Goldman?"

"How do you think?"

Hansel was now consulting his buddy, this skinhead who looked like a poster child for the Aryan Youth, before he walked around the table to take a crappy shot that he missed. I sometimes get lost in my own head when I play pool for money. I get caught up measuring angles and thinking two or three shots ahead, and I was now intently focused on taking the table away from Hansel along with his twenty dollars, so I didn't notice John Henry get up and leave Billy sitting there alone with his thoughts. I didn't see John Henry step to the bar or sit down on a stool behind me either. Instead, I dropped solids into corner pockets one after another as I talked myself through caroms and measured all the leaves. It was a decent run that left me one solid away from the eight ball, so I turned to ask some dope in a white sweater vest to get out of the way of my draw, and that's when I saw her again.

She was at the bar, swirling the ice in her drink with a red cocktail straw, smiling her enormous smile, and hanging on John Henry's every word. They were so close I could've rammed the butt of my pool cue right through the back of his head. There was no longer a tan line where an anklet used to be, but it was unmistakably the girl from the lingerie store, beaming like the cover of a magazine. I don't know how long I stood there staring, but it was long enough to finally get Hansel's attention.

"Are you gonna play or what?" he said.

I didn't move, and as I watched her smile, a familiar knot grew in my stomach—a knot that formed tentacles and reached into every inch of me.

"Is he fucking deaf?"

My thoughts began to swirl.

"*Hello*?!"

But it was also like I was breathing again—like I'd been hit by a bolt of lightning that reminded me I was alive.

I finally turned back to Hansel, but my brain was scrambled, and I couldn't think straight.

"I just needed some room," I said.

"For what? You're not doing anything."

"Is it my shot?"

"Is it your shot?" Hansel looked down, mystified as the waify girl and the poster child for the Aryan Youth smiled at my stupidity. Then he looked back at me. "Are you the dumbest fuck at Yale or what?"

I forgot about the Lingerie Store Girl and set my cue on the table, but before I could do anything else, John Henry was between us.

"Don't do this," he said.

But I wasn't doing anything. Hansel was the one coming at me. John Henry turned to stop him. He started to say something that I'm sure would have been really clever and disarming if it ever made it out of his mouth.

Hansel cross-checked him with his pool cue and sent John Henry stumbling toward Billy, and as he went to the ground, he fumbled to grab the little round table before he dragged the whole thing down on top of himself. The clatter of breaking beer mugs caused the whole place to stop and look at the mess.

Hansel was amused now that John Henry was covered in Billy's dip spit, so I grabbed him by the neck and lifted him about six inches off the ground before I drove his head back down into the concrete. He didn't look too amused after that. I don't know how many times I hit him, but when I was done, all you could really see was a trail of snotty blood connecting his nose to the cold hard floor. The Dread was gone, but I'd forgotten where I was, and then somebody smashed me in the side of the head with what felt like an iron skillet. The next thing I remember, I was outside with Billy under one arm and John Henry under the other.

"We gotta get out of here," said John Henry.

"What happened?" I said.

"You lost," said Billy. "Again."

# Chapter 23

I still had a lump the size of a nectarine pit on the side of my head the next day, only now I was standing on the top step of the third base dugout at Yale Field waiting for Ralph the Groundskeeper to finish spreading cat litter on the puddles near second base so the game could start again even though it was still raining. Somebody once said there aren't any rainouts in heaven. There aren't any rainouts in hell either. They throw cat litter on the standing water and you keep playing.

My teammates elected me the 108th captain of the Yale baseball team. My picture hangs to this day in one of the upstairs rooms at Mory's—me in my cream letter sweater, one leg up on the genuine replica Yale Fence that sits in front of a sunny-day backdrop in the dingy studio where the photo was taken.

We were in the middle of the second game of a doubleheader against Cornell. Norman and John Henry were down inside the dugout under the overhang spitting sunflower seeds at a cup on the first step while Larry iced his arm in between them. They were both holding clipboards. John Henry charted the hitters, and Norman charted the pitchers.

Canelli was down there too, slumped in the corner of the dugout closest to home plate, despondent since we'd just blown a five-run lead.

"I don't understand why you invited her to Vandershar's twenty-first birthday," said Larry. "*You* don't want to go to Vandershar's twenty-first birthday."

"I thought she might say yes," said John Henry.

"How is Vandershar only now turning twenty-one?"

"He skipped the second grade," I said.

"Of course he did."

"This is the girl you bought the boxer shorts from?" said Norman.

"Her name is Annie."

"The one who thinks you're gay."

"She does not think I'm gay."

"Silk boxer shorts are pretty gay," said Larry.

"Who was the other pair for?" said Norman.

"You know what I did last night?" said Larry.

"No," said John Henry, happy for the subject to change. "What did you do last night?"

"I got baked. I put *R.B.I.* on demo, and I watched the '86 Red Sox play the '84 Tigers. Clemens against Morris."

"Did it take this long?" said John Henry.

"Jim Rice hit a three-run homer off Willie Hernandez in the ninth to win it. Not as exciting as your night, but still pretty good."

The rain blew sideways into the dugout for a second.

"My dad wouldn't shut up about the seasons after I got in here," said John Henry, looking up at the weather. "All he could talk about for weeks was how great the seasons were... like no one in California has ever seen a leaf turn brown. I coughed up something the size of an egg this morning. I might have pneumonia. I can do without the seasons if you want me to be honest. I officially do not like the seasons."

"What color was it?" said Larry.

"My phlegm? Is that what you're asking me?"

"I'm trying to determine if there's an infection."

"I wasn't serious."

"Larry's taking the MCATs after all," said Norman.

"Isn't it a little late?" said John Henry.

"I'll have to take a year off before I can apply to med school."

"Well played," said John Henry, spitting a seed at the cup. "It looked like tapioca."

"What did?"

"What I coughed up this morning."

"I thought you said you weren't serious?"

"I wasn't serious about the pneumonia."

"Would you people shut up?" said Canelli from his side of the dugout. "There's a game going on if you hadn't noticed, and stop spitting that crap all over the place. It's disgusting."

The only time we won two games in a row that whole season was a doubleheader we swept against Embry Riddle Aeronautical School on our spring trip to Florida. We would win, then lose, then win, then lose, then win, then lose, until finally it just got to be where Canelli thought we were doing it to him on purpose. Norman unloaded a wad of sunflower seeds into the mud like he was a Gatling gun.

"What time is it anyway?" said John Henry.

"Quarter after five," said Norman.

"Why are you wearing a watch?" said Larry.

"So I can know what time it is."

"Who cares what time it is in the middle of a game?"

"Ask John Henry."

"Norman," said Canelli. "Where are we in their lineup?"

Norman looked down at the chart in his lap.

"Esposito, Brandt, and Bade," he said.

"The numbers," said Canelli with this pained look on his face. "I don't know what their names are."

Norman feigned confusion and fumbled with his chart until it fell on the ground at his feet.

Canelli stood from his spot and took a couple steps toward Norman like he wanted to wring his neck, but Norman and John Henry had been waging a guerrilla war from inside our dugout ever since Canelli'd left them behind at Dartmouth, so he stopped about halfway, unsure what to do next. There was a weird pause as he looked at each of us one by one, almost like he was wondering who could be trusted. I was still on the top step, and he looked up like he wanted to say something to me in particular, like he wanted to remind me that I was there to win baseball games—not punch pay phones or get stabbed in the throwing shoulder or fuck around in dugouts, but he didn't.

"You're all horseshit," he said instead.

And it just kind of lingered there for a minute. Then Norman picked up the clipboard.

"Three, four, five," he said.

Canelli just turned and headed back to his corner of the dugout where he slumped back onto the bench at the thought of our freshman pitcher, Cary Brown, facing the heart of Cornell's lineup again.

Cary was about my height, but pale from a long winter and frail because he was only seventeen, and he had a thick swath of blond hair that hung down in front of his face like that elf who wanted to be a dentist. He was from St. Petersburg, Florida.

Now he was standing in a puddle of coagulated mud outside a dugout in New Haven, Connecticut, wet and suffering from hypothermia.

I was freezing my ass off too as I pulled on batting gloves. The next pitch got slapped into the hole between short and third where it hit a clump of the cat litter Ralph spread in the third inning of the first game and crawled up the Cornell shortstop's wrist for a hit. I slid a donut onto my bat and moved aimlessly in front of the dugout to get the blood all the way to my extremities.

"You think I'm the hardest throwing Jew that ever lived?" said Larry, unraveling the Ace bandage holding the ice on his arm.

"Sandy Koufax is the hardest throwing Jew that ever lived," said Norman. "You're not even close."

"Maybe I'm the hardest throwing right-handed Jew."

Billy crushed a fastball into the gap in left center field.

"That a way to be a ballplayer, Billy!"

Canelli was screaming in his castrated falsetto as he jumped off the bench and raced up the dugout steps.

"That a way to be a ballplayer!"

The game was tied again. I could pretty much feel my heart beating in the nectarine pit as I dug in to hit. My feet were freezing. The batter's box was basically quicksand. The cat litter squished under my feet. As a kid, I got in the habit of swinging early in counts to avoid striking out. All of my at bats were uncomfortable like this. I rarely ever let a pitcher get two strikes on me. I always went up there to hit the first pitch I could handle, mostly because I wanted it over with as soon as possible. It just so happened that this approach worked pretty well for me. Canelli hated it. He wanted me to work counts, but he gave up trying to change me when I started hitting home runs. The first pitch I saw was a fastball. It was high, probably not a strike, but I took a rip at it anyway and hit a fly ball to center field to end the inning. Canelli looked disgusted when I got back to the dugout.

Cary Brown just looked terrified. The rain was coming down full force again, and it was nearly dark. I hopped up and down a few times at third, but I still couldn't feel my feet. Then Cary's first warm-up toss hit the mud in front of home plate and took a funny sideways bounce to elude John Henry who was out there to warm him up. The ball rolled all the way to the backstop.

"Why do they call you the catcher?" said the Throaty Fatboy from the end of Cornell's bench.

That voice was so irritating. It made you want to strangle the kid every time you heard it, but nothing could shut him up.

Canelli signaled for our outfield to shift into what he called his "Gap Defense." Canelli designed the Gap Defense to take away doubles into the outfield gaps, but it usually ended up in triples down the outfield lines. It didn't matter anyway. Cary Brown walked the first two hitters he faced, and after ball eight, Canelli collapsed back into the dugout, dropped his chin to his chest and waited for it to happen.

I was freezing and standing in about three inches of mud and cat litter while Billy Clark screamed from right field, "Where the fuck is that!" after every pitch.

"Be tough out there, kid!"

"Battle him now!"

"Hey, Cary," said the Throaty Fatboy.

"Throw strikes!" yelled Canelli.

"What were they gonna call you if you were a boy?"

"I know one thing," said Canelli. "If you can't throw strikes, you can't win baseball games."

It was hard to tell who was making Cary more miserable—the other team's bench or his own coach. He backed off the mound to clean the goop out of his cleats with a tongue depressor like he was trying to run out the clock.

"Throw the ball!" yelled Canelli, marching back up the dugout steps. "Get up on the goddamn mound and throw the baseball! I want to see your best pitch!"

So with Canelli waiting, Cary Brown got back on the mound and threw his best pitch—a straight fastball right over the heart of the plate—and it got ripped right at me. That's the way it always was. Every time I ever wanted to go take a hot shower, somebody ripped a baseball right at me, and Ralph was never good at his job. No matter how many times I asked him to fix the launching ramp where the infield grass met the infield dirt in front of third base, he never got it right. My feet were stuck in mud and cat litter as the baseball hit that lip and shot straight at my face. I turned my head to avoid it, but it hit me anyway— right in the nectarine pit.

"To err is human," said Canelli. "To suck is Mazio."

Then he turned and descended back into the darkness.

"Defense wins championships," said the Throaty Fatboy.

We lost eight to seven.

# Chapter 24

Two hours later we were flying down the Merritt Parkway in John Henry's Blazer on our way to the party Vandershar was throwing himself for his twenty-first birthday. Norman was up front with John Henry while I was wedged into the back seat between Larry and Billy. My head was already spinning. I didn't even bother to call shotgun and now I was riding bitch in the middle of the back seat, jammed back there uncomfortably listening to Larry drone on about some vegetarian girl he met in the Silliman laundry room while Billy spit dip sludge into a red keg cup. I needed a drink, but John Henry wouldn't let anyone have an open container in his car, so I was left festering in the back seat with my nerves spiraling as we got closer and closer to the City.

"You checking the fluorocarbon output or what?" said Larry, interrupting his own story and looking into the front seat.

"Seriously," said Norman. "You're going a hundred miles an hour. Not figuratively either. You're actually driving a hundred miles an hour."

"If she gets there before us, she'll leave," said John Henry.

"You can relax," said Larry. "She's not gonna be there."

"How do you know this girl's a vegetarian?" said Billy.

"She told me," said Larry.

"That just came up? You asked her what kind of meat she likes doing a load of laundry?"

"Can you change this?" said Larry. "I don't want to listen to The Cure all the way to New York."

"Play the stupid shit," said Billy.

"So then who are the Old Critics?" said Norman.

"There aren't any Old Critics," said John Henry as he changed the music.

"How can there be New Critics if there aren't any Old Critics?"

"There's just New Critics."

Norman reached down and pulled a binder off the floor and turned his Itty Bitty Book Light on so he could see as he flipped through the pages.

"You brought notes?" said Larry.

"The drive's an hour and a half. I'm not wasting this time."

"It's New Critics," said John Henry. "Capital 'N,' Capital 'C.'"

"So are the deconstructionists New Critics?" said Norman.

"No. They're deconstructionists."

"But they're newer than the New Critics."

"They're totally different. It's not even a hermeneutics really."

"Hermeneutics?" said Billy. "That's a word?"

"It's a way of analyzing a text," said John Henry.

"It sounds like something you'd do to a cat."

"Then which one's right?" said Norman.

"Which what is right?" said John Henry.

"Which hermeneutics?"

"What do you mean?"

"Well, they can't all be right. What's the right way to analyze a text?"

"There is no right way. I think that's the point."

There was nowhere to park when we got into the City, so we circled the block for another ten minutes until John Henry finally couldn't take it anymore, and he stuck the Blazer in front of a fire hydrant.

We were supposed to live in that loft space after graduation—me, Billy, John Henry, and Jonathon. Vandershar was supposed to buy it. Three thousand square feet, twenty-foot ceilings on the fifth floor of a funky-looking building in SoHo. There weren't any doormen, so the door downstairs was propped open with a rolled up newspaper. A bunch of sketchy-looking dudes were loitering in the hallway when we got off the elevator, and a lot of noise was coming from down the hall. A temporary plywood bar ran nearly half the length of the loft, and the music was cranked so loud you could hardly think once you got inside. I'll bet there were a hundred people in the place by the time we got there—huddled in little masses or pressed up against the bar or dancing on the makeshift dance floor in front of a DJ who had piercings everywhere and a beard that stretched to the middle of his chest.

"What do you think?" said John Henry.

"I think I need a dip," said Billy as he looked up at the ceiling.

"Can't you go one night without that shit in your mouth?" said John Henry.

"I can't go fifteen minutes without that shit in my mouth," said Billy. "Wasn't there a package store around the corner?"

"Who knows?" said Norman. "We drove around the block a hundred and fifty times."

I felt shaky in the doorway, so I went straight for the bar and slugged three whiskey sours before I even turned around. It was an odd crowd really. Vandershar knew everybody. He went to Yale. He got thrown out of two prep schools on the way, and he hung out in dive bars and underground clubs in the City, so next to any given Hotchkiss alum in a pink button-down oxford, there was a gaunt high school dropout dressed in black and suffering from some sort of drug-induced stupor. I saw Vandershar first. He was holding court from a purple velvet chair at the far end of the loft, and there was a pixie-girl perched next to him on the chair's velvet arm. Her name was Sabine. She had short brown hair and giant blue eyes, and I could tell he was working his usual bullshit because Annie, from the purple velvet chair next to them, was leaning in behind Sabine to get a better listen while John Henry hovered right behind her with a solid grip on the seat back. I grabbed what was left of my whiskey sour and headed over there.

"The whole thing is made of cast iron," he said.

"So?" said John Henry.

"So it's supporting itself from the inside. That's what enables all the glass. You don't see too many buildings like it in Manhattan."

"You mean besides all the ones made of steel?"

"I mean the older buildings. It's an incredible find. Donald Judd used to own it. He lived here. I didn't think he'd part with it, but he needs the money."

"Who's Donald Judd?" said Sabine.

"An artist," said Vandershar. "This is a prototype Judd sculpture." He kicked the steel cube sitting in front of the chairs. "It's a coffee table... because it doesn't aspire to be anything else."

"That's the point though, isn't it?" said John Henry.

Vandershar craned his neck to get a better look at him.

"Someone knows their Minimalism."

"The object represents nothing more than itself," said John Henry.

"And the artist is irrelevant."

"Why does there have to be a hierarchy of artists?" said John Henry. "Maybe no one is better than anybody else."

"This is a coffee table."

"Since when is art a competition?"

"Since forever. What artist worth a shit doesn't have eyes in the back of their head?"

"It's honest."

"It's lazy."

"Judd didn't consider himself a Minimalist anyway."

"And he shouldn't. Rothko painted emotion... and succeeded. This is a failure as a work of art. It's cowardice."

"It's a pretty valuable failure," said John Henry. "Maybe the artist is what's relevant after all."

Vandershar looked kind of irritated.

"It's like taking art back from the fucks who hijacked it," he said.

"Aren't you afraid somebody'll steal it?" said Sabine.

"It weighs like two hundred and fifty pounds," said Vandershar.

"But strangers are so untrustworthy," said Larry.

"Are they?" said Vandershar.

"His mother had a bed incinerated due to the nastiness of strangers," said Norman.

"She did not," said Sabine.

"She did, actually," said Vandershar.

"Why?" said Annie.

"It started just like this," said Larry. "An unwieldy gathering. Too many people to keep track of."

"It was the Fourth of July," said Vandershar.

"So what happened with the bed?" said Annie.

They loved to talk about the pictures. One time in some girl's room in Silliman, Larry and Norman recreated the whole scene with the stuffed animals on her bed. At one point they had a purple hippopotamus taking it back door from a pink kangaroo, and they were talking about the whole thing like they were trying to figure out who shot Kennedy.

"My sister spread cameras all over the house so our guests could take pictures of the party," said Jonathon. "She's documenting her life. It's a school project."

"Seriously?" said Annie.

"Yeah, but she only keeps the pictures she wants you to see, so the whole thing is a lie really. Anyway, when we got the pictures from the party back, my sister sifted through them only to discover that several had been taken from inside my parents' bedroom."

"What were people doing in your parents' bedroom?" said Sabine.

"Fucking," said Billy.

"Oh my god," said Annie. "Who was it?"

"That's the mystery," said Larry.

"There are actually two schools of thought when it comes to what happened that night," said Norman.

"Norman here is a champion of the Single Shooter Theory," said Larry.

"And what's that?" asked Annie.

"Two participants," said Larry, holding up two fingers, then only one. "One taking the pictures."

"And what's wrong with the Single Shooter Theory?" said Annie.

"The pictures aren't taken from the same spot," said Larry, "and from what we know about the bedroom... and I believe our information is accurate... there was a long dresser next to the bed, French doors at the foot of the bed, and then nothing on the other side of the bed for at least twenty feet, which means, if you believe Norman, in order to have taken these pictures, this camera would had to have levitated off the dresser and paused... in mid-air, mind you... to take a photograph every five feet as it circled the bed. Does that sound plausible to you?"

"How many pictures are there?" said Annie.

"Five."

"So what's your theory then?" said Annie.

"A second pornographer," said Larry.

"And what's the flaw with that one?" she said, now looking at Norman.

"The camera didn't levitate," said Norman. "He used a tripod."

"He thinks this guy hopped in and out of bed five times to fuck around with a camera," said Larry.

"What makes you think the girl didn't do it?" said Annie.

"What?" said Larry. "No. Either way, no one hops in and out of bed five times to move a tripod around while they're in the middle of banging. John Holmes wouldn't stay hard under those circumstances."

"This isn't the kind of thing you want witnessed," said Norman. "And the pictures are all out of focus. If there was a second pornographer, he was the worst pornographer of all time."

"They're out of focus on purpose," said Larry. "You see what he wants you to see. The angles. The light. The composition. Whoever took those photographs knew exactly what they were doing."

"So what do you see?" said Annie.

"The first shot is just the girl," said Larry.

"She's standing at the foot of the bed," said Norman. "You see her from behind through the French doors."

"But you can't tell who she is?" said Annie.

"Just some blond girl," said Larry.

"Healthy girl," said Billy. "You get a little side shot of her tits."

"Then what?" said Annie.

"Then there's two of her sucking dick," said Billy.

"Extreme close ups," said Larry.

"But she's definitely sucking dick," said Billy.

"And the next one?"

"It's chaotic," said Larry. "Hard to tell exactly because you're so close to the action."

"He's dogging her fucky style."

"Billy," said Vandershar. "There is a time and a place for everything, and this is neither the time nor the place for you."

"That still leaves one picture," said Annie.

"It's a money shot," said Larry.

"Cum on tits," said Billy.

"But that one's in perfect focus," said Larry. "Perfect light. Perfect skin. Perfect everything really. It's actually breathtaking."

"And that's why my mom had the bed incinerated."

Julia wanted to get with Vandershar that night, not me, but something that conventional bored him, so it became a game to see if he could talk her into those last four photographs before he had his way with her himself. He told her how perfect her skin appeared in the frame. He promised the photos would be unfocused and unrecognizable. He told her he wanted to watch her as her authentic self, that the photos would be only theirs to share—the secret of durable pigment, he said. Then he slid them in with the rest from the party before his sister had even begun the process of constructing her own lie about that night. He thought it was funny. I just didn't care. I was a prop, and Julia didn't matter. Nothing did. I treated her like some bluefish I'd gaffed and thrown bleeding to the sharks, and as I watched Annie, I wondered if maybe it was finally time to stop slashing tires.

Vandershar didn't want to talk about those photographs any more than I did, so he grabbed a shot of tequila and a saltshaker off the little tray sitting on the Donald Judd coffee table and raised his glass.

"To the beautiful people!"

Then he threw the saltshaker over his shoulder, did the shot, and dumped the glass of limes out all over the tray. Vandershar would throw a saltshaker over his shoulder and dump a tray of limes, and I'd try to memorize it like it was a poem.

"You know what I think," said John Henry.

"No," said Vandershar, looking up at him. "What do you think?"

"I think *you* took those pictures."

"Really," said Vandershar, craning his neck again to get a better look at John Henry. "And who do you think was in them?"

But Annie wasn't listening anymore. She was looking at me now—me standing there like a fluorescent bug light, frozen as the tentacles of Dread wormed their way through the whiskey.

"You know, I saw you last night," she said as she stood out of that velvet chair. "It was great the way you hit that guy in the heel of his boot with the side of your head."

"It felt more like a brick."

"I'm Annie."

The moment she said her name the Dread vanished.

"Who kicked me?" I said.

"The one who looked like a poster child for the Aryan Youth."

"What about the other one?"

"That one they took away in an ambulance."

"Well, maybe he shouldn't have shoved my friend."

"He's a prick," she said. "Don't worry about it."

I didn't have anything else to say, and I wasn't really sure what to make of this person who had the power to both summon the

Dread and send it away, but I was suddenly comfortable in the silence.

"I still don't know your name," she said.

"Spencer," I said. "Spencer Mazio."

"Well... Spencer Mazio. Come with me."

She grabbed me by the forearm and led me toward the bar. Of course, the crowd parted in front of her, and the bartender ignored about ten people to give her his complete attention when we got over there.

"What is that?" she said, looking at my glass.

"Whiskey sour."

"What are you like eighty? Who drinks whiskey sour?"

"Vodka gives me a headache."

"Perfect," she said. "You probably already have a headache."

Then she ordered two greyhounds.

"It tastes like lighter fluid," I said.

"How would you know what lighter fluid tastes like?"

"I don't... but it sounds about right. It definitely smells like lighter fluid."

"A lie right out of the blocks. How will I ever trust you?"

"If you knew my brothers, you wouldn't think I was lying."

"You're saying if I knew your brothers, I'd find it plausible that they made you drink lighter fluid?"

"That's exactly what I'm saying."

"How many brothers do you have?"

"Two. They're both idiots."

"The benefits of being an only child are endless."

"You don't have brothers or sisters?"

"I do not."

"Where are you from?"

"Beautiful New Haven. East Haven actually. I live in Branford now. What about you?"

I thought about that for a second.

"I don't know," I said, only I said it like it was the truth.

"What do you mean? How can you not know where you're from?"

"I'm not from anywhere, I guess."

"There must be some place you call home."

"My dad lives in Newark, but I never go there."

"What about your mom?"

"She died when I was eleven."

She didn't say anything for a second. She just looked at me like she was taking some kind of inventory in her head.

"What happened to her?"

"She had cancer."

The drinks came right as I said it. She turned to grab them, handing me mine without even looking back, and I found myself wanting to tell her more, wanting to tell her everything, but she spoke first when she finally turned to face me.

"It's okay, you know."

"What is?"

"Being alone in the world." She clinked her glass into mine. "I am too." She didn't take her eyes off me as she lifted the glass to her mouth to take a sip. Then the music changed and she slid off her bar stool. "Wait here."

Annie never stopped moving. I don't think I ever saw her actually finish a drink. There was always someone across the room, always something else to see. She made a beeline for that pierced, bearded DJ, and when she came back, she grabbed my hand and dragged me out onto the makeshift dance floor where I ricocheted off other bodies until we finally got separated in the madness. I settled into a backwater to catch my breath as I watched her move across the floor. It was like she engaged with everyone and no one all at once. She was this uninhibited, irresistible force, an out-of-control rave girl, but she also had a way of making every dipshit in the place think he had a shot at her, so one by one the pink-shirted Hotchkissers and the drug-stupored dropouts took aim, all fumbling for words and struggling to find the stamina to keep pace. But she always managed to find me at the edge of the insanity, and when she did, she'd flash her enormous smile like I was the only other person there. That's when I caught a glimpse of Vandershar sizing me up from the shadows like Imke had just boarded my yacht.

I have no idea how I got to her car. I drank so much that night that what I do remember is in still shots that get progressively smaller and smaller as the night wears on, until finally they occupy a space about the size of a pinhead, and only if I concentrate really hard am I able to run the last few frames fast enough to make seamless movement. She drove a piece-of-shit white BMW 318i. The door on the passenger's side didn't work, so I had to crawl in over the driver's seat and gearshift. When you've had four whiskey sours, five greyhounds and god knows what else, something like that can take a little while. We fooled around in the parking lot of our building back in New Haven, but you can only get so much done in the front seat of a 318i, so I tried to get her in the back seat, but that was a total failure, and I was ridiculous by that time. I was so messed up I needed her help just to get in the elevator. I blacked out after that. I have no memory of anything else until John Henry yanked the blinds open the next day.

"They towed my car," he said.

I was suddenly very aware of my hangover and struggling to piece together where I was and what had happened to get me there.

"Did you hear me?" he said.

"I heard you."

"They towed my car."

"Can you go away?"

I let my head drop back to the pillow, wondering if I'd done anything to embarrass myself. Then the phone rang.

"You didn't tell me you were leaving."

"How'd you get back if they towed your car?"

"The train."

You could hear Billy's voice on the answering machine: "Pick up. Pick up, motherfucker."

"What time is it?" I said.

"Where is she?" said John Henry.

"I don't know."

"Pick up the phone," said Billy.

"Where'd *you* sleep?" I said.

"The loft," he said. "Vandershar nailed that Sabine girl. I think they did it right on the Donald Judd coffee table."

"Why didn't you stay down there to get your car?"

"You fuck her or what?" said Billy.

"I didn't know where you were," he said. "You didn't tell me you were leaving."

He started to turn a milky shade of green as he slumped onto his bed, and I could tell he was on the verge of a cataclysmic hypoglycemic meltdown.

"You didn't eat, did you?"

"Did you leave with her?"

He sounded delirious, like he was about to pass out, so I got up and went for the kitchen.

"She drove me back," I said from the hallway.

"So you did leave with her."

"How else would I have gotten home?"

He didn't say anything for a moment, but I could hear him sort of crumple back onto the bed.

"I can't believe this happened again."

"I was just standing there," I yelled from the kitchen.

"What happened when you got back?"

"I don't know."

I grabbed a jar of Jif and a spoon.

"What do you mean you don't know?"

"I don't know," I said now in the hallway again. "I was too fucked up. I sort of remember getting in the elevator with her... and then that's it. I blacked out."

"We're never gonna see her again."

I reentered the bedroom.

"What are you talking about?" He looked pitiful, sort of twisted on his side, but with his feet still in contact with the ground. "I don't even know what happened... and what do you mean *we*?"

"You don't know what happened?" he said, sitting up so I could hand him the jar of peanut butter. "Let me ask you this then: What are the odds any of it was good?"

I tossed the spoon at him.

"Shut the fuck up and eat your peanut butter."

# Chapter 25

*Summer 1992*

In the dream, I'm in distress as I rummage through the garbage under the seats at Yale Field. I'm wearing my uniform. I have nothing but sanitary socks on my feet, and I'm searching for a pair of cleats that don't exist. Only this time I wasn't in distress at all. I was perfectly happy watching the wind blow the hot dog wrappers into the air and stir the paper cups. I wasn't even looking for the cleats. I was just chasing the wrappers as they floated up into the air like ketchup-soaked butterflies. I'd reach higher and then higher still, only for some reason I couldn't leave the ground. My vertical leap was like zero, so I could only watch as the wrappers floated away.

"Stop it!"

It was the Throaty Fatboy from the end of Cornell's bench, only his voice was muffled like I was under water, like I was suspended in a warm, cozy fluid.

"Stop it!"

I reached for another hot dog wrapper, but I was too slow to grab it, so I watched it drift out of reach too, higher and higher, until finally it drifted up above the grandstand, and I was staring straight at the sun, this bright white luminescence expanding until it ultimately filled my entire field of vision, and it stayed like that for a while, you know, like I was in suspended animation. Then I woke up.

I was staring straight into the ceiling lights of my room at Widworth.

"Stop it! Alan! Let go."

It was Duddle, not the Throaty Fatboy, and even though it was the middle of the night, the lights were on in our room. Duddle was struggling to pry Alan loose from crisp white bed sheets. I tried to lift my head, but I couldn't move it. I was too deep in the sludge now. The horse pills had worked to keep the Dread away, but I'd been backsliding into a sticky, viscous sludge since I'd started taking them. I'd missed entire days with my grandmother, just lost in a toxic fog so dense it interfered with my ability to do just about anything, so the best I could do now was let my head fall to the side in time to see Leonard creeping on all fours to the foot of his bed. I tried to say something. I wanted to stop him, but nothing came out. I couldn't speak, and then Leonard went flying like a giant, homicidal frog and landed square on Duddle's back. He wrapped those skinny frog legs around Duddle's bloated midsection and then his wiry arms around Duddle's neck.

Duddle appeared only mildly concerned at the sudden possibility of being strangled to death by a lunatic. He staggered back from the bed and pawed at Leonard over his shoulders. I could see Alan more clearly now. He was stiff as a board, convulsing inside his rigid body, almost vibrating, and his eyes had rolled all the way back into his head.

"Leonard, get off," said Duddle.

Duddle backpedaled into the wall next to the door, but Leonard wouldn't let go, and only then did Duddle appear to be laboring. He rammed Leonard into the wall again, and then again with more urgency, but Leonard only squeezed tighter, so Duddle finally put his full weight into it. The drywall gave, and Leonard fell to the ground. Duddle bent over to catch his breath. I could see Alan now raking at his face like he was trying to dig his own eyeballs out of their sockets. Then Duddle stood upright, all sweaty and panting while Leonard took aim again. He took one stride and launched himself, but this time Duddle snatched him out of midair in an awkward bear hug and threw him into the wooden chair next to the door. Leonard crumpled into a broken heap, all twisted and contorted in a way that didn't look fixable.

"Shit," said Duddle like he'd done something irreparable to his nursing career. "Shit, shit, shit, shit."

It wasn't long before a small army of psych techs scraped Leonard off the floor. Then one of them injected Alan with something that knocked him into next week before they loaded his sedated body onto a gurney.

"What about that one?"

"What about him?"

Then I heard them wheel Alan away.

They didn't touch me. They didn't even bother to ask me what had happened. They didn't bother with me at all. I was just another wing nut too drug-addled to lift his own head, trapped inside his own body, and even though the Dread was nowhere in sight, I felt cold and alone lying there—like I'd crossed some point of no return with no way back and nowhere to go, and all I could do was lay there staring at the ceiling, shaking until the sun came up and the pleasant nurse with the absurdly long fingernails arrived with yet another white paper cup containing a single orange, horse-sized capsule.

# Chapter 26

*Spring 1992*

The Career Services Office at Yale was in a building that looked like a place Vlad the Impaler might have spent some time. It was all castle-like, burnt orange, and medieval. It was also just the second time I'd ever set foot in the place. Up to that point, I'd relied almost completely on Larry and Vandershar for my career services. All the rooms were tiny and the floors warped, so they rolled and creaked every time anyone moved. When somebody got up to take a piss, you could hear it three floors below. It was hard to imagine anyone's career getting started there.

My Prudential interview was on the third floor in a cramped room with a couple rent-a-chairs and a rickety wooden desk. The old man Prudential sent to do the interviews was on the other side staring down at a sheet of paper. He looked like Darth Vader without the mask—this huge Humpty-Dumpty head with an enormous oval face and an overgrown nose covered in a billion exploded capillaries. Sometimes you look at an old man, and you can sort of see the young man he used to be, but other times, like when his head looks like Humpty-Dumpty and his nose has outgrown his face, you really have no idea, and you have to wonder what the fuck happened.

"How are you today?" he said.

"Pretty good."

And I did feel pretty good. I had no interest in working at a bank Vandershar referred to as a "piece of shit." I just wanted the interview to tune up for Goldman, but I immediately sensed something was wrong. Humpty-Dumpty was just sitting there glumly.

He nodded and then looked back down at the piece of paper in front of him.

"I'm supposed to ask you these questions."

I waited, now replaying in my head all the stock responses I'd memorized, but he didn't say anything for an uncomfortably long time as he continued to look down at the sheet of paper, so it was like I was suddenly way out ahead of him, formulating answers in my head to questions he'd never asked.

"These are tough times, aren't they?" He looked up and smiled. It was a nervous smile. "The recession persists." He took a deep breath and slumped back into his chair. "I have an entire day of this ahead of me. A death by a thousand cuts really." His smile was even weaker now. "You know, I once made six hundred thousand dollars in a single year."

I wasn't sure what I was supposed to say to that, so when I said nothing, he picked up that piece of paper again and started to read from it, only he wasn't asking me the questions. He was just reading them. *Why do you want to be an investment banker.* I tried to focus on my memorized answer to that softball when he moved on to the next one. *Why do you want to work at Prudential.* But I couldn't hold on to what I'd memorized for the first question because he just kept talking. *Tell me about a class you're taking.* Then I forgot the first question altogether as other memorized answer-fragments bubbled up into my head. *What are your three strengths*. And then I didn't hear the next question at all or the one after that, until finally he ended with *Walk me through a discounted cash flow analysis*.

He looked up, relieved, like he'd made the happy decision to set himself free, and that's when the tables sort of turned. Forgotten answers to forgotten questions now boiled in my brain.

"Fine questions, aren't they?"

"Five?" I said, half hearing him.

"Fine."

"Do I answer one?"

"It's not necessary." He crumpled the piece of paper into a ball and threw it in the trash. "I'm afraid I don't have a job for you."

"But I can answer."

"Well, it's not you. I don't have a job to offer anyone. There are no job openings at Prudential Securities."

He smiled.

"Then what are you doing here?"

He paused and seemed to gather himself before he answered.

"What you see before you is the occupational hazard of a washed-up trader. My true value to Prudential on display for all to see."

I had no idea what he meant.

"This is someone's idea of funny," he said.

"What is?"

"I'm very sorry. In fact, I've decided to spend my day apologizing to each and every one of you."

"For what?"

"This farce. On behalf of Prudential Securities, I'm sorry we wasted your time. I'm sorry you have to graduate into such a terrible job market." He righted himself and smiled again. I think he could tell his apology was actually making me more uncomfortable. "Maybe I can still be of service to you. Perhaps you'd like to ask *me* some questions?"

"You want me to ask *you* questions?"

"Surely there's something you'd like to know about the beast you have your sights set on. I've been in its belly for quite some time now."

"What do you mean it's a terrible job market?"

He looked at me for a moment after that, this pitiful look like he felt sorry for me.

"Come on," he said. "On your feet." Then he stood. "Here you go. Take this." He handed me a white handkerchief as I got up. "I have nothing but fond memories of my time here. They can never take those away. Don't forget that. They can never take away your memories." He cleared his throat and started to sing in this crusty old man voice:

> *Bright College years, with pleasure rife,*
> *The shortest, gladdest years of life;*
> *How swiftly are ye gliding by!*
> *Oh, why doth time so quickly fly?*
> *The seasons come, the seasons go,*
> *The earth is green or white with snow,*
> *But time and change shall naught avail*
> *To break the friendships formed at Yale.*
> *In after years, should troubles rise*
> *to cloud the blue of sunny skies,*
> *How bright will seem, through memory's haze*
> *those happy, golden, bygone days.*
> *Oh let us strive that ever we*
> *may let these words our watch-cry be.*
> *Where'er upon life's sea we sail:*
> *For God, For Country and For Yale.*

I didn't know the words. All I could do was mumble along with my mind racing until he got to the end of it all teary-eyed, and then he motioned like he wanted me to wave that handkerchief all over the place, so that's what I did, and then we stood there, him on his side of the desk and me on mine, until finally in that odd silence he extended his hand.

"Good luck to you," he said.

And that was it. That was my tune-up for Goldman.

It rattled me so completely I forgot to meet John Henry for lunch in Berkeley. Instead, I wandered home in a fog, wondering if there were no jobs at Goldman either, thinking maybe Vandershar just didn't know. He never said a word about a shitty job market. All he ever said was it was a done deal. He didn't even think I needed to do the Prudential interview, but none of that mattered now. It was like the full force of the future hit me right in the face. It didn't even make sense. They just throw you out into the rest of your life? So what had Yale actually done then—besides take my money? Where were my happy golden bygone days? The only certainty now was that I owed some unknown enterprise eighty-five thousand dollars just for having had the privilege of being the dumbest fuck at Yale. What kind of bullshit was that?

Our doorman tried to say something when I got on the elevator, but I was so lost in thought I didn't even acknowledge him as the doors shut. Where would I go? I certainly wasn't living in the loft if it turned out Vandershar was full of shit, and I could never go back to Newark. I felt weightless as the elevator headed up even though the forces should have been holding me to the floor. Everything was upside down, and then the Dread exploded into my head to remind me that the world owed me nothing. I felt unstable as I stepped into the hall, mumbling about the shitty job market, thoughts crashing from back to front and front to back until finally it no longer felt like I would remember to breathe, like I had to consciously consider every breath, like I had to remember to inhale... and then there she was.

Annie was sitting on the floor in front of our door.

"You clean up nicely," she said.

She hopped up from her spot and smiled, only I couldn't shed the negative thoughts.

"What are you doing here?" I said.

"Not exactly the welcome I was hoping for. Your doorman let me up. We're buddies now."

I was struggling and suddenly very aware that I'd pitted through my suit jacket.

"Are you okay?" she said.

"What? Yeah. I just... I wasn't sure I'd see you again."

"Whiskey does not agree with you."

"It was the vodka."

"Well," she said, brushing something off my lapel. "Surprise!" Then she stepped back and gave me a once over. "Why are you in a suit?"

"I had an interview."

"For what?"

"I'm not sure," I said, my mind drifting again.

"Are you sure you're okay?"

"Yeah. I'm fine. I just... I forgot I was supposed to meet the guys for lunch."

"Perfect," she said. "I'm starving."

But I just stood there staring at her, still wondering why she'd camped out on our doorstep.

"You didn't tell me what you were doing here," I said.

The question seemed to surprise her.

"I came to see you."

"Yeah, I know... but why?"

She just smiled that enormous smile like it was the most ridiculous thing she'd ever heard.

"Because I like you, Spencer. Why else would I come to see you?"

# Chapter 27

When we got to the Berkeley College dining hall, John Henry was at a round table toward the back near the table where the Black kids sat. All the dining halls at Yale were pretty much the same: high-beamed ceilings, wood-paneled walls, wooden tables, wooden chairs, semi-edible food and, for reasons I never completely understood, a table where all the Black kids sat. I signed Annie in as a guest, and we made our way back there. The guys were all done eating, and Billy was sucking on a wad of chewing tobacco and spitting into a glass half-filled with dip sludge and apple juice.

"Annie," said John Henry all surprised.

Then he jumped up and pulled a chair out for her.

"How'd it go?" said Larry.

"It was weird," I said, now that I could think again.

"What happened?"

"He told me there were no jobs at Prudential and then we sang."

"What's weird about that?"

"The guy's head was as big as Larry's," I said. "He looked like Humpty-Dumpty. Full on Darth Vader without the mask. I sit down, and he's just fumbling with this piece of paper, all nervous and weird. I'm sitting there wondering why Prudential would even send this guy. Then he looks up and tells me there's no jobs."

"What do you mean you sang?" said Norman. "What'd you sing?"

"I don't know. At the end of it, he made me wave a white handkerchief all around."

"You sang the Whiffenpoof Song?" said Larry.

"That's not the Whiffenpoof Song," said Norman. "The Whiffenpoof Song is about Mory's and goats and there's no handkerchief at the end."

"What are they doing here if there's no jobs?" said Larry.

"They have to be here," said Billy. "It was the same with Bear Stearns. It looks bad if Goldman is here and they're not, and I heard Goldman's only got five slots."

*Five slots.* That was all I heard. The confidence that had slowly returned as Annie and I made our way from my building's elevator to the Berkeley College dining hall drained instantaneously. How was it possible that the dumbest fuck at Yale had one of only five jobs at Goldman Sachs?

"Did you actually sing?" said Larry.

"No, I didn't sing. I didn't know the words. It was totally weird. I just wanted to get the fuck out of there. The guy cried at the end."

"What is that?" said Annie, pointing at the remnants of John Henry's lunch.

"Chicken patty," said John Henry.

"Where are they?"

The food sat in trays behind glass under heat lamps. After four years of the semi-edible, we all pretty much stuck to the chicken patties. They were harmless breaded patties that seemed to be made out of chicken. You basically knew what you were getting when you ordered a chicken patty. They were reliable. They could be counted on. The alternative that day was scrod. The scrod was not reliable. It could not be counted on. A pimple-faced fairly miserable-looking work-study girl in a white paper hat loaded our plates, but when I looked up from the soft drink dispenser, Annie was gone and I was face to face with Ernie Rickman's pear-shaped roommate, Kevin Strommer.

Kevin was a Tunnel Dweller too, and he loved baseball, so he was constantly cornering me to talk about it, but he had a stutter, and it only seemed to get worse when I was around, so it always took forever. Larry called Ernie and Kevin the "Nars," which was short for something in Yiddish that had to do with their ability to waste my time. As Annie slipped away, Kevin struggled to say something about the Cincinnati Reds' bullpen, and then Ernie showed up with his own tray of chicken patties.

"Duke plays North Carolina tomorrow," he said through his nose.

"I haven't even looked at it," I said.

"Well, look at it."

"I'll have to call you."

"I want to parlay with three other games."

"I told you I'm not running parlays anymore."

"Why not?"

"It's too much work."

"What is? All that adding and dividing?"

"You can always take it to another bookie."

"How are you even a math major?"

Annie was now weaving through the tables without me, so I steadied my tray and did a three-sixty to split the Nars. Then I accelerated away from them before they could waste any more of my time.

"This was a lot easier when you lived here!"

Larry was playing with the lone surviving Brussels sprout on his plate when I got back to the table. He was now dating the vegetarian girl from the Silliman laundry room, so that's about all he ever ate.

"So do you all play baseball?" said Annie.

"We do," said Larry.

"Is that why you're always together?"

"We were tortured by the same twelve assholes," said Norman.

"I played baseball when I was little," she said, banging on the bottom of a long-necked mustard bottle. "I played for Grannis Corners in the New Haven Annex Little League."

"What's Grannis Corners?" said John Henry.

"It was a pharmacy," she said. "I quit though. I never really liked organized things. I was a Brownie too, but the uniforms were ugly."

Larry put his foot up on the table and lifted his pant leg to show her the muscled two-inch cartoon bulldog on his ankle.

"See that," he said. "We've all got one."

"I've seen it," she said.

Then she inhaled half a chicken patty.

"Pretty good, right?" said Larry.

"You traced it from a refrigerator magnet," said Norman.

"There's something wrong with its ear," she said with her mouth full.

"What?" said Larry. "No, there's not."

"Look at its ear," she said, still chewing.

Billy pulled his sleeve up to get a look at the bulldog on his shoulder.

"What the fuck?" he said. "The ear is on the wrong side of the dog collar."

Larry gave his ankle a closer inspection.

"Well, look at that."

"Well, look at that?" said Billy. "This shit is permanent."

"At least it's an original," said Larry. "I told you I didn't trace it."

"What happened to yours?" she said to me. "It's all scarred."

They all looked at me, waiting for me to say something, but I never know how to tell that story.

"He got stabbed," said Billy.

Then he spit into his glass.

"Seriously?" she said. "Somebody stabbed you?"

"It happened at The Moon," said Larry.

"Up Whalley?" she said. "That place is awful."

"I realize that... now."

"What were you doing there?" she said.

"It was Vandershar's idea," said John Henry.

"He wanted to see Nirvana," said Larry. "Who the fuck had heard of Nirvana?"

"We get there and it's all disorganized," said Norman. "It was like there was a line to get in, but it wasn't a line really, so there were about a hundred people just standing around doing nothing. Just waiting to get in, I guess."

"We had no business being there," said Larry. "John Henry was wearing a black turtleneck and pegged jeans like it was a poetry reading, and Norman was in tie-dye."

"I thought they were a Dead cover band."

"Everyone else looked homeless," said Larry.

"We were standing there," said Norman. "Minding our own business, you know, trying to figure out what the fuck was going on. Just trying to figure out how to get in really, when the chubby dude in front of us turns around and asks John Henry if we all go to Yale."

"It was nothing though," said Larry. "I barely noticed the guy."

"So John Henry starts to talk to him," said Norman. "What'd he even say to you?"

"He asked me if I dressed like that all the time."

"Fair question," said Larry. "You looked like Dieter from *Sprockets*."

"He said he thought we all had to wear khaki pants every day," said John Henry.

"What do you mean?" she said. "Like a uniform?"

"I guess."

"Was he serious?" she said.

"No," said Larry. "He was not serious."

"So right in the middle of this conversation about John Henry's attire," said Norman, "this other guy shows up. This one's got the untucked flannel shirt. The long greasy hair. The whole grunge thing going on, and he's a big dude. Huge head. Bigger than Larry's."

"He's also really fucked up," said Larry. "He was half-cocked the moment he dropped into the conversation."

"He listens to John Henry for about two seconds," said Norman, "then he cuts him off and says, 'I hear there's a lot of faggots at Yale. One in four... maybe more?'"

"What a piece of shit," said Annie.

"Then he gets in John Henry's face," said Larry, "and he says: 'Which one of you is the faggot?'"

"Now this is all starting to attract some attention," said Norman. "There's like ten of them watching all this now."

"So John Henry looks up at the big one," said Larry, "and he says, 'But there's six of us.' Now, it did not appear that the big one understood that John Henry was trying to de-escalate the situation with mathematical humor because he got all serious and stuck a finger in John Henry's chest and said, 'I bet you're the faggot.'"

"What'd you do?" said Annie, now looking at John Henry.

"He didn't do anything," said Billy.

"Why not?"

"Because Spencer dropped the guy," said Billy.

"He just showed up out of nowhere and put the guy on the ground with one punch," said Larry. "The guy just folded. Out cold. I don't think he ever got up, did he?"

"Yeah, well it was a fucking nightmare after that," said Norman. "Just this human tsunami rolling over us."

"We were basically running for our lives at that point," said Larry.

"The entire mob turned on us," said Norman.

"I tripped over the curb and fucked up my knee," said Larry. "I guess they lost interest in me because they let me lie there unmolested. So now I'm on the ground watching this whole thing. It was surreal. Spencer and John Henry are doing figure eights in the parking lot trying to outrun this mob while Billy and Norman end up fending off a lunatic who looked like the beef jerky version of a high school slut."

"She was out of her fucking mind on something," said Billy. "It was like fighting Mike Tyson on PCP."

"Billy went to jail by the way," said Larry.

"I did not go to jail," said Billy. "She dropped the charges."

"That's because you pressed charges against her," said John Henry.

"You punched her in the face with a closed fist," said Norman.

"I couldn't get her off me."

"I'm still on the ground at this point," said Larry. "Vandershar is long gone."

"Where'd he go?" asked Annie.

"He says he ran for the car," said John Henry.

"Wherever he was, he wasn't there," said Larry. "So the crazy bitch now has Billy pressed up against chain-link. Norman is trying to peel her off him, and that's when the mob catches up to John Henry. They got you by that fucking turtleneck. They were spinning you around." He paused as a thought seemed to enter his mind. "Is it centrifugal or centripetal?"

"Centripetal," said Norman.

"Are you sure?"

"Centrifugal isn't even a force."

"Anyway, I just remember the sound of your turtleneck ripping as they spun you to the ground, and then it was up over your head, you know, so you couldn't see anything, and that's when they just started to beat the shit out of you. At first it was like five guys... five flannel shirts with long hair, taking turns kicking the fuck out of John Henry, but then the rest of them stopped chasing Spencer so they could get in on it too, so then it was like twenty guys beating the fuck out of John Henry. There were so many I couldn't even see him anymore."

"I was fine," said John Henry like he was suddenly drowning in the story, like he was suddenly gasping for air.

"Really?" said Larry. "You were fine? Were you gonna outsmart the bad guys from the fetal position? I wasn't even sure you were still conscious. Then I hear the sirens, and I remember thinking, *There's no way they're gonna get here in time.*"

"In time for what?" said Annie.

And then there was silence. It's the same strange quiet every time someone tells the story, when it sinks in what could have happened, and it's during this odd pause that it always occurs to me to confess how wired I was when I threw that punch... but I never do.

"To stop it," said Larry.

"Well, you're all here," she said. "What happened?"

"Spencer dove on top of John Henry and took the rest of the beating himself."

"That's how you got stabbed?" she said.

"He ended up in Yale New Haven for two weeks," said Norman.

"Why would they stab you?"

"I don't know," I said without looking up from the table. "They thought it was funny, I guess."

"How is that funny?"

"I don't know, but they were laughing. That's all I heard. That's the only thing I really remember."

Larry started to fuck around with the Brussels sprout again to take us away from the parking lot at The Moon. He put it under a glass, and then he moved it around like he was running a shell game on a street corner. He had the glass with the Brussels sprout, a coffee cup, and a salt shaker, and he was moving them all around—this way, then that way, then this way, then that way, then back again, only you could see the sprout right through the glass the whole time. Then he pulled his hands away with a ridiculous look on his face.

"Where's the alfalfa sprout?" he said.

"It's a Brussels sprout, genius."

# Chapter 28

I called Vandershar's number for forty-five straight minutes until he finally picked up.

"What difference does it make how many jobs there are?" he said. "You have one."

"I have an interview."

"You need to relax. You'd have to be a complete idiot to fuck this up."

Then Annie showed up a full hour before she was supposed to. I'm not even sure I said anything to her when I opened the door. I still had the phone up to my ear, and when I hung up, I immediately started rummaging through our kitchen for Wayne the Law Student's number. I had routines. I had schedules, and I needed to get back to them as soon as possible, but Annie wouldn't leave me alone. She was pestering me for something to drink. I wasn't used to someone nipping at my heels. I existed semi-alone inside a comfortable bubble with *Days of Our Lives* and *R.B.I. Baseball* to keep me company. She smashed all that to pieces. I finally handed her the remote to the TVs thinking maybe that would keep her occupied. She looked at it like it was a bag of dog shit and pretty soon she was opening and shutting the very same kitchen drawers and cabinets that I was, until finally she stopped at the refrigerator door.

"Who's the Yankee fan?" she said, looking at the autographed photo of the 1961 Yankees that hung on the wall above the phone next to the fridge.

"That was my little brother's," I said, still searching.

"I loved Bucky Dent."

"Bucky Dent's not in that picture."

"I know. I'm just saying."

"What are you guys doing?" said John Henry, emerging from our bedroom the moment he heard her voice.

"Looking for something to drink," she said.

So now John Henry was opening and closing cabinets too.

I felt an odd obligation to make her something, so I dumped some vodka into a twenty-four ounce plastic Batman cup and filled it the rest of the way with Tang.

"What is this?" she said as I handed it to her.

"Screwdriver."

"There's Tang in this," she said. "I watched you make it." She took a whiff. "Jesus Christ, Spencer. This smells like lighter fluid."

Just about every Tunnel Dweller had some bullshit betting system based on a sketchy algorithm or bad math. I'm not sure any of it ever really worked, but once I had all the math figured out, I knew who would bet on what, so it helped me set lines. Wayne's system for college basketball was weighted heavily toward home teams and the home court advantage, which ultimately boiled down to home crowds influencing referees. Ernie looked for statistical oddities in college basketball which he believed could only be explained by point-shaving or point-making. Then he'd bet on the side of the fix. He came to the conclusion that the North Carolina Tar Heels were not point-shavers but point-makers. He claimed they had a mathematically unexplainable ability to beat spreads even if it meant a layup or two in garbage time, and since Ernie thought most of college basketball was rigged, it wasn't much of a leap for him to believe the Tar Heels were just another team in on it. He liked to say he was "dollar cost averaging" the Tar Heels, but he always said it like a prick, so I never asked him what it meant.

Duke was at home and the number one team in the country, so I thought I could get Wayne to take Duke and give seven and a half because I was pretty sure I could get Ernie to take North Carolina and get only four. Two hundred and fifty bucks was the bet. It was something the bookie who flicked cigarette butts at my head in Bobo's taught me. If North Carolina lost by less than four, or won for that matter, I'd lose my bet with Ernie, win my bet with Wayne, and make fifty bucks in juice. If Duke won by eight or more, I'd lose my bet with Wayne, win my bet with Ernie, and still make the fifty bucks in juice, but if Duke won by five, six or seven, I'd win both bets and all five hundred and fifty bucks. I just needed to find Wayne's fucking phone number, and I was running out of time.

"Let me ask you this since Spencer has no opinion on the matter," said John Henry as he poured Annie's screwdriver into the sink. "You know what Skull and Bones is, right?"

"My grandfather thought they killed Kennedy."

"Skull and Bones?" said John Henry. "Why would Skull and Bones kill Kennedy?"

"I don't know. What do they really do?"

"They don't do anything," he said. "About a hundred years ago some nitwit got ahold of some pre-Nazi German philosophy and decided to found a secret society to take over the world. Now I think they just meet twice a week."

"Well, my Poppy loved all that shit."

"Did he go to Yale?"

"No. He was just from here."

"Well, now women want to join. It's been men only forever, and now women want to be in it, so I said to one of the other editors, I said why don't we do a story on how pointless this is?"

"The editor of what?"

"*The Yale Herald*," he said, now concocting something in a coffee mug.

"You write?"

"I'm an editor now, but yeah. I want to be a journalist."

"You're not gonna be an investment banker?"

"No," he said. "I have a job at *The New York Daily News*. So they actually tapped girls this year for the first time, but when the Bones alumni found out, they all went apeshit and sued."

"Sued who?"

"Skull and Bones."

"For what?"

"To keep these girls from meeting twice a week, I guess, and now it's this whole thing, so I said I wanted to do something on Yale's history with women... to point out how inconsequential this is in light of the last twenty years of progress."

"Sounds consequential to me."

"I mean, Skull and Bones is antiquated. It doesn't mean anything anymore. When you compare the progress of women at Yale over the last twenty years to this, it seems to me it's not a fight worth fighting... for either side... but when I bounced the idea off this other editor, she told me not to do it. She said coming from a male it would sound paternalistic or pandering."

"Pandering?"

"Yeah… pandering. What do you think?"

"It might be pandering if you're doing it to get laid," she said. "You're not doing it to get laid are you?"

"White Russian!" he said, handing her the mug. "I found some vanilla."

The stray piece of paper with Wayne's number scribbled in the margin was stuck in an old spiral ring notebook I found behind the bar, so I grabbed the cordless and ducked into Vandershar's room for some quiet as I dialed the number.

"I don't have any money," he said after I made the proposal.

"That's a little pessimistic, don't you think, Wayne?"

Wayne took Duke and gave the seven and a half, so I hung up before he could change his mind. I called Ernie with only a couple minutes left before tip-off, only Kevin Strommer answered.

"Kevin, is Ernie there?"

"Yeah," he said, but then there was a pause where I did not hear him attempt to get Ernie's attention. "That w-w-was a great p-play you made against P-Penn."

"Kevin, I need to talk to Ernie."

"The b-b-barehand on the b-bunt."

"You were there?"

"I t-try to go to all your h-h-home games."

"Kevin, can you just give the phone to Ernie?"

"I've been m-meaning to ask you. What kind of a b-b-bat do you use?"

"What? I don't know. It's an Easton with green letters."

"I f-found a bat with a r-really n-n-narrow handle," he said.

"Kevin."

"I think I'll b-be able to g-g-generate more c-c-cen-tri-trifugal f-f-force with it."

"Centripetal," I said.

"W-what?"

"It's centripetal force, not centrifugal."

"Are you s-s-s-sure?"

"Kevin... it doesn't matter. Can you just put Ernie on?"

"Centri-tri-tripetal f-f-force then."

"Kevin."

"It s-s-still has the oversized b-b-barrel, but with the th-th-thin handle, I th-think I can ge-ge-generate more ce-ce-centri-tri-tripetal force."

"Kevin. Please give the phone to Ernie."

"I w-w-want to u-use it in intram-m-murals. Wh-wh-what do you think?"

I heard a scuffle for the phone on the other end.

"It's almost tip-off," said Ernie through his nose. "How much longer were you gonna make me wait?"

"North Carolina and four," I said.

"That's not the line."

"The game's about to start."

"I should get at least six points. Duke is the best team in the country."

"North Carolina and four," I said. "Two-seventy-five for two-fifty. That's it. That's the best I can do for you. Do you want it or not?"

"It's not the right line," he said.

"You have sixty seconds."

There was a long pause, but I could still hear him breathing.

"Fine," he said. "They'll cover. They always cover."

I felt oddly satisfied when I hung up. I forgot Annie was even there. I switched Vandershar's TV on to watch the tip-off. John Henry used to say I would have these petit mal seizures whenever I got in front of a TV. According to *Webster's*, a "petit mal seizure" is a seizure involving staring spells. That night I had a petit mal seizure that lasted until halftime. I didn't come out of it until

I felt our apartment vibrating from the music cranked up in the common room, and when I stepped into the hall, I felt off-balance again. I actually had to put a hand on the wall to steady myself. I wasn't really sure what was around the bend. The lights were off when I turned the corner, and all these candles I didn't even know we owned were lit, and there they were: Annie's arms outstretched high over her head as she grooved to John Henry's shitty music on that oxblood red shag carpet while John Henry just stared up at her from the couch mesmerized. I couldn't tell if it was a séance or a lap dance.

"What the fuck are you doing?" I said as the Dread slithered into my gut.

"What am *I* doing?" she said without stopping. "I've been here for an hour. What the fuck are *you* doing?"

# Chapter 29

Annie sublet a spare room from an old high school friend in a weather-beaten apartment building near the water in Branford. It wasn't the plan to stay with her, but I spent the next night out there, and the next, and after that I just settled in, I guess. It was comfortable there, away from the worry of my impending interview with Goldman, not to mention John Henry's omnipresence. Annie's room was nothing but an old thin mattress slapped down under a Levolor blind-covered window with the rest of her shit strewn all over the floor. It was just me and her and piles of clothing, but I was soon blowing off class to stay there.

We would walk the dirt roads and trails along the estuaries in the mornings. She had a way of grabbing me every time she burst into laughter, and it made me want to keep her laughing all the time, so I'd tell her goofy stories until I realized the best ones all involved John Henry. How long does it take to get to know a person? Is it a day? A week? One conversation? A lifetime? At what point do you know the person you're with is the person you think they are?

Our first morning out there, we were on a dirt road all the way down near the yacht club. It was a cool morning, and there was a layer of mist over the water with all the big boats way up ahead of us. The tide must have been high because the river seemed swollen beyond its normal depth, driving the shorebirds up onto the banks, and every now and again I'd find a rock and chuck it as far as I could into the river.

"So do you not work?" I said, curious how she paid for even that sty of a room.

"I'm a nanny. It sucks, but they only need me three days a week."

"Pretty soon you'll be washing lettuce."

"And that's when the big bucks start rolling in."

"No more lingerie?"

"Hell no."

"How many kids do you watch?"

"Two boys. They're twins. The dad's like sixty, and I think the mom's my age. It's so gross."

"Is she hot?"

"What is wrong with you?"

"How old are the twins?"

"Eight."

"John Henry has twin sisters about that age."

"What are *they* like?"

"Kind of amazing actually. They're musicians."

"No. The two I watch are little shits. One of them grabbed my ass the other day and told me it was 'squishy.'"

"John Henry's sisters are legitimate musicians. You have to hear it to believe it. Your ass is not squishy if it makes you feel any better."

"You want to hear something terrible?"

"Sure. Tell me something terrible about eight-year-old kids."

"I picked them up from school the other day, and I was in a huge hurry, and I'm just kind of sick of their shit to be honest. So I hustle them out to the car, with their fucking backpacks and school shit flopping all over the place, and I get them strapped into their seats. Neither of them says a word the whole time. About two blocks later, I look in the rearview mirror, and I have the wrong kid. I have one of them, but the other kid is the wrong kid. I left a twin at school and grabbed some random eight-year-old."

"What'd you do?"

"I freaked out. They're fraternal twins. They don't look exactly alike, but still, it's so embarrassing, so of course the ragamuffins in the back seat are laughing hysterically, and I'm freaking out because I lost a kid."

"Did you find him?"

"He was on the playground like he didn't give a shit. I think they planned it, and then he got all irritated when I told him it was time to leave. I have no idea whose kid I had. Thank god his mom wasn't there yet. That would have been even more mortifying."

"I don't know how to break this to you, but you might be in the wrong line of work."

"You think? I honestly wonder if I have a subconscious desire to off these kids, and then I was terrified they'd tell their mom."

"Did they?"

"No... which is worse. Now they have something on me."

"How is an eight-year-old gonna use this information against you?"

"I don't know... but they're crafty. Maybe you're right. Maybe I should just forget about it. What's the most embarrassing thing *you've* ever done?"

I thought about it for a second since there were so many contenders, but one stood out head and shoulders above the rest.

"I was in some club in New York," I said, "and I was wearing this new shirt. I was very proud of this shirt. I'd picked it out myself at this boutique in Soho. It was like a hundred and forty bucks or something like that. Basically, the most expensive thing I'd ever bought with my own money."

"What'd it look like?"

"I think it's made of silk, but half of it's red and the other half is blue."

"You mean like a jester?"

"Like a what?"

"You know... a jester."

"No. It's sweet. Even Vandershar asked where I got it."

"Or maybe a jockey."

"Can I finish the story?"

"The embarrassing part's not the shirt?"

"No."

"Do you still have it?"

"Of course."

"I haven't seen it."

"That's because I keep it for special occasions."

She whacked me on the arm.

"Can I finish now?"

"Can I stop you?"

"So I've got this shirt on, and I go to take a leak. It's pretty dark, and I turn the corner to where the bathrooms are, and there's this guy right in front of me, and he's wearing the same shirt, so I'm like, 'Hey buddy, nice shirt'... and then I walk straight into a mirror."

"Oh my god. Did anybody see you?"

"Yep."

"Did they hear you compliment yourself on your own shirt?"

"Oh yeah."

"So what'd you do?"

"I hauled ass into the bathroom and hid in a stall for like ten minutes."

She was laughing and hanging on to me the way she did, but then I saw a nice round rock, so I stopped and picked it up and hucked it about fifty yards into the river.

"How come you don't want to play baseball?" she said as it splashed down.

"What do you mean?"

"If you're so good, why not baseball? Why be an investment banker?"

"What's wrong with being an investment banker?"

"All the bankers I've ever known are assholes."

In the unconscious calculus of working at Goldman Sachs—both before Humpty-Dumpty and after—a downside had never weighed against it. I never thought about how shitty the job might be or what it might do to you. I just knew it was the thing that would free me from the Dread. I thought about pocked-face, capillary-exploded Humpty-Dumpty and his death by a thousand cuts. The job had certainly not been kind to him. He didn't seem like an asshole, but then again maybe that's what the job did to you when you *weren't* an asshole. I staggered a few more steps toward the yacht club before I jettisoned the whole thing. It was simply too late for that kind of second guessing. I was already second guessing enough.

"I'm not that good," I said.

"That's not what John Henry says."

"Well then he doesn't know what the fuck he's talking about."

"He seems to know a lot about you, and he says you're really good."

"Anybody with a decent slider can get me out."

"What's a slider?"

"It's like a curveball, only harder to hit."

"Then learn to hit a slider."

"You want to hear the odds on getting to the major leagues?"

"No." She spun away from me and did a little pirouette in the gravelly road. "Fuck that. Who cares? Why would you even think about that shit?"

"Maybe it's just time to stop," I said.

"What does that mean?"

She was facing me now with a funny frown on her face.

I looked at the yachts for a second before I picked up another rock and tossed it.

"I don't know," I said. "Just... it sometimes feels like a burden, you know? Like I'm not playing for me."

"Who's it for then?"

"At first my mom, I think. Then Nathan. My grandmother. Larry. John Henry. I never know how to quit without disappointing someone. It just feels like it's time to stop, you know?"

She came back to take my hand, and we started down the dirt road again.

"I'm so sorry he got sick," she said.

"What?"

"Your little brother."

There had been a moment right before I dropped the note about Nathan in that girl's locker when I couldn't wait for her to read it because not only would someone else finally help me carry the weight of what had happened, but that someone else would also know that I'd chosen her to do it. I just didn't fully understand how heavy the weight was until it was obvious she wanted no part of it. I've hated that girl for as long as I can remember, but all she really did was protect herself from what was in that note, so I have to be very careful who I share Nathan's story with to make sure they're ready and willing to bear it with me. I wanted to tell Annie. I wanted to unwind the lie, but I couldn't take the risk. I picked up another rock and threw it even farther than the first one, beyond all the yachts moored in the deepest stretch of the river.

I lounged around her apartment for the next few days, but I really couldn't stop stewing on Goldman. I was still worried I'd fuck it up, so I got back to running interview questions through my head for hours on end so I wouldn't sound stupid when the time came. I hardly ever got up from the couch, but all that uncertainty bored a hole right through my head. I'd lie awake at night, worried about the future, until I realized the only thing that ever really enabled me to clear my mind was Annie, so I stopped trying to memorize meaningless answers to bullshit questions and just watched her sleep. What was she afraid of? Nothing it seemed, and it was like I was immune from the future when I was with her, like there was nothing it could do to me as long as she was around... and that's when her roommate threw the bedroom door wide open.

"Where the fuck are my Triscuits?!"

She was a stocky girl who looked a little like Betty Rubble, wearing nothing but an oversize blue T-shirt with the words "Van de Lay Industries" printed on the front, and she was distraught over an empty box of crackers.

"Jesus," said Annie, snapping awake. "What's wrong?"

"Where the fuck are my Triscuits?"

"Calm down," said Annie. "I don't know."

"No. I'm not calming down. He can't stay here."

"What happened?" said Annie.

"This is *my* apartment."

"What did we do?"

"It's *my* apartment, Annie."

"I didn't realize it was such a big deal."

"We have one bathroom." She was wiping tears from beneath her eyes. "One TV. He watched college basketball for like five hours yesterday. You weren't even here."

"I had to work."

"This morning you two took a forty-five minute shower. I paid for that, Annie. I paid for your dirty fuck water."

"I'm sorry."

"You think I want to hear you all night?"

"Okay. I'm sorry."

"He can't stay here," she said as she turned. "He leaves tomorrow... and he ate all my fucking Triscuits."

# Chapter 30

We had to move back into my place after that. We took Vandershar's room since he was never there, and before long Annie's stuff was all over the floor and food had magically appeared in the refrigerator. But Annie had this odd fascination with Yale, and since I didn't know shit about Yale, John Henry always seemed to be necessary.

We embarked on a never-ending campus tour. He'd point out the windowless crypts and stained glass panels. He'd pause under stone gargoyles, then show her the remnants of the real Yale Fence. We watched the Whiffenpoofs in Woolsey Hall. He showed her the stacks in Sterling and the weenie bins in Cross Campus. We saw the worst play in the history of theater at the Yale Rep. There was even a trip to the Beinecke Library for a white-gloved pawing of a "real Gutenberg Bible," whatever the fuck that is, and pretty soon she was tagging along with him to Shakespeare: Comedies, and Nineteenth-Century French

Art. What the fuck was I supposed to do? Make her sit through Applied Calculus and a Mandelbrot lecture on fractals?

I had my first real panic attack wedged in a hard wooden seat way in the back of Statistics 430b. I squirmed in that seat for forty-five minutes unable to focus or hear a word of the lecture. I just obsessed about what she was doing and who she was doing it with, until the dark finally closed in from all sides. I backed my way out of class with about fifteen minutes to go, before anyone else could see that I was hyperventilating, and then I ran home like a twat only to find her curled up on the couch with a book. I had to hide in the bathroom for half an hour just so she wouldn't see the hives all over my body. I told her there was something wrong with my stomach, which was somehow less embarrassing.

I emptied my bank account fending off John Henry after that. There were trains back and forth to the City—cabs, clubs, movies, dinners, cocktails, all of it financed by Chase Bank courtesy of one of the eighteen million credit card offers I got that semester. I dropped a hundred and eighty bucks one night on seaweed, sake, and fish parts that tasted like spare tire. It was a Tuesday. I know it was a Tuesday because Annie told me all about some chef she'd dated in New York, and how you never eat fish on Monday because the fishmongers were still unloading crap from the weekend.

I also know it was Tuesday because my Aunt Barb called on Wednesday to let me know my dad had died. John Henry was already in class and Annie was off taking care of scheming eight-year-olds, so I was alone in bed when she told me he'd had a stroke, but it was odd the way she said it, like she didn't really believe it, and it made me wonder if she was even telling me the truth. I didn't react really. I didn't say a thing. I just thought about Barb the whole time with her irritating voice and rotten daughters, but even after she hung up, I didn't really feel any different. She told me I could have his car. All I had to do was get down to Newark and pick it up. She didn't invite me to a memorial or a funeral or anything else, and I didn't think to ask. I didn't think to ask about anything. I just got dressed and headed to Statistics.

That night Annie took me up Dixwell Avenue to the three-family dwelling where her dope dealer lived. We edged up the side of this house in the pitch black to get to a concrete rectangle of backyard that smelled like dog shit. Three cracked concrete steps led to a rickety wooden door, and in the middle of the door was a rectangular hole. Annie put a finger up to my lips to keep me quiet. Then she knocked. A few seconds later a panel slid away. She slapped a ten dollar bill down, and then a disembodied hand took the money and set a Ziploc bag of weed down in its place. All I could think about the whole time was the Once-ler— this character from a Dr. Seuss book my mom used to read to my little brother. The Once-ler was a dick who destroyed an entire forest and everything in it just to make a three-armed sweater, but you never got to see the Once-ler. The most you ever got to see was a disembodied hand as it reached through a hole in a wall. I don't know how long I stood there like that, thinking about that book, seeing my mom turn the pages in my mind—seeing that green disembodied hand. It's a miracle nobody blew me off the stoop with a shotgun.

I backed down the steps real slow when I realized where I was and made a break for it. Annie was waiting, driver door open, and I dove in like we were Bonnie and Clyde, but my belt got caught on the gear shift, and I ended up just about having to take my pants off before we could go anywhere. Normally, that would have had her laughing hysterically before she swatted me, but now she seemed lost in her own thoughts and didn't find it funny at all. She hardly said a word as we crossed over the Quinnipiac

Bridge to buy a bag of Oreos and a six-pack of Coors Light at a gas station near the water in Branford, and after that, she quietly wound us through sandy streets and parked in the dirt driveway of the house her dad was building.

I could smell the salt of the Sound as I grabbed a blanket out of the trunk. We hopped a low concrete seawall onto the beach. The house seemed skeletal in the moonlight, this monumental cavernous thing with the ocean breeze blowing through windowless holes covered loosely with plastic tarp. I spread the blanket while Annie dumped a beer in the sand so she could make a pipe out of the can. Then she pulled a few buds out of the baggie and fired them up before she took a hit.

"Here," she said, holding her breath and handing the can to me.

I waved her off and got comfortable on the blanket.

"Are you for real?" Then she exhaled. "You just risked your life for this shit."

"It makes me a little paranoid."

"Fine." She lit up again, then took an enormous hit. "But I'm getting baked."

"Your house is gonna be huge."

I was still looking at it as I pulled a beer out of the six-pack.

"It's not my house."

"You're not gonna live here?"

"Are you kidding? I'm not gonna live with my dad."

She'd complained about him before, just a few backhanded comments that made him sound like a bullshit artist who had a habit of promising Annie things he didn't deliver, and then it occurred to me that I really hadn't thought about my own dad the whole day. I started to tell her what had happened, but I stopped because I really wasn't sure why she was so upset, and I was worried my dad's dying would only make her feel worse. But then

I couldn't stop thinking about him, and it was like I suddenly wanted to see him again, which only made *me* feel worse.

"What's he do anyway?" I said.

"He's a 'developer,'" she said with air quotes. "But mostly he does nothing."

"Do you even know where your mom is?"

"Oh, yeah," she said, ripping open the Oreos. "She's in Ocala. I'm eating these. You can have like two of these. My dad would go forever without 'developing' anything. She got tired of his bullshit and left... without me." She popped an Oreo in her mouth. "He finally built something again—some piece of shit strip mall down in Bridgeport. So what's he do?" She gestured toward the house. "He pisses every penny away on this money pit, and now he's not doing jack shit again. I don't know if this place'll ever get finished. He says it's the weather every time I ask him why it's taking so long, but it's total bullshit. He's out of money again."

The moon was full, and I could see the shore break lapping at the beach about twenty yards in front of us.

"How old were you when she left?"

"Ten."

"She didn't say anything?"

"Nope. One day she was there. The next day she wasn't."

"You ever talk to her?"

"No. Why would I do that?"

"I don't know. Why would you not do that?"

"Because I don't want to talk to her."

"You don't think about her?" I said.

"She left. What is there to think about?"

"I don't know. I wish it was that easy."

"It's different," she said. "Your mom was sick. She didn't abandon you. You can't blame her for that."

She didn't realize I was thinking about my dad and not my mom, but she could tell I was about to go down some dark hole too, so she pulled herself up into my lap to make us both feel a little better.

"Tell me about her," she said. "What was she like?"

I heard myself begin to speak, rattling off the benign waypoints of my mom's life like I was reading an obituary—born in Widworth, Massachusetts, tomboy, basketball star, met my dad in college, never worked outside the house, had four kids, *one of them dead, two of them incarcerated, the fourth a total pussy.* It all sounded perfectly normal the way I said it, except there was nothing normal at all about my mom's abbreviated life, and if I was being honest, I would have said that she was sad, and that when something pleasant ever did happen, she always seemed surprised, like she didn't deserve it, only I never understood why. But then I got to the part where she's lying in her bed, refusing to take any more of the drugs, surrounded by everybody but me.

"I wasn't there," I said, still staring at the water.

"You weren't where?"

"In the room."

"What are you talking about?"

"I was in the basement when she died."

"Why?"

"I didn't want to be there."

"Why?"

"Because I couldn't understand why she wouldn't take the drugs. It was like she wanted to die, you know, like she wanted to leave us, and I couldn't understand that. I was mad at her."

"You were just a kid."

I finally cracked open the Coors Light as I stared out into the night sky.

"Yeah... but I've always wondered if she knew."

"Knew what?"

"That I wasn't there. That I wasn't with her."

"What difference would that make?"

"I don't know. You don't think it made it worse, do you?"

She pulled my arms around her so I could hold her tighter.

"This feels good," she said. "I feel safe when I'm with you. When I was a little girl, I used to lie like this in the backyard with my Poppy and wait for the first star so I could make a wish."

"What would you wish for?"

"Usually ice cream."

She wolfed down another Oreo.

"Ice cream?"

"I was seven. What would *you* wish for?"

"If I was seven?"

"No. Now. What would you wish for right now?"

"I don't know."

"Come on. There must be something?"

I thought about it, but I didn't want to tell her what I'd really wish for, so I said something else.

"A job at Goldman."

"Seriously?"

"What's wrong with that?"

"Well, for starters, you already have that."

"I have an interview."

"Please. Jonathon hooked you up with a job. Not a job interview."

"I still have to do the interview."

"You have to go through the motions of an interview. It's not gonna matter."

"It will if I fuck it up."

"Are you seriously that worried about it?" She sat up to root through her purse. "Here," she said. Then she threw a bottle of pills at me. "Take these."

I set my Coors can in the sand and popped the top of the bottle open. It was filled with tiny green pills.

"What are they?"

"You need to stop stressing about this interview," she said. "It's driving *me* crazy. Just listen to their questions and be honest. That's all anybody gives a shit about. Just be a real person for fuck's sake. You're trying to remember all this other bullshit. If you do that, you won't hear what they're actually asking you, and that'll make it worse. It's like stage fright."

"What do they do?" I said, still looking down at the pills.

"They'll keep you from freaking out. Take one."

"Right now?"

"Yeah, they don't kick in for like a week. Take one every day. You can have the whole bottle if you want. I have a doctor friend who gets them for me."

I popped one and chased it with some Coors Light.

"You need to stop obsessing about this interview."

"What did you think you were gonna do when you graduated?"

"I didn't graduate."

"I thought you went to Providence."

"For two years."

"And then what?"

"I quit. I didn't like it."

"So what'd you do?"

"I went to Tokyo."

"Tokyo?"

"It was for a job."

"You want to hear something fucked up?"

"Sure," she said. "Tell me something fucked up about Tokyo."

"When I was at John Henry's a couple summers ago, there were all these Christmas cards stuck to the refrigerator, and in every one of them his whole family was dressed up in some stupid shit from wherever it was they went that year. You know, like a family trip. One of them was Tokyo."

"That is some really fucked up shit. A Christmas card stuck under a refrigerator magnet. Great story, Spencer."

"No. That's not the fucked up part. The fucked up part is it was all bullshit. They never went to Tokyo. His mom doesn't fly. They never went to any of those places."

"How'd they take a picture in Tokyo then?"

"They took it in front of a pagoda at SeaWorld."

"Why would they do that?"

"I don't know. It's fucked up though, isn't it? One year John Henry had to wear lederhosen and act like he was having the time of his life in Bavaria."

"Why don't they just wear Armani and pretend to be in Milan?"

"Good question."

"Does John Henry smoke weed? We should've invited him."

"John Henry's high school voted him most likely to become a truancy officer. What do you think?"

"That's not true."

"He does not smoke. I promise you."

"I love how you know everything there is to know about John Henry, and he knows everything there is to know about you."

"He doesn't know everything."

If she'd just asked, *What doesn't he know?* I think I would have told her about the Dread. I would have told her everything that was wrong with me. But she didn't.

"What kind of a name is John Henry anyway?" she said. "Who names their kid John Henry?"

"Henry is a family name on his mom's side. John is a family name on his dad's side. His first name was supposed to be Henry, and his middle name was supposed to be John, but his dad switched the names on the birth certificate."

"Where was his mom when this happened?"

"Intensive care."

"He did it on purpose?"

"He says he was tired."

"Jesus. I thought my dad was a jackass."

"No one's dad is a bigger jackass than John Henry's, but his mom's a piece of work too. She wouldn't let it go."

She sat up and took a long hit from her beer can pipe and then crawled back into my lap.

"When you saw him on the ground that night, how did you know what to do?"

"I don't know. I just didn't want him to get hurt. I wasn't going to let him get hurt."

"But you had to know they were going to hurt you instead."

"I don't know," I said, staring at my beer can. "Maybe I deserved it. Does that even make sense?"

"No. Why would you have deserved that?"

"I wish I didn't hit that guy. How's that for a wish?"

"Doesn't count."

"So what happened after Tokyo?"

"The job ended and I came back. That's when I worked at Maxime's."

"Maxime's?"

"John Henry's lingerie store."

"And then where'd you go?"

"Los Angeles."

"What'd you do there?"

"Nothing. That's why I came back."

"Great story, Annie."

"The real story is boring. It involves lawyers and a creep." She sat up to face me. "Those wishes don't count. Investment banking is lame. What would you really wish for?"

"I don't know."

"You really should have a wish handy. That way when someone asks you what you'd wish for, you'd already have something to say."

"I wish you'd stop asking me what I'd wish for."

"I'm serious. I'm being serious. What would you wish for?"

"You really want to know?"

"Yes. What is your wish?"

I took a sip of beer and thought for a minute.

"I wish I was from someplace like Maine."

"Maine? Why the fuck would you want to be from Maine? I just granted you one wish, and you pissed it away on your Goldman interview, and then I give you another wish, and you use it to be from Maine? What the fuck is wrong with you?"

"All you wanted was ice cream."

"I was seven."

"I don't know. It just seems like you'd be a part of something if you were from a place like that."

"A place like what?"

"Where you just did whatever your dad did, and that was it. Where you knew everything you ever needed to know and there was nothing to worry about."

"But you'd be in Maine."

"So?"

"So I'd want the fuck out of there."

# Chapter 31

*Summer 1992*

I started to refuse the horse pills and the little green pills and anything else that might leave me stupid and dickless for the rest of my life. The problem was Kyong wouldn't let me quit. We arm wrestled in broken English, until I realized he was trying to say the word "taper." He wanted me to taper my dose over time, but that shit was killing me. I was convinced that I'd wake up one day and never be able to climb out of the sludge, so I needed to be rid of it immediately. I hid the pills under my tongue each morning and spit them in the toilet the moment the nurse with the long fingernails was gone.

The first few days of cold turkey were miserable. A dense fog settled in, no different than the fog that rose in my head from taking that shit. It was like the pills refused to let me go. All I wanted to do was sleep, but then for a few days after that, it was like there was something alive just under the surface of my skin, creeping and crawling, and that misery made it impossible to sleep at all, and after I got through that, I was left fending off something more like smog, like the residual pharmaceutical sludge had ignited in the space behind my eyes and was now burning in the front of my brain. It was difficult to concentrate, so I'd read and reread the same paragraph about a hundred and fifty times when Nafziger showed up in the library that day. He grabbed one of the Signet Classics and sat down across from me.

"Finally taking on *Ulysses*, I see."

"Just started," I said.

"What do you think?"

"I don't love it... but I'm going to read it anyway."

"I've never seen someone so determined to suffer."

"I have a lot of catching up to do."

"Maybe you've suffered enough already."

"I meant the books."

"How about *A Portrait of the Artist as a Young Man?*"

"I finished it."

"And?"

"I think you'd have to be a complete pussy to like that book."

"Have you thought about writing yourself?"

"Writing what?"

"I don't know, but you might find it useful. You seem to dislike everything you read. Maybe you can do better."

"The Dedalus in *this* is okay, I guess."

"It's the same Dedalus."

"Yeah. I know."

I put the book down for a second, shut my eyes, and rubbed my temples.

"Maybe this will make you feel better," he said. He cracked open his own Signet Classic and started to read from it. "'Whenever you feel like criticizing anyone,' he told me, 'just remember that all the people in this world haven't had the advantages that you've had.'"

"I read that one too."

"Don't interrupt. We have a long way to go."

"That's gonna make Alan come in here."

"I doubt it," he said. "He thinks you're an undercover agent with the FDA."

"The what?"

"The Food and Drug Administration."

"They have undercover agents?"

"I have no idea actually."

He smiled when he said that like the whole idea was absurd.

"Why does he think that?"

"I don't know the answer to that either."

"What happened to him anyway?"

"To whom?"

"Alan. It looked like he had some kind of a seizure."

"Alan did? When?"

"The other night."

"What night?"

"The night Duddle tossed Leonard into the drywall."

"Timothy Duddle did what?"

"I don't think he meant to hurt him. Leonard kind of jumped him."

"Timothy caused Leonard's injuries?"

"He was trying to help Alan, but Leonard attacked him from behind. Alan was a mess. He was like... rigid... like stiff as a board, and his eyes were all rolled back up into his head."

"You saw this?"

"I'm not totally sure what I saw to be honest. I was pretty out of it." Nafziger had this faraway look on his face like something was horribly wrong. "I'm not an undercover agent with the FDA if it makes you feel any better."

I looked back down at the words I'd read over and over already, but then I stopped and looked back at Nafziger, who suddenly seemed unsteady, and I just felt like he deserved the truth.

"My grandmother lives in the East Wing," I said.

"I'm sorry?"

"That's what I'm doing here. I'm not a patient. I mean, I don't really belong here. I just didn't have anywhere else to go."

"Your grandmother?"

"I thought I could help her. I mean, I thought she could help me. I needed help... for something, but she's... she doesn't even know who I am."

"I see," he said, shifting in his chair.

"They keep telling me there's nothing I can do for her, but she doesn't have anyone else either... so I stayed."

"What happened that you needed her help?"

"I got thrown out of school."

"I see."

"Are you gonna make me leave?"

"Why would I make you leave?"

"Because I'm a liar. Because I shouldn't be here."

"Spencer, if I threw out all the liars, there'd be nobody left."

I looked back down at *Ulysses* with the smog still smoldering.

"You don't have to keep doing this," I said.

"Doing what?"

"Coming in here. You don't have to come in here every time you see me. There's nothing you can do for me either."

"What makes you think I come in here for you?"

My head now hurt too much to say anything else, so I just stared down at *Ulysses*.

"You know, one of my neighbors as a boy growing up in Chicago was blind as a bat, but she could hear the postman's footsteps a block away. My mother told me this was Mrs. Foley's gift from God. According to my mother, God had given Mrs. Foley extraordinary hearing because *He* had deprived her of sight."

"So?"

"Some years later I participated in a study that demonstrated that the loss of a sense results in the enhancement of the other senses as a matter of physiology, not metaphysics. We showed that the brain actually reallocates the unused computing power to, in effect, supercharge the other senses. As it turned out, God had very little to do with Mrs. Foley's glaucoma or her extraordinary auditory sensitivity."

"What does that have to do with anything?"

"We don't yet understand your grandmother's condition, but the brain is a system of infinite complexity with an extraordinary capacity to repair itself. Perhaps there's no need to give up hope."

# Chapter 32

*Spring 1992*

Annie lost an earring on the beach. That's how I met her dad. We went back out there the next day to look for it. Her dad was standing in the driveway staring up at the house. His name was Jack. He was taller than me and weathered in a rugged Marlboro Man sort of way. All I could think about was how horrible it must be to meet the guy who's drilling your daughter. I stumbled on the gearshift trying to get out of Annie's car and fell down right in front of him.

He gave me a death grip handshake. I did my best not to show the pain. Then I noticed a tattoo on his right forearm—one of those old faded green ones that looked like it had been there for about a hundred and fifty years. I started to tell him about mine, figuring it was good to have something in common, but I fumbled for the words when it occurred to me that my mangled cartoon bulldog really didn't have much in common at all with the crusty, green thing on his forearm. I shut my mouth and looked at Annie. She just smiled and mouthed the words *I'm sorry*.

"What brings you by?" he said.

"It doesn't look any different," said Annie.

"It's the weather. July's the month. Maybe August. A couple more months is all it'll take."

"You've been saying that for six months."

"July," he said. "Maybe August."

Now, in the daylight, I could see all the scaffolding everywhere and the construction debris. It didn't look anywhere near finished.

"I've been thinking about the landscaping," he said.

"You can tell Spencer about the landscaping," she said.

Then she left me there and hopped the seawall to go find her earring.

"You'll never fool that one," he said, shaking his head. "Always one step ahead." Then he looked at me. "So you're over there at Yale?"

"Yeah."

We started to walk around to the side of the house.

"What do you study?"

"Math."

"Math?" he said, surprised. "What's that lead to?"

"In terms of work?"

"Yeah. What do you do with a degree in math?"

"Investment banking."

"An investment banker," he said. "Now there's a change. Annie usually dates guitar players." He bent over and pulled a weed out of the ground. "How do you feel about Jesus by the way?"

"Jesus?"

"Yeah... Jesus. What's your stance there?" he said, sort of shaking the weed at me before he tossed it to the side.

"I'm a Methodist."

I'm not really sure what I am to be honest, but I figured when some girl's dad asks you what you think about Jesus, you have to be something.

"I guess that's alright. The last guy she brought around here was a born-again Christian. You ever have to deal with one of them born-agains?"

"I sat next to one on a plane once."

"Pushy bastards. This fella didn't care too much for me. I was involved in some litigation a few years ago and some people said some not too nice things about me, and I guess Annie must've told him something. Anyway, I won't bore you with the details. He come out here passing his religious literature around and pretty soon he'd converted my best drywallers and half the framers. They all walked off the job. They're all unemployed now. Doesn't make a goddamn bit of sense. They were building a house. Now I have the worst goddamn drywall job of all time."

"Annie dated a born-again Christian?"

"He didn't last very long. Thank God for that."

We turned the corner and came around to the back of the house with the beach right in front of us. Annie was on the spot where we'd spread the blanket the night before, now staring pensively out at the Sound.

Jack stopped when he saw her and watched for a bit.

"The thing about Annie is she disappoints too easy."

"She just dropped something over there last night," I said.

"The problem is, you go and throw away all the people who ever disappointed you and pretty soon you're just alone. Not everybody is disposable. No matter how bad they let you down."

He kept looking at her, like he was running through his head all the times he'd failed her, all the white lies he'd heaped on top of other white lies, like he was trying to figure out how to undo it all, and it made me feel kind of sorry for him. You could tell he'd fucked something up so unforgivably that he'd regret it for the rest of his life, and as I stared down at the sand, I wondered if my own dad had ever looked at me that way—like I was something he wanted back instead of something that reminded him of what was gone forever.

Jack turned to face me when he knew nothing could be done.

"So where will you work then?" he said. "New York City? Wall Street?"

"That's the plan."

"Which one of those banks you looking at?"

"Goldman Sachs."

"I don't believe I've worked with them. Goldman Sachs. What the hell's the name of that place? Morgan. Something Morgan."

"Morgan Stanley?"

"Yeah, that might be it. They were in on a deal we did out here a few years ago."

"What kind of a deal?"

"Shopping mall," he said. "I build shopping malls. One of those New York banks helped us finance a deal we did out in Wallingford a few years ago." He stopped and looked up at the back of his house. "All I ever wanted to do was build houses. There's art to it, you know. Meaning." Then he looked back at me. "Nobody should ever pat themselves on the back for building a shopping mall. There's no art to that. That's for goddamned sure."

We stayed outside for another few minutes. He walked me all around and told me all his plans for landscaping, but I really wasn't following much of it. We finally went in through the French doors on the far side of the house.

"Place was a mess when I bought it. In the end, I said to hell with it. We took it down to the studs and started over."

"The house that Jack built," I said.

"What's that?"

"Oh, nothing. Just a book my mom used to read to my little brother."

I followed him into a wide-open rectangular space with pipes sticking up out of the ground.

"This is the kitchen," he said. "Industrial specs. I don't even cook, but I love industrial kitchens. The roughed-in plumbing is already done. You can see here where they started in on the electrical." He pointed to a naked electrical box nailed to a stud about four feet off the ground. "We blew out two walls to open this up."

He couldn't keep his hands off the walls and the cabinets and the counters and everything else. I kind of miss Jack McIntyre. He just seemed like the kind of guy you might want to talk to every once in a while.

"It's the hourly guys that kill me," he said. "They show up and unload a bunch of crap out the back of their trucks. They mill around for a while. Half an hour goes by before they even get inside the house. I was a welder. I know how these guys operate. Half the time it's just a game to see what I'll give up on or what I'll forget. Nothing ever gets done right the first time. I can't believe how poor the trades have been on this job, and it's my own house. It's not just the drywallers either. None of 'em give a damn about what they're doing, and they're all pointing fingers at one another. You've got to build something you're proud of. Something that endures. That's the secret."

It occurred to me that I'd never built anything. When I was a kid my dad built a wooden platform that he attached to the aboveground swimming pool in our backyard. It didn't endure though. I spent a whole day coating it with what turned out to be some pretty fucking flammable shit because when Troy set it on fire, it burned a hole in the side of the pool in about five seconds, and five seconds later a thousand gallons of water filled our basement. Nobody built much of anything after that.

"The original sink was way the hell over there," said Jack, pointing at the far wall. "I wanted two sinks, and I wanted them side by side on an island that floated out over here. Those right there are the original drain pipes." He pointed at two capped black pipe stubs sticking out from the wall. "We'll hide those behind some cabinets. The PVC are drain pipes. The copper is the water supply. We had to drill holes right through the subfloor to run pipe down into the basement. Of course, when we did that, we found out the subfloor was rotten, so we had to replace it. That delayed the job two months. The weather and the Sound eat these places alive. This whole house was nearly rotten. Come on through here. This is the living room."

It was the size of a small gym with a twenty-foot ceiling and a wall of French doors looking out the back to the Sound. The sun was going down, and the house cast a long shadow all the way to the water, which made the place seem enormous.

"Just look at this," said Jack. "Drywall has to be the easiest goddamned trade of them all. Look at this."

He was running his hand along a sheet of drywall that had been hung in the living room. I leaned in closer to see what it was that had him so bent out of shape. There were tiny bubbles and pockmarks everywhere.

"I can't paint this," he said. "Somebody's gonna have to come in here, remud this and sand it down until we can put a coat of primer on it." He ran his hand along the wall, and I could see that old green tattoo again. "You see where the drywall meets the wood beams in the ceiling? You see how ragged that looks? Any time two different surfaces meet, that's where the art is. There's art in this. Don't ever punch a clock. Make your work a part of you.

A man can find himself in a job like this, and there's nothing you can buy that'll ever make you that happy."

"What's the tattoo of?" I asked.

"This?" He turned back to face me as he ran his other hand over it. "You can't read it anymore."

We could see Annie through the French doors, still staring at the water.

"What was it?" I said.

"Nothing special."

"I've got one too."

I pushed my shirt up over my shoulder so he could see my mangled little bulldog.

"Jesus, what happened to it?"

"It's kind of a long story."

He took a closer look.

"What's wrong with its ear?"

"That was a mistake."

"Hell, son. That's not a mistake. Tattoo a woman's name on your arm. Now, that's a mistake."

# Chapter 33

We played the University of New Haven a couple days later. We played them every year in a thing they called the New Haven City Series. It was UNH, Southern Connecticut, Quinnipiac, and Yale, but UNH went to the Division II College World Series just about every year, so they usually beat the shit out of the rest of us. New Haven's head coach was a foulmouthed, potbellied little man everyone called Porky. The local baseball people worshipped him, and he and Canelli had known each other forever. Somebody once told me they shared the backcourt at Shelton High School an eon before. Canelli would follow Porky around the whole City Series, comparing notes, acting like they were equals, but mostly he was just kissing his ass.

"It was pizza," said Larry right before the game started.

We were still down in the dugout waiting for the PA announcer to finish blathering about something to do with the City Series so we could take the field.

"What was pizza?" said John Henry.

"Pizza is what was invented in New Haven."

"No," said John Henry. "Well, that too, but I was talking about the hamburger. I was there."

"You were there when they invented the hamburger?" said Norman.

"Nobody invented the hamburger," said Larry. "It's a fucking hamburger."

"Louis' Lunch," said John Henry. "You don't believe me, just go there. It's on Crown across from our building. Annie took me."

"What the hell are you doing?" said Canelli, peering into the dugout.

"John Henry says the hamburger was invented in New Haven," said Larry.

"The game is about to start."

"Pizza maybe... but the hamburger?"

"You think you can pull your head out of your ass long enough to get on the mound?"

"Is it this way?" said Larry, pointing up the steps.

The sun was actually shining when we took the field. The temperature was in the seventies, and we had a real crowd for a change since all the teams were local. I kept looking for Annie in the grandstand, but I couldn't find her. There were too many people, so I gave up and threw my last warm-up toss across the diamond before the umpire brushed off home plate to get the game started. Larry's first pitch was right down the middle. The umpire called it a ball anyway. Every umpire within a hundred miles of New Haven worshipped Porky too.

"Where is that?" said Larry, but he didn't get an answer. "Is it up?"

"Let's go!" yelled Canelli. He was already on the top step of the dugout. "Throw strikes."

The next pitch got lined straight over Larry's head. The pitch after that got ripped into the gap in right center for a run scoring double, and just like that Canelli threw his hands up and disappeared back into the dugout. UNH just seemed to hit everything. Inside, outside, up, down. It didn't matter where Larry threw it, they hit it, and they hit it hard. A booming double that short-hopped the left field fence. Another line drive single up the middle. Then a double down the right field line. A walk. Another double, but Canelli just sat there and did nothing. It was 5–0 and still there was no one warming in our bullpen. The next pitch got lasered into left, but I cut the throw home. A relay was pointless, and then I saw Larry bent over at the back of the mound. I walked the baseball over to him. He took it and looked up at the green wall in center field.

"That pitch was six inches outside," he said. "He hit it like he knew it was coming."

"Let's go!" yelled Canelli from the shadows.

"He's gonna let me die out here, isn't he?"

"It looks like it."

"What happens if I can't get an out? Does this just go on forever?"

"You're gonna get an out."

"That's not much consolation. I actually need three."

He bent down and picked up the rosin bag and then looked over at Porky.

"It would've been nice to beat these guys just once."

"Porky might be a bigger dick than Canelli."

"Well," he said, tossing the rosin back down onto the dirt. "We might as well enjoy ourselves."

That's when it got a little weird. First of all, when I turned to head back to third base, I spotted Annie. She was right there in the first row along the third baseline with her white sneakers up on the railing. I got so anxious worrying the next rocket would be launched right at me that I was actually looking down at my feet when Larry delivered the next pitch. Fortunately, it was a ball and nobody swung at it. Then Larry started to talk to himself. I was too far away to hear what he was saying, but it was this whole Mark Fidrych routine between pitches, like he was psyching himself up or something. Then he started talking to the umpire. He started telling the home plate umpire where he thought every pitch was. It seemed like it might get a little contentious, but Larry just kept complimenting the guy for getting most of the calls right, and all this continued until Larry finally got an out—a lazy fly ball to Billy in right field—but by the time the inning ended, it was 7–0.

"Hardest throwing right-handed Jew my ass," said Canelli to no one in particular when Larry sat back down on the dugout bench.

The bombardment continued in the second inning as the clouds rolled in, but Larry talked himself right through it. It was like he'd been ordered to push a rock up a hill forever, but instead of letting it make him miserable, he just started pushing. He varied his windup—Luis Tiant one pitch, Dwight Gooden the next. He threw pitches he didn't even have—knuckleballs, forkballs, a circle change. It was like he was trying to complete some pitcher's bucket list in the space of an inning, but the whole thing really had only one purpose. Larry just wanted to keep everyone preoccupied and amused so he could get outs, but none of it amused Porky, and the crowd was only getting more hostile. They were there to see UNH, not Larry, so when he struck out one of their best hitters and took a bow, it only made it worse.

"Have some class!" yelled Porky.

So Larry turned to Porky and bowed again, only this time it was one of those elaborate, aristocratic bows with one leg straight out in front, his hat in hand with a sweeping grandiose gesture like he was greeting Louis XIV. That's when Canelli came flying out of our dugout. It usually took him about six weeks to walk from the dugout to the mound, but this time I had to hurry to get there before him.

"This clown show is over," he said.

"What clown show?" said Larry.

"You're embarrassing yourself."

"That's weird. I'm not trying to embarrass myself. Is it happening anyway?"

"Not trying to embarrass yourself? This is an *abortion*."

He said it loud in his whiny fly voice, only he tried to throw a little laughter in at the end to make it sound like he didn't care, but then he looked into the UNH dugout to make sure Porky had heard him.

"They were just better than me today," said Larry, handing Canelli the ball as he walked off the mound.

"Where are you going?"

Larry did a sort of pirouette as it started to drizzle.

"You shouldn't take it personally."

Then he spun back around, leaving Canelli there on the mound holding the baseball with no one warm in our bullpen. He had to pull somebody straight out of our dugout to finish the inning.

He emptied our bench after that. Then he banished Dicky Janice from the third base coaching box. The last place in the world Canelli wanted to be was inside our dugout with us, so he took the field and exposed himself to the ridicule of that crowd instead, but then he stood there at the back of the third base coaching box with his arms folded across his chest like he had nothing to do with our performance, like he was trying to remind everyone in that stadium that he was one of them and not one of us.

The intermittent rain was pretty unremarkable really, but with the score the way it was, you could tell the umpires were looking for any excuse to put us all out of our misery, so when the drops started to come down a little fatter in the sixth inning with the score 13–0, the home plate umpire took his mask off and motioned for Canelli and Porky to join him. Canelli just stood there for a second, arms still folded, and then a little smirk came to his face as he took a step forward, knowing he had one more indignity to endure. It was like a contest to see which of them could take longer to walk the fifteen steps to home plate. Porky won, but by the time he got there, it wasn't raining anymore.

"You ever notice how obsequious Canelli gets around Porky?" said Norman.

"You ever notice how nobody knows what obsequious means?" said Larry.

I don't know why, but Canelli just refused to accept his fate. He coached an Ivy League team, not a team of hard-nosed pricks whose last names all ended in vowels. He was Sisyphus too—only miserable.

Then I noticed John Henry down the third baseline chatting up Annie.

"Does it bother you that John Henry is dating your girlfriend?" said Larry.

No matter how many countermeasures I deployed, no matter where I took her, no matter how much money I spent, John Henry was always waiting there when we got back, relentlessly pursuing his long game while I had to pretend not to care.

"They're friends," I said.

"You know, Melody told me she'd fucked nineteen other guys."

"Why?" I said, still watching John Henry.

"Why'd she tell me or why'd she fuck nineteen other guys?"

"Why'd she tell you?" I said as the game resumed without us. "I can guess why she fucked the nineteen other guys."

"Exactly," he said with his index finger in the air. "Exactly. That's why I asked her. Think about it. For a girl who's out there, in the game, the blow job-to-sex ratio has to be at least three to one. So if she's fucked nineteen guys, that means she's sucked what? Fifty-seven dicks?"

It turned out Melody the Vegetarian Girl's primary source of protein might have been dick. Number twenty was Larry, of course, but number twenty-one was the guy who lived upstairs from Larry. That one she got reverse cowgirl while we were on a road trip to Harvard. The guy told his entire suite, and when Larry found out, he went on a two-day bender that involved a bottle of Wild Turkey and a tray of veal parmesan.

"You're the math guy," he said. "If you've sucked fifty-seven dicks, and you've been fucked, let's say three hundred times, because you know some of those guys were plowing her for weeks at a time, plus an extra couple hundred blow jobs just to be conservative, how much is that?"

"How much *what* is that?"

"Well, just... assume I'm right. Let's say a load is an ounce. How many ounces in a gallon?"

"I have no idea," I said.

"You're the math guy," he said again.

"I'm the math guy, not the weights and measures guy."

"Isn't it sixteen?"

"I think that's mass," I said. "It's different for volume."

"Eight ounces in a cup," said Norman. "Two cups in a pint. Two pints in a quart. Four quarts in a gallon."

"So do the math," said Larry. "Five hundred fifty-seven ounces. How many gallons is that?"

"Around four," I said.

"The girl's only twenty. She'll have another fifteen, twenty gallons of semen through her before she's done."

"Cole," said Canelli, peering under the overhang. "Where's Cole?"

"He's down there," said Norman, nodding toward Annie.

Canelli shot a glance down at John Henry and an odd look crossed his face like he'd finally seen everything.

"Tell him to stop playing grab-ass and go warm up."

"He's not playing grab-ass, sir," said Norman. "They're just friends."

The game was now waiting for Canelli with the home plate umpire holding things up until he got back in the coaching box, but Canelli wouldn't budge. He stayed right there on the dirt in front of the dugout, looking at Norman almost like he wanted to take a swing at him.

"This is a big joke to you, isn't it?" he said. "What do you care? You're all gonna go off to Wall Street and make a million dollars. You know what's gonna happen to me? They're gonna fire me!"

"That's Spencer's girlfriend," said Larry.

"Shut up," said Canelli. Then he turned back to the plate to find Billy Clark, one foot still in the batter's box, patiently waiting for Canelli to flash the signs. "What do *you* want? Hit a thirteen-run home run. How's that? Can you do that?"

"Be tough out there, kid!"

"Battle him now!"

"How many guys has Annie fucked?" said Larry.

"I have no idea."

"Well, you should find out. You want to spend the rest of your life with a pig? You want to pledge your existence to a sex addict?"

"Annie's not like that," I said as I thought of guitar players and born-again Christians and that chef from New York.

Norman grabbed John Henry to lead him away from Annie and down to the bullpen.

"How do you know?" he said. "You're not asking because you're afraid of the answer, and if you're afraid of the answer, you're ruined anyway because you'll always wonder how many dicks she's sucked. Your imagination will ultimately supply a number. It'll be generous. You'll start to do the math and the next thing you know she's fucking your upstairs neighbor."

Billy's at bat lasted forever. I started to feel this odd animosity as he worked the count full. He fouled off one meaningless pitch after another like he was grinding out an at bat in the seventh game of the World Series while I pondered how many dicks Annie'd sucked, but the animosity wasn't directed at Billy or Larry for that matter. For some reason, I was mad at Annie—like how dare she suck so many dicks? Then Billy hit a rocket into the gap in left center field that got caught on the dead run for the final out of the inning, and our dugout instantaneously emptied of underclassmen. Canelli had to wait for them all running around like chickens with their heads cut off to take the field before he could descend back to his corner of the dugout, so he was still up on the dirt when John Henry and Norman got back from the bullpen.

"Where do you want me?" said John Henry, all eager to take the field for the first time in his Yale baseball career.

"Where do I want you?" said Canelli. "I don't want you anywhere."

"Norman said you wanted me to warm up."

"I wanted Norman to warm up. I wanted you to warm up Norman. Jesus Christ." He looked at Norman. "Did you warm up at all?"

"I played catch with John Henry."

"You played catch... with John Henry."

He looked out beyond them with a pained smile like there was nothing left we could take from him. Then he shook his head and looked over his shoulder at Porky, who was still stationed with one foot up on the top step of the first base dugout, ready to score thirteen more. And just like that, Eddie Canelli turned and strolled down the left field foul line. He tipped his cap to Annie as he passed her by and stopped only when he reached the bullpen, where he stood motionless for a while. He stared pensively into the expanse of that giant outfield as Norman took a baseball and headed to the mound to keep the clown show rolling. Then, before the game could begin again, he opened the side gate next to the bullpen mound and just left, and as I sat there struggling to prevent my imagination from supplying a number, it occurred to me that Canelli wasn't like Sisyphus at all. He was the Lorax right as he lifted his tail to disappear through a hole in the clouds. The Lorax quit. Sisyphus never stops.

# Chapter 34

Annie's little green pills didn't seem to be doing anything, so I took two more the morning of my Goldman interview, but I was still freaking out about an hour before I had to head up to Vlad the Impaler's, so I called Vandershar in a panic.

"What is wrong with you?" he said. "You're gonna fuck it up if you can't calm down. Do me a favor and don't even say anything. Alright? Just sit there. And be on time for fuck's sake."

I threw up in the kitchen sink. My mind was racing with all the shit I worried Goldman might ask about—manhole covers... standard deviations... Flannery O'Connor... dollar cost averaging. It was a cyclone of unrelenting thought. I didn't want to look stupid. I couldn't let them see I was an idiot. Then I worried I'd puked up the drugs, so I took another pill and realized I'd also puked on my only tie, so I rushed to put one of John Henry's on while I started to pit out my suit.

The guy from Goldman was all polished and shiny like a Navy pilot. I shook his hand, sat down, and immediately forgot his name.

"Spencer Mazio," he said. "I've been looking forward to meeting you."

I followed Vandershar's instructions and sat there with my mouth shut.

"You're leading the Ivy League in home runs," he said. "Impressive at Yale Field. That park is huge and the ball carries for shit."

His tie had the biggest knot I'd ever seen. It was like a knot tied on top of a knot tied on top of another knot, and it was perfectly triangular, this perfect triangular knot. I couldn't stop looking at it.

"I played shortstop at Princeton," he said.

It was a perfect equilateral triangle.

"I graduated in '81."

This time he waited an extra beat for me to say something, but I was pleasantly glazed over, and I couldn't take my eyes off his tie.

"You guys had Ron Darling," he said. "We never beat him. He shut us out three years in a row. I was actually at the Northeast Regional when Yale played St. Johns. Darling against Viola. That might be the greatest college baseball game ever played."

"We screwed up a first and third," I said.

It came out so smooth and creamy I wanted to say it again.

"Exactly. St. Johns scored an unearned run in the tenth. How does that even happen?"

"We have a defensive playbook an inch thick," I said. "Nobody can figure it out."

All we did was talk baseball after that. The guy loved the Yankees. Everything fell into place. My thoughts somehow synched to what I actually wanted to say. He told me his all-time favorite player was Bucky Dent. I told him my girlfriend had a crush on Bucky Dent. I told him about my autographed team photo of the 1961 Yankees, and how it was hanging right at that moment from a nail in my kitchen. Then I rattled off the top row like I had the memory of a bull elephant: *There they are, the league-leading, pennant-minded Yankees. From left. Ford, Skowron, Maris, Tresh, Hegan, Crosetti, Houk, Sain, Moses, Boyer, Mantle and Richardson*—the names of strangers seared into my head after staring endlessly at a photograph that reminded me of my dead brother.

He did ask me about the toilet I smashed in the locker room after a doubleheader at Princeton, but he didn't seem too bothered by it. He told me that was the kind of competitor he was too. We talked about nothing but baseball. That was it. That was the whole interview, and when it was over, he told me he wanted to bring me down to New York to meet more people.

"I think you're gonna do great at Goldman," he said. "Get a new tie though. What is that thing?"

I felt like I'd just gotten away with something unspeakable, and for like a second I thought about all the suckers grinding away just for the chance to interview for a job I got by basically doing nothing, and I wondered how anyone could ever think that all the effort in the world meant more than a single connection and a couple home runs at Yale Field, but as I got further from Vlad the Impaler's and the euphoria dissipated, I actually convinced myself that I deserved that job. I deserved it precisely because I didn't deserve it. I didn't know shit about anything, but how was that my fault? It was like I'd cashed in on all my bad luck, like all the shit that had happened was a debt owed to me.

I couldn't wait to tell Annie, but when I got home, she was nowhere to be found. I started to get anxious again looking for her. I was coming down off the little green pills, so I took another and called Vandershar, thinking that might make me feel better, but I barely listened to him after I told him about the interview. I did my best to contain the distress, but all I could really do was wonder where Annie was. Why wasn't she there waiting for me? Why wasn't she the first to hear the news?

"What'd I tell you?" he said. "I just talked to Jerry. We're gonna meet at his place tonight."

"For what?"

"We're celebrating."

"Is that a good idea?"

"Don't be an idiot. He runs the high-yield desk at Goldman."

"I need to get to my dad's tomorrow."

"That's in Newark, right? Stay here tonight, then head over in the morning."

"John Henry's supposed to take me."

"Just have Annie do it. Or get a car."

"I don't know where she is."

"He's expecting us," said Jonathon. "You need to do this." I could hear keys in the front door. "This is how it starts."

The front door flew open. Annie and John Henry came crashing through, giggling like fools.

"There he is!" said John Henry. "How'd it go?"

"Where've you been?" I said.

"Doing laundry," she said. "John Henry says you haven't washed your sheets since he's known you."

"Is that my Christmas tie?"

I put the phone back up to my ear.

"What time do you want us down there?"

# Chapter 35

Jerry's doorman was dressed like an organ grinder's monkey. He took us up in an elevator that opened straight into an apartment that was all white marble and white rugs and white walls. It felt like an ice cave, except for this mural in the living room that was supposed to be some Portuguese seaport. That's where Jerry was—in the living room with that little pixie-girl Sabine. You had to walk a couple steps down to get there. He was sitting on a white daybed, and Sabine was stretched out on a white shag rug next to a life-size porcelain dalmatian, rubbing Jerry's feet. Vandershar introduced Annie. Then Annie gave Sabine a big hug since she had no idea Sabine would be there.

"And you remember Spencer," said Vandershar.

Jerry stood as I stepped forward to shake his hand.

"How can I forget the man who threw twenty-seven thousand dollars worth of art and furniture out the penthouse window of the Waldorf Astoria?"

The Dread overwhelmed what was left of the little green pills inside me—my first taste of how imperfect those pills really were—and I felt lightheaded.

Then Jerry looked at Annie.

"Did you know this?" he said. "He got trashed in my suite and threw half the place out the window."

"It was three years ago," said Vandershar. "Go get Spencer and Annie some drinks for fuck's sake."

"The glasses are Waterford," said Jerry. "He's not gonna throw them out the window is he?"

Jerry disappeared into the kitchen, and a familiar knot tightened in my stomach, and not the perfectly equilateral Goldman knot either. This was the perfectly fucked up Gordian knot that made me want to vomit. Everything felt wrong, but all Vandershar did was pop in a CD and dance his way back over to me like it was nothing.

"What was that?" I said.

"He's messing with you."

"What'd you tell him?"

"I was the one who paid for it. The least you can do is be the one who did it. We might want to go easy on the Goldman shit tonight."

"What the fuck does that mean? What else are we doing here?"

"Relax. I'm in escrow on the loft. We'll be in there in six weeks. It's all good. I'll take care of it."

"Take care of what?"

"Why don't you calm down and try to enjoy yourself for once?"

Sabine was now explaining to Annie the significance of the Portuguese seaport.

"What is *she* doing here?" I said.

"I can't get rid of her. We went out a couple times. She asked me to take some headshots. I told her it was over. She put her mom on the phone, and this woman spent half an hour telling me why I should date her daughter. She had a whole list of reasons fired up and ready to go. It was fucking nuts."

Jerry came back from the kitchen with a couple gin and tonics.

"Come on," said Sabine, grabbing Annie by the hand to lead her back up the stairs. "Let me show you around."

"What is she gonna show her?" said Vandershar as they wandered off. "She's only been here an hour."

"An hour is enough for me," said Jerry.

"Not interested, are you?" said Vandershar.

"No thanks. I have enough neurotics in my life. I was kidding by the way when I asked her to rub my feet. I didn't think she'd actually do it."

"What happened to the girl you were dating?" I said.

Jerry looked at Jonathon like I was speaking another language.

"He means the Dog Food Heiress."

"I haven't seen her in over a year. Nice girl, also neurotic, but a totally different kind of pain in the ass. These two are easy." He stuck a finger in Vandershar's chest. "You're nothing but a free dinner and a house in the Hamptons to these girls. If you play nice, pretty soon they're calling all the time. They're cluttering up your life. It's not worth it."

We ate at some Italian restaurant on the West Side. I can't remember the name of it. There were maybe fifteen tables. It was crowded and loud, and the whole place seemed to be lit from the ground with a dim golden glow. Jerry paid the maître d' a hundred dollars just so he could seat us at a round table near the kitchen. Our waiter had a bald dome of a head and a dark bushy mustache, and he stared pompously off into the distance when he spoke, so when Jerry wouldn't look up from the wine list while he ordered the champagne, they had an entire conversation where they never saw each other. Then the Dome-Headed Waiter disappeared through the kitchen doors and Jerry turned back to me.

"So I still can't book a room at the Waldorf," he said, dragging a piece of sourdough through olive oil. "What the fuck? Help me understand your thought process."

I still wasn't sure if he was serious.

"Hello? Anyone home?"

"I don't know," I said.

"You don't know? You don't know what?"

I looked at Vandershar, hoping he might put an end to the joke, but Jonathon was now staring at his plate.

"Is that it?" said Jerry. "Is that all you have to say? You throw half the suite out the window, and you don't even know why. It's pretty fucked up, don't you think?"

It was like he was inside my head, banging on the bottom of a stainless steel pot with a metal spoon.

"So is asking somebody to rub your feet before dinner," said Annie.

Jerry hung on looking at me for a beat, just long enough to make sure I knew he thought I was an idiot. Then he set his sights on Annie.

"Sabine tells me she's a model," he said. "What is it that you do?"

"I'm not really working… right now."

"Are you sure?"

"Modeling is beneath Annie," said Sabine.

"I wore underwear in the Sunday newspaper. That's nothing to be proud of."

"My agent says if you can wear lingerie, you can wear anything," said Sabine.

The whole time a small army of little Italian guys took plates off our table and put other plates on our table while I wondered what exactly this guy could do to me and my offer from Goldman.

"If selling underwear is not the apex of your ambition," said Jerry, "then what exactly does Annie McIntyre plan to do?"

"It's a secret," she said.

"Really," he said, leaning forward onto his elbows. "I'll bet I can figure it out."

"Why don't you tell us how *you* got to be such a huge success?" she said.

"Okay." He sat back into his chair. "Fine. I'll go first. I certainly don't have any secrets. It was lucky how I ended up on the debt side. I'll admit that." He ran another piece of sourdough through the olive oil. "After I finished Harvard, they randomly assigned me to fixed-income. The debt side was supposed to be boring. The equity guys all thought we were dipshits, but it was the best thing that ever happened to me. The credit markets move the equity markets. It's not the other way around, and a loan is nothing but math. I was good at math, and math, along with the arcane documents that come with it, is a barrier to entry to all the fucktards in equity who don't know shit about anything. I started in sovereign debt. They had me flying back and forth between Buenos Aires and New York every other week for a year. It turned my hair gray, but when it was over, they wouldn't let me leave to go back to business school."

"Why not?" said Annie.

"They didn't want to lose me," he said. "They promoted me instead."

"What's sovereign debt?" said Sabine.

"I wasn't finished," he said. He turned back to Annie. "The equity guys are morons. They're sheep, and what's better, we have an army of propeller heads right now coming up with algorithms so computers can trade equities for us. These guys are gonna get fucked out of their jobs, and they're so stupid, they don't even know it. They think all this software is making life easier. It's making them obsolete... but the thing is, a computer can only make trades based on the algorithm you put in it. A computer's not an entrepreneur. It doesn't create products. Don't let anyone ever tell you they came up with the collateralized mortgage obligation or mortgage-backed securities. I was doing that shit before anyone. We made that market. *We're* the entrepreneurs.

I had lunch just the other day with a guy at JP Morgan who's working on a thing he calls a credit default swap. It's basically insurance against something that will never happen. It's brilliant. We'll sell that shit forever."

He wiped his mouth on his napkin.

"Now it's your turn."

"How can I possibly top that?" she said. "You're successful because you're smarter than everyone else."

"I'm successful because I work harder than everyone else."

"Are you sure?"

"You don't have a problem with work, do you?"

"Annie wants to be an actress," said Sabine.

"Now that was a little anticlimactic, don't you think?" said Jerry. "Did you not understand the game?"

The Dome-Headed Waiter stepped between them and proceeded to spend five minutes telling us about the specials even though nobody cared. I couldn't concentrate. All these worried thoughts were racing through my head, so by the time the Dome-Headed Waiter was done, I'd forgotten what I actually wanted. Then Sabine wouldn't eat anything. Vandershar tried to order a Caesar salad for the whole table, but Sabine said she'd rather die than eat an anchovy. She wanted a plain salad with "regular lettuce" and not the kind that looked like "weeds in the backyard." She wouldn't eat the calamari or the clams or the beef carpaccio, and she made the Dome-Headed Waiter go through the entire menu and tell her what had oil, cream, or butter in it, and after all that, all she ordered was a plain chicken breast.

"He's gonna spit in our food for sure," said Vandershar when it was over.

"Fine with me," said Sabine. "I'd rather eat somebody's spit than butter."

"Okay," said Jerry. "So Annie here wants to be an actress... even though the odds against that are astronomical. I mean, let's be real. No offense, but you might want to have a plan B. Nevertheless... for fun, let's assume she's in good faith. What about you Sabine? You can't be a model forever. What are you going to be when you grow up?"

"Can we talk about something else?" said Annie.

"What would you rather talk about?" said Jerry.

"How about anything?"

"Okay," said Jerry. "How about books? Do you read?"

"I am capable of reading, yes," said Annie.

"Good," said Jerry. "I just started Joyce's *Ulysses*. It's my second time actually. I'd love to get your perspective. Have you ever read anything by James Joyce?"

"Not really," she said.

"How about the life insurance salesman and hater of crystal decanters everywhere? You haven't said shit all night. You ever read Joyce?"

I wanted to shut him up, but all I could really think to do was grab the back of his head and dredge his face through the olive oil. Why didn't I just tell him I was a math major? That probably would've stopped him right there. I could have told him about my algorithm—about how intragame betting on baseball was no different from intraday trading on the stock market, how it made no sense that betting on sports ended when the games started— but I was frozen in my seat, terrified that if I opened my mouth, he'd cut me to shreds and end my future at Goldman right there, so I said nothing and left Annie to fend for herself.

"I prefer Jane Austen," she said.

"Really," said Jerry. He shoved another piece of bread in his mouth and started chomping on it. "You prefer Jane Austen. How can you prefer Austen if you've never read Joyce?"

"I've never finished anything by James Joyce," she said. "I don't like it. It's tedious."

"*Ulysses* is the finest novel ever written," he said. "It's only tedious if you can't understand it."

"What's it about?" said Sabine.

"Loneliness," said Jerry. "Betrayal. Exile. How love is an illusion. Joyce swallows Austen whole."

"That's not what *Ulysses* is about," said Annie.

"I thought you didn't finish it."

"That doesn't mean I don't know what it's about."

"Then what's it about?"

"*Ulysses* is about love."

"Is it?"

"She loves him in the end."

"She fucks another guy," said Jerry.

"But they still love each other."

"I think Bloom's just a colossal pussy who doesn't do shit when his wife starts banging the concert manager."

"Maybe love is worth more than that," she said.

"Worth more than what?"

"Than whatever might come between you and it."

"Love is more like a pain killer," he said. "But the pain never really goes away. You just can't feel it for a while. The thing is, when you dull it like that, it just gets stronger. It starts to feed on whatever you're suppressing it with, until finally it's just fucking monstrous. So do you really want to count on somebody else for your own happiness? I mean, do you really want to take that risk?" He nodded at me. "What about him? Can you count on him? He's sitting there with his thumb up his ass while I have my way with you."

"You're not having your way with shit," she said. "I feel sorry for you."

"It's better to see the world as it is than the way you want it to be, don't you think?" Then he took a sip of champagne. "T. S. Eliot thought *Ulysses* was a landmark in art because it would destroy civilization. Now T. S. Eliot was an asshole, but he got that right."

"He got what right?" said Vandershar.

"We're not in this together," said Jerry. "It's every man for himself."

"That's not what T. S. Eliot was saying," said Vandershar. "*Ulysses* is vulgar. It's honest. Civilization is the lie. Honesty was going to destroy the bullshit of civilized bourgeois hypocrisy in England. That's what he was saying. Where do you get this shit?"

I'd never read Jane Austen. I'd never read James Joyce, and I'd never heard of T. S. Eliot. It really is awful to know nothing about anything. At some point in your life, you have to open up your mouth and know what the fuck you're talking about.

Jerry monopolized the conversation after that. It wasn't even a conversation really. It was just him talking about himself— one boring story after another. The first was about a typhoon in the Seychelles, then a leak at his vacation home in Miami, then something about a knee injury in Park City, and then a broken putter at Pinehurst. He finished with a story about a plane crash he survived in Idaho. I couldn't take my eyes off Annie, but she wouldn't look at me. She stared straight down at her food the whole time. I don't think she even touched it. Jerry droned on about this G4 and how it had too much weight on it and how it couldn't get enough lift at takeoff so it ended up perched in the pine trees at the end of some runway. Nobody even got hurt, but when he was done, there wasn't any oxygen left in the room, so nobody said a thing. Jerry sat back, oblivious that no one else had spoken in half an hour, slugged a shot of espresso, then got up to pay the bill since the Dome-Headed Waiter was back to ignoring us. When he came back, he shook Jonathon's hand, leaned over and whispered something in his ear, and then took off before Annie and Sabine were even back from the bathroom. He didn't say a word to me. He just left the restaurant and got in a cab.

# Chapter 36

I had a horrible ringing in my ears when we got into our own taxi, and there was an unbearable downward pressure on my shoulders. I couldn't even turn my head. All I could do was look straight into the oncoming traffic. Jonathon leaned forward into the front seat to tell the cab driver to take us down to Bleecker Street. Then he flopped into the back seat.

"Who wants to drop some X?"

"I do," said Annie. "That guy was a prick."

"Not me," said Sabine. "I heard a kid in Tribeca got paralyzed from one hit. It dries up your spine."

I would've freebased dog shit to get the thought of Jerry Sandoval out of my head, so the three of us did it right there in the cab, these little white tablets (along with the little green one I took too for good measure), and by the time we were drinking twelve-dollar cocktails at a sidewalk table on Bleecker, I was rolling in la-la land—sipping away at a gigantic fruity daiquiri drink, mesmerized by the brake lights leaving trails of red, like the whole street was one giant time-lapse photograph. All I wanted to do was sit there and feel nothing. I didn't want to go anywhere else, but Vandershar was always pressing, always doubling down. He said he could get us into the Tunnel, so we hopped a cab back up to Chelsea so Jonathon could weasel us through yet another line.

The drugs wore off the moment we got inside—all the drugs—like the chemicals that keep my shit together headed down the same drain as the chemicals that made me forget about losing my shit, so I was suddenly in my natural state, and that was terrifying. We made our way into a long, narrow space like the nave of the most irritating church on Earth. It was dark with flashing lights, and the whole place throbbed with house music. I couldn't take another step. I tried to grab Vandershar to stop him, but he was just out of reach, laughing as he and Annie charged into the crowd. It was like the current was carrying me in the other direction until finally I couldn't see them anymore. They just left everything behind—me, the last two hours, the last two days, the last two years, the last two centuries. It was like nothing had come before that very moment. I tried to keep up. I tried to push forward. I tried to catch them, but it was impossible. That nave was crammed so full of people you could just about lift your feet off the ground and keep moving—all these idiots banging into me, faceless strangers attacking me from all sides while Vandershar and Annie pulled farther and farther away. I would catch a glimpse of her in the flashing light and chaos and then push through strangers in her direction, only to get to an even louder and more crowded area to find her gone.

I struggled up the stairs to get a better view, to get away from people, but from the second floor balcony it was nothing but a molten pit of bodies below. I couldn't see Annie anywhere, and that's when this hole opened up inside me. I just wanted to find her, you know. I just wanted to pull her close. Hold her tight. Never let her go. I staggered back to the stairs, but the panic swallowed me about halfway down. I grabbed the rail to stay upright, but I was paralyzed not knowing where she was, not knowing what she was doing or who she was doing it with. The music entered me through a billion raw nerve endings. I began to vibrate like every cell in my body was about to explode. I have no idea how long I stayed there, clinging to the railing halfway down the stairs, but that's where Vandershar found me.

Somehow they dragged me into a cab, and then they carried me into the elevator—Vandershar under one arm and Annie under the other, since Sabine wouldn't touch me. They flopped me down on the couch right beneath that old wrinkled butcher and his chicken.

"Who took that?" said Annie, as I lay there shaking.

"I did," said Vandershar, heading to the kitchen.

"I love it. It's so creepy."

Vandershar reappeared holding a bottle of red wine. He sat down on the floor next to the coffee table where Annie and Sabine joined him.

"Imagine being that chicken," he said, peeling the aluminum off the top of the bottle. "Every day is the same. You're confined. You know nothing of the outside world, but you're taken care of. They feed you. They clean your cage. They unburden you of the unfertilized eggs cluttering your nest. Then one day some motherfucker cuts your head off, but you're so oblivious to the possibility you don't even bother to struggle as he sticks your neck in a notch."

"Gross," said Sabine.

"Maybe you're the butcher then, Sabine. Is that any better?"

Sabine didn't seem to know how to answer.

Then he looked at me.

"Spencer, Spencer, Spencer," he said as he twisted the corkscrew into the cork. "What are we gonna do with you?" He looked at Annie. "Spencer ever tell you about the first time we met?"

"No," said Annie. "Where was it?"

"We were both in line for something. It was right at the beginning of freshman year. I can't remember now. It doesn't matter. I see him, and he's mumbling to himself like a loon, looking all annoyed, and then he drops the one thing he's holding, and I'm like, *How retarded is this guy?* Totally fucking helpless. Now look at him. I thought I could help. Four years later and nothing's changed." He uncorked the bottle and spilled wine all over the coffee table and didn't give a shit. "How'd you two meet?"

"We lived together in Amsterdam," said Sabine.

"Amsterdam," he said as he filled Annie's glass. "You lived in Amsterdam and still you have no stories to tell? How is that even possible?"

"It was only three weeks," she said.

"Three weeks in Amsterdam is enough time to get implicated in a murder and still turn a few tricks."

"Why do you have to say things like that?" said Sabine.

"You go to the Rijksmuseum?"

"What's that?" said Sabine.

"It's a museum," he said as he filled his own glass. "In Amsterdam."

"No."

"That's a shame."

"What's so great about it?"

"The van Gogh runneth over."

He took a drink.

"The what?" said Sabine.

"Van Gogh?" he said. "Vincent van Gogh. The artist?"

"I know who he is," she said. "I didn't understand what you said."

"Van Gogh was hopelessly misunderstood too." He raised his glass. "Let me submit to you, ladies of the jury, since our gentleman has expired, that the life and death of Vincent van Gogh is the most tragic of our time. If you get close enough, if you get right up next to a van Gogh, it looks like something a child might have painted, but if you step away, if you put a good fifteen or twenty feet between you and the canvas, the same painting looks like a photograph. The truth revealed by God himself. How heartbreaking did it have to be to see things the way they truly are? That, my sweet ladies, is what the seraphs envied. That's what killed him."

"What killed him?" said Sabine.

"The seraphs' envy," he said. "Were you not listening?"

"Yeah, but how'd he die?"

"It was very sudden," said Vandershar, now spinning the cork off the corkscrew.

"He was dying for years," said Annie.

Vandershar looked up and caught her smiling.

"Sure," he said, "but the end was very... very sudden."

"He was in intensive care for eight weeks."

"Yeah, but I mean the very end when he actually died. That was extremely sudden."

Annie and Jonathon laughed hysterically until she spilled wine on the rug.

"I'm serious," said Sabine. She had no idea what was so funny. "How'd he die?"

"He shot himself in the heart," said Vandershar. "Pinot?"

"You know I don't like red wine," said Sabine.

"No, I'm generally aware that you don't like much of anything, but I didn't know it was specific to red wine."

"That's not true. I like a lot of things."

"Really? Name one thing you like, Sabine."

"It's four in the morning, Jonathon."

"Is it too late to think of something you actually like?"

"Hermès," she said, showing him her bracelet. "I like Hermès. Are you happy?"

"No."

"Why not?"

"Because that's boring. You're boring. Just like Spencer," he said, filling his own glass with more pinot. "The trick in life is to be neither the butcher... nor the chicken."

"I'm not boring."

"You're regular lettuce and grilled chicken breast."

"I am not."

"Have you ever heard the devil trombones, Sabine? The angel trumpets?"

"The what?"

"Do you have even one story to tell?"

"I have stories."

"You don't have any stories. Tell me one story. Tell me your best story from Amsterdam."

She looked at Annie for a second, uncertain at first, but you could see the confidence come as she remembered something.

"Okay," she said. "Annie and I lived together in this tiny flat. We shared everything. And we would buy these cookies at the market. I can't remember what they were called, but they reminded us of home because they were basically Oreos. So I was eating these Oreos one day, and I realized they barely had any filling in them, so I showed Annie, and she promised me there was nothing wrong with them. She said they were low-fat. Low-fat Oreo cookies, and this went on and on until one night I got up late, and I went out to the kitchen, and there was Annie. She was opening these cookies up and scraping the filling out with her teeth and then jamming them back together to stick them in the box again. They weren't low-fat. She was eating all the filling!"

There was a moment of nothing.

"That's it?" said Vandershar. "That's your best story from Amsterdam?"

"It's a funny story," she said.

"You know what we need to do?" he said, looking at Annie.

"What's that?" said Annie.

"We need to help Sabine."

"And how do we do that?"

"We need to give Sabine a story she can tell."

"What kind of a story?"

"I don't know," he said. "Something shocking. Something salacious. Something that after you tell people, they know you're not afraid to be alive. What do you think, ladies? Want to have some fun?"

The room started to spin the moment he said it, and I could feel sickness everywhere, my brain now submerged in a liquid sick that drowned out the sounds and blinded me to whatever there was to see. I woke up broken on the floor between the couch and the coffee table next to a towel covered in fruity cocktail-colored vomit, and my back hurt like a motherfucker.

"You're alive," said Annie, only she didn't sound too excited about it. She was all put together like there'd been no night before. "I don't understand how you got so fucked up. We all did the same shit. Haven't you ever dropped X before? You were like... beyond fucked up."

I felt like if I opened my mouth, I'd puke again, so I kept it shut. I wasn't really sure if the sickness was real or imaginary. I was falling backward in time, like I was eleven years old again. The Dread just wouldn't let me go. I reached for my bottle of little green pills, but it was gone. It must have fallen out of my pocket at some point.

"What happened?" I said, forcing myself to speak.

"You barfed your guts out."

"Where's Vandershar?"

"He's gone. It's almost one."

"My back is killing me," I said as I sat up. "You think it was the ecstasy?"

"You slept on the floor. That's why your back hurts. I'm not cleaning that shit up either. I've cleaned up enough."

"What happened after I passed out?"

"We rolled you onto the floor so you wouldn't choke on your own puke."

"I saw you head into the bedroom."

She stopped and looked at me like I was an idiot.

"What?"

"The last thing I remember is Jonathon saying he wanted to give Sabine a story."

"Yeah. That's when you started to puke."

"What was the story?"

"What do you mean 'What was the story?' You projectile vomited for like twenty minutes. That's the story. We almost called 911."

She pretended to tidy up, but there was nothing left to clean really besides the puke-covered towel next to me, so she was basically just nervously moving things around.

"So nothing happened?"

She finally stopped and looked down at the ground again.

"We had fun last night. Can you not ruin it?"

"I'm just asking."

She finally looked at me.

"I can't take you to your dad's," she said.

I never told her my dad died. She thought she was just driving me to Newark to pick up a car, but as I sat there covered in puke,

I wished I'd told her. She never would have left me there if she'd known, but now it was too late.

"I need to get back," she said.

"For what?"

"I have to go."

She just looked so disappointed. I wanted to tell her why I didn't say anything to Jerry. I wanted to tell her why a thousand faceless strangers turned into a twisted horror show that froze me to a wall inside the Tunnel, but she grabbed her purse and left before anything came out of my mouth, so I guess the Dread won that round too.

I took the subway alone to Newark and then a cab to my dad's house. The key was right where Aunt Barb told me it would be. My dad had been gone a week and still that house had the unmistakable smell of dying in it—the cleaning products couldn't mask the stink of body rot and incontinence. That tiny compartmentalized townhome with its narrow hallways was as cramped and uncomfortable as ever—even without any furniture in it. It had been picked clean, of course, hardly anything left besides a bedroom full of rented hospital equipment that had yet to be picked up by the rental service—a bed, an IV stand, a wheelchair, a plastic booster for the toilet, an aluminum chair for the shower, a portable triage center like the one Duddle hauled around—but as I looked at the scene, it didn't really make any sense. It looked like my dad had been sick for a long time, like he'd had this stroke months ago, but if that was true, why did Aunt Barb wait until he was dead to tell me? I didn't learn until some time later that she'd taken care of him for weeks before he died and in that time she'd persuaded him to sign over his rights to the Lake Anna house along with any claim he might have to anything else that belonged to his parents. As for the money he still had from selling our house in New Brunswick, he left that to Garbage and Wretched. They bought brand new cars with the cash. I got the Buick. If there was an algorithm into which you could feed my family's data, it would have predicted this outcome exactly.

Then I noticed all the bottles left in a plastic bag on the bed, tiny amber bottles still filled with pills. I read the prescriptions to see if any of them were worth taking, but the names were all unfamiliar. I couldn't tell what any of it did, except one that seemed to be an antiviral, and none of them were little and green, so I left them there and looked around one last time, and as I did, it occurred to me that I had no memories from that place. I wanted to remember something. I wanted to remember one good thing about my dad, but it was like I'd never lived there.

The key to the Buick was on the kitchen counter next to a small box of personal items that were apparently not valuable enough for Aunt Barb to steal—an old pocket watch, my dad's driver's license, an odd assortment of cheap cuff links, but there was also an old baseball mitt and a stack of letters. The mitt had been mine. It was my first baseball glove. I have no idea where he got it, or why he kept it. The leather was still in good shape. It was nice and broken in, but it was hard to imagine my hand ever being that tiny. The letters were still in their opened envelopes. There must have been at least twenty-five. I set the glove down and slid a few out to give them a read. They were all in different handwriting, but they said basically the same thing—random parents thanking my dad for molding their boys into fine young men, and I couldn't help but feel cheated as I read them, as if he'd kept those letters for all these years to persuade himself that he hadn't failed miserably at a job he never wanted to do. I took the car keys and left the rest of it behind.

# Chapter 37

By the time I got back from Newark, Annie had already cleaned her shit out of the apartment. I kept the door to Vandershar's room shut so John Henry wouldn't see she was gone. Then I called her number in Branford. I just wanted to hear her voice, but she wouldn't pick up, so I called it again. I started to leave a message, this rambling, semi-psychotic message, but I was pretty sure her roommate would hear it first, so I cut myself off and hung up before I said anything coherent. I drove out there the next day and lurked around her building, but nobody was home, so I sat there waiting in my car for another four hours like a total psycho. I was just waiting for Annie to come or go, but she never did, and eventually I had to take off. The bus to Brown was leaving, and I had to get to Ernie Rickman's first. I was broke. I didn't have a dime in the bank, and thanks to Annie, I'd also run my Chase credit card up to its limit.

Kevin Strommer opened the door. Ernie was reclined in an old brown La-Z-Boy full of rips and holes all held together by a roll of duct tape, and he was watching a nineteen-inch black-and-white television that sat on a stack of gray egg crates connected to an illegally spliced cable wire he'd run up from the Master's house. He pretended not to notice me, but I was standing right there in front of all his stolen glass half-yards. There were three of them on the mantel above the fireplace—eighteen inches of fluted glass with a small bulb at the base—and all of them carefully wedged into white Styrofoam blocks to keep them upright like trophies. I waited, and I waited, but Ernie wouldn't look over, and then Kevin started to browbeat me.

"W-What do you think about the s-split-f-f-fingered fastball?"

"The what?"

"The s-s-split-f-fingered fastball."

"I don't think anything about the split-fingered fastball."

"I think they're too h-h-hard on the arm."

Ernie still wouldn't look at me.

"Have you ever f-f-faced one?"

"I don't know. Maybe."

"What about a f-forkball?"

"Ernie," I said.

"Bruce S-Sutter's f-f-forkball was r-ridiculous."

"Ernie," I said again, only this time louder.

"A f-f-forkball is more like a ch-changeup."

"Yeah, I know what it is."

"But it's s-s-still b-bad for the arm. Mike S-S-Scott throws a s-split."

"Why is he not listening to me?"

"It's the fingers."

"Why are *you* not listening to me?"

He had a baseball with him, so he started to show me how you hold it, depending on which pitch you want to throw.

"For a forkball, the f-f-fingers are really w-w-w-w-wide. You n-need to have long fingers. My f-fingers aren't even long enough. To th-throw the split, the fingers are j-just outside the seams, but that's still t-t-too wide. Either w-way, the elbow v-varus torque is high, but without f-fingers on top of the b-baseball, there's n-no support. All the strain is on the f-f-forearm and elbow. Kids sh-sh-should not be throwing these pitches."

"Can you shut the fuck up? I mean, is it even possible for you to stop talking?"

He stopped talking, but he wouldn't leave. He just kept staring at me, like I'd hurt him. I was the one shaking. I was the one breaking out in hives, but I got the feeling he was ready to stand there for as long as it took for me to apologize so he could get back to his inane conversation.

"I don't give a shit about split-fingered fastballs, Kevin." Then I turned back to the La-Z-Boy. "Ernie, what the fuck?"

Ernie finally grabbed the handle on the side of the La-Z-Boy and yanked it to un-recline, but something snapped and the footrest didn't move, so he ended up having to climb out of the thing while Kevin moped his way back to his bedroom.

"Jesus," said Ernie through his nose when he was finally upright. "You look like shit. What the fuck is all over you? Are those hives?"

"I'm fine."

"I guess you're here for your money."

"Two hundred seventy-five bucks."

"I talked to Wayne."

"So."

"We thought it was kind of strange I could bet on North Carolina and he could bet on Duke, and yet we both still managed to lose."

"Why is that strange?"

"You gave us different lines."

"I move my line all the time."

"Two minutes apart? You talked to him literally two minutes before you talked to me."

"You didn't have to bet it."

"How many times have you done this?"

"Done what?"

"You don't see anything wrong with this?"

"No. With what?"

"You gave me a different line."

"That's how it works."

"That's how what works?"

"I set the line. You don't have to bet it."

"No, this is different," he said. "You cheated me."

I grabbed one of the half-yards off the mantel.

"You took these?" I said.

"Put it back."

He tried to snatch it from me.

"Give me my money, and you can have it."

"I'm not paying you. You're a fucking thief. Go ahead. Break it. Break 'em all. I don't give a shit. I'll just get more."

I ripped the half-yard out of the Styrofoam block, and all this white Styrofoam shrapnel went flying all over the place.

"Show me how you took it," I said.

"What? Why?"

"Shut the fuck up and show me how you took this."

I jammed the thing into his chest, and that's when I think he finally realized I wasn't myself.

"Alright," he said. "Jesus. You don't have to get pushy."

He went to the La-Z-Boy for the roll of duct tape. Then he knelt on the dusty wood floor and set the tape on the ground next to the half-yard so he could lift his T-shirt over his head, and for the first time I could actually see the impossibility of his scrawniness. He was nothing but knobs and ribs and shoulder blades.

"The bartender at Richter's was ignoring me as usual," he said. He couldn't stop himself from telling me a story he'd already told me ten thousand times. "It took forever to get a round of Jaeger shots, so I left a dollar on the bar as a tip… commensurate with the level of his service."

He tore an eight-inch length of duct tape from the roll and laid it across the half-yard.

"But he wouldn't pick it up. It sat there, and it sat there, and it sat there in the very same spot on the bar, so it started to bother me that he wouldn't pick up this dollar, you know, like he was the one showing *me* up, so I finally said, 'Hey, I left that for you,' you know, just so he would know what I thought of him, and without even looking up from the glass he was washing, he said, 'I don't want your fucking Jew dollar.'"

He tore another length of tape.

"I complained to the manager, but of course the manager did nothing… other than tell the bartender I was complaining."

He laid that length across the half-yard too.

"I went back twice to work out the details. They guard these like it's Fort Knox. Most people think this is a yard. It's not. It's a half-yard."

He tore a third length of tape.

"You can only do this on a cold night when it's busy. It's got to be jacket weather, and there needs to be a bunch of these lined up on the bar so they don't notice right away if one's gone. The first time I did it, I ordered from the same Nazi who wouldn't take my money. He didn't recognize me of course because that's what assholes do. They don't recognize people they've met fifty times. I finished the beer, and when he was busy ignoring me again, I slipped it under my jacket and headed for the bathroom. The trick is to get it on your back because they make you open your coat on the way out."

He lifted the thing over his head and then ran his other hand across the tape to secure it to the scrawniness of his back like a quiver of arrows.

"There," he said.

Then he started to get up, only I didn't let him. I shoved him face down to the floor and climbed on top of him to keep him from squirming. Then I took a firm grip of the half-yard.

"What are you doing?" he said. "Get off me."

I started to pull on the glass.

"You fucking asshole. That hurts."

"Where's my money?"

"Kevin!"

"Shut up."

"Kevin!"

"Kevin's not gonna help you."

"Fuck you."

"Where is it?"

"I'm not giving you shit."

I pulled harder. I pulled until I could feel the tape ripping away from his skin. He made a noise that sounded like it came from the inside of a slaughterhouse, and then Kevin appeared in the doorway to his bedroom.

He was red-eyed and holding a narrow-handled, big-barreled bat that looked more like a lead pipe, but I could tell he didn't want to use it.

"Kevin!"

Ernie was pleading at this point, but Kevin just stood there in the doorway with tears in his eyes.

"Kevin, get him off me!"

But Kevin didn't move. He just kept looking at me, like he was begging me not to make him do it, but I wasn't going anywhere.

"It's Kevin," I said. "C-c-coming to k-k-kill me."

That's when his expression changed. He hoisted that bat over his head like a Samurai warrior and charged. He came at me, screaming unintelligibly. Then he took a wild, halfhearted swing and missed, only before he could regain his balance and have another go, I ripped the half-yard off Ernie's back and hit him over the head with it.

He dropped the bat and crumpled to his knees, holding his bleeding head while Ernie rolled around on the dusty wood floor in agony. I stood there for just a second actually considering how to finish the job. Then I dropped the jagged, bloody mess of glass and tape and left.

# Chapter 38

*Summer 1992*

I thought a lot about what Nafziger said—how the human brain is infinitely complex—and now that the pharmaceutical smog had lifted, I could think straight again—even if the Dread was lurking everywhere all the time. Complexity in nature is an interesting phenomenon that we'd spent a fair amount of time studying in Mathematics in the Real World. Complexity breeds fragility. That's why every complex system worth a shit is redundant, and the more complex, the more redundant it should be. But watching my grandmother deteriorate made it seem like the brain was about as redundant as the hydraulic system of a DC-10. How could a system that fit, that complex, be that susceptible to failure? And what about Ira Gershwin? Something about Ira Gershwin flipped a switch that took us on an alternate route to a memory of my mother. The obvious, direct pathways had all failed, but maybe there were other redundant wormholes waiting to be discovered? Maybe the brain was not just redundant, but functionally redundant. Maybe it was biologically degenerate? So one night as I sat in the West Wing dining hall, the caterwauling of wing nuts all around me, I had an idea, so I left my green beans and pushed away from the table to go grab Nathan's autographed photo of the 1961 Yankees out of the trunk of the Buick.

When I got to the front desk, the Admitting Nurse greeted my enthusiasm with her usual irritation. She was busy, and I could barely get her to look at me, let alone release me. I noticed her braces were gone, so I complimented her on how straight her teeth looked, thinking that might earn me some points. She just rolled her eyes and told me the braces had been off for three weeks. Then she turned her back again in a hurry to finish whatever needed finishing before she could take off now that her shift was over. She was gone by the time I got back from the Buick with the Yankees.

Gram was already in her frumpy flannel nightgown and ready for bed when I got to her room. I gently took the hairbrush from her hand and replaced it with the Yankees. She sat on the bed and looked at it, running her fingers along the edges of the frame for the longest time.

"It's lovely," she said.

"Do you know what it is?"

"Oh, I don't think so."

"I think you do."

She tried to hand it back to me.

"Gram, look at it again."

"I'm sorry. I don't know these people."

"It's not the people in the picture."

"I don't think I want to do this."

"It's not the picture," I said as I took it from her. "You were there. We were all there. You and Papa drove down to be with us."

"Oh?"

"Nathan was sick. He was really sick, so we were all there."

"We were where now?"

"At the hospital in New York City. It's the only time we were all together. You don't remember that?"

"No."

"Whose picture was this?"

"I don't know."

"It was Papa's."

"Oh?"

"And who did Papa give it to?"

"I don't know."

"Yes, you do. Think. Who was it?"

"Please don't ask me any more questions."

"Look at it."

"I don't want to look at it."

"Look at it," I said, shoving it back in front of her. "Papa gave it to Nathan that day in the hospital. It was Papa's. You don't remember any of this?"

"I don't want to do this."

"How the fuck can you not remember this?"

"I don't think I want to talk to you anymore."

"Just look at it, Gram. Look at it!"

"You stay away from me."

Then she darted for the bathroom.

"Gram?"

She slammed the bathroom door shut, so I left the Yankees on her bed and tried to open it, but I could feel her leaning on it from the inside, and I felt tired all of a sudden. I couldn't even push her away from the door.

"I don't know what to do," I said. "Tell me what to do."

"You stay away from me!"

"I just need somebody to tell me what to do."

"Don't you come near me!"

"I'm sorry. I thought it would help."

I pushed on the bathroom door again, only this time it opened, and when it did, I found her on the ground unspooling toilet paper as fast as she could straight into the toilet, so I grabbed her wrist to stop her.

"Don't you touch me!"

Her dentures were gone, and when I looked to see if they were on the floor, she pulled free and hit me.

"Gram."

"You get away from me!"

She hit me again—this time with two clenched fists right in the chest.

"Why are you doing this?"

"I hate you!" she screamed. Then she shoved me with what seemed like superhuman strength right out the door, and I fell backwards into the bedroom onto my ass. "I don't ever want to see you again!"

The panic came from somewhere deep. I felt dense, like something collapsing on itself, like I was being compressed into nothing. She pulled the emergency cord when I tried to stand, and even though it only took fifteen seconds for the room to fill with nurses and the lab tech who found her teeth at the bottom of the toilet, I grabbed the Yankees and was out of there before anyone could ask me what had happened.

I staggered back to the edge of the parking lot to the light of a single flickering bulb that burned on the side of the lawnmower shed. I sat there in the driver's seat of the Buick with the headliner of that piece of shit sagging in my face, and all I could think about were all the drives to Weequahic High with my dad in that car and its faded silver paint and smashed front grill, every morning in that Buick, just the two of us, exchanging not a single word, having not one fucking conversation.

I put the key in the ignition. I wanted to get as far away from that place as possible, but then I saw a hose on the ground next to the lawnmower shed, and I put the car in park instead. That hose weighed about a thousand pounds, so it took a minute to drag it back over to the Buick, but once I had it there, I fed one end into the tailpipe and the other end through a crack in the driver's side window. Then I got back in the car. That was all the thought I gave it. But nothing changed. My mind didn't empty. There was no eerie calm. I just kept thinking about all the people I'd lost and the ones I'd never see again, but that hose was a mile long, and the smoke took forever. I couldn't help but notice a familiar sound somewhere off in the distance as I waited, something pleasant I was pretty sure I'd heard before, so I turned, but all I could see out the back window was Diamond Dave's powder blue Jaguar rocking in the moonlight.

I rolled the window down a bit further to get a better listen, but that wasn't enough to really hear it either, so I opened the door and slid outside. It was Beethoven's Something in Something Minor—the music the twins had played for me at John Henry's all those summers before—and the moment I saw their tiny determined faces in my mind, I thought of John Henry throwing a silk pillow at Maggie, and I couldn't help but smile. I could see everyone. The ones I'd lost and the ones I worried I'd never see again. I wanted to remember them all, only differently—the way I do now, instead of the way I did then. I wanted to start over. I wanted to fix as much as I could, but the back window of Diamond Dave's Jaguar slowly opened and the Admitting Nurse's head popped into view.

"Fuck me!" she said.

She seemed to be insisting that someone fuck her as she looked back over her shoulder into the back seat with her tits on full display, and then I could see Diamond Dave slumped over her from behind.

"Fuck me, baby! Fuck me!"

The Admitting Nurse was not nearly as hard to look at with her shirt off, and she wouldn't shut her mouth. She was putting on an absolute Fuck Show in Something Minor. I ducked behind the Buick so she wouldn't see me, but I couldn't take my eyes off the performance. For the first time in weeks, I felt my dick move.

"Are you gonna do it?" She was looking back over her shoulder again. "Are you gonna fuckin' do it?"

Whatever it was she wanted him to do, it didn't seem possible from that angle, so there was a changing of the guard. She struggled to reposition herself, and during the commotion, all I could think about was Diamond Dave's perfect wife, and his two perfect kids, and their elderly golden retriever. It wasn't much of a fuck show after that. It was just kind of pathetic really, and pretty soon, all I could see was the Admitting Nurse's kneecaps and a shadowy figure on top of her doing his best to keep her quiet while the solitary light of the lawnmower shed flickered and black smoke billowed from the driver's side window of the Buick.

# Chapter 39

*Spring 1992*

I sat up front on the bus to Brown. I didn't want anybody near me since I still didn't know where Annie was, and I was worried I'd have another panic attack at any moment. Thinking about panic attacks might be worse than the panic attacks. It's like thinking about going crazy is the surest way to actually go crazy. The ride was awful. I bit my fingernails until they bled. It probably only took two hours. It felt like two days, and we didn't stop until we reached a shitty Days Inn in Providence.

I roomed with John Henry. We were studying for our Mambo final, and it was pretty late. The class was actually called New York Mambo: Microcosm of Black Creativity. I took it because it was a gut. John Henry took it because it was New York Mambo: Microcosm of Black Creativity. The midterm was a participatory capoeira demonstration and an essay on the African influence on modern American music. I killed the capoeira demo even though it was pretty clear to me that anyone busting that shit out in a fight would have their ass kicked in about fifteen seconds. I wrote the essay on A Tribe Called Quest, parroting a bunch of bullshit I remembered Vandershar telling me about how their music was "jazz-infused" and how jazz's dissonant roots were really African. It was the only "A" I ever got on anything that didn't involve numbers, and in the margin of my blue test booklet, underneath my "A," were the following words:

*Love the Quest Groove! Good luck with the season!*

*Master T.*

It kind of made me want to do well on the final, but it was technically an art history class, which meant the final involved slides. Every lecture was basically a graduate student projecting slides onto a screen while the professor, who also happened to be the Master of Timothy Dwight College, danced around the room trying to explain the significance of each image to the migration of African culture to the Western Hemisphere. The final was a bunch of essays based on a random subset of these slides. Most people had to spend about a week inside a room in Linsly-Chit staring up at a twenty-foot wall of laminated images trying to memorize every single one of them and their significance, but since we played a varsity sport, and we were on the road, we got to take a slide-filled binder with us.

"When's the funeral?" said John Henry, jotting a note in a spiral ring notebook.

"It already happened."

*SportsCenter* was on in the background, and Dan Patrick was interviewing some basketball player who was going on and on about how unstoppable he was.

"What do you mean it already happened? You didn't go?"

"I wasn't invited."

"You don't need an invitation to go to your dad's funeral."

"They didn't tell me where it was."

"You didn't ask?"

"I think it was in New Brunswick."

"I would've taken you."

"I didn't want to go."

"Why?"

I grabbed the remote and hit mute.

"I can't listen to this anymore."

"Why? What'd he say?"

"He's used the word 'respect' like a hundred times in two minutes. It's fucking irritating."

John Henry looked up from his notes.

"You do see the irony here, don't you?"

"It's like if you say the word 'marshmallow' a hundred times in a row it doesn't mean anything anymore."

"Are you okay?"

"I'm fine."

"How was New York?"

"Fine."

"You meet the guy from Goldman?"

"Yep."

"How was that?"

"Good."

"Nothing eventful to report?"

"Not really."

"Annie drive you to Newark? Did you get the Buick?"

"This is just shit hanging in trees," I said, looking at a picture of plastic bottles dangling from tree branches in some dilapidated Southern neighborhood.

"It's a bottle tree."

"What the fuck is a bottle tree?"

"It's a superstition from the Congo. It came to the South in the slave trade. They hang the bottles in the trees to ward off evil spirits."

"It doesn't sound like they work very well."

"It's an example of the migration of culture."

"It's bottles in trees. Who gives a shit?"

"You sound like Vandershar."

"Really. What does Vandershar sound like?"

"A cynic."

"Nobody gives a fuck about this shit."

"Master T does. If you listened, you'd know that. Go to class... take notes... condense the notes into an outline... study the outline. Every professor leads you right to what they care about. I've been telling you this for four years, and you still don't do it."

"Never take a class with slides," I said. "That's the lesson."

"Here," he said. He started to read from the outline in his spiral ring notebook:

> *A moral voice is imbedded in the African-Atlantic aesthetic. White world refuses to see it. No crisis that cannot be weighed and solved. Nothing achieved through hysteria or cowardice. Step back from the nightmare. Call for parlance, congress and self-confidence.*

"I don't know what that means."

"It's what he said on the last day. No matter what he asks you to write about on the final, bring it back to that."

"Bring it back to what?" I said.

He paused, trying to figure out where to go next.

"I didn't see Annie today."

"Maybe you should stop looking for her."

He sat back again and considered his next move.

"You know I'm not dating your girlfriend."

"I'm not the one who thinks you are."

"That's not to say I didn't want to."

"That's not to say you could."

"I'd never do that to you," he said. "She's the only thing that's made you happy since you've been here." Then he turned the volume down on the TV. "I need to talk to you about something else."

I flipped to the next slide and was now staring at a picture of a college football player executing a spin move.

"I'm not going to New York," he said.

"What are you talking about?"

"I got an offer from the *L.A. Times*."

"You already have a job."

"*The Daily News* is in bankruptcy."

"Vandershar is buying a loft."

"It's a better job."

"It just occurred to you to tell me this?"

"I've been trying to tell you all day, but when you got on the bus, you sat up front and stared out the window mumbling to yourself for three hours."

"The *L.A. Times*?" I said.

"Yeah."

"In Los Angeles?"

"That's where the *L.A. Times* is, yes."

"So you'd be moving to Los Angeles."

"I thought I wanted to be as far away as possible, but that's not what I want. I need to be closer to the twins."

"You just happen to be moving to the city where Annie wants to end up."

"What?"

"You know where she is, don't you?"

"What are you talking about?"

"Don't bullshit me about a fucking job," I said as I got up. "You know where she is."

"Where are you going?"

I left to wander the streets of Providence until daylight, only I didn't get any farther than the potted plant I heaved off the balcony into the parking lot. When I beat that toilet with a bat at Princeton, all they did was make me pay for it. I figured a potted plant was nothing compared to a toilet, so when the Dean of Berkeley College asked me to come see him when we got back from Brown, I really didn't think much of it.

# Chapter 40

Dr. Moseley's office was in the South Court of Berkeley College at the far end in the corner. He looked ten years younger than he probably was with these round, wire-rimmed glasses, and his short dark hair all parted neatly to the side. It was a small office for someone in charge of hundreds of people, but it was perfectly put together, not a piece of paper out of place, ninety-degree angles no matter where you looked.

"How are you feeling?" he said as I sat.

"Okay, I guess."

"I'm told you've had an outstanding baseball season."

"If it's about the potted plant, I'll pay for it."

He looked at me like he had no idea what I was talking about.

"I also understand your father died recently."

Now I wasn't sure what he was talking about.

"He had a stroke," I said.

"I was about your age when my dad died." He waited for a response, but I didn't say anything. "I felt gypped," he said. "It made me angry for a very long time. And that's okay... to feel angry."

He looked at me again like he expected me to say something, like he needed me to say something to complete his administrative task, but I just sat there.

"Spencer, I had a disturbing conversation with Ernie Rickman over the weekend. You'll be happy to know his injuries aren't permanent. Neither are Kevin Strommer's. I've also persuaded them not to press charges. I've arranged it so that you can take a family-related leave of absence this semester and return in the fall."

"What does that mean?"

"Well... it means you would take the rest of the semester off and return in September. Ernie's hands aren't exactly clean either. Under the circumstances, your readmission would be a formality. I'm hoping a little time away will be useful for you. Of course, Ernie and Kevin will both have graduated by then."

"I'm not graduating?"

"Not exactly. If all goes well, you'd graduate in December."

He smiled like his job was done.

"That doesn't make any sense. I need to graduate. I'm done."

"No... you're not done, and I can't allow you to graduate under these circumstances. Not this semester at least."

"My job starts in July," I said. "I have a job at Goldman Sachs."

"Spencer, I hope you appreciate the lengths to which the University is going to deal with this inconspicuously, but you assaulted two students, and you seem to have been running a gambling operation here for the better part of three years."

"I need to graduate," I said. "My job starts in July."

"I'm willing to look the other way under the circumstances, but there have to be consequences. You understand that, right? I'm afraid this is the best I can do for you. I'm sure Goldman will understand. You just have to explain it."

A jumble of disjointed and cracked thoughts made my brain hurt, and there was a horrible ringing in my ears.

"What do I do?" I said.

"Well... I'd start by going home. You should be with your family at a time like this. Everything will be waiting for you when you get back."

But that wasn't the question I'd asked. It never once occurred to me that what I'd done was awful or that Yale was doing me a favor by covering it up. I just wanted it to disappear. The question I'd really asked was *How do we make this go away?*

Dean Moseley walked me out to the courtyard and wished me well. He told me he looked forward to seeing me in the fall, but I was barely listening to him. I looked around that empty courtyard. It felt like starting over in a place I never wanted to be to begin with, and I was falling forward into an uncertain future again. I couldn't take any chances. I needed Vandershar's concierge-diddling dad to talk to Jerry or the Navy pilot or Julia's dad or whoever the fuck he knew there and explain it all so everything would be back to the way it was supposed to be. I actually thought someone at Goldman would call Yale and unwind this, so I grabbed the keys to the Buick before the panic made the drive impossible, and I headed straight for New York.

I have no idea how long I sat in front of Vandershar's door waiting for him to get home, but I was mumbling to myself, rehearsing what to say when the elevator doors finally opened and Jonathon stepped into the hall. I don't think I've ever felt so relieved. The Dread vanished the moment I stood to face him, but he looked surprised. I fumbled for the words to explain myself, so in the end, the only thing that came out of my mouth was: "My dad died."

His expression didn't change though, just a quizzical *What the fuck are you doing here?* look on his face.

Then Annie stepped off the elevator right behind him.

It was just the three of us motionless for a second before Jonathon smiled—this little *fuck you* of a smile.

"It's totally what you think," he said.

Then he shrugged like it didn't matter, because nothing mattered, so I did the only thing I ever think to do: I drilled him right in the mouth. He staggered, but he didn't go down, and he wouldn't stop smiling, so I hit him again. And then again, but I could've hit him a million times and I still wouldn't have wiped that *fuck you* off his face. Annie was in tears, but the Dread had its hooks in me, and I didn't want her to see it, so I crashed down twelve flights of stairs, slid behind the wheel of the Buick, and drove off with the world spinning around me as I tried to outrun the panic all the way to Widworth.

# Chapter 41

*Fall 1992*

I left Widworth a few days after Diamond Dave fucked the Admitting Nurse's head out the window of his Jaguar—a hundred and thirteen days after I got there. I still had no money when I got back to Yale, so I stopped by Ray Tompkins House to see if Canelli could get me a job through the athletic department. He wasn't there though. His redheaded secretary told me he'd resigned. He just packed his office one day and left. She also told me how Billy Clark signed a free agent contract with the St. Louis Cardinals and was now in Johnson City, Tennessee, playing Single-A ball, and how Norman was off to law school at the University of Chicago, and how Larry had followed him there for his year off before medical school, but she didn't know a thing about John Henry. She had no idea where he was.

"You seem different," she said as I turned to leave.

"I do? How?"

"I don't know, but I've watched you come and go for four years, and you've never said two words to me before today."

I went back to my old building after that, hoping they might still have some of the stuff I left behind, but all the doorman had for me was an envelope. I opened it right there in the lobby and inside was a note written in John Henry's unmistakable half-cursive, half-print handwriting.

*Spencer,*

*I've waited as long as I can. I don't know where you are or why you left. I don't really care to be honest. All I know is I want my friend back. Please call me when you get this.*

*John Henry*

I asked the doorman to use the phone behind the front desk, and even though I had to talk to John Henry's mom to track him down, I finally found him behind his desk at the *L.A. Times*. It was awkward at first. He seemed to want to know what had happened and where I'd been for the last three-and-a-half months, but I found myself unprepared and too embarrassed to tell him.

"You were right," is all I said.

"About what?"

"Everything."

I'd always thought I was the one looking out for John Henry, but it turns out, he was the one always looking out for me, and when he sensed that was all I had, he pivoted and told me how he'd been fact-checking articles about the Rodney King riots for weeks, until, short-staffed, the *L.A. Times* finally pressed him into action. He told me this whole story about how he'd been sent to investigate the disappearance of bicycles in Santa Monica, something that at first sounded totally depressing and inconsequential, but by the time he was done, he'd spun all these facts into a whole thing about a city stretched thin and ready to buckle, and all I wanted to do was listen. Maybe I just wanted to hear someone else talk for a while.

I've been back to Widworth once to see Gram. She doesn't remember anything now. I hung Nathan's photograph of the 1961 Yankees on the wall above her dresser, hoping one day it might do for her what it was never able to do for me. Then I asked to see Dr. Nafziger. I just wanted to thank him and let him know I was back in school, maybe tell him a thing or two about *Ulysses*, but the nurse at the front desk—who was not the Admitting Nurse—told me he was on administrative leave. I guess Diamond Dave got busted in some FDA investigation that involved patients who didn't exist and a shit ton of falsified clinical trial data. They arrested Nafziger the same day. I was ready to tell him I thought *Ulysses* was just a story about regular people treating each other like shit to survive the bad luck of their own lives since no one in that book is any better than anyone else, but when I thought about Nafziger being led away in handcuffs, I couldn't help but wonder if maybe it was about the people you love and how they're the ones who can really ruin you. At some point, I guess you have to decide if you're going to let them.

I moved back into Berkeley College. I had to take three more classes to graduate, but I'd already finished my major, so I was able to take them all through the computer science department— two in programming and a third on algorithm development. School had already started, so I had to stand in that same line outside the bursar's office to sort out my tuition. I was way at the back again, outside on the sidewalk, and the line was barely moving as usual, only this time it was the girl in front of me who seemed flustered. She kept looking at her watch, and I could tell she wasn't exactly sure she was where she was supposed to be. I wasn't about to guess where she was from. I was thinking maybe Southern Italy since she reminded me a little of the local girls I'd met in Brindisi, but she also had a few dark freckles on her face and the most unusual green eyes I'd ever seen.

"This line doesn't move very fast," I said, but she didn't hear me, so I tried again. "I've been in it before."

"I'm sorry?" she said.

"This line. It's slow. We're gonna be here for a while."

She looked at me skeptically, like I couldn't possibly know what I was talking about, but I think she finally realized I was just trying to help her, so she reached into her bag and pulled out a piece of paper.

"Do you know what this is?"

"It's a bursar hold notice," I said, looking at it.

"Why did I get it?"

"You probably fucked up a student loan. It happened to me once. I forgot to put my social security number on something. It's not that big a deal."

And that was it. She stuck the piece of paper back in her bag and began to turn away, but right as our paths were about to uncross forever, she stopped and looked back at me.

"Thank you," she said.

"What's your name?"

"Helen."

"Helen?"

"Is that a problem?"

"No. Just... unusual."

"Unusual how?"

"It's kind of an old person's name, isn't it?"

"No."

"Well, I've only ever known one Helen, and she was like ninety."

"What's your name?"

"Spencer."

"What kind of a name is that?"

"It was my grandfather's."

"Well, how old is he?"

"He's dead," I said.

"Are you always this blunt?"

"No one called him that though. Everyone called my grandfather Bud. *Bud* is an old person's name."

She smiled a dimply smile.

"What are *you* doing in this line?" she asked.

"You don't want to know that."

"Why not?"

Her smile faded, but I didn't feel like giving her some bullshit answer.

"I was supposed to graduate last May."

"Then why didn't you?"

"It's a long story."

She looked back toward the door to the bursar's office to gauge the wait.

"I think we have the time."

I thought about it for a second. I mean, where does any story really start? When is there ever really a beginning or an end?

"You ever have the same dream?" I said. "Like over and over again?"

"No. I don't think so."

"I used to have this dream. It was the same one every time."

# Epilogue

*Fall 1992*

So this is the story I told Helen—not all of it right there, of course—but on long, meandering walks through campus. There is now something different about Yale. It's suddenly a place I need to be, a place I will never give up, and we meet on Cross Campus in the afternoons to explore it. Helen Lemartiniere turns out to be half Creole. She's from New Orleans and has this sprawling, complicated family I haven't met yet and stories upon stories that go back to the days of the French and Spanish.

She's an art history major—a bookworm—but I still have no idea why anyone would want to stare up at the white walls of Linsly-Chit memorizing the art of the Bronze Age. I tried to impress her once with my knowledge of the Rijksmuseum. She looked perplexed and explained that most of van Gogh's paintings were actually next door in the Van Gogh Museum, and I just had to shake my head and wonder why Vandershar would lie about something so trivial, but I knew the answer. *Rijksmuseum* sounded better. It made the story more engaging. It was the kind of detail he used to manipulate you. The truth is mostly boring—or so I thought—but as Helen and I continued to stroll up Hillhouse Avenue and talk about my little brother, I remembered an odd detail I had long forgotten.

The fish in the tank were African cichlids. It's a small thing, I guess, but my dad had let me pick them out, and until the day Nathan spilled the fish food, I'd always thought of those fish as mine. I guess I hadn't thought of them as anything after that, but it was just me and my dad that day in the pet store, staring at a wall of fish tanks as I pointed to the cichlids I liked—blue peacocks, red zebras, electric yellows, and this tiny freshwater puffer fish that followed my finger down the glass like it knew me—and as I slid further away from the story I was actually telling Helen, I got lost in happy thoughts about my dad, and I wonder if I felt right then the way my grandmother did the moment her memory fluttered back, and then it all slipped away like I was looking through some turning kaleidoscope of broken glass, like the truth never stops moving, like I'll never be able to figure anything out.

"Is everyone this fucked up?" I said.

"I don't know. Maybe."

"Who am I? Who am *I* to feel this way?"

"What kind of a question is that?"

"Look at me. Look at where we are."

"What difference does that make?"

"What about you then?"

"What about me?"

"Do you feel this ripped off?"

She didn't answer right away. We took a few more steps down Hillhouse until finally she stopped in front of the Department of

University Health, home to the infirmary where John Henry and I met all those years ago. Then she turned to face me.

"Yeah," she said with sad eyes. "I do."

I couldn't understand why she was so sad all of a sudden, and then it hit me that I didn't really know her story at all. I mean, how could I? She smiled through tears, and I felt unprepared for what was coming, but I braced myself anyway. We were in it together now, and it was my turn to listen.

# *Acknowledgments*

I want to thank all the friends and family who helped me persevere through early and incomplete drafts by providing me with the insights that prove elusive when you're so inside something.

In particular, John Darrow, who helped me understand I couldn't just leave Spencer splattered on the ground. Alexa Scoma, who inspired Rudolph Valentino. Dan Mickelson, who demanded a more sympathetic anti-hero, and David Williams, whose comments gave rise to Helen Lemartiniere.

Then there were the later readers whose kind words gave me the confidence to keep at it: Eric Kaup, Chris Kouri, Teri Campbell, Kevin Allen, Alex Fitzpatrick, Matt Garretson, Jody Greer, Erin McConkey, Sandi Nelson, and Jacqueline Rimel.

And my family: Jill, Tatum, and the real Spencer. Everything I do is for you guys.

But I don't think this book ever sees the light of day if I had not found Tom Fiffer and Christmas Lake Press. Tom is my editor and publisher and the person who somehow instantly understood what I was trying to do and saw the potential and value of doing it. He invested an unexpected amount of time reading and rereading, poking and prodding, making sure I'd uncovered every opportunity to dig deeper and push harder. I am eternally grateful. He also introduced me to the hybrid publishing world, where I had the pleasure of working with fantastic cover designers, copyeditors, proofreaders and typesetters. I am proud to be a part of an ecosystem where those who want to write are free to write what they want.